The winner of eight BAFTA awards, Graham Norton is one of the best-known faces on British television. His long-running and ever-popular Friday night chat show, *The Graham Norton Show*, continually features some of the world's biggest stars. Since 2009 he has presented the *Eurovision Song Contest*. He also charms Radio 2 listeners each week on his Saturday morning show. Born in Dublin and raised in West Cork, Graham now lives in London. *Holding* is his first novel.

HOLDING

The remote Irish village of Duneen has known little drama, and yet its inhabitants are troubled. Sergeant PJ Collins hasn't always been this overweight; mother of two Brid Riordan hasn't always been an alcoholic; and elegant Evelyn Ross hasn't always felt that her life was a total waste. So when human remains are discovered on an old farm, suspected to be those of Tommy Burke — a former love of both Brid and Evelyn — the village's dark past begins to unravel. As the frustrated PJ struggles to solve a genuine case for the first time in his life, he unearths a community's worth of anger and resentment, secrets and regret.

Books by Graham Norton
Published by Ulverscroft:

THE LIFE AND LOVES OF A HE DEVIL

GRAHAM NORTON

◆

HOLDING

Complete and Unabridged

CHARNWOOD
Leicester

First published in Great Britain in 2016 by
Hodder & Stoughton
London

First Charnwood Edition
published 2017
by arrangement with
Hodder & Stoughton
An Hachette UK company
London

A catalogue record for this book is available
from the British Library.

ISBN 978–1–4448–3323–2

Published by
F. A. Thorpe (Publishing)
Anstey, Leicestershire

Set by Words & Graphics Ltd.
Anstey, Leicestershire
Printed and bound in Great Britain by
T. J. International Ltd., Padstow, Cornwall

This book is printed on acid-free paper

For Rhoda — finally one you can read!

Part One

1

It was widely accepted by the residents of Duneen that, should a crime be committed and Sergeant Collins managed to apprehend the culprit, it would be very unlikely that the arrest had involved a pursuit on foot. People liked him well enough, and there was no name-calling as such, but it was still quite unsettling for the village that their safety depended on a man who broke into a sweat walking up for communion.

This particular morning, however, nobody seemed overly concerned. Main Street, being the only street, contained most of the action. The village was still waiting for winter to arrive, and yet Susan Hickey looked like she was preparing for an Arctic expedition. She was huddled over awkwardly with a wire brush, trying to remove a few patches of rust from her gate. She was also keeping a silent tally of the wine bottles Brid Riordan was placing carefully into the recycling. Sixteen! Had the woman no shame? On the other side of the street, outside the pub, Cormac Byrne coughed up a very satisfying lump of phlegm and dispatched it through the air to land in the gutter. Over by the phone box, the dusty black and white collie dog that belonged to the Lyons from the garage looked up, satisfied himself that everything was as uninteresting as he had assumed and put his head back down between his paws.

Outside O'Driscoll's shop, post office and café, the Garda car, sitting low over its tyres, gave the impression of having been there for some time. In the driver's seat, with his stomach wedged against the steering wheel, sat Sergeant Patrick James Collins. The names had been chosen because his mother's father Patrick had died just six weeks before her son was born, and because his mother was a big fan of James Garner, the actor that starred in *The Rockford Files*. His father had provided the surname. In retrospect, the care put into his christening was misplaced, since everyone simply knew him as PJ.

PJ Collins had not always been fat. On long summer evenings he had played with the other children in the lane at the back of his parents' shop in Limerick. Kick the can, hide-and-seek, what time is it, Mr Fox? The high-pitched laughter, accusations of cheating and occasional crying filled the still air of dusk until the clang of a colander or the sizzle of frying onions called them in for their dinner. He missed that feeling of just being one of the gang. He could hardly remember what it felt like not to be noticed or judged. Puberty had brought with it a combination of appetite and inertia that led to a thickening of the skin and the end of his days as one of the lads. He hadn't needed his mother's nagging to see what was happening, but somehow, despite constant private vows to get his weight under control, he just got bigger and bigger, until by the time he left school, he felt the task of slimming down was beyond him.

Looking back, he could see that he had hidden behind his size and used it as an excuse so he didn't have to compete in all the trials of adolescence. No need to summon up the courage to ask a girl out on a date, because which of the Margarets or Fionas with their long pale necks and shiny hair would want his warm clammy hands holding them on the dance floor? The other boys tried to outdo each other with fancy leather-soled shoes or bright stickers on their bikes, but PJ knew that no matter what he did, he could never be cool. Being overweight hadn't made him happy necessarily, but it had helped him avoid a great deal of heartache. It got him off the hook.

Life as a guard suited PJ. The uniform and the car didn't make him feel any more alien than he always had, and keeping a strict professional distance between himself and the neighbours he had to police was no great challenge for him. He stared out of the window at the long, slow hill that led the tourists' cars on towards the coast and the beauty they had been promised. People didn't stop in Duneen. In defence of the casual traveller, there was little reason why they should. There was nothing to make the village stand out from any other. Wedged into a gentle green valley, jagged terraces of two- and three-storey buildings lined the road, painted long ago in the sort of pastel colours usually associated with baby clothes. At the bottom of Main Street there was an old bridge across the River Torne. Beyond that, the solid grey chapel kept watch on a small hill. No one living could recall a time when it had ever looked any different. Time didn't pass in Duneen; it seeped away.

PJ dabbed a damp finger on the toast crumbs in his lap, brought it to his mouth and sighed. Just gone eleven. A good hour and a half till lunch. What day was it? Wednesday. Pork chops. He supposed they'd have the leftover crumble from last night, but then he remembered he had finished that standing in front of the tall fridge just before he went to bed. He blushed slightly as he thought of Mrs Meany, the housekeeper, finding the bowl in the sink. Tutting as she washed it under the hot water while at the same time planning what new confection she could conjure up to tempt him with. He swore that if it weren't for her he'd be half the size. Sure, a sandwich would do him for his lunch. He didn't need two dinners or, come to that, two puddings. He only had the cooked breakfast every morning because she plopped it down in front of him before he could protest. His arm twitched as he imagined slamming the fridge door against her small frame and letting her slump to the floor, no longer able to widen her eyes as she cleared his plate: 'Well, no need to ask if you enjoyed that, Sergeant!'

A knock on the car window interrupted his violent reverie. It was Mrs O'Driscoll herself from the shop. Normally it would be the daughter, Mairead, or the skinny Polish girl whose name he couldn't remember but was too embarrassed to ask again. He turned the key, held the window button down and cleared his throat. He hadn't spoken since he said goodbye

6

to Mrs Meany at a quarter to nine.

'Nice enough again.'

'It is, thanks be to God. I brought you a cup of tea there, to save you getting out.'

Mrs O'Driscoll bared her small neat teeth and laughed. She was being kind, and yet all PJ heard was a woman laughing at a man his size squeezed into the driver's seat and revelling in her own slim figure. She held out the cup and saucer with its cloud of steam. Then her other arm shot out, thrusting a plate with a jam-covered scone up to his face.

'They're just out of the oven, and that's the jam from the rector's wife.'

'You're too good to me,' he said with a forced smile. Who knew a simple scone could provoke such a confusion of emotions? He felt patronised, angry, greedy, hungry and defeated all at the same time.

'Enjoy that now, and don't worry, I'll send Petra out in a minute for the plate. Sure you'll make short work of it!' Another laugh and she scuttled across the footpath back into the shop.

PJ placed the cup and saucer on the passenger seat and picked up the scone. He forced himself to finish it in two bites rather than one and licked the smears of jam from the corners of his mouth. Plate down, saucer up, he took a slurp of tea. On the radio the presenter was asking movie trivia questions. Name the original *Ghostbusters*. Well, that's not a hard one. Bill Murray, Dan Aykroyd, and . . . who was that other one? He shut his eyes to imagine the face of the actor but instead conjured up the grinning face of

Emma Fitzmaurice. *Ghostbusters* had been their date. He felt the heat of embarrassment course through his body as if it were yesterday. His awkward attempt to angle himself in the small cinema seat so that he could try and put his arm behind her shoulders. The way she looked at him and laughed. No attempt to spare his feelings, just sheer derision. Why had she agreed to come with him? No matter how awkward or humiliating the 'no' might have been, it would have been better than staring straight ahead at the screen trying not to cry while her shoulders shook beside him. He had never made that mistake again.

Another knock at the window. He turned expecting to see . . . what the hell was her name? . . . but instead saw a face he didn't recognise: a tall man in his late forties with weathered skin and a head shaved to mask the baldness that had come all too soon. He wore a bright yellow hi-vis jacket and carried a hard hat under his arm. PJ assumed he must be working on the new housing development up behind the primary school. The window slid down.

'Guard. The foreman sent me down to get you. We're after finding something up above.' The builder waved his hand in the general direction of the school.

This was a good feeling. He was needed. After an unhurried sip of tea, PJ looked up and asked, 'What sort of thing?'

The investigation had begun.

'It might be nothing. Some of the lads said work on, but myself and the foreman thought

8

somebody better have a look.'

'Right so, I'll head on up. Will you sit in with me?'

'Oh thanks. I will so.'

PJ remembered he was holding the cup and saucer, and of course there was the plate as well. This was awkward. It was not the slick sort of modern policeman he wanted to be. He hesitated for a moment and then reminded himself that he was a sergeant and this a mere labourer. He held out the crockery.

'Would you run those back into the shop there for me like a good man?'

The builder didn't move. Was he going to say no? Was he simple? But then without speaking he took the items and headed into the shop, before returning and climbing into the passenger seat. Once inside the car, he seemed much larger than he had on the street. Their shoulders touched. As Sergeant Collins started the engine and put the car into reverse, he placed his hand behind the other seat so he could get a better look out the back window. The awkward manoeuvre, the physical proximity of another warm body: all at once he was back in the darkness of the cinema with Emma but this time, he thought, nobody was laughing.

The car rolled backwards with a satisfying crunch of gravel, and then with a smooth change of gear moved quickly across the road and headed up the hill to the east of the village, past the school, towards what had once been the Burkes' farm. Both Susan Hickey and the collie looked up as the Garda car vanished, leaving a cloud of ancient dust. Sergeant Collins let out an involuntary grunt. For some reason he felt good. He felt like a winner.

2

Before the soft growl of the Garda car's engine had died away, the door of O'Driscoll's shop opened and Evelyn Ross stepped into the street. With her bright red woollen coat, wicker basket and dark blue beret, she looked out of place on Duneen's main street. Tall, with chestnut hair and the sort of fine features that meant her age was very hard to guess — fortyish? — this was a woman who organised tennis parties in the Hamptons, or served trays of mulled wine to riders before the hunt, not a woman who trudged past the phone box and the garage with nothing in her basket but a small bag of oat flakes and a copy of that week's *Southern Star*. She picked her way carefully across the short stretch of uneven pavement and unbuttoned her coat. So mild for late November. The collie followed her for a few yards but then peeled off on to the garage forecourt and home. Susan Hickey didn't even look up.

In the village and surrounding parishes Evelyn was what might be called 'well known'. Not famous, exactly, but everyone knew who she was and if they didn't they'd soon be told. She was one of the Ross girls from Ard Carraig. There were three of them: Abigail, Florence and the youngest, Evelyn. All unmarried, they lived together in the large stone-fronted family home about a mile outside the village.

11

Their parents had been the wealthiest people in the area, with a prosperous farm and vague talk of investments. Robert Ross had provided the land while his bride Rosemary, being the only daughter of a bank manager in Cork city, had the shares. Everyone worried about how the little girl from the big city would cope on the farm, but she had in fact blossomed. Soon there was hardly a committee or a board that didn't boast Rosemary Ross as a member.

The young couple had been delighted when their first daughter Abigail had been born, but even though they never spoke of such things, that joy had turned to a palpable sense of disappointment by the time a third baby girl had arrived. It felt unjust. Where was their son? After Evelyn there were two miscarriages and then nothing. Robert began to feel that his desire for Rosemary and a son was causing his wife harm. The full wet kisses became chaste lips barely touching after he turned the light off. Two people lying in the dark full of love but both thinking they had failed the other. Some marriages combust, others die, and some just lie down like a wounded animal, defeated.

Strangely, it was the cancer that brought the marriage back to life. In Rosemary's final months, she and Robert found their love did still exist; it had just been buried beneath layers of misunderstanding and missed opportunities, waiting to be unearthed like those perfectly preserved bodies found in bogs. Of course the feelings remained unspoken, but every unasked-for cup of tea, too milky or too strong, every dripping saucer placed by rough dark fingers on her bedside table beside her rosary beads told her that he still loved her. And in those dark endless hours before dawn when she allowed him to hold her thin bony frame as she wept, he understood that she still loved him.

Evelyn's first day back at school after her mother's funeral had been hard. Most of the girls avoided her, unsure of what to say or how to act, and the couple that didn't just wanted to know if she'd seen the body. It was a relief to reach the gates of Ard Carraig, and as she trudged down the tree-lined driveway towards home, her schoolbag heavy on her back, she allowed herself to cry. She had remained dry-eyed all day and she knew her mother would have been proud of her, but now as she looked at the dark windows ahead, it was all too much. Everything seemed grey and bleak and would for evermore because her mammy was gone.

As she went around the back of the house into the yard, she could feel the chill of the wind drying her wet cheeks. Her footsteps slowed as she tried to delay facing the cold, gloomy kitchen. No radio. No baking filling the air as it cooled on a wire tray. She had reached the back door when she noticed a light coming from the workshop in the far corner. Over the years, she would often retrace this short journey and examine every detail. The dozen paces across the greasy cobbles, her small hand pushing open the heavy wooden door with its flaking paint, the shadow on the floor moving slowly from side to side, the work boots with dirty soles and one lace untied, the hands that had patted her on the head that very morning, now hanging limply. The creaking of the rope. That was where her memories ended. She could never see his face. The face of her father who couldn't face a world that didn't have his Rosemary in it.

To begin with, nobody was quite sure what would become of the three Ross girls. Women from the village had come to the house to help with meals and various men had assisted with funeral arrangements, but it soon became clear that they were neither needed nor welcome. The eldest girl, Abigail, took charge in a way that almost suggested that she had been waiting for this very circumstance. She arranged to rent the land to a local farmer, and that money meant Florence was able to go away to teacher training college. Evelyn, though the youngest, ran the house, doing the majority of the cleaning and cooking. She had imagined that this arrangement would come to an end at some point, but somehow she never found a time when it felt right to abandon Abigail; and then, when Florence came back to Duneen to teach in the local school, it seemed that they were simply meant to stay together, bound by sadness and their big house that had forgotten every happy memory it had once contained.

Twenty-six years later, though, as she walked down the same avenue with her wicker basket, Evelyn Ross was not thinking about the past. Abigail's ladies were coming for bridge after dinner and Evelyn was planning what supper she would wheel through on the trolley with the tea.

She thought she might use the good china with the yellow roses. Was that a bit over the top? Would Abigail roll her eyes? Evelyn decided that she didn't care. It was pretty, and anyway, what were they saving it for? What occasion at Ard Carraig would ever be special enough to truly warrant its use?

Once inside the house, she hung her coat on the rack by the freezer, turned on the radio and started to get lunch ready. She glanced at the clock: 12.15. Florence would be home from school soon and she was always in a rush. The soup was steaming on the hob and the slices of soda bread were fanned out on a plate when she heard the familiar *ting* of the bicycle bell as Florence threw her bike against the wall outside the back door and rushed in with a blast of cold air.

Of the three sisters, Florence was considered the prettiest. She kept her light brown hair shoulder length and swept to one side. Evelyn envied her 'curves', as the magazines called them, though Florence never dressed to make the most of them: the kilts and thick knits that made up most of her wardrobe always gave her the slight air of a head girl. She seemed more out of breath than usual. Evelyn sensed at once that she had news.

'Great excitement!'

'What is it?'

'Well, I was just finishing geography when the Garda car went flying by.'

Florence put her anorak on the back of a chair and sat down. She picked at a piece of the bread and paused for effect.

'And?'

'I thought nothing of it, but when I was leaving just now, I could see it parked up at the new development. I didn't want to look too nosy so I didn't cycle up, but then as I came through the village I saw a couple of the builders outside the shop, so I stopped and asked what was going on. You'll never guess!'

'You're right, I won't,' Evelyn said as she took two soup bowls down from the dresser. They had played this game before.

'Something was found when they were digging out the foundations, and they think it's a body!'

The soup bowls hit the floor with a crash, the pieces scattering into every corner of the room.

3

Duneen had somehow managed to slip through the World Wide Web. No 4G, no 3G, no signal. PJ stared at his useless mobile phone, unsure of what to do next. There was little doubt that the builders had uncovered a body, or at the very least, part of one. The long white bones that had first aroused suspicion had now been joined on the large pile of dark earth by what was clearly a human skull.

He was very aware that the foreman and the other men standing around were staring at him expectantly. They stood perfectly still, each one wearing the regulation bright yellow jacket, white hard hats perched awkwardly on their heads. PJ might have been a visiting dignitary or the priest come to bless the works. He tried to ignore the trickle of sweat that was tracing its way along the side of his nose. This was clearly a time when he needed to exert authority, but in reality, all he wanted to do was contact a higher power. This would require detectives, coroners, those rolls of plastic Garda Síochána tape used for major incidents. He knew he had some of that, but God alone knew where. Vague memories of his training at Templemore were telling him that under no circumstances should you leave a crime scene unattended, but equally he knew that he would have been added to the pile of bones by the time a senior officer happened to be passing by. He looked away from the excavations back down towards the school and took out his notebook, playing for time and hoping desperately that he was giving the impression of a professional following protocol.

No building site had ever been so silent. A wood pigeon was purring quietly in a nearby tree and in the distance a tractor engine was idling in a yard. A builder stifled a cough. Should he abandon the human remains to go and raise the alarm or should he stay at the scene and dispatch someone else to tell the outside world about the most exciting thing that had ever happened during his entire career? Suddenly certainty coursed through his veins. He snapped open the notebook and looked back at the foreman.

'Have you any rope?'

'We do.'

'Right, I want you to rope off this section here, from around the bones to the other side of the foundations. Can you do that for me?'

'No bother.'

'Then I need you to ensure that absolutely nobody enters that area,' he began to walk towards his car, 'until I return with . . . '

Shit! He had lost the word. What was it? Please, please, please, he begged his brain.

'Forensics!' he announced a little too loudly and with a wide smile that made sense to no one, only himself.

★ ★ ★

The building that served as Duneen's Garda barracks had started life as a retired teacher's

18

bungalow: a pebble-dashed box with a central porch and a large rectangular window to either side. The former living room, with its peach tiled fireplace and Artexed ceiling, now housed PJ's office, while the rest of the rooms were his living quarters. Some of the more basic furniture had been provided; the rest was a combination of charity shop finds and a few pieces that his sisters hadn't taken after their parents died. It was the sort of haphazard interior design that one might find in a run-down bed and breakfast or a retirement home. Not uncomfortable, as such, but nor was it a place to feel at home.

PJ parked the car on the short drive that separated the house from the main road. At the back of the house was a long, thin garden that went down to the river, which meant that most winters there was flooding, though so far the water had never made it past the back door. Full of purpose, the sergeant manoeuvred his bulk with some speed around the car towards the small glass porch. The smell of pork chops filled the air.

Mrs Meany was waiting in the hall, holding a tea towel. The old lady was PJ's full-time housekeeper, though she lived alone in a cottage on the other side of the village. She had been the priest's housekeeper for quite a few years, but when Miss Roberts had retired as the manager of the hotel in Ballytorne, she had asked Mrs Meany to come and look after her, as she had no one else, and as an incentive promised the woman her cottage when she died. The arrangement had suited Mrs Meany well. She liked the little cottage and the feeling that it was all hers. No one could take it away from her, and like an animal spraying its scent she had covered every available surface with much-dusted china figurines and small glass ornaments. Since the passing of Miss Roberts she had cooked and cleaned for various people around the village before starting work full time in the Garda barracks.

'There you are, guard. I was beginning to think something had happened.' She flapped the tea towel and turned towards the kitchen.

'Well actually, Mrs Meany . . . ' He heard his own voice. He sounded angry. Why did he sound angry? 'Something *has* happened.'

The old lady turned, her expression suitably shocked and intrigued.

Pleased by her reaction, PJ continued. 'I'm after finding a body.'

'You what?'

'A human body!'

He had waited his whole life to utter those words, and it felt as good as he had always imagined.

'God spare us!' Mrs Meany gasped and raised both hands to her neck as if gathering close an imaginary cardigan. 'Where?'

'I've no time. I must let Cork know,' he announced, and went into his office, leaving Mrs Meany doing a strange little dance of uncertainty outside the kitchen, like a figure on a weathervane unsure if it was rain or shine.

★ ★ ★

20

When PJ hung up the phone, he felt strangely deflated. Help was on its way, which was what he wanted, what he needed, but once it arrived this would no longer be his case. He would just be another useless man standing around at the scene, a sort of crime butler servicing those who would find out the identity of the body and how it died. Were they ancient remains? Was it a crime? The suits from Cork wouldn't get to the village for at least another hour. Was there anything he could do? Maybe he could crack the case in the next sixty minutes. He smiled at his own foolishness.

A knock at the door, and before he could speak, Mrs Meany opened it, carrying in a steaming plate of food. PJ pushed his chair back from the desk.

'No time for lunch today, Mrs Meany.'

'No lunch?' Her voice suggested he had announced his plan to commit suicide that very afternoon. 'You'll have a bit before you go?' she said, her head bowed like a dog that wants you to scratch its ears. She put the plate on the desk and pulled a knife and fork out of her apron pocket.

'I'm sorry, Mrs Meany, but I have to get back up to the building site. They're sending down some uniformed lads to secure the scene.'

Mrs Meany drew her imaginary cardigan close once more.

'Burke's farm? Is that where you found the body?'

'It is.' PJ was pulling his jacket back on.

'What class of a body?'

21

'Just bones — too early to tell.'

The old lady steadied herself against the desk and gulped at the air like a goldfish with grey hair. Her voice came out as a whisper. 'Jesus, Mary and . . . Could it be Tommy Burke?'

The sergeant took a step back into the room.

'The fellow who owned it? Sure he's not dead.'

'Isn't he?' Her eyes narrowed as if she was trying to send PJ a message telepathically.

'He just ran off, didn't he? After some girl trouble, wasn't it?'

'That's what we all thought, but I've never heard of a single one in the village who ever heard from him or caught a glimpse of him, and that must be seventeen — no, more, because sure you're here nearly fifteen, so it's more like twenty years since he vanished. It would make an awful lot of sense if it turned out he'd been up on the farm the whole time.' She pushed a strand of grey hair behind her ear and slowly rubbed the side of her face. 'It doesn't bear thinking about. Cold and alone all these years and not a stone to mark him.'

PJ was appalled to see that the old woman's eyes had filled with tears.

'Ah, Mrs Meany, now don't upset yourself. We have no way of knowing yet who it is or how the bones came to be up there. Go and put the kettle on and I might have more news later.' He put his hand on her shoulder and encouraged her towards the door.

'Thank you, guard. I don't know. The thought of it . . . him. I just don't know.' She closed the door behind her.

Sergeant PJ Collins hardly dared to breathe. Not a suit in sight, no other uniforms had even arrived, and he had a lead. He saw himself standing, one foot on the pile of soil, indicating where the farmhouse used to be and getting the rest of the team 'up to speed'.

He picked up one of the pork chops and took a large bite.

4

A limp spring onion draped itself over the edge of the wicker basket that displayed the fresh produce in the O'Driscolls' shop, café and post office. It shared the space with a shrivelled red pepper, while the basket above it held a few sweaty-looking bags of carrots. On the ground was a large sack of potatoes. Brown paper bags dangled from string to allow eager shoppers to make their own selection from the enticing display. The sales representative who explained the refurbishment had mentioned something about a 'French market feel' and tried to include some sort of oven-to-bake frozen baguettes. Mrs O'Driscoll had drawn the line at this suggestion. There was no call for French sticks in Duneen. They had a daily delivery of sliced loaves, and her daughter Mairead had a nice little sideline making her own soda bread, thank you very much.

Nobody did what might be called their 'main shop' in O'Driscoll's. It was where you popped in for a forgotten pint of milk or emergency toilet paper; the sort of shop where you could buy every ingredient for a full Irish breakfast but would be faced with slim pickings for any kind of dinner. They made their money by being open long hours so that when it was too late or early to be bothered driving the forty minutes into Ballytorne, the nearest market town, people would drop in happy to pay a little more for the convenience.

Mrs O'Driscoll liked the mornings best. Counting out the change bags, putting the little board out in the street, bringing in the paper delivery. After that the day was punctuated by regular flurries of activity — people going to work, a light surge around lunchtime and of course when the kids were being picked up from school.

This afternoon was no different, except today the small gathering of mothers seemed to be growing and in no rush to leave. By a quarter past four there must have been at least eight of them, plus their bored children being ignored as they tugged on their mothers' sleeves and skirts. At the centre of the group was Susan Hickey, still wrapped in thick layers to protect herself from the impending winter. Her small round face with its mouth pursed like a balloon knot was red and shiny from a mixture of heat and excitement. Her nephew worked up on the development and had told his aunt everything. A big pile of bones — it could be a mass grave. The place was crawling with guards, some down from Cork. There were various noises indicating dismay and approval. One woman reached down and slid her hands over her son's ears.

Behind the counter Mrs O'Driscoll sat silently contemplating her equally silent cash register. She didn't mind customers chatting, but most of these women hadn't actually bought anything. There was poor Petra trying to sweep around them; of course she'd have no interest because the Burkes were long gone when she had arrived. A whispered piece of speculation reached her from the hastily assembled coven.

'Do you think your man Tommy was some sort of serial killer?'

This was met with the sound of a giant airbed being deflated. Mrs O'Driscoll could hold her tongue no longer.

'Oh for God's sake. If that boy was a killer, wouldn't he have started with his own father?'

All eyes turned to her. They wanted more and she found herself reluctantly opening her mouth and forming words.

'Big Tom was the only one in that family with any badness in him. Young Tommy might have been a bit of a fool, but there is no way on earth he was Ireland's answer to the Yorkshire Ripper.'

The women herded themselves to the till to learn more. Susan Hickey did not appreciate her role of expert being usurped in this way.

'Well,' she said loudly, 'whatever happens, the police will certainly want to track him down in England to ask him some questions.'

Much nodding. Mrs O'Driscoll rolled her eyes. She knew it was Susan Hickey who had objected to their wine licence in the café.

'England? Who told you that, Susan?'

'Everyone knows that.'

'I've heard it as a rumour, but as far as I know not a soul has actually heard from him since he left. He could be anywhere.'

A small woman with hair that used to be blonde put her hand up as if she was at a committee meeting.

'You don't think . . . could he be one of the bodies up above?'

The airbed deflated sharply. They liked where this story was going.

A loud crash suddenly ripped through the shop, followed by the shrill wail of a child. The mothers looked around for their various charges.

'Fintan, where are you?' Great gasping sobs came as a reply. 'Fintan! What have you been doing?' As the boy's mother came around a stack of shelves, the answer was clear. A tear-stained face stared up from the floor, surrounded by at least a dozen cans of creamed rice.

'Oh Mrs O'Driscoll, I'm so sorry. Fintan, what do you say to Mrs O'Driscoll?'

Apparently all Fintan had to say involved a long scream of dismay as his mother dragged him by the hand from the scene of the carnage. Mrs O'Driscoll waved away the various expressions of apology as she came from behind the counter and called for Petra to come and help her. Secretly she was quite pleased. There was no damage done and it had put an end to the pointless speculation of the mothers' meeting.

Once order had been restored and the shop was empty, she retook her post behind the till. Wiry but strong, she sat perched on a high stool, her back slightly hunched from her years at the cash register, her scrubbed face giving nothing away. This was not a woman to go to for a hug or a 'there, there' pat on the back, but still there was enough warmth in her eyes to let people know you could rely on her in a crisis. Just the right side of formidable, she gazed out at the world

27

passing by with her own unwavering sense of what was fair and right. She helped those she felt were capable of at least trying to help themselves, but didn't hesitate to judge people she considered to be the architects of their own downfall. Running a shop, post office and café showed her every shade of humanity.

She saw a Garda car drive by. Its indicator flashed orange and it headed up the hill to the old Burke farmstead. She wondered what on earth had gone on up there. She felt a twinge in her stomach; an uneasiness about the secrets that might be unearthed to disturb this little village. Of course she was aware of the various dramas that had taken place over the years, but somehow they had occurred off stage. The scandals had been contained. What if these bones threatened to drag the whole community into the spotlight?

She chewed at the side of her thumbnail and remembered Little Tommy Burke and his mother. She had only been a child herself but she'd loved to sit at the back of the shop, pretending to do her homework while in reality hanging on every word the grown-ups said. If the voices were whispers, even better.

Nobody thought Mrs Burke would ever have a baby, but then after about ten years of marriage came the miraculous news that she was expecting. It wasn't only her belly that grew; the whole woman blossomed. Over the counter or on the steps after mass, she wore a newly acquired beaming smile. She was literally bursting with joy. A few weeks before she was due to give birth, it was only Mr Burke who was seen around the town. His wife was resting. Headscarves muttered to one another, getting ready for bad news, but then came the joyful announcement that the baby had been born. A boy, Little Tommy, named after his father, who immediately became known as Big Tom.

It was a few weeks before anyone saw the new mother, and the little boy seemed very small. The headscarved mothers of the parish spoke in hushed tones once more about their prognosis. Nobody expected Little Tommy to thrive. Mrs Burke returned to being a figure of pity.

Time proved everyone wrong. The baby grew quickly, becoming a sturdy little boy who went to school, and the smile returned to his mother's face. It was not to last long.

Most people in the village would have said that Big Tom drank the farm, but Mrs O'Driscoll had heard her parents talking. She knew there was more to it than that. He gambled a big part of it away and mismanaged the rest. She remembered Little Tommy, hardly able to see over the counter, and his mother, bright red in the face, stumbling over her words as she asked for a line of credit. It was the first and only argument Mrs O'Driscoll had ever heard her parents having. Her father holding out a ledger asking her mother if she was mad. Why had she agreed to give the Burke woman tick? Her mother had shouted back at him. Had he no heart? It was a simple act of Christian charity. Anyone would have done the same.

Dying was the only sound business decision Big Tom ever made. It turned out that, unbeknownst to his wife and son, now eighteen years old and ready to farm himself, a life insurance policy had been purchased. For the first time in their lives they had some money in the bank. The other bit of good fortune that befell them was that bad business out at Ard Carraig with Robert and Rosemary Ross. The Ross daughters had land but needed money. Little Tommy didn't have enough to buy a farm, but he was able to pay a fair rent. Everyone was pleased to see these two dark tales find some sort of happy ending. Mrs Burke went to her grave knowing that she had raised her son well. He never touched a drop and had no interest in the horses.

After his mother died, a change came over Tommy. He had always been a hard worker, but now it took over his life. He was always trying to sell you something, and all he ever wanted to talk about was land. The price of it, who had it, who was selling, where it was. His fervent wish to be nothing like his father seemed to have taken a sinister turn. Everyone liked a young man to be ambitious, but this was different. It meant too much to him. It wasn't natural. A good-looking young lad like Tommy should have friends and be falling out of the pub at closing. Mrs O'Driscoll remembered thinking to herself that he would never be satisfied, and sure enough, it had ended in tears.

The door to the shop opened and brought her back from the past. A late-afternoon breeze rustled the paper bags hanging from the vegetable baskets. She didn't recognise the man in the suit who walked in, but after nearly forty years behind the counter she knew the type and she didn't like it. Too much time had gone into picking out that tie, and his smile was the sort he might have used meeting a group of special needs children on a day out.

'Twenty Camel Lights, please.'

She reached behind her for the packet.

'Oh, and a box of matches.'

Mrs O'Driscoll rolled her eyes. He might think he was some sort of hotshot, but he was never going to make her rich.

5

Abigail stood by the open front door for a few minutes, watching the lights of the cars make their way down the avenue. The branches of the trees caught the headlights and reared up against the black sky. She took a couple of deep breaths and stared at her own shadow stretched out across the gravel. The stillness. She liked this time of night.

Normally Florence went to bed first, taking a book and a small glass of milk, then, once Evelyn had set out the breakfast things, she too would make her way up the stairs. Abigail relished the half an hour or so when the house was hers alone. It wasn't that she didn't like people; she just didn't need them. Sometimes she saw this self-reliance as a character flaw. Was there something wrong with her? But mostly she felt it was a strength.

It didn't take Dr Freud to figure out that her emotional reserve was deeply connected to the death of her parents. She would have said she loved both of them equally, but in truth it was her father she adored. Her earliest memory was holding his big shovel of a hand and walking unsteadily in oversized wellingtons across a ploughed field. They had fed the calves together. She had sat on his lap as he drove the tractor up to the back paddock. Even when Florence and then Evelyn came along, her special bond with her daddy went unbroken. While the other girls stayed in the house with their mother or played around the garden, Abigail remained by her father's side. With her serious little face framed by an angular fringe, she became a familiar sight wherever Robert Ross went. The men who worked on the farm took to calling her 'Shadow', as if she was a loyal collie.

Of course she missed him when he died, but what broke her heart was discovering that he hadn't loved her enough not to leave. When her mother had died, she had been sad, but there was another feeling, too. An energy and strength that flowed through her as she prepared to be her father's partner. Together they would run Ard Carraig. When she howled into her pillow in the days and nights after Evelyn found the body, what hurt her the most was that her father hadn't shared her vision of their future. It was the first time in her short life that she had realised she was alone. Pain like that can do strange things to a young heart.

Abigail stepped inside and closed the heavy front door behind her. She turned the upper lock and slid the thick brass chain across. Making her way slowly down the hall, she switched off the lamp on the long oak table. A pale blue bowl held some bunches of keys and a few lines of raffle tickets. Beside it, framed photographs of the three girls at various ages in school uniform stood in order alongside a larger silver frame that held the black and white image of Rosemary and Robert on their wedding day. Abigail had often stood and stared at those faces, searching for a sign or a clue, something that foretold the sadness that was to be heaped upon them. Nothing. Smiles so certain of the future and all the joy it would bring. Florence in her first communion dress and veil. God, she looked so like her mother.

She made her way into the living room and put the fire guard in front of the dying embers in the grate. The polished wood of the side tables glowed golden beneath the light of the lamps. She made her rounds of the room, switching them off one by one, then picked up a stray wine glass to return to the kitchen. Once there, she put it on the draining board ready for Evelyn to deal with in the morning. Turning away, she caught a glimpse of her own reflection in the black sheen of the window. She stopped and stared. As the ghostly image floated in the oily darkness, she could clearly see the bags under her eyes and the deep lines cutting across her forehead. Abigail was not a vain woman, but even she was taken aback. When had she become so old? Not yet fifty, but this was the face of an ancient crone. It seemed unfair. She still felt like a girl who was just taking care of the place, waiting for the grown-ups to come back. She rubbed her eyes and went across to the dresser to get a glass for some water. Time for bed.

Tonight had been a disaster. Nobody had had any appetite for bridge. They all just wanted to gossip and speculate about the bones. Even Mavis, who never spoke in much more than a whisper, had been moved to shriek at the assembled players, 'It was on Sky News!'

Big Tom, Little Tommy, Sergeant Collins: the names went round the circle like pass the parcel. The actual bridge game never really took off, and then Evelyn had been fussing around making a fool of herself. Who forgets to put the tea in the pot? Abigail had been embarrassed. Of course she knew well what had upset her sister, and doubtless the others would speculate about it in the morning, but nobody would have dared say anything in front of them.

Yes, she thought as she started up the stairs, I'm glad today is over.

Everything about Abigail suggested a practical woman, from her cropped grey hair to her flat brown shoes. It wasn't just the solitude of the night she enjoyed; it was the routine. The familiarity of habits she had developed over decades. A house run according to her rules. The click of light switches marked her progress to the top landing and along the corridor to her bedroom. As she turned off the last one, she was surprised to see a glow coming from beneath the door of Evelyn's room. Abigail hesitated. Normally she would have been annoyed. Her sisters knew she didn't like them to leave their lights on, but tonight she felt differently. Should she go back and knock gently, enquiring with a whisper if everything was all right? Of course she knew that she should, but the truth was that she was afraid Evelyn might say 'no', or appear at the door with a face streaked with tears. Then what would she do?

It wasn't that she didn't care. She did. Evelyn wasn't like Florence, who never gave Abigail cause for concern. The school and the children seemed to provide Florence with everything she needed in life, but Evelyn, sweet, innocent Evelyn, well, she was different. Had Abigail been wrong to keep them all together? It had felt like the right thing to do. Florence hadn't hesitated to come back to Duneen for Evelyn's sake. Evelyn had been through so much and appeared to be so fragile. It was only proper that her sisters would take care of her, but now it seemed that act of concern had turned in on itself. The refuge of Ard Carraig, Abigail had to admit, was now a sort of prison for the three of them. Evelyn should have more in her life than cleaning this house and cooking for her sisters.

Christ, thought Abigail, I think I'm the antisocial one, but even I have more friends than Evelyn. It pained her to think it, but what that girl really needed was a man. Leaving the light seeping out across the threadbare carpet, she went into her room and shut her door.

*   *   *

At that very moment, Evelyn was flicking through a copy of *Vogue*. It was from March 1995 and came from the neatly stacked piles of the magazine beneath the window. Every year, someone donated them to the book stall at the Church of Ireland fete. Abigail wouldn't have approved of her wasting money buying them new, but when they were so cheap and it was all going to charity, even she couldn't do more than raise an eyebrow.

The pages were being turned with a slow, steady rhythm, but Evelyn's eyes weren't focused on the photographs of Madonna wrapped in Versace. She was staring straight ahead at the opposite wall of the bedroom. The drab wallpaper was a tangle of green and brown leaves and had certainly been there in her grandmother's time. She traced her eyes along the branches looking for where the pattern repeated itself, as she had done so many times before. There was no way she could have gone to bed and fallen asleep. Not now. She hoped she could calm down. She had been so embarrassed tonight with the supper fiasco. Pouring out cups of hot water. Her face flushed at the memory of it.

March 1995 was finished. She folded it shut in her lap and then got up to return it to the pile. As she stood, she too saw her face in the cold glass of the window. She paused. Yes, there were a couple of grey hairs and she looked a little tight around the mouth, but this face was basically unchanged. She remembered another night over twenty years before when she had stared at her reflection in this bedroom. Tears had been running down her cheeks and her chest had been heaving as she tried to gather breaths in between her stifled sobs. She had longed to run to her sisters but she couldn't tell them what had happened. Looking back, she realised that they must have known. It turned out most of the parish had been watching the soap opera of her life play out, but neither Abigail nor Florence had asked her how she was, or even touched her arm as she stood hunched in the boot room doing a hand wash in the big butler sink.

She felt a strange pressure building behind her face. No. She would not cry. She might have carried the pain for twenty-three years, but she would not release it now. Her face contorted into a thin smile.

She knew who it was buried up above and the thought of it gave her pleasure. It must be Tommy Burke. He hadn't left her. He hadn't run away. He'd been in Duneen the whole time, unable to reach her. She sat on the bed and then stretched out and hugged her pillow. She was seventeen again. Tommy hadn't stopped loving her.

She breathed in the clean smell of the pillow-case and tried to make sense of her feelings. There was relief, but also sadness and a rage, because her life, her whole life, with kisses and children and picnics and laughing, had been stolen from her. She held her breath. How had shiny-haired, tanned-skinned, wide-mouthed, lovely, perfect Tommy ended up buried in an unmarked grave? Maybe now after all these years the mystery of her life would be solved. The loneliness and misery weren't her doing after all. Someone had robbed her of her happiness, and now that they had found his body, she knew exactly who was to blame.

6

At this rate he might lose weight. Mrs Meany had gone home the night before without leaving him any dinner, and this morning he had left the barracks before she arrived. She'd never forgotten to feed him before. He hoped she wasn't sick. A pâté sandwich last night and a bowl of cereal eaten standing up in the dark kitchen this morning was all he'd had. He felt a little light-headed but also more energised than he had for years.

The detective superintendent from Cork crushed his third Camel Light of the morning underfoot. PJ looked at him. Christ, he was an awful prick. The slicked-back hair, the long, thin hook of a nose, the suit and clean pressed shirt. What sort of man wore socks that matched his tie? Since 7.30 the nasal whine of his voice had been droning on. 'If it was a vagrant', 'if it was a suicide', 'if it was a murder'; he had a detailed theory for every possible outcome and was more than happy to share them. Somehow everyone else had managed to make themselves look busy, leaving PJ to become an unwilling frozen audience of one. The wind blowing across the site seemed to have brought winter with it. He had feared the worst when he had googled Detective Superintendent Dunne the night before and discovered that his Christian name was Linus. Linus? What sort of a name was that?

How could he solve a crime if he couldn't even figure out that his name made him sound like a gobshite?

The forensic team had arrived late yesterday and taken the bones up to the lab in Cork for testing. Now they were back examining the area and looking for any more remains. PJ felt that in the absence of new or contradictory evidence they should be following his lead. The young man who had been farming this land twenty-odd years ago had left the village and not been heard of since, and now a body had turned up. Surely it seemed fairly safe to assume that Tommy Burke was either the victim or the murderer. These so-called experts only seemed interested in the things they didn't know. The use of mechanical diggers meant they weren't sure if it was a shallow or a deep grave. In turn this meant they were going to have difficulties getting any sort of accurate timeline for the death. The one thing they could say with any certainty was that the remains that had been found so far belonged to a young adult male.

After all the clearing and excavations it was hard to tell what part of the old farm they were actually standing in. The builder did have a map, but for some reason it was in the Skibbereen office. It was on its way. Sergeant Collins' stomach gave a deep gurgle of impatience, but it went unnoticed under the never-ending lecture on criminal investigation. He looked around the flattened site, trying to get his bearings.

The first time he had come across the Burke farmhouse was just a couple of weeks after he'd been transferred to Duneen. It wasn't just the promotion that had excited PJ; he liked the idea of being a one-man band. After graduating from Templemore, he had been stationed in Thurles. He liked the job well enough; it was the nights in the pub, the banter in the barracks that he found tough. Nobody ever said anything to his face, but he found it hard to shake the way the uniforms looked at him when he arrived. In every pair of eyes he saw the unasked question, 'How the hell did you get through training?' The truth was that PJ had just scraped through, and that was mostly thanks to his written work. In Thurles he worked longer hours than anyone else and was always the first to volunteer for the shifts that nobody else wanted, but it never seemed enough to make him accepted.

As the new sergeant in Duneen, he was keen to make a fresh start. He felt he could really be of service. For years the village had had some old codger who, from what he'd heard, did most of his police work from a bar stool in Byrnes. PJ was the young blood. He had decided to go for walks around the village on Sunday evenings. You saw things differently by foot, and it was a chance to exchange a few words with anyone he met on his travels.

He remembered that it had been a warm evening in early September. He had made his way up past the school but was beginning to regret his route. The road was much steeper than he had imagined and he was getting quite short of breath and was coated in a slick of sweat that was making his clothes stick to him. As an

41

excuse to rest, he stopped by a thick bit of hedge and pretended to be looking for a nice length of branch he could break off to use as a stick.

As he peered into the darkness of the shrubs, he was surprised to see a glint of light about twenty feet ahead of him. What was it? A piece of metal, a bird's wing? He stepped into the ditch to get a closer look. Glass. It was a tiny bit of exposed window, the rest of it covered by a mass of untamed foliage. He stepped back and went to the other side of the road. Sure enough there was a small rusty gate almost lost in the dense hedge, and there, high up, he could see the very top of a chimney pot. An entire house swallowed whole by nature. PJ wiped the sweat from his eyes and let out a long sigh. The sadness of such neglect was somehow superseded by a wonder at the vigour and power of nature. The scratchings of man so easily erased. He had continued his walk, making a mental note to find out the story behind the buried farmhouse.

'Shit.' It was suddenly silent. The superintendent's whine had come to an end and he was looking at PJ expectantly. Had he asked a question? It was like being back at school, caught out by the teacher. There was nowhere to hide. PJ swallowed and tried a tentative 'Sorry?'

'Who? Which resident?'

'Who what now? I'm sorry, I just . . . ' His voice trailed away.

The detective superintendent picked a phantom piece of tobacco from the tip of his tongue and lowered his eyebrows until he was almost squinting.

'Sergeant Collins, I had hoped to use you in this investigation. I had hoped your local knowledge would be an asset to myself and the rest of the team, but if you're not interested . . . ' He raised his hands in a gesture that suggested he was taking no responsibility for what would happen next. PJ looked at him and decided that not speaking was probably his best course of action.

'Who was the last person to see the farmer lad?'

'Tommy Burke? People say he went to London.'

The superintendent closed his eyes and lowered his head. A beat and then he looked up again with a sigh.

'I'm aware of that, Sergeant. Who saw him go? Who has been in touch?'

PJ's face lit up. He knew this one.

'As far as I know, nobody has heard from him since he left, but I don't know why people think that's where he is. I'll ask around the village . . . unless . . . Is that all right? I don't want to go against proper procedure.'

A weak smile from the detective.

'No. That would be helpful.'

'Should I talk to the women at the same time, or is that your job?'

'Women?' His head cocked to one side.

PJ groaned silently. He hadn't told him. Well, it wasn't his fault. This slimy fuck wouldn't shut up, but of course now it was himself who looked like a bungling incompetent.

'The story was that Tommy left because of a

43

messy love life. I've never really got to the bottom of it, but I believe he was stringing a couple of girls along and it all came to a head with a fight in the village.'

'Names?'

'Well, I know one of the Ross girls was involved, but I'm not sure who the other one was. Would you like me to find out?'

A long, narrow cloud of cigarette smoke was followed by a quiet 'Yes. Yes, that would be good.' His voice was a patronising blend of bored, sad and resigned. PJ had an almighty urge to punch him hard in the face.

The rustle of paper in the wind made both men look behind them. A guard was coming towards them across the site, struggling with a large map. He weaved through the excavations like a small dinghy in rough seas having trouble with its sails. The map reared up and slapped him in the face and he nearly fell.

Christ. What a fucking clown, thought PJ.

'Jesus. Here comes another fucking clown,' said the detective. PJ could feel himself blushing.

A few spots of rain began to drum against their coats and the dark sky promised more. Detective Dunne shooed the approaching guard back.

'Head for the Portakabin,' he shouted into the wind, and pulling his collar up he moved off back towards the small makeshift site office. PJ hesitated for a moment then followed a few feet after him.

They stood around the brown Formica-topped table and stared down at the old map folded out before them. Strange names of townlands were written to the north and east of the area that was now the building site. The old house was marked just back from the road, and behind that a series of outbuildings and what would have been a large garden or paddock. The detective stared out of the window and then back to the table several times before speaking.

'So the body was found about here,' he said, pointing just to the east of the row of farm buildings that must have formed the farmyard at the rear of the house. He looked at PJ and opened his mouth to speak. The sergeant braced himself.

'How many acres?'

A wave of relief. He sort of knew this.

'Well, I'm not sure how big the farm was, but all that's left now is about six acres. The Flynn brothers bought it a few years ago to build a big scheme of houses, but then sure the arse fell out of everything.'

As he spoke, he had an idea, a brilliant idea. If the Flynn brothers had bought the land, they must know where Tommy Burke was. He blurted out, 'Oh, do you think . . . ' but before he could finish, the detective had turned to the other guard.

'One of these Flynns must know the whereabouts of the Burke fella if they bought a house off him. Track them down.'

PJ wasn't sure what he wanted to do exactly, but it was violent.

'One of them is just there, Detective.' The guard was pointing through the grime-smeared window at a large silver car parked by a couple of builders' vans just beyond a pile of gravel. Both PJ and the detective peered out and saw a bald middle-aged man sitting in the driver's seat talking on his phone.

'Well get him in here,' the detective barked, making it very clear that he considered himself to be the captain of a ship of fools.

With the other guard gone, PJ felt this was his chance to redeem himself. Surely he had some local insight to offer, some line of enquiry to suggest. He searched his brain, but to no avail. The two men stood silently side by side, the sound of the rain on the thin roof filling the silence. A heavy winter fly made its way slowly across a 2013 Bank of Ireland calendar hanging by the door.

★   ★   ★

The Flynn brothers, Martin and John, had taken over their father's small building company in the mid-nineties and quickly transformed it into the magnificent company Flynn's Future Homes, which, on the advice of a brand management company from London, had been shortened to Flynn's Futures. The idea was to use the millions they were making during the boom to diversify the company. Martin and John had lots of other ideas, but sadly so too did the economy. The great crash happened and now all the Flynns owned were their homes and cars, and they were lucky to have them. The offices and permanent employees were all gone and people wouldn't even talk to them after mass, they owed that much to so many. This modest development in Duneen was supposed to be the beginning of their comeback, and now this. A dead body. Martin was not a very religious man, but as he sat in the car talking to his brother John about whether or not the insurance would cover them, he decided that if there was a God, he was an awful bollocks.

'His name is Connolly. I think it's Fergus Connolly. He's based up in Dublin. He approached us. Said it was land that belonged to a relative.' Martin sat on the orange plastic chair opposite the detective and answered the questions as best he could. All he could think of was the amount of money they had paid at the time, when it seemed the golden goose would never stop laying. Suddenly he had a question of his own.

'Tell me this. If your man Connolly knew there was a body buried here, would I have a claim against him?' He could almost feel the wallet in his jacket pocket getting heavier.

Detective Dunne shut his notebook and gave him a smile, more out of pity than anything else.

'I really wouldn't know. Best speak to a solicitor about that. Thank you for your help.' He stood up, signalling that this interview had been terminated. As Martin got up to leave, he remembered that he had an even more pressing question.

'When do you think we'll get back to work on the site?'

The smile of pity again.

'I really wouldn't know. We'll be in touch.' The detective opened the small door and ushered Martin down the steps into the rain.

The policemen watched him scurry back to his car.

'Right. Let's find this Connolly. In my experience most bad things in this world happen because of sex or money, and we just found a whole lot of money.' Linus Dunne buttoned his coat and headed out towards his car.

PJ rolled his eyes. Had he really just said that out loud? He'd bet good money he was a graduate that had been fast tracked through the ranks. PJ stood in the door of the Portakabin watching him picking his way across the mud towards his car like a dressage pony. Yes, he really was a complete and utter prick.

7

Duneen slept. A ragbag of smoky clouds drifted across the half-moon sitting low in the sky. A fox trotted daintily down the main street, enjoying his freedom to strut in the open rather than cower in the clump of rhododendrons at the back of the priest's house. The street lights bled the shadow of his tail along the pavement behind him like a dark cloak. Almost as if he were keeping someone waiting, he quickened his pace as he got to the alley beside O'Driscoll's. The anticipation of browsing the bins without interruption gave his paws a slight bounce as he disappeared from view.

The fox was not the only resident awake. In four houses, four women found that sleep was eluding them.

Mrs Meany tossed and turned. Normally if she couldn't sleep she prayed a few rounds of the rosary, but tonight she couldn't even keep her mind on that. She kept losing count of the beads and the Hail Marys until it felt disrespectful. If she couldn't sleep, she reasoned, she might as well read her book, but the words refused to fall into place and become sentences that told a story. She shut the book and rubbed her hand across its shiny cover, tracing out the large embossed gold lettering. She felt so tired, why wouldn't her mind yield to sleep? Of course she had continued to think about the body they had

49

uncovered up at Burke's, but it was more than that. It was an uneasiness, a nervousness that tugged at the pit of her stomach. The past was opening up like a great dark bottomless pit, and she felt herself falling. Squeezing her eyes shut, she let out an audible whimper and pushed her book to one side, letting it hit the floor with a muffled thump.

Susan Hickey knew exactly why she couldn't sleep. Excitement. She had stayed up far too late getting everything ready. On the third Friday of every month she had a little coffee morning to raise money for the hospice in Ballytorne. Normally she made around fifty euros and she got a little thank you in the announcements at mass. Of course that wasn't why she did it, but it was a nice gesture. She enjoyed doing something to help others less fortunate, but at the same time it was amazing how quickly the third Friday came around every month. Tomorrow morning, however, couldn't come fast enough.

She smiled to herself as she added another stack of paper napkins to the already precarious tower on the sideboard. The timing couldn't be better. Guards swarming all over the village and an actual body unearthed in Duneen. True, she had been disappointed when she found out that it wasn't a mass grave, but in a way this was almost better. A single mystery. People would be coming from all over the parish. How lucky for her that her coffee morning was happening before that Sunday's mass so this would be everybody's first opportunity to discuss every little detail. She wasn't a gambling woman, but having talked it over with, well, everyone she had met in the last forty-eight hours, she was fairly certain the bones were the last remains of Little Tommy Burke.

She skipped up the stairs to bed. Whoever those bones belonged to, they hadn't buried themselves! She felt breathless as she pulled her duvet up and turned out the light. She hoped she had enough cups.

Like the Lady of Shalott, Evelyn lay on her back, her arms crossed over her chest and her hair fanned out on the pillow. Her breathing was deep and regular and yet her eyes remained wide open, staring into the gloom that engulfed her. She wondered if this was the start of her dark, lonely journey into madness. The last two days had been hell. She had lost count of the number of times she had had to run upstairs or rush into the downstairs toilet to have a quick cry. She hadn't dared step foot in the village, because she knew exactly what it would be like. All beady eyes and whispers, and just when you thought that was bad enough, some interfering bitch rubbing your arm and asking pointedly, 'And how are *you*?' Evelyn's flesh shuddered under the covers at the thought of it.

She knew Abigail was watching her carefully, but she honestly thought Florence hadn't noticed a thing. Evelyn suspected that she had spent so much time with children that she had begun to view the world as they did. She was the centre of her own universe and if it wasn't affecting her directly then it was as if it wasn't really happening. She sat at the table cheerfully recounting the comings and goings of the Garda cars up the hill past the school oblivious to what part her own sister might have played in the mystery. Mind you, why would anyone suspect that things that had happened — or more importantly hadn't happened — all those years ago would still have such a vice-like grip on her heart? At least when her parents had died, or when Tommy had left, she knew why she was crying. Back then the sleepless nights had felt real, felt natural, but what was this? How could her heart and mind make sense of these feelings when she couldn't name them? Was it sadness, regret, love? No, she decided, the most overwhelming emotion was fury. She wanted to slap the face that looked back at her from the mirror. This stupid woman who had allowed her whole life to slip by in a dull blur.

She put a hand up to her face to wipe away the tears that had begun to roll down the sides of her face into the pillow. The young girl with all that passion, where was she now? Wild, that was the word; Evelyn Ross had been wild. She had stood with her feet wide apart on Main Street and howled. She could remember the first punch, and the mad rush of adrenalin as people tried to drag them apart. Why had she banished that version of herself so completely; why had she replaced her with this prig? This woman who worried about cleaning tile grout and putting borage flowers in her salads? And for who? Not even a man — just her sisters, who neither cared nor noticed! What a fool! What a stupid, stupid woman she was.

She turned on the light and closed her eyes for a second to avoid the sudden glare. When she opened them again, she scanned the room as if searching for something, anything, that she could do to change her life. She couldn't go back, but she could start again. *Vogue!* Her ridiculous shrine to the clothes she would never own and the places she would never go. She almost jumped out of bed and started heaving bundles of the old magazines over to the door, where she stacked them in haphazard piles. When they had all been moved, she looked with satisfaction at the pale square on the carpet where they had been, making a mental note to give the room a good hoover. In the morning she would continue the *Vogues* on their journey. She would bring them to the back of the long shed and have a bonfire.

She closed her eyes and imagined the heat on her face and the flames dancing like flags in the wind. Something to look forward to at last.

Sleep had found Brid Riordan but now she had escaped its hold and was wide awake. She blamed the screw tops. It was so easy when you finished a bottle around ten to think to yourself that just one more glass was a good idea, then suddenly it was one o'clock in the morning and you were stumbling around the kitchen half-cut trying to get things ready for the next day. It was sort of funny, but also a bit mortifying, that time Carmel came home from school after finding a bottle of washing-up liquid in her lunch box. Brid had made a bit more of an effort after that. Well, after that and the time she got breathalysed taking the kids to school. Thank God she'd gotten away with a fine. Anthony had looked at her as if she'd tried to kill the kids, but she knew she'd been perfectly fine to drive. Failing one of those tests was very different from being drunk. Everyone knew that.

She had woken up face down on the kitchen counter at 3 a.m., and now, two hours later, she was still sat there half listening to the radio. She knew she should head upstairs. She'd feel awful in the morning, but she couldn't bear the disapproving sigh as Anthony rolled over when she got into bed. That was part of the problem. He went up so early and she had no one to talk to, so of course she had a few glasses of wine. She was bored! The kids were holed up with their computers all the time. Anthony wouldn't let her get another dog after she'd run over Trixie, even though the whole family knew it hadn't been her fault. Yes, she was bored.

The days weren't so bad. There were things to do. A bit of housework, a trip into the village or over to Ballytorne for provisions, dinner to make, but once Anthony, Carmel and Cathal had wolfed down their food, she was left alone with nothing to do and no distractions. She used to be a big reader when she'd been young, but somehow she had got out of the habit. As a girl she had welcomed the refuge novels had offered. In their pages she had imagined so many futures for herself, but time had run out for those fantasies. She was living her future. No book now seemed able to hold her, though she still bought the odd one and left them around the house just in case the mood would suddenly take hold of her. In reality they were just more things to dust.

Tommy Burke. She had needed a drink that lunchtime. Why had no one told her? She was sure Anthony must have heard but supposed he hadn't wanted to upset her; or maybe he simply didn't want to talk to her. He rarely did these days. The shock of it. She had been changing a bulb in the lamp in the hall. She'd asked Anthony to do it, but you might as well be talking to the wall. Through the frosted glass of the front door she saw the outline of Pat the postman. Carmel and Cathal used to get a real kick out of that. Their letters were delivered by a real-life Postman Pat. The excitement when they had a day off school so they'd be at home when he called! She'd opened the door to get the few bills or circulars she knew he'd have for her, but mostly just to see another face, hear another voice. They exchanged the usual observations about the weather, deciding it was mild for nearly December, certainly compared to last week, but then as Pat turned to leave he said, 'Fierce business up at the building site.'

Of course she couldn't have known what had happened; she just assumed one of the lads on the site had been injured or even killed.

'What's that, Pat?' Such a simple question. She leaned forward to get the news and he told her about the bones, and then he said his name. She hadn't heard that name spoken out loud for so many years, and here was a voice telling her that Tommy Burke was dead and buried in his own farmyard.

She had slumped into the spare dining room chair she kept by the hall table, a light bulb in one hand and her letters in the other. Pat had rushed forward. 'Are you all right there, Mrs Riordan?' Brid had immediately rallied and reassured him as she stood up that everything was fine. She waved him on his way and shut the door. Then, without ever deciding to, she headed straight for the fridge and poured herself a large glass of white wine.

★ ★ ★

Brid Riordan had never been the prettiest girl in Duneen. Her mother's weak chin combined with the broad features and stocky build of her father meant she had always had the look of a much older woman, even as a child. At school she had relied on being clever and the first to make jokes at her own expense in order to survive. After school she continued to live at home on the farm with her parents and got a job doing the books for the largest chemist's shop in Ballytorne. She made the most of herself, spending her wages on make-up and clothes, and went to all the dances, but somehow, despite her longing for a boyfriend, she knew that none of the boys who spoke to her were good enough. She flicked through magazines and gazed into the moist eyes of John Travolta, or imagined David Soul placing his hand on the small of her back as he helped her step into a low open-topped car.

By the time she reached her mid-twenties she had still never had a boyfriend. Her friends from school were one by one announcing their engagements, and a few were even pushing prams. Brid had been a bridesmaid three times, and of course everyone told her as she stood at the reception wearing some ill-fitting dress in a colour that didn't appear in nature that she would be next. She would smile and nod even though she knew it wasn't true. Despite all of this, though, she didn't panic. She knew the other girls had their assets — the shiny hair, the beautiful bodies, the perfect teeth — but she was also aware that she would develop her own allure.

Early one Sunday evening, while her father was still out finishing the milking, her mother had sat her down at the kitchen table for 'a talk', in an act of parenting that was as breathtaking as it was brutal. When the radio was switched off, Brid knew it was serious.

Her mother started to speak to her about boys, and Brid instantly dreaded the conversation that was about to happen. She had heard some of the older girls at the convent talking and laughing about 'willies' and 'hard-ons'. It all sounded awful. In fact the conversation took a very different turn as her mother carefully explained to her that she wouldn't find it easy with boys. They would always be more interested in the pretty girls. Brid's eyes filled with great globe-like tears and her mother stroked her hand, telling her calmly that she mustn't worry. Her father was getting on and not in the best of health, and when he went, the boys would be knocking the door down for the farm. Brid would find her man in time, and he'd be a good steady worker who would make a great father, because he'd have his head tied on straight. It wasn't what any teenage girl dreaming of princes and pop stars wanted to hear, but it had prepared her for the next ten years of her life.

Once her father had been hospitalised for what seemed to be the last time, various friends of her mother's would arrive with cake, or a stew, to save her cooking, since she was having to make the journey up and back to Cork every day. They also brought with them sons. Giant children who sat awkwardly in the kitchen staring at the floor while their mothers talked to Brid for them.

'Brendan did the Leaving Cert a couple of years after you, but he was very good at English. Don't you like reading, Brid?'

'Kevin is just back from the agricultural college over in Darrara. He did very well. He's mad for the farming. Aren't you Kevin?'

These evenings were torture for everyone, and of course pointless. There was only one gentleman caller in the village who was going to get any sort of welcome, and that was Tommy Burke. He wasn't very tall, but Brid kind of liked that. With his dark hair and shy smile, he had the look of a Spaniard about him. She wondered if something as simple as land could really get her a man like that and decided that, until she knew for certain, she wouldn't even consider any of the dolts in their Lee jeans and baggy sweatshirts bearing the names of American cities they would never see.

Her courtship of Tommy lasted for several

months without him knowing anything about it. On Fridays she would follow him from stall to stall at the market in Ballytorne. From a distance she began to know him. He was a great man for cheese and he liked white pudding more than black. She stored away these details ready for when they started their life together. After mass, she stood as close to him as she dared in O'Driscoll's when he was getting the papers. He smelled lovely. Nothing like the other boys.

When her dreams finally came true, it all seemed to happen so fast and effortlessly. He had waited until after her father's funeral, which she thought was a nice touch, and then he drove up to the house to pay his respects. She remembered her mother taking the bottle of red wine he offered and passing it to her to put in the back kitchen with all the other unopened bottles that people had brought with their words of condolence. Tommy and her mother had made stilted conversation. He asked long, serious questions about the amount of acres and the yields, while she stared at him with the wide, gormless smile of a girl who did not appear to be too upset at the death of her father.

After Tommy left, her mother was transformed into a giggling schoolgirl, gushing about his eyes and his lovely skin. Brid felt decidedly uneasy. She didn't want to think about her mother having those sorts of feelings towards any man, but especially not the one who was going to make her the happiest girl in all of Ireland.

The next contact came after mass, when he approached them on the chapel steps. With no preamble of any kind he blurted out an invitation to go to the pictures in Ballytorne on the following Friday. It wasn't entirely clear if he was asking her or her mother, or possibly both of them. Only the sight of her mother glaring at her prompted Brid to utter a breathless 'Yes. That would be lovely.' The expression on Tommy's face didn't change. He just grunted and said, 'I'll be up for you about seven, so.' And then he was gone. Out of the corner of her eye she could see her mother looking at her with eyebrows arched and lips pursed.

'What?' Brid asked. 'It's only the pictures!' The two women smiled at each other, and then, as they walked back to the car, they both began to laugh.

As it turned out, none of the dates were quite how Brid had fantasised. There were no long, passionate kisses. His rough cheek never rubbed against her smooth white neck. No walking hand in hand in the moonlight. That first trip to the cinema, to see *Robin Hood: Prince of Thieves* — Kevin Costner looked fierce old — had set the tone for the six or seven dates that followed. He opened doors for her and bought her a box of Maltesers, but sitting in the dark he never once tried to put an arm around her or take her hand. Brid had sat too close so that their arms touched and even through the wool of her cardigan she could feel the heat of his body.

Afterwards he had bought two bags of chips and they had sat in the car, eating more than talking. He asked a couple of questions about her father's funeral and talked a little about how strange it was being in his house by himself, with no mother or father. Brid made small noises of agreement or sympathy as she piled chip after chip into her mouth. She thought of the two of them alone in his house. It would be different there. Hands would be everywhere, they would be tangled up in large white sheets, and then . . . Her imagination drifted in a vague warm mist.

When the car pulled into the yard to the back of Brid's house, Tommy had jumped out at once and run around to open her door. She stepped from the car and found her face very close to his. She could feel his breath, the smell of vinegar. She waited. Tommy cleared his throat.

'Right. Thank you very much. Would you like to go out again?' She stared at his face but it gave nothing away. He showed more enthusiasm when he was choosing cheese.

'Lovely, yeah,' she replied, and then, more out of desperation than desire, she leaned in and kissed his cheek. Still nothing. It was as if he was embarrassed for her, and his lack of response was his way of sparing her further humiliation. Brid had behaved the same way when her Aunt Rhona's dressing gown had gaped open, revealing a pale, veiny breast.

She stood in the hall with her back pressed against the front door and listened to his car drive off, unsure of what had happened. Had she done something wrong? Was this just what first dates were like? She made sure not to air her doubts when her mother quizzed her about the evening, and by the morning she had managed

61

to reconstruct the whole date in her mind. He was the perfect gentleman and clearly he saw her as his princess, not some trollop who would let any boy kiss her tits for a glass of wine.

Two months later, they still hadn't kissed, and he certainly hadn't tried to undo her bra, but despite that, she still found herself opening a small white box with a ring inside. They were parked in Tommy's car in the main square of Ballytorne on a Saturday afternoon. Brid watched people walking by with their shopping, some talking, some laughing, but most looking bored and beaten by their lives. She looked back down at the small diamond ring, and then at Tommy. He turned away and, staring straight ahead through the windscreen, said, 'I wondered would you like to get married?'

Brid imagined she was standing in the street looking at their car. That girl was being proposed to by Tommy Burke! That girl was clearly the luckiest girl alive, and yet whatever she might be feeling at that very moment, Brid was fairly certain that it wasn't lucky. She longed to ask him questions. Do you love me? Do you want me to be happy? Will you . . . She opened her mouth and, a little louder than she expected, said, 'Yes.'

She reached forward in her bulky coat to hug him. He let her kiss him on the mouth. His lips felt warm and very dry. Then he gently pushed her away and started the engine. As they drove in silence back out to Duneen, past the familiar bungalows, fields and junctions, she pulled herself deep inside her coat and wept great jagging tears.

As news of the engagement spread, so did the joy. Everyone loved a wedding, and especially after all the tragedy that had befallen the village of late. There had been far too many funerals. It was Brid's mother's idea to put the announcement in the *Irish Times*. She wanted everything done perfectly. She knew how keenly her little girl had dreamed of this day, and she was going to make sure it was everything she had hoped for and even more.

After the awful scene with the Ross girl, and in the days following Tommy's disappearance, Brid often wondered if everyone had known all along. Had all those people shaking her hand and beaming their congratulations at her been secretly pitying her? She had decided they hadn't, partly because that was what she believed but also because to think otherwise would have driven her insane. It was hard enough to imagine how life would continue as she and her mother sat in the kitchen wrapping up wedding presents ready to return.

★　★　★

The door of the kitchen opened with a jolt. Anthony stood there, his face gleaming red and still wet from the shower. His plaid shirt clung to his thin frame where he hadn't dried his back.

Shit. Had she been asleep? She didn't think so. Pushing her hair back, she made an attempt at a smile.

'Good morning.'

Anthony gave her the look. The look that said

63

everything that was wrong with their lives but mostly told her that she disgusted him.

'Have you been up all night?'

She was at the sink now, turning the tap on, trying to look like she had a purpose.

'I had a little nap down here. I didn't think I could sleep and I didn't want to keep you awake as well.' She tried another small smile.

Anthony muttered something as he made his way to the fridge. She saw him making a point of ignoring the empty wine bottle on the counter. She rolled her eyes. Another day in paradise.

8

Detective Superintendent Dunne had decided to drive up to Dublin to talk to the cousin who had sold the land. Of course he didn't have to go himself, but it was as good an excuse as any to spend a night away from June and the new baby. It was agreed that one of his colleagues would come down from Cork to conduct the interviews with both of the women who had been associated with Tommy Burke. PJ was to be in effect a combination of driver and local guide.

Linus had just left Cork behind him and was driving north towards Dublin on the M8 when his mobile rang. He waited for the Bluetooth to pick it up, but it didn't. Of course it fucking didn't. He hesitated before reaching down for the handset and prayed he wasn't stopped by the guards. Listening without comment to the news that a fatal stabbing overnight in the city meant his colleague was no longer available, he reluctantly agreed that Sergeant Sumo could make the initial contact with the former girlfriends and conduct the interviews. He reasoned that surely even Sumo could get the bare facts; if they needed any further information, he could always see the women later himself. As he hung up, he glanced down at the petrol gauge. He figured it would get him as far as Urlingford.

★   ★   ★

Somebody knew. One of the faces that he passed must know who was buried up there and how it had happened. Maybe they all knew. Was there a conspiracy of silence amongst the good people of Duneen? Certainly PJ had never been made to feel like such an outsider in all his time in the village. Conversations stopped when he was spotted, and if people caught his eye, they seemed sheepish and furtive; even Mrs Meany served his meals in silence. PJ didn't like it. Did they all have something to hide or were they just unsure of how to treat him now that he finally had a real crime to investigate?

He wondered how this morning's visit would go. What was that saying about answered prayers? He had been cursing the fact that he wouldn't get to do any interviews by himself, but as the gates of Ard Carraig came up on the left, he found himself dreading it. He had taken his unexpected responsibility as a vote of confidence, but now, as his car slowed to a stop and his heartbeat increased alarmingly, he began to wonder if that confidence had been misplaced.

He switched off the engine and took a moment to collect himself. Though he had passed the gates many times over the years, this was the first time he had ever had cause to come down to the house itself. The grey-plastered facade was less grand than he had imagined, and although it had the large Georgian fanlight above the front door, and tall sash windows, the rest of the house seemed very plain and bare. Still, it had an air of quiet elegance, sitting at the edge of a wide sweep of gravel driveway. To the left, behind a high stone wall, he could see a plume of grey smoke drifting up into a matching sky.

Right, he thought, somebody must be in. He had feared they weren't when he had arrived and seen no sign of a car parked outside. He hoped that the sister he was looking for — he checked the scrap of paper on the passenger seat: Evelyn — was at home. He opened the car door and placed one foot on the gravel, but then, as if the ground was covered with burning coals, jerked his leg back into the car. How was he going to play this? Was he going to pretend he was hearing the whole story for the first time? No. That would be stupid. Sure, why was he here if he knew nothing? Would he be all friendly with her? Maybe it was better to try and intimidate her?

He noticed he had started to pant again. He gripped the steering wheel and took a few deep breaths. Evelyn Ross was not a dangerous woman. He would simply play it by ear. Before he could talk himself out of it, he hauled himself from the car and slammed the door. He hesitated for a moment before deciding to head straight for the source of the smoke. He walked past the house and made his way to a small door in the high garden wall. He noticed that the paintwork was very well maintained.

Good, he thought, I'm noticing details. That's good. I'm good at this. He tried the handle, and with a slight jolt and a long creak it opened. On the other side he found himself in a small cobbled courtyard, lined with various outhouses. The smoke was coming from somewhere behind them.

Evelyn Ross was beginning to think the bonfire had burned down low enough for her to leave it and head back inside. Her eyes were red, but that was from the smoke rather than from any tears at the loss of her *Vogue* hill. The reality hadn't left her quite as elated as the thought of doing it had the night before, but still she felt she had taken the first few steps on some sort of journey to a new life. She looked about her. The arch of the trees behind the chimneys, the fields sloping away down towards the overgrown banks of the stream where their childhood pets were buried, the damp patches on the stone wall of the long shed, all so painfully familiar that they seemed to gently mock her: 'What are you still doing here?' Evelyn glanced down at the dark green of her Wellingtons, which she'd had for so long she couldn't remember buying them. Why was she rooted to this spot?

She had never imagined that this house and these few fields would be her whole life. Somehow she thought there would come a moment when it felt right to leave, but it appeared that she was still waiting for it. She remembered so well the day Florence had come back from college. The bags in the hall bearing the names of impossibly glamorous shops in Dublin: Brown Thomas, Switzer's, Boyers. The tissue paper on the kitchen table where she had unwrapped her gifts — a hairband covered in tiny pearl-like beads and a pair of slippers trimmed with rabbit fur. She had felt truly happy that day for them all to be back together, but when Florence had made her big announcement about her new job at the school in Duneen, Evelyn's joy, even then, had been tinged by guilt. She knew that Florence had only come back for her, but what could she do about it? She had never asked her to. It wasn't her fault. If Abigail had made her return, then blame her! But she knew in her heart that both of them had stayed for her, and if she had decided to go it would be like telling them they had wasted their lives, that she had never needed them. It was ludicrous. Was it really possible that she could have wasted so much of her own life out of a demented sort of politeness?

Looking up, she saw the dark shape of a man come around the corner. Who was that? It looked like Sergeant Collins, but why would he . . . Oh, of course. Evelyn had expected someone to come. She raised her hand and waved. The guard returned the gesture and then stood and waited as she picked her way through the weeds and long grass towards him.

'Good morning, Guard.'

'Hello. It's Evelyn Ross, isn't it?'

'It is. I was just . . . How can I help you?'

'We just wanted to ask you a few questions about the disappearance of Tommy Burke. Just any details you can recollect. Would that be . . .' He trailed off.

Evelyn smiled broadly. 'Of course. Will you come inside?' She indicated the way he had come and began to move off even before the sergeant had grunted his assent. They walked around the shed in silence and crossed the cobbles towards the back door of the house.

Evelyn was wondering where she'd put him. Did the kitchen seem too casual, overfamiliar? Yet the front room seemed wrong too, and besides, she hadn't drawn the curtains in there yet, or cleaned out the fire. PJ found he was pleasantly distracted by the way the soft grey material of Evelyn's trousers clung to the curve of her hips. He wondered how old she was.

Well, he thought, in a minute I can ask her.

Evelyn gave a slight start when she saw her sister Florence sitting at the kitchen table with a small stack of books. Then she remembered that the night before she had said she was getting a half-day because of some plumbing issue up at the school. Florence looked up and smiled, but before Evelyn could make any introductions, PJ had marched forward with a burst of unexpected confidence, his arm outstretched. 'Miss Ross.'

'Sergeant,' came the reply of recognition along with a vigorous handshake. PJ noticed the puzzled expression on Evelyn's face.

'I go in a couple of times a year to talk about road safety to the kids in Miss Ross's class.'

'Of course,' Evelyn said, as her sister stood, pushing away her books.

'Oh please, we're not in the classroom now. Call me Florence.' She finished her sentence with a strange high-pitched giggle that Evelyn had never heard before. Was it possible that her sister was flirting with this shiny-faced lump? Oh God. Look at him. He was blushing.

'Florence, I wonder if you could excuse us? The sergeant wanted to ask me a few questions.'

Her sister looked puzzled for a moment but then quickly realised what was going on. She gave Evelyn the same smile of encouragement she used for children before an exam. 'Of course, of course.' She began to gather her books. 'I can do this in the other room.' As she got to the door, she looked over her shoulder. 'Nice to see you, Sergeant Collins.'

'And you . . . ' he hesitated, 'Miss . . . Florence.' He attempted a smile. Evelyn silently noted that smiling really didn't suit him.

Tea. Should she offer him tea?

'Would you like some tea?'

'No, I'm grand, thanks. Well, unless you're making some.'

'I am, of course,' Evelyn replied and brought the kettle over to the tap. 'Sit down there.' The sergeant did as he was told.

Over at the dresser, she decided on mugs. This was not a cup-and-saucer situation.

'I'm not sure how helpful I'm going to be. It was all such a long time ago, I've probably forgotten everything,' she said out loud, though of course she knew that was a lie. She could remember every detail of what had happened. As she poured boiling water on the tea bags, she wondered how much she would actually tell this man. Why couldn't she tell him everything? She had nothing to hide. Walking back to the table, she felt an unexpected twinge of excitement.

The tea poured, the milk and sugar added (Evelyn watching in horror as the sergeant added three heaped teaspoons to his mug), they both settled themselves for the main event. PJ reached for his notebook. Oh for fuck's sake! He pictured the small black notebook lying on the passenger seat of the car. He took out his pen and held it in the air like a wand with which he could conjure some paper out of thin air. He was glad there was no gobshite from Cork with him to witness this. He cleared his throat.

Evelyn leaned forward. 'Oh Sergeant, would you like something to write on?' PJ knew she wasn't trying to mock him, or make him feel foolish. She was just being helpful and kind. He beamed.

'Yes please.'

Oh, she thought, that smile suits him better. She caught a glimpse of the man behind the Garda uniform. He seemed sweet, almost vulnerable. Despite his enormous bulk, there was something boyish about him. She handed him an old spiral-backed jotter she used for making lists, and the interview began.

It lasted for just under half an hour. His questions were simple and thorough: 'What was the nature of your relationship with Tommy Burke?' 'When did you last see him?' 'Have you heard from him since then?' 'Do you have any idea of his whereabouts?'

Evelyn spoke calmly. It felt so strange to hear her voice saying his name out loud again after so many years. She hoped her tone came across as measured and reflective. Sometimes, just for effect, she paused as if trying to recall exactly what order certain events had occurred in. PJ took copious notes. Linus the prick would not catch him out on this one.

She told him how Tommy had needed some help around the house after his mother died. He must have mentioned it to Abigail when he was paying the rent money, and she had suggested that Evelyn could do it so she'd have a little bit of cash in her pocket. Back then her sister thought she might still have a life of dances and boyfriends away from Ard Carraig. She detailed the day she had been getting ready to head over to Burke's when Florence had read out the engagement notice from the *Irish Times*. Glossing over the way both her sisters had teased her, she described going to the farm and finding the house locked up. She had never seen Tommy again. No, she didn't know his current whereabouts.

She answered truthfully and in as much detail as she could, and yet as the sergeant began to bring things to a close, tearing the pages from her jotter and thanking her for the tea, Evelyn knew she had not told her story. This man had garnered some facts but he didn't know what had really happened. She thought of all the things she hadn't told him.

She hadn't described her feelings when Tommy had walked into the kitchen one morning with his shirt unbuttoned. He was startled to see her and immediately began to cover his chest, but not before she had seen the ridge of dark hair that led down to his belt, and his smooth white skin and honey-coloured nipples. His blushes. His smile. How her heart had thumped; how she had closed her eyes so many times to see him come around that door once more with his wet hair and shirt flapping free.

She didn't tell the sergeant how she had fussed around the house, imagining a time when she would live there with Tommy. A jug of flowers on the dresser, two bath towels, making sure the toilet seat was down. She couldn't talk to Tommy directly, but by coaxing the house into accepting her, she felt the rest would follow. She could just slip into his life. She stood and watched him eat his lunch before taking the empty plate over to the sink, her hands shaking after the way he had looked up at her and smiled his thanks, a lock of hair hanging over his eyes.

No mention had been made of the small brown paper parcel she had found on the kitchen table one morning. Tommy had thrust a finger towards it and, not looking at her, said, 'That's for you.' She opened it slowly, trying to hide her excitement. After all, it might just be a few tea towels or some dusters. As she peeled back the paper, she let out a little gasp. Pink roses on a silky cream material. She held it up, wafting it through the air.

'It's a scarf,' Tommy had explained.

'Sure, I know. It's only gorgeous.' And then she had hugged him. This policeman would never understand the heat of Tommy's body, how solid he felt, the smell of him, grass and soil and a musky maleness. After she had broken away, there was an embarrassed silence between them. Evelyn slid the scarf between her hands and held it up to her face.

'Thank you.' His smile. His flushed cheeks.

That had been the last time she had seen him.

For years she had thought the scarf was some sort of leaving present, but now she knew that she had been right that morning when she had folded it back up ready to bring it home to take pride of place on her dressing table. It had been a love token.

She failed to mention her humiliation outside O'Driscoll's, or how when she had found the house locked up she had let herself in. Part of her had wanted to see him so she could tell him that she would never be coming back to clean or cook for him again, but the coward in her was glad to find the house empty. She wondered when he'd move in with his new wife. Just thinking about it had made her feel unsteady on her feet. How could he prefer that girl? How could he want to live with her?

She didn't tell the sergeant how she had washed the one dirty plate and cup that had been left on the counter, how she had climbed the stairs and thrown herself on Tommy's unmade bed, drinking in the smell of him and leaving his pillow drenched with her tears. There was no mention of her placing the silky scarf neatly folded on the kitchen table. She had considered leaving some sort of note as well, but then thought about Tommy and Brid reading it together and laughing, or even worse, pitying her. She left the door wide open and put one leaden foot in front of the other as she walked back to her loveless past that seemed to also be her future.

'It's Tommy, isn't it?' she blurted out.

'Sorry?'

'Up above. The remains. They're Tommy's, aren't they?'

'Too soon to know who it is. There will be tests, I'm sure, and then we'll find out.' PJ paused and looked at Evelyn's face. Her eyes darted around the room. There was a twitch in her upper lip. 'Why are you so sure it's Tommy?'

She hesitated before she spoke. She had told no one, but then no one had asked her before. She had found this interrogation unexpectedly pleasant. She couldn't remember the last time another human being, and certainly not a man, had been so interested in her. She knew he was only doing his job, but she felt flattered.

'It just makes sense that it's him. When I heard about the bones, I knew at once. He . . . You'll think me very foolish, Sergeant, I know I was only a girl at the time, but Tommy Burke . . . well, he loved me.'

She felt a sudden engulfing tsunami of emotion come over her. She grabbed the mugs and stood up with her back to the sergeant, determined not to collapse, a sobbing mess, in front of this man. She moved quickly to the sink and let the cold water run over her hands. A few deep breaths. She tried again. What did she want to say? She decided to forgo any preamble about Tommy's feelings or how she could be so sure. There was only one thing she needed to tell this man:

'Brid Riordan killed Tommy Burke.'

She turned and stared at Sergeant Collins, awaiting his response. She wasn't exactly sure of what reaction her accusation would provoke, but she had certainly expected more than this. The sergeant sat perfectly still, staring back at her, breathing through his slightly open mouth.

PJ was thinking.

Of course Brid would be a suspect, but surely Evelyn Ross must know that she too was under suspicion? He was beginning to feel uncomfortable. Somehow being alone in this room with a woman who was clearly very emotional didn't seem like one of his better ideas. He wondered if he should call for Florence to try and defuse things. Evelyn's statement sounded less like the facts and more like a deeply intimate secret that she shouldn't be sharing with a stranger. Neither of them was looking away, so that the stare was now locked. PJ felt very warm and his mouth was dry. He swallowed and spoke. 'Thank you for the tea, Miss Ross. We'll be in touch should we have any more questions.' He smiled in what he hoped was an encouraging way.

'Did you hear me, Sergeant? I told you who killed Tommy.'

'Yes, of course. Well, it is an ongoing investigation and I, we . . . they will be exploring many different roads . . . not roads, sorry, avenues.' PJ longed to be out of this room and back in his car. One glance at Evelyn's face and the twitching muscles in her neck told him that wouldn't be happening as quickly as he'd like.

'Do you not believe me? Am I just some deluded old spinster to you?' Like a fuse being lit, Evelyn felt outraged that rather than thanking her and heading off to arrest the ugly drunk bitch, this man was talking to her as if she were one of the old biddies who came down from the mountains to collect their pensions from the post office counter in O'Driscoll's.

PJ was standing now and speaking as he moved to the door. 'It's not that at all. But you must understand that we have to wait to learn all the facts. The investigation has really only just begun, and we don't yet know who the bones up there belong to.' He hoped these sentences sounded plausible. He just wanted Evelyn to go back to being the calm, charming woman he had met just half an hour earlier. He was in the hall now.

'Goodbye, Sergeant!' It was Florence's voice, coming from a room to his right. The front door was steps away. His hand was on the large brass lock when Evelyn pressed herself close to his face and whispered urgently into his ear. 'You'll see. I'm right. That woman knew he'd never really love her.' PJ could see the fine hairs above her lip.

Evelyn stepped back, startled by her own intense outburst. She knew she was right, but she was also suddenly aware of how unhinged she must seem to this poor policeman so clearly desperate to escape.

'Sorry, Sergeant. Let me.' And she reached up and opened the door for him.

They stood together for a moment in silence. The wind moved through the trees and the cold air felt good on their faces. She looked up at the sergeant. 'I do apologise.'

'That's quite all right. We'll be in touch.' And

then without thinking he found that he had reached out and stroked her arm. It wasn't a gesture that came easily to him and yet it felt like the right thing to do. Evelyn too found the hand on her arm surprising but appreciated that this man wanted in his own clumsy way to help her heal. She smiled and he started across the gravel towards the police car.

Out of the rustle of the branches came the sound of a car engine. PJ stopped and looked. A small red hatchback was making its way down the drive. It was going slightly too fast, and as it reached the expanse of gravel in front of the house it skidded to an abrupt halt. Behind the wheel was the horrified, wide-eyed face of Brid Riordan. Three sets of eyes met, and then the hatchback did a violent U-turn before taking off with a screech in a cloud of dust and gravel, heading back towards the gate. Inside the car, Brid gripped the steering wheel and bellowed a long, loud 'Fuuuuuuck!'

9

Linus sat hunched in a small cave of light at the end of the dark abandoned office. In the grey gloom, empty desks were arranged in rows like hospital beds; the glint of a street light coming through the blinds, the green glow of a fire exit sign, the flickering light from a computer screen saver at someone's desk. Detective Superintendent Linus Dunne had the privilege of his own glass-and-plywood cubicle. At this time of night he left the door ajar for air, but during the day he tended to keep it firmly shut. If he couldn't hear their stupidity, he reasoned to himself, then he might forget for a few hours that he worked with idiots.

Mind you, he thought, as he scrolled through endless emails from various departments, brains weren't helping him much here. O'Shea, the fuckwit, had by fluke got the guys who did the stabbing, and when they went to the house to arrest them had found it packed with stolen goods, meaning that in the space of two hours he had closed about fifteen cases and was now downing pints.

A long, weary sigh escaped from Dunne's lips. This was not going well. He reached out to his mug of coffee. It was cold. He considered going to make another but decided against it. The kitchen area was downstairs, and besides, he should go home. He was making no progress here.

The trip to Dublin hadn't really answered any questions. He had quickly found Fergus Connolly in his well-maintained terraced house in Ranelagh. They had sat in an overdesigned kitchen-diner extension at the back of the house while Mrs Connolly set about getting refreshments for the 'Super Detective'. Linus had looked ruefully at a pristine Gaggia machine sparkling on the granite worktop as Mrs Connolly placed a steaming mug of weak instant coffee in front of him.

Fergus told his story. When his mother died, she had left him far less than he had been expecting. They suspected that a neighbouring widower had convinced her to invest in various doomed business ventures, but they could prove nothing, and in any case the money was gone. Fergus had remembered his mother talking about how her nephew down in West Cork had gone missing and by rights how that land should be hers. Over the years he had forgotten about it because it was only a few acres out in the wilds. What would it be worth? By now, however, land was gold, especially if you could get planning permission. He had got a lawyer involved and eventually the High Court had agreed to issue a death certificate for Tommy Burke. At this piece of information Linus had choked on his coffee and his face turned rhubarb pink. The old couple looked at him with surprise. Even they were taken aback that the investigation hadn't unearthed such a basic fact. The old man continued. He was his sole heir. Fergus smiled widely at his wife and she in turn grinned at Linus and made a gesture with her right hand like a gone-to-seed magician's assistant. *Voilà!* A ridiculous seventy-thousand-euro kitchen!

It was a good trick, thought Linus as he made his way back out to his car. Christ, was that a Sean Scully hanging in the hall? He made a mental note to check just how much money they had got for the scrap of a farm. Could Connolly have killed Burke? He looked back at the couple on the doorstep waving him off with inane grins, both of them wearing cardigans that didn't quite meet over generous bellies. No, he decided, they were not killers.

Linus had opted not to stay in the city after all but instead drove straight to Cork to scream at his worthless team of fuckwits. There was a death certificate for Tommy Burke and nobody had thought to look for it. It beggared belief! A group of ten-year-olds armed with nothing more than Google could do a better job. At least the reports he found waiting for him from the technical bureau were more efficient. The body was that of a male between the ages of sixteen and twenty-two. The cause of death was blunt-force trauma to the side of the skull, and they estimated that the remains had been in the ground for over two decades but less than three. The end of the email contained the bad news: neither dental records nor DNA could provide an identity for the body.

The detective's brain collated what he knew and what he wanted to find out. It was a young man who was murdered, over twenty years ago. Good. He paused. Unless they could establish who the man was, there was no way they could move forward. They had to ascertain if the body was Tommy Burke or not. Much as it pained him, he realised he was going to have to apply for an exhumation order for the parents. Linus wasn't squeamish about blood, or even finding a limb, like that leg they'd come across up by the lough last spring, but there was something about disturbing remains that he found deeply unsettling. Still, it had to be done. He would alert Sergeant Sumo so that he could let the locals know why it was necessary.

He reached forward to turn out his lamp and glanced at the wooden-framed photograph to the right of his computer. A small, thin woman with dark hair that hung limply down the sides of her face stood holding a baby whose face was hidden in a lemon blanket. Linus thought back to the day he'd taken the picture, just a few hours after they had come back from the hospital. He pressed with his thumb and plunged the cubicle into darkness. He sat still for a moment, and then, as he got to his feet, decided he might just swing by the pub for one before he went home.

10

Brid hated herself. Why had she been so stupid? What had possessed her to drive over to Ard Carraig? How could that have ever been a good idea?

She blamed her tiredness. Somehow she lacked the energy to fight her impulses. There had been a thousand times since that day all those years before when she had wanted to attack Evelyn Ross. So smug and perfect. Walking through the village in that coat that hung so well, with her fucking wicker basket. Every step she took a declaration to the world that her love for Tommy had been pure and she was waiting for him to return. Not like Brid, with her blouses straining around her breasts, too large on the shoulders. Brid with her noisy children; Brid, who had given herself with extraordinary haste to that boring Riordan fella.

Evelyn didn't understand. Brid's mother had left her with no choice, telling her in no uncertain terms that she had ruined her life. A virgin with a farm was one thing, but trailing a broken engagement behind you like a soiled sheet was something else entirely. When Anthony had come sniffing around for the unclaimed farm, her mother had virtually locked them in the front room together until some talk of marriage had occurred. Brid had known all along it wasn't right, but, she reasoned, it was better than the alternative. The wedding had been a welcome distraction and Anthony to begin with had been pleasantly attentive in ways that Tommy had never been. He liked to kiss her, he ran his hands over her breasts; he did all the right things, but he was the wrong man. He wasn't Tommy.

She thought she could forget Tommy and move on with her life, but how could she, because there was Evelyn fucking Ross. Calm, cool Evelyn, walking through the village at an even pace. Never sweat patches under her arms, never a thick clump of hair that refused to lie flat even when you'd slapped it down with cold water. It didn't matter what Evelyn was doing — buying a paper, browsing the stalls at the summer fete, trotting down the steps after mass; what she was really doing was judging Brid Riordan. Ugly, fat, sweaty Brid Riordan.

With Tommy on her mind, Brid had sat in the car before nipping into O'Driscoll's for a sliced loaf. She had glanced in the direction of Ard Carraig and suddenly no time had passed. It was all so real. The light was the same, the heavy clouds moving across the sky, the shadows racing around the street as if the whole village doubted itself. It had been about this time, half nine in the morning, and she had just left the shop with a box of eggs. Her mother wanted to make meringues to give people who came up to see the wedding presents before the big day. She heard her before she saw her. Evelyn's feet clattering down the road. At first she wasn't sure who it was; all she could see was a skirt swinging wildly from side to side above bouncing knees. She remembered how Evelyn's hair had swung in the opposite direction, and then there she was, standing in front of her breathing heavily. Brid thought of the cows snuffling from behind the wooden door of the milking parlour.

'Why?' The voice was so loud that immediately bodies had gathered at the door of the shop.

Brid tried to remain calm. 'Why what?'

Evelyn brandished a piece of silky material.

'Why would you go after somebody when they're in love with someone else?' Her voice had now become a scream.

'I'm . . . I'm engaged to be married.' Brid was aware of how hot and red her face was becoming.

Evelyn was sobbing now and almost howled out, 'He gave me this scarf!'

'Well,' Brid's voice was louder now, 'he asked *me* to marry him!' She tried to sound victorious, but as she looked at the soft pinks of the scarf and the slim young girl before her, somehow she knew the truth.

They stared at each other, both crying now, their lips moving, looking for something to say, but suddenly there were no words.

Then Brid felt a sharp, stinging pain in her left cheek. It took a moment before she fully comprehended that Evelyn Ross had slapped her. It was as if someone had fired a starting pistol. They flew at each other, like animals fighting over a half-eaten carcass. Brid struck hard and Evelyn was on the ground. The eggs went flying as Brid straddled her, but Evelyn was too quick to pin down. She grabbed Brid's hair and pulled her head down to the pavement. She squirmed and punched and now she was on top. People had gathered in the street, and more were hurrying down the hill to witness the action. Brid felt a sharp pain in her ear. Evelyn had dug in with her nails! She raised her hand to slap her but instead managed to elbow her hard just below her right eye. Panting and grunting, they had rolled into the gutter and on to the street.

The spectators, much as they were enjoying it all, felt they had let it go on long enough, so a few stepped forward and dragged them apart. Gasping for air, the two girls had glared at each other. Brid's coat hung loose where several buttons had come off, and a delicate trail of blood was trickling down her neck. Evelyn's blouse was torn and her flesh-coloured bra strap was there for all the world to see.

Old Mrs Byrne, long since gone, was the one who urged them both to leave the scene. 'He's only a man, and sure aren't there plenty of them. Go home!'

Someone had helped Brid, shivering and crying, along the main street towards home until she had assured them she was fine. She had no idea what had happened to Evelyn. She walked home slowly, not knowing what to think. Should she tell her mother? She felt certain that somehow this would all become her fault. As she began to calm down from the fight, she was overcome with shame. The whole village had seen her acting like some tinker in the street at the end of market day in Ballytorne. Everyone knew Tommy Burke didn't love her. But he *was* going to marry her. He would be hers. That skinny bitch could wave scarves in the street all day, because he hadn't proposed to *her*. She wiped her streaming nose on her coat and began to feel a little better.

Her mother didn't know what to think either. One of the Ross girls? In broad daylight? She wasn't sure she had the whole story, but here was her daughter crying and begging her not to make her go back down into the village to get more eggs. She let her go to bed for an hour and thought they'd get to the bottom of it all when Tommy came up that night for his tea. She had some smoked mackerel; with a bit of boiled egg and potato salad, that would do.

The day dragged by for Brid up in her room. She couldn't read. About four in the afternoon she ventured downstairs and had a cup of tea with her mother, who was being very nice for a change. When her mother told her not to worry, she did actually feel better. By seven, when there was no sign of Tommy, she didn't feel so bright. Her mother had stopped speaking and wouldn't look her in the eye. Eventually, at nine o'clock, Mam went out into the hall for her coat, buttoning it as she came back into the kitchen.

'Brid, this is ridiculous. I'm going down to the village to look for him. I won't be long.'

Brid was astonished. Her mother had never been so nice to her. The situation had to be serious.

Less than an hour later, she heard the latch on the back door. Brid turned the volume down on the television she hadn't been watching. 'Mam?'

The door opened and her mother walked in. Silently she took off her coat and sat down, draping it across her knees.

'Well, I went into Flynn's and the Long Bar, but they had nothing. Then I went into Byrne's, and young Cormac had it that Tommy was seen in Ballytorne this afternoon. He had a bag and he was getting on the Cork bus. Cormac said there's been no sign of life up at the farm all day.'

Brid stared at her mother, waiting for more.

'What does that mean, Mammy?' She could feel her chin beginning to quiver.

'Well, I don't know. We can't be sure and you mustn't stop hoping yet, but I'd say there might be a . . . a delay with the wedding.'

'A delay?' She leaned forward.

Her mother chewed her bottom lip while she examined her daughter's face. She took no pleasure in it but the girl had to know the truth.

'Oh Brid. I'm that sorry for you, pet, but I'd say that the wedding is probably off.'

Brid's hands covered her face and she gasped. On the far side of the room a table had the first few wedding presents arranged on it. A slow cooker still in its box, a set of salmon-pink table linen, a cut-glass bowl. Brid had imagined Tommy coming in from the cows and asking what smelled so delicious when she took the lid off the slow cooker; his smile of delight when she scooped him a big bit of trifle out of the bowl. She felt empty. There were no tears, no dreams; there was nothing. Her mother got up and went to hang her coat up in the hall, leaving her daughter more alone than anyone should ever feel.

So that morning, as she had sat in the car reliving that awful day, she had suddenly known with a deep and violent certainty that she should go and confront Evelyn Ross. Brid was sure the woman knew what had happened to Tommy and had allowed her to suffer all these years. The police would take forever to do anything; she was going to sort it out for herself now. As she drove up the road, she muttered encouraging words to herself: 'long enough', 'lying bitch', 'this is over'. It was only when she was suddenly confronted by the Garda car, with Sergeant Collins standing beside it, and Evelyn in the doorway that her scheme was revealed to be madness. She dreaded to think what those two must have thought she was doing. She had taken in their looks of astonishment, turned her own car around and fled.

When she got back on the road, she decided she shouldn't go home. Sergeant Collins was bound to follow her, and she wasn't ready. She couldn't speak to him yet. Not sure where she was going, she turned left and just drove.

About an hour later, she found herself in Schull. She glanced at her watch: just after twelve. She parked her car up behind the supermarket and walked down into the main street. Thank God! The first pub she came to wasn't empty. She never liked to be the only one in a bar. It looked terrible. She ordered a large glass of wine. The young barman (was he even old enough to drink?) told her they didn't do wine by the glass. They just had small bottles like those they sometimes handed out on a plane.

'A white one of those then, please.'

'We have two types.' He pointed at the display of tiny bottles on the shelf behind him.

Brid peered at the unfamiliar labels. 'Whichever one is nicer.'

The barman smiled sheepishly. 'Well one of them has a green label, the other one is yellow. I'm not a big wine drinker, to be honest.'

'Yellow then,' she barked, impatient for her drink, followed by a softer, 'please'.

After two more of the little bottles, which held more than you thought in actual fact, on top of an empty stomach, she didn't feel that well. She was finding it hard to focus. Deciding that she'd better eat something, she made her way to the supermarket to get a sandwich. She had great difficulty finding what she wanted, and a number of sandwiches ended up falling on the floor. They were very badly displayed. Eventually she selected a cheese and ham one and approached the bored girl on the till.

'Two sixty, please.'

Brid looked down. Jesus, hadn't she left her handbag in the pub. She tried to explain to the girl what had happened, but it was complicated. Abandoning the sandwich, she went back to the pub. The barman smiled when he saw her and held up her bag.

'Thank Christ!'

The young man then offered to walk her down the street. He seemed bizarrely interested in whether she had a car or not. Brid didn't like it, so she told him nothing and escaped back into the supermarket, but the thought of trying to get a sandwich suddenly seemed like a herculean task, so she just went straight through to the back of the shop and up into the car park.

So many red hatchbacks. Like an inept witch casting useless spells, she jabbed her car keys into the air. Finally the familiar beep and she was back in the driving seat. As soon as she sat down and before she had even closed the door, she had fallen asleep.

When she woke, she had that familiar feeling she got when she found herself coming to at the kitchen counter or on the couch, where she felt more exhausted than before she had slept. Her mouth was thick with wine and she had a dull ache behind her forehead. She glanced at her watch. That couldn't be right. She looked again, but it was still a quarter to four. She sat bolt upright, properly awake now.

'The kids! Shit, shit, shit.' She was sometimes — well, quite often — a little late, but this was going to be bad. She shoved her hand into her bag to get the car keys, but rummaged in vain. There was no sign of them. 'Fuck!' She glanced frantically around the car. Nothing. Then . . . 'Thank you, Jesus!' There was the familiar fob sticking out of the plastic cup holder.

She started the engine and edged her way out of the car park. She had driven cars in this state quite often. Her reactions muffled by the wine, but sober enough to know she had to be extra careful. She wondered if she should phone the school, but decided not to. It would just waste time, and surely, she thought, if they got really worried, they'd call her.

It was almost half past five when her red hatchback pulled up outside the school gates. The journey had taken longer than she had expected. She had got stuck behind a lorry from the Co-op, and then just before she got to Duneen, some fucker had been moving a herd of cows back down for milking. She stared at the railings, but there was no sign of anyone. Knowing she couldn't park here, she stuck on her hazard lights and got out of the car to have a better look. Back to the right of the main school she could see that the teachers' car park was empty and the bike racks stood in rows abandoned. The only sign of life was a limp crisp packet being slapped by the wind against the bars of the gate. Brid tried to swallow, but her mouth was very dry. Too dry.

On the drive from Schull, she had managed to stop herself from panicking too much, but now she felt it building up inside her. She leaned her hand on the bonnet and tried to catch her breath, becoming aware of just how eerily quiet it was. Not a car on the road, nobody walking by. A random thought popped into her head: how long was I asleep for in that car? Has something happened?

Back in the car, she checked herself in the rear-view mirror. She didn't look too bad. Well, not crazy, at least. Taking long, slow breaths, she started the engine. A neighbour would have dropped Carmel and Cathal back home. Maybe one of the teachers had taken pity on them and given them a lift. They knew where the spare key was. It'd be fine. She'd get home and they would be stuck in their rooms, as usual, tapping away at the keyboards on their computers as if they were working on things of international importance. Brid managed a smile and did quite a respectable three-point turn before heading back to the farm.

No lights. This wasn't good. The wheels of the car came to a crunching halt, the engine was switched off, and then all that remained was silence. A grey stillness engulfed the house and yard. As Brid hurried towards the back door, she could hear a funny high-pitched juddering sound and for a moment wondered what it was, then realised that she had begun to whimper like a frightened pup. She began to pray to a re-found God, 'Please let them be here. Please. I'll go back to mass. Let them be here. No more drink.' The door was locked. Brid put her hands on either side of the wooden frame and leaned forward with her head bowed. She was defeated. Where were her children, and why had she been such a fucking irresponsible moron?

The back door opened directly into the large kitchen, and the moment she switched on the light she saw it. The back of an old ESB envelope covered in blue writing. The biro lay across it.

Standing perfectly still, Brid considered the scene. She knew that this note could contain no good news, and yet she would have to read it. Even from across the room she could recognise Anthony's neat, even handwriting. She took a deep breath.

Brid,

I have taken the kids to my mother's for a few days. I know you are upset at the moment but it's not fair on the children.

The school rang me. We are all fine.

I'll be in touch.

Anthony x

Reasonable, sensible Anthony. Why wasn't he here? She wanted him to be standing on the other side of the table, screaming at her, berating her for being the worst mother that ever lived so that she could fall to her knees and sob her apologies and beg her little family to forgive her. What was to be gained from this? The three of them sat in their granny's bungalow eating their tea in silence, her sat here in her coat with nothing but the ticking of the clock above the cooker for company. How could this solve anything? She glanced at the fridge. No. No, the last thing she needed now was a drink.

A little over an hour later, she was still sat in the same chair, still wearing her coat, but she now had a wine glass in her hand and on the table in front of her stood a bottle, two thirds of its contents gone. She wasn't going to finish it. After the first glass Brid had remembered that she still hadn't eaten anything. She had stood in front of the open fridge, but everything seemed so complicated; even the idea of heating a bowl of soup was beyond her. In the end she had eaten the end of a wedge of Cheddar cheese.

Staring at the wall, she pondered how many nights she had spent sitting alone in this room. It must be in the thousands, yet tonight felt so different. The house almost seemed to sense it was empty. A single heartbeat wasn't enough to fill it, and Brid felt as if it were shutting down around her. A glance at the clock told her it was only twenty past seven. Still early, but yet far too late. The thought of the big empty bed waiting just for her was the first glimmer of comfort she had encountered all day. Heading upstairs didn't hold such dread without the thought of his sighs and grunts; the wall of back that always met her as she slipped beneath the duvet.

It took a moment for the shrill electrical interruption to register. The doorbell! Brid jumped to her feet and rushed to the kitchen door, but even before she reached it, hopelessness had overcome her. Of course it wouldn't be the children or their father. They had keys. Wondering who would be calling on the house at this hour, she went into the hall and turned on the porch light. Behind the frosted glass was a large dark shadow too big to be just one person. She noticed a slight tremor in her hand as she reached for the lock and, holding her breath, slowly pulled open the door. Their eyes met and then she simply hung her head and stepped back. Sergeant Collins made his way into the hall.

11

It wasn't the first time PJ had called at the Riordans' house that day. After Brid's car had fled Ard Carraig, he had wanted to follow her immediately but instead found himself putting on the kettle to make tea for Evelyn and her sister Florence, who was comforting her at the kitchen table. Evelyn's screams had brought Florence to the front door, and then PJ felt he could hardly leave the two of them alone. He stepped into the role of responsible adult and ushered the two women back towards the kitchen.

Evelyn had recovered herself quite quickly and told PJ the full story of the love rivalry that had gone on between herself and Brid. She told him about the scarf and the awful fight in the village. As she gave him all the details she had omitted earlier, PJ thought to himself that it was little wonder people in the village believed Tommy had simply run away. Any man would have done the same.

Florence kept her hands wrapped around her mug of tea and stared at the grain of the wooden table. She felt awful. Of course she had known some of what had gone on, but not this detail. She remembered the whole incident as Evelyn having a teenage crush. When had it become this tale of long-lost love, and why hadn't she known? Because she had never asked. Never asked her own sister; it was easier not to. Even now, she knew she should just reach her hand out to Evelyn, but she couldn't. It wasn't like that between them, between any of the sisters. Life had taught them well. Feelings were to be feared, pain was to be avoided at all cost, and if that meant not experiencing joy, then so be it.

Evelyn stopped speaking. Florence looked up and found her sister looking into her face with an expectant expression. 'I'm so sorry, Evelyn. I had never . . . well, never fully realised.'

A weak smile. 'Don't be silly. It was a long, long time ago.' But all three people sitting around the table knew that was a lie.

PJ stood up. 'Well, if you don't mind, I suppose I should go and talk to Mrs Riordan now. Will you be all right?'

'Yes, yes, I'm fine,' Evelyn replied as she too got to her feet.

'Thank you for being so open and, well, honest.'

They exchanged smiles, and as PJ drove away, leaving her at the door with her right arm raised in farewell, he felt changed. He glanced in the rear-view mirror at her elegant frame disappearing into the house, and when he stopped at the gate he found that he was smiling for no discernible reason.

Up at the Riordans' place, he had found no car and nobody at home. He pushed an official-looking postcard through the letter box with his contact details on it and drove back into the village. He was going to start asking around for the names of Tommy Burke's friends and who had seen him leave or been in contact since, but by the time he reached the main street he found that all the tea he had drunk at Ard Carraig was very keen to come back out. Looking at his watch, he decided to use the toilet back at barracks and then have a bit of lunch.

Friday meant fried plaice and boiled potatoes. The new and unimproved Mrs Meany put the plate of food on the table with an air of distraction and shuffled back towards the kitchen. PJ almost missed the days when she would have stood at the table watching him eat while an endless stream of words tumbled out of her. Who had cancer. The problems with her outside tap. That awful business up the country. He knew he should probably ask her what was wrong, but the thought of having to listen to her reply exhausted him. He settled for silence.

Normally after lunch he would have done some paperwork or shown his face in the village, but today all he could think of was Ard Carraig and why he should go there again. He finally decided that reporting back on not interviewing Brid Riordan was enough of an excuse. He imagined himself sitting across from Evelyn saying something about putting her mind at rest, and the expression of gratitude that would spread across her pale, thin face. He knew he was being a fool and that nothing would come of this, but there was no harm in flirting.

He couldn't remember when he had last felt like this. Had he ever felt like this? Of course he had found other women attractive, hundreds of them, all the time, but this seemed different. It was the way she looked at him — he knew that she could never find him attractive, but he felt as if she saw something more than his weight, looked beyond the tight, uncomfortable uniform, and when she spoke, she was speaking to a man. What did it matter anyway? He would never do anything as stupid as act on his feelings. That lesson had been learned very early on.

When he got to Ard Carraig, the doorbell went unanswered and the house appeared to be deserted. PJ stepped back and looked up at the dull shine of the windows, wondering which bedroom was Evelyn's. He walked around the side of the house, enjoying the crunch of his shoes on the gravel. The despondent calls of a few crows seemed to add to the sense of silence. To the right of the house was a lawn that stepped down in a series of terraces towards a field. The grass was well kept and the various beds seemed to a non-gardener's eye to be carefully planted and maintained. Suddenly from one of the lower beds a grey-haired head popped up. PJ let out an involuntary 'Jesus Christ.'

'May I help you?' The head rose up, revealing a stocky woman wearing baggy jeans and an oversized cardigan. She looked as if she was neither expecting nor pleased to see visitors.

'Sergeant Collins from the village.' PJ stepped towards her but realised too late how steep the incline on the lawn was, and so found himself hurtling towards the woman with precarious haste. His hostess looked suitably alarmed, but he managed to stop and steady himself just before he had sent the two of them rolling towards the field.

'Abigail Ross.' She held her gloved muddy hands aloft to explain why she wasn't offering to shake his. 'Anything wrong?'

'I was actually looking for Evelyn.'

'Why?' Abigail scowled at him. He wasn't sure if it was because of the low winter sun in her eyes or if it was caused by the mere sight of him. If her sister made him feel like a man, Abigail made him feel like a little boy who had come over to ask if Evelyn could come out to play. He sensed the answer would be no.

'I . . . we are investigating — '

'I know,' Abigail interrupted him. 'Evelyn told me. She's not here. May I pass on a message?'

'Eh, no. That's all right. I'll try back another time. Nothing that can't wait. I'll leave you to it.' With a half-hearted wave of his hand he turned to walk back up to where he had parked the car.

'Oh Sergeant!' Abigail called after him. He turned. 'I'd prefer it if my sister were not needlessly upset. She can be rather sensitive and . . . well, whatever went on up on that farm had nothing to do with Evelyn. Of that I'm quite certain.'

She held his gaze, and unsure of what to say, he simply nodded and turned away once more.

'Do you understand me, Sergeant?'

PJ froze. A line had been crossed. He slowly turned to face her and waited for as long as he dared till he spoke.

'Yes. Yes, I understand.'

As he clambered up the incline, he thought to himself that he really hadn't the slightest clue what Abigail was getting at.

The rest of the day had passed slowly. He checked emails and trawled through the various Garda alerts he got sent, and then, because Mrs Meany left early on a Friday afternoon, he treated himself to a bit of daytime telly.

He wasn't sure how long he'd slept for. It was dark outside and the small former back bedroom he used as a sitting room was dimly lit by the flickering glow of a news programme. He turned on the lamp next to the chair and checked his watch. A quarter to seven. PJ sat up and decided to head back to the Riordan place to see if there was any sign of life.

As the headlights of the Garda car swept across the yard, he could see Brid's car at the side of the house. The driver's door was open and the interior light was on. There was no other sign of life. He walked up to the car, and after a cursory glance inside shut the door, leaving the yard in total darkness. Using his small torch he made his way carefully to the front door and rang the bell. Nothing. He was just about to press it again when the porch light came on with a violent glare and Brid, wearing a dark blue woollen coat, opened the door. Her mouth fell open when she saw the sergeant, and then she sank back against the wall, silently inviting him to come in. He stepped forward and she shut the door behind him before leading him down the corridor towards the kitchen, neither of them feeling the need to speak.

The scrape of a kitchen chair against the tiled floor seemed unnaturally loud as Brid gestured for PJ to sit.

'I'll stand if you don't mind. This shouldn't take too long,' were his first words to her. She was leaning against the kitchen counter now, just staring straight ahead. He noticed the wine bottle and remembered the abandoned car in the yard.

'Is everything all right, Mrs Riordan?' he enquired, peering down into her face. She didn't meet his gaze, but her breathing had begun to change. Long, slow breaths escaped her lips, each one a louder rasp than the last. It sounded as if she were steeling herself to lift something very heavy or run up a steep hill.

'Mrs Riordan?'

Her large eyes swivelled towards his.

'My children.' Each word deliberate and measured, like an incantation. 'He's taken my children.' And with that her shoulders collapsed, her head tilted back and she let out a long, deep moan.

Before PJ could react in any way, Brid had thrown herself against him. Her short arms reached around his belly and her head was buried into his chest. Her whole body rose and fell with each wave of sobbing. PJ considered pushing her away, but it seemed easier just to hold her. His hands felt wide and strong on her back. He lowered his head to whisper a soft 'ssh' in her ear, as he might have done to a crying baby left unexpectedly in his care. Brid gripped him tighter, and PJ could feel the weight and shape of her breasts resting on the top of his stomach.

The awkward embrace seemed to be lasting

103

for a very long time, but the truth was, neither of them wanted it to end. It felt good to just hold the warmth of another human being and they both knew that once the spell was broken one of them would have to speak. With his eyes shut, PJ inhabited a dark, all-consuming world. The strands of her hair that were stuck to his cheek, her fingers digging into his deep flesh, the undeniable pressure of his now hard cock against her body . . .

Brid lifted her face from his chest and he knew what was going to happen next. Was it her, or had he . . . It didn't matter who had initiated it, because now they were kissing. As their lips met and their tongues became a hot, wet knot, it was as if they were set free. Hands roamed, seeking out bare flesh; now they were on their knees, now rolling on the floor. A chair was knocked over. PJ knew he should stop, that he must stop, he was going to stop, but then she slid her hand along the inside of his thigh and all hope was lost.

12

The bedroom was filled with the murky half-light that spilled through the window, its curtains left undrawn. A soft rain was tapping on the glass. No birds sang. Brid had been awake for about an hour just watching the great bulk of a man lying next to her. The soft pink of his flesh, the wiry blackness of the hairs on his back, the slow, even rise and fall of his breathing. She felt remarkably calm. Gazing at the ceiling that hadn't been painted since her mother died, she made an inventory of her feelings, but search as she might, she could find no guilt. Flashes of what had gone on the night before kept running through her mind. The buttons of her coat scattering across the floor, the weight of him on top of her, their sweat-soaked bodies writhing on the landing, the noises they had been making! Her face reddened and a small smile played across her lips. She leaned over and gently kissed PJ's back. She had no idea what was going to happen next, but in this stolen moment between sleep and the rest of her life, she felt truly happy.

The mound of flesh next to her stirred. PJ raised himself on one arm and turned awkwardly to look at Brid.

'I must go to the toilet,' he whispered.

'Right. Well off you go.' Brid smiled and PJ smiled back. Sensing his embarrassment, she looked away to allow him to get out of bed. She felt the great weight being lifted off the mattress and heard him picking through some of the clothes on the floor. She glanced over and saw him struggling to get his thigh through the leg hole of a pair of underpants. Her hand shot up to cover her mouth.

'I think those are Anthony's.' He turned to look at her and froze for a second, before the two of them began to laugh. He let go of the underpants and sat back down on the bed.

'That's terrible.'

'I think yours are on the stairs somewhere.'

Another wave of laughter washed over them.

PJ caught sight of the red numbers glowing on the digital clock.

'Shit, it's nearly a quarter past eight. I've got to get back.'

He stood up again and started looking for any items of clothing that belonged to him.

'Go pee. I'll gather up your things,' Brid said and stroked his shoulder.

★　★　★

PJ was almost back at the barracks when he remembered that it was Saturday and there would be no Mrs Meany. He needn't have worried. No awkward questions. Driving out from the Riordans' yard he had felt confused. He'd had a good time and Brid seemed like a lovely woman, but she was married and he was the sergeant. It couldn't happen again. But that didn't stop a stirring in his trousers just thinking about it.

This was not the first time PJ had had sex. When he was much younger he had gone to Dublin and visited a prostitute: a tall, thin woman who had called herself Anna. She had spoken with some sort of accent, east European perhaps, but all he could really remember was how pale her skin had been and the way her neck was stained pink from her red hair dye. He had seen her three times over two years, but each time was less exciting than the last. Her counting the notes before taking off her bra and panties; the way she handled his body without even the pretence of desire. She was at work, with a job to be done, and after the last visit he vowed never to return.

It turned out that it wasn't sex he'd been looking for. What he was trying to find was someone who wanted him, and that was what had been so amazing about last night. Brid had desired him completely There had been no moment when she flinched. Even this morning when they had said goodbye she had planted her warm, damp lips on his without hesitation and stroked his stomach with both her hands. He smiled and thought to himself that he must stop thinking about her or he'd crash the car.

'Sweet Jesus, not the prick!'

PJ had arrived back at the Garda station to find a silver Mercedes parked on the driveway, and leaning against it, cigarette in hand, Detective Superintendent Linus Dunne. He turned off the engine. Even before he got out of the car he could see the smirk on the detective's face.

'Good morning, Sergeant! You're out very early for a Saturday.'

PJ suppressed the violent feelings welling up inside him.

'I just popped out to get the papers.'

'Did you now?' The detective almost laughed and gestured at PJ's empty hands.

PJ brazened it out.

'You're out early yourself, Detective.'

'Yes. Sorry to just show up, but I was trying to call the station.' He paused and smiled. 'There was no reply.'

The sergeant toyed with the idea of trying to explain the unanswered phone, but thought better of it.

'Will you come in? I'll put the kettle on.'

'Right. I was wondering how you got on yesterday, and I needed to check a few files you have here.'

Minutes later, the men were sitting opposite each other at the kitchen table with their tea between them. PJ was starving and longing to fry up some breakfast, but he had no intention of cooking anything for the prick. Linus revealed what he had found out in Dublin and explained why there would have to be an exhumation order. PJ nodded and chewed on his thumbnail. He knew that putting a mechanical digger up in the cemetery would upset a lot of people. As if reading his mind, Linus continued, 'I don't like it either, but it's the only way we can get a positive ID on the body. We know it's not just some John Doe — this guy was murdered, and that means someone killed him. What vibe did

108

you get off the women?'

PJ hesitated. He mustn't give anything away. Jesus, if it ever got out what had happened, he'd be finished.

'Well, there's a lot of bad blood between them, that's for sure. Evelyn Ross thinks Brid Riordan killed him, but I'd doubt that very much. If anything, I'd say Brid has managed to move on with her life. It's still very raw, like shockingly raw, for Evelyn Ross. Would I think either of them could murder someone? I'd say no, but then God knows who those women were twenty-five years ago.'

'Any contact with Burke over the years?'

'No. Just the same story about him getting on the bus to Cork.'

'And have we anyone who actually saw that happen?'

'Not yet, but I was thinking of going down to the pubs tonight and asking around. You know how a drop taken can help.'

Linus raised his eyebrows in mild surprise.

'Good man. Yes, do that and call me if you get anything.'

As PJ nodded, it struck him that this conversation hadn't been as hellish as he'd been expecting. He had to concede the prick was fairly good at his job, and for the first time in days, he felt like they might actually solve this case.

'Now, a bit of homework, and I'm happy to help. I want to go through the files and see if any of our key players — the Ross sisters, the Riordan woman or Burke — have had any other run-ins with the law.'

PJ beamed. 'I've done it!'

The detective smiled back. 'And?'

'Nothing. The eldest Ross girl has a few points on her licence for speeding, Brid Riordan has a DUI, and Tommy Burke complained about some farm diesel being stolen but no one was ever charged. That's it.'

'Well, I've got to hand it to you, Sergeant, I'm impressed.'

PJ hated how pleased he was to hear those words out of the prick's mouth.

'Turns out it's all fucking useless, but I'm impressed.'

He got up from the table.

'I'll head away. Let you get on with your breakfast.' A wide and knowing smile spread across his face.

PJ felt himself turning a deep red, but kept silent.

★　★　★

After two fried eggs, a bit of black pudding, two rashers and a sausage, the sergeant was contemplating heading back to bed for a short nap. He hadn't got much sleep the night before and knew it might be a late one if he was heading down to the pubs later. He was just putting his plate in the sink when there was a knock on the front door. Odd. He hadn't heard a car.

He opened the door and was confronted by a smiling Evelyn Ross. Her cheeks were flushed pink after her walk and she was carrying a basket.

'Sergeant!'

'Evelyn. How can I . . . What can I . . . Is everything all right?'

PJ felt as if a naked Brid Riordan was at that very moment spread-eagled on his duvet in his bedroom. This was ridiculous.

Evelyn held out her basket.

'I was baking some loaves this morning and I made a couple extra. I just wanted to thank you for your kindness yesterday. I was being a bit foolish and it was good of you to indulge me.' Their eyes met. 'Oh, and from what Abigail told me, I gather she was less than friendly when you called back. Sorry about that.'

'She was just being a big sister, don't worry about it.'

'What did you want me for, by the way?'

For a second PJ couldn't remember, and then it came back to him. He blurted out, 'Brid Riordan.' Just saying her name aloud and he felt like he'd made a sex tape that had gone viral.

'I just wanted to let you know that I still haven't interviewed her properly. I mean, it will happen, but I'm not sure when. Please know I was taking what you told me seriously.' They exchanged a quick smile.

'Will you come in?' PJ took a step back from the door.

'No. No, I'd better get back.' She turned to leave and then as an afterthought said, 'My sisters and I are going to the music by candlelight event up in the chapel on Tuesday night. If you wanted to come with us, you'd be more than welcome.' She spoke quickly but without blushing. She even managed to catch PJ's eye once or twice.

111

The sergeant was at a loss. Was she asking him out on a date? Had the sisters taken pity on him and decided to include him in their night out? He searched Evelyn's face for clues, but her passive expression gave nothing away. He decided he needed more time.

'That sounds lovely, though I'll have to check with the bigwigs in Cork to see if they'll be needing me. Can I let you know?' He was pleased with himself. He had sounded calm and unflustered.

'Of course. Well, fingers crossed.' She stepped down from the porch and raised a hand in farewell. 'Goodbye . . . Oh, the bread!' She laughed. 'I'm a fool!' She held out the two loaves and PJ took them.

'Still warm,' he remarked, cupping a loaf in each hand. Jesus, he thought to himself, had that sounded a bit sexual? Evelyn was still smiling, so he assumed she hadn't thought so. 'Thank you very much. They'll be grand.'

'Not at all,' replied Evelyn, walking back towards the road. 'Let us know about Tuesday,' she called over her shoulder.

'Will do!' PJ called back.

After he shut the front door, he looked down at the crusty loaves. Was it possible that he, PJ Collins, at the age of fifty-three and for the first time in his life, had not one, but two women who were interested in him? He gently squeezed the bread. Still warm.

13

The chapel was not a pretty building. It stood squat and square on the brow of a hill. There was no spire reaching towards God, just a raised enclosure on the westerly gable end that housed a bell. Grey stone walls led to a grey slate roof, which in turn, on this morning, led to great high banks of heavy grey clouds that promised rain before too long. A ridge of overgrown leylandii trees separated the priest's house from the graveyard, and on the other side of the chapel was a lone monkey puzzle tree. The only splash of colour was the vibrant yellow of the small mechanical digger working in the cemetery.

The priest was standing to one side along with Linus Dunne and a man and a woman from the technical bureau, fully suited in their white overalls. PJ had stationed himself at the top of the steps to prevent anyone from the village getting too close, or any of the journalists who had been asking questions outside O'Driscoll's showing up with a photographer. As it turned out, nobody had any appetite to come and watch the Burkes being returned to the light of day. Susan Hickey had slowed to a near stop when she had driven by earlier, but even she didn't want a closer look.

An abrupt silence prompted PJ to look over towards the grave. The engine of the excavator had been turned off and the small group of bystanders had huddled closer to the mound of earth. PJ didn't want to abandon his post, yet he felt he should be closer to the action than this. Dunne had begun to treat him like a colleague, and he was keen to be at the heart of this investigation. He shuffled a few feet forward but his view wasn't much improved. Were the technical team in the grave? He glanced behind him to check no one was coming up the steps and took a few more paces forward. This was better. He could see the woman in her white overalls kneeling down fiddling with something. It must be the lid of the coffin. No, that would be gone. Was she just tugging at a bit of bone? Was the wife nearer the surface or were they side by side? His face crumpled into an involuntary grimace at the thought of it all and he turned back to his post.

What was that? Something had moved. He thought he had caught a glimpse of colour — had it been green? — at the far corner of the chapel. He hesitated. His eyes could have been deceiving him, but no, he had seen something, something green, and it had moved. PJ did his version of a run that was really more of a low fast stride towards the end of the chapel wall. As he came to the corner, he caught another glimpse of the green coat as it disappeared past the leylandii down the path that led to the priest's house. He also saw the grey hair and the red-and-white-striped shopping bag. There was no doubt in his mind. The figure in the green coat scuttling away was his own Mrs Meany.

* * *

In her heart she knew the sergeant had seen her. She made her way as quickly as she could down the path, shoulders hunched and head bowed forward, willing herself to become invisible. Of course she shouldn't have come. It had been a stupid idea, but when the sergeant had told her what was happening, she felt so sorry for ... well, Mrs Burke really, but they had both been good to her in their own way. Maybe he wouldn't say anything to her. Oh but he would. She had to come up with some story. Parish business? She had been looking for the priest. That would put him off. The sergeant was always terrified she was going to try and get him involved in something.

Looking down, Mrs Meany saw the hardened soil of the path with its thin carpet of dead pine needles and moss. She wanted to run but her feet picked their way carefully, afraid of a fall. When she got beyond the trees, she paused to catch her breath and thought of the girl who had dashed up and down this path forty years before. That was when she had been the priest's housekeeper, after the Burkes had given her a second chance at life. How was it that all these years later here she was again, still frightened, still hiding? She looked at girls now and was amazed at all the choices they had. They could go anywhere and do anything. Sometimes she was eaten away by jealousy, but on other days as she watched them with their long hair and short skirts laughing and pushing each other as they

115

waited for the school buses in Ballytorne, she wondered if even now her younger self would have had the courage to step away from Duneen.

There had never been a Mr Meany. After Father Mulcahy had left, the new priest had been an elderly Jesuit called Father Carter. One afternoon the young girl had been scrubbing the tiled floor behind the stairs when she heard the bell ring, summoning her. She stood up quickly, drying her red hands on her apron. When she knocked on the door of the priest's study, a voice that sounded like it was deep inside a velvet-lined box had intoned, 'Come in.' Father Carter was seated behind his desk, the lamplight reflected in his small round glasses. It had always felt like night in that room. She approached the desk, and since the priest didn't invite her to sit down, she simply stood before him with her hands behind her back.

After a bit of throat-clearing, Father Carter slowly explained that he had been thinking. He felt it was inappropriate to have such a young unmarried girl working in the house, so in the future she would be referred to as Mrs Meany. She had bowed her head in acquiescence and made her way back to the kitchen, but in her mind she had been incredulous. Sure, everyone knew she wasn't married. What was the point of calling herself Mrs? But such was the power of suggestion and the implied papal seal of approval that after a few months there were no more raised eyebrows or questions. She had become the wife of a mysterious Mr Meany, and then, as the years passed by, his widow, but the important

116

fact was that she had been a married woman. Sometimes even she herself forgot that she wasn't single out of a sense of duty to her dead husband. She had learnt to embrace the fiction, not wishing to dwell on the truth that she had always been alone.

Creeping down the side of the priest's house, Mrs Meany checked her hair and coat before stepping out into the road to continue her walk into the village.

★ ★ ★

The chapel fared slightly better by night, largely because you could see less of it. In the early nineties there had been a great fundraising effort led by Susan Hickey to provide floodlighting. Initially the effect was a little strong and gave the impression to the unfamiliar nocturnal visitor that Duneen was now the home of a nuclear reactor, but twenty years later, lack of maintenance meant there was just an uneven orange glow that highlighted random parts of the building.

A large group of shadows gathered by the door, twenty people or more talking quietly in the darkness, their breath riding on the light that was spilling from the wide stone porch. Evelyn Ross was making her way carefully up the steps, flanked by her two sisters. This was a rare outing for the three of them, and rarer still given that it was Evelyn who had suggested that they attend the music by candlelight event. Neither Florence nor Abigail had been keen when Evelyn produced the thin pamphlet printed on mint-green paper with its wispy illustration of a burning candle set below a few notes of music, but they both in their different ways felt a certain guilt about their sister, so here they were.

The three women were about halfway up the steps when they heard a strange wheezing behind them. Florence looked over her shoulder and called out, 'Sergeant Collins!'

Evelyn chimed in with 'You found us!' and Abigail, albeit with a smile, simply said, 'We meet again.'

All three women attempted and failed to hide their looks of astonishment at the sight of the sergeant in his 'casual wear'. On his feet were heavy-soled brown canvas shoes that were somewhere between a sneaker and an ortho-paedic boot. The jeans were a pristine navy with a severe Mrs Meany crease ironed into each leg. The crotch seemed to start somewhere around the knee. A green-and-beige-striped collared T-shirt was stretched across his stomach, and over that he wore a navy anorak that revealed that PJ's shoulders were in fact just an illusion created by his uniform.

The outfit had been purchased on the internet. As he left the barracks, PJ had glanced in the mirror and decided that he looked casual and relaxed, but now the faces of the Ross sisters told him that he resembled an overinflated schoolboy. He swallowed hard, planted a smile on his face and half-heartedly raised his right hand into something resembling a wave.

He was immediately filled with a paralysing

doubt. Why on earth had he accepted this strange invitation? He had made enquiries in O'Driscoll's and the evening had been described as a mixture of opera arias and harp music. It had been organised by Mairead Gallagher, who was studying in the Cork school of music. No one seemed very clear why it was by candlelight; it wasn't Christmas yet. PJ took comfort in the thought that at least the musicians mightn't notice when he fell asleep.

The weekend had been quiet, too quiet. There had been far too much time for thinking and rethinking. Sleep had not come easily, even after the skinful he had had in the pub on Saturday night. At least the hangover he had nursed on Sunday morning had distracted him from what was going on in his personal life. His personal life! The very idea appalled him. Since when did he have one of those? He had managed to get through decades of adulthood without emotional attachment, and now, without intending to, he felt embroiled in . . . he didn't know what. When he was calm and rational, he reasoned with himself that Evelyn was just being polite and taking pity on a lonely man, and Brid had simply been a drunk, unhappy woman who had made a mistake. Somehow, no matter how much he told himself these facts, it didn't alter what he was feeling. How drawn he was to both these women in their different ways. He felt unnerved and uneasy. This was not a man he knew.

'I'm so glad you decided to come,' Evelyn said as the unlikely quartet continued up the steps. 'Young Mairead sang a solo last Christmas, and

119

she has a marvellous voice.'

'I taught her and she has always been a great singer. Terrific that she's making use of it,' Florence added.

'Yes, yes,' the others concurred. This was followed by an awkward silence.

'It's chilly enough.' This was PJ's attempt to break the ice, but the atmosphere remained frozen. They walked towards the lit porch in silence.

Evelyn knew she should speak, but her mind was a blank. This man was an oaf. If someone had shown her a photograph of him, she would have recoiled, but in the flesh he emanated a kind of heat. It confused her. She found that she wanted to touch his skin, stroke the side of his face, maybe press her lips against his. It was madness. Since Tommy had left her broken-hearted, she had shut down that side of her life. For a quarter of a century she had not allowed herself to feel anything for a man; indeed, she had met scarcely any. But now it was as if her heart had been rediscovered along with those bones. Was all of this simply because Sergeant Collins was the first man she saw after her long flight from the world? Was she like one of those silly deluded girls in fairy tales who had been given a love potion? She didn't know, but nor did she hate how any of this was making her feel.

★ ★ ★

As the Ross sisters took their seats in a pew halfway down the church, another car was being parked on the street below. The Riordans were both wearing variations on their Christmas mass outfits, Anthony in a dark suit with a white shirt but no tie, and Brid in her best coat buttoned to the neck, the amber brooch Anthony had given her for their tenth wedding anniversary on the collar, and wearing the sort of red lipstick that no woman would wear to confession. She took a couple of steps away from the car, but then paused while Anthony turned back to lock the doors. The lights flashed and it gave a small beep. The two of them exchanged weak smiles and headed towards the stone steps.

After PJ had made his discreet departure on Saturday morning, Brid had sat at the kitchen table and tried to figure out what to do next. It felt overwhelming. There didn't seem to be a single thing in her life that she didn't want to change. The enormity of the task loomed so large before her that it hardly seemed worth starting, but then she thought about Carmel and Cathal. She wanted her children back. She wanted to bury her face in their clean hair and wrap her arms around them. If she could rescue them, then maybe she could rescue herself. She had stood up and started cleaning the kitchen.

That afternoon, freshly showered and without even half a glass of courage inside her, she had driven to her mother-in-law's bungalow. She had gone to the back door and after a brief knock let herself in. She would not ring the front doorbell like some visitor. This was her family.

When she saw the children, she opened her arms wide as if she'd just been away for the night. Carmel came to her at once, but as subtle as he tried to be, Brid saw Cathal give a glance to his father for a nod of approval before he crossed the room and kissed her on the cheek. Her heart was fluttering like a small bird, but she was being the best version of herself she could manage. She asked the kids if they had been good for their granny. Did they eat everything they were given? Had they slept well? Anthony and his mother, after an initial awkwardness, had joined in with the forced impression of a happy family.

'They were no bother.'

'Sure, Cathal would eat your arm, wouldn't you?'

Tea was made, and without being asked, Brid had taken her coat off, hanging it on the back of her chair rather than on one of the hooks in the hall. Baby steps. She looked at Anthony leaning against the kitchen counter holding his mug. He had hardly changed since the first day she'd seen him. He had never put on weight, and if it wasn't for his dark hair slowly retreating from his forehead and the lines around his eyes, he might have been twenty years younger. He wasn't a vain man, but there was still something in the way he looked at her that made her think that he felt he deserved better.

Her hands were on the table, palms down. She felt like she needed to anchor herself to something or she might fly around the room screaming out her pain like a hysterical balloon. Taking a deep breath and arranging her face into a neutral expression of unconcern, she announced, 'Now,

kids I must have a quick talk with your father.'
She tried to ignore their frightened faces. What
did they think was going to happen next? Did
they really think she would ever leave them? She
looked at her mother-in-law. 'Is it all right if we
use the sitting room for a minute?'

The older woman stood and addressed Brid as
if she were a visiting dignitary with a limited
command of English: 'You are very welcome to
use any room in this house.'

When they were alone, there was a moment of
silence.

'I fucked up.' Before Anthony could speak, she
continued, 'I've been fucking up. I am sorry.'

He opened his mouth, but Brid held out her
hand. 'No, Anthony. Let me . . . I know I've said
sorry before, but this is different. I haven't been
a good mother. Or a good wife. I know that, but
this time I am going to change. I promise you
that I will stop with the wine. I know you won't
believe me and trust takes time, but I have never
been so serious about anything in my entire life.'

She reached forward and grabbed his hands,
looking directly into his eyes and holding her
breath. How was this going down? It sounded
convincing enough to her. She knew if she was
going to get a truce that she had to take all the
blame. There was no point trying to defend
herself. No mention would be made of his
coldness or long silent moods. She was the awful
unworthy wife and he was the long-suffering
saint. She was deadly serious about not drinking,
but that was for herself and the children, not this
sanctimonious cock. She squeezed his hands and

. . . yes, her eyes filled with tears. If that wasn't enough, she had no idea what else she could try.

Anthony sighed. 'It's not fair. How do you think the kids felt yesterday standing outside the school? People talk. There's name-calling. Those children want to love you. We all want to love you, but you're a joke. An old joke that isn't funny any more.' He pushed her hands away.

The tears were real now. They had started when he had said that thing about how they all wanted to love her. Did he want to love her? Had he ever loved her? It was news to her.

She sat down on the low hard sofa and stared at the floor. 'I know, Anthony. I've been a monster, but this time I swear to you it will be different. What can I do to get you to believe me?' She looked up, her face a flushed mess of tears and snot. 'I will not drink again. No more. Not a drop!'

'Jesus, Brid, are you drunk now?'

'No!' She let out a wail and jumped to her feet. She wanted to implore him to believe her, but she simply had no more words.

He rubbed the back of his neck and paced the short distance between the door and the china cabinet like a cat in a cage. His breathing became a series of sighs and gasps. Finally he stopped and looked at her. As they stood facing each other with stooped shoulders, they looked like fighters in the ring waiting for the final round.

'It's the children, Brid.'

'They don't want to be here.'

'I know that, but they can't be around you when you're . . . '

'I won't be.'

'Ah Brid. I want to believe you, for the kids, I truly do, but how can I?'

'Give me a week. One week. Can't you see this is different? If I fuck up this time, I'll leave. You and the kids won't have to run away. I'll just pack my things and go. Please!'

And in that moment she really felt like she was asking Anthony to come back as well. Maybe she didn't want a new life. She just wanted her old one to be better, like polishing a familiar pair of shoes.

Anthony ran his finger along the bevelled glass in the door of the china cabinet. He didn't look up, just whispered, 'One week. You have a week.'

She wanted to hug him but sensed that it was the wrong thing to do. This was her victory but she knew she mustn't give any hint of triumphalism. A simple nod and a demure 'Thank you, Anthony.'

Even better than shepherding her own children out of their grandmother's house had been the look on the old woman's face when Anthony had announced they were all going home. It was an act of extreme self-sacrifice on Brid's part not to flash her the wide, smug smile of a winner.

Music by candlelight was the start of their new life together. This was both of them making an effort. As they climbed the steps, Anthony took Brid's arm. Any stranger might have thought what a sweet couple they were, whereas most of the population of Duneen just assumed Brid was a bit unsteady on her feet.

The concert was about to begin when they got into the chapel, so they slipped into a pew at the back of the church.

Mairead Gallagher stepped in front of the altar in a dress that would have been more appropriate for the Oscars than an amateur musical evening in Duneen. Presumably the desired effect of having so much skin on show was to be sexy, but in the stony chill of St Michael's chapel, it just made men and women alike wonder how cold she must be.

With both hands clasped tightly together to prevent shivering, she introduced a harpist and a pianist from the school of music in Cork. The two young men stepped forward to lacklustre applause and took their places by their instruments. The programme began by confirming everyone's worst fears when Mairead sang two arias by some obscure Polish composer. PJ became painfully self-conscious of every little movement, so tried to ration his number of fidgets. Evelyn sat perfectly still, staring straight ahead, while Abigail examined her fingernails. Florence allowed a range of emotions to play across her face so that the simple people of Duneen could see that she fully appreciated this shrill discord.

Things improved somewhat when Mairead announced that she was going to perform a medley of songs from *Oklahoma!*. Everyone relaxed into the familiar tunes, and even the most reluctant husbands began to enjoy themselves. There was some more opera, but it was Mozart and Puccini — crowd-pleasers — then the harpist performed a solo piece, and while nobody could claim to have actually enjoyed it, they could at least marvel at the technical achievement in the playing. Mairead finished the show with such a powerful performance of 'You'll Never Walk Alone' that it sounded like more of a threat than a promise. The chapel erupted into applause and cries of 'More!' The trio had clearly not envisaged any need for an encore, so made do by leading a strange sing-along version of John Denver's 'Take Me Home, Country Roads'.

It turned out that everyone, without realising they had ever learnt the song, did in fact know all the words. Evelyn was surprised to hear PJ's smooth baritone voice: 'West Virginia, mountain mamma!'

The sergeant was enjoying himself. He had forgotten how much he liked to sing. His career in the school choir had been cut short when he became too self-conscious to stand in front of an audience and had quit. He strained to hear Evelyn's voice, since she was singing in almost a whisper. Florence was the musical one and threw her head back as if trying to contact country roads somewhere on the other side of Ballytorne.

Afterwards people jostled towards the doors, pulling on coats, nodding to neighbours and all agreeing with each other that it had been very good. 'Wasn't it good?' 'It was. Very good.'

Brid and Anthony were almost the first to leave, while PJ and the Ross sisters had become stuck in the crowd surging towards the exit. Evelyn touched PJ's sleeve. He looked down at her and was struck by her smooth skin and the hint of a smile. 'It's still early, Sergeant. Will you come back to the house for a cup of tea or a drink? I made a few sandwiches before we came out.'

The thought of making small talk with Abigail and Florence while wedged into a low uncomfortable chair didn't really appeal, but it was such a rare kind invitation that he didn't feel he could refuse. Besides which, he was actually quite hungry.

At the bottom of the steps, they stopped while it was decided that PJ would take his own vehicle and follow the sisters up to Ard Carraig. He was just about to turn away when a car inched slowly by trying to avoid the dispersing crowd. He saw Brid's face in the passenger seat. She noticed him and smiled, but then she must have registered Evelyn standing next to him and her expression changed. PJ glanced over to Evelyn, who had also spotted Brid. Her expression was hard to read, but there was certainly no hint of a smile. PJ had suddenly lost his appetite.

14

It wasn't raining, but it didn't need to. The air was thick with a wet mist and the horizon was lost in the various shades of grey that blurred the sky and sea into a single mottled canvas. The small red car parked on the cliff looked like a wound in the vast bleakness.

Brid stared out at the white-tipped waves and the small leafless trees bent against the wind. The driver's-side window was open and she was taking great gasps of the damp sea air. The drive up here wasn't exactly what she had intended, but she knew that she couldn't stay at home when she was feeling like this. A glass of wine was so appealing, she'd had to escape the kitchen with its heavy fridge door. She hoped that pausing for breath on the clifftop might help her sort out what she wanted to do.

For most of her adult life Brid had never allowed herself to examine or question too closely the life she was living. She simply got through the days and, when she needed it, used wine to chase her feelings into the shadowy recesses of her heart. It had been a shock last night when she had seen PJ standing by the Ross woman. Without hesitation she was able to label what she had felt. It was a deep, irrational jealousy. What she found less easy to identify was whether it was because that man she hardly knew was with someone else, or if it was purely to do with it being Evelyn Ross. It was all so shamefully juvenile.

Anthony had eventually asked what was wrong, because without realising it she had not said a word for the rest of the journey. Poor Anthony. Yes, he was priggish and annoying, but at the same time, no man deserved this treatment. His life hadn't been easy and Brid often wondered why he stayed. Was the farm really that important to him? More important than his happiness? More important than being with a woman he actually loved? Maybe the children were enough. They had been for her, after all, hadn't they?

Jealous. She had no right to feel anything after their drunken tryst, but even the next day she knew that she had felt something more. Perhaps it was as simple as the physical connection. She still had sex with Anthony occasionally, but nothing like the hungry clawing and biting that had gone on with the guard. In fact she had never in her life felt desired like that, and it was overwhelming. Still, that didn't make it a relationship, and she knew that if he had been standing with any other woman besides that Ross creature, she would not have felt the same.

Brid stepped out of the car and, pulling the collar of her coat up, walked to the edge of the cliff. Despite all the dark days, she had never felt like ending her life. Still, today as she stared down at the water boiling around the rocks below, she could imagine just letting go. The wonderful lightness and freedom of flying through the air and then the cold dark of the water washing away every single care and concern. She smiled to herself. Of course she'd never do it. It wasn't just the children; she still believed that life had more to give her. It had to, because so far it had offered her precious little.

She wondered if she should say something to PJ. Would an affair help her or make things worse? How strange that she could imagine sharing a bed with him again but couldn't envision looking into his eyes and asking him what it was he felt.

Her thoughts were interrupted by the growl of a car engine coming along the road, and she saw the distinctive blue and yellow of the Garda car. It was too late to duck or hide, but happily it drove by, disappearing behind a thick hedge. Brid sighed with relief. She wasn't ready to have any sort of conversation right now. But then she heard the engine at a slightly higher pitch and turned to see the car, with PJ at the wheel, reversing slowly down the slight hill. He stopped about fifty feet away and turned off the engine.

Brid attempted to compose herself, running her right hand through her hair, knowing that she must look . . . well, someone kind might call it windswept, but she knew that bedraggled was closer to the truth. PJ walked towards her, leaning into the wind. He was smiling.

'I thought that was you.'

'Yes.'

'What a God-awful day.'

'Yes.'

He looked out to sea as if what he was about to say was written in the clouds.

131

'I was just wondering if you sorted everything about the kids.'

'Yes. It's fine . . . fine.'

Another pause, then Brid saw PJ's lips moving, but the waves and the wind drowned out his words.

'I can't hear you,' she shouted over the elements.

PJ came a couple of steps closer.

'I was just asking if we're all right?'

'All right?'

'Well, you know, after the other night?'

He looked so serious and concerned she couldn't help smiling back at him.

'It was a mad thing to happen, but I don't regret it. I had fun. Are you all right?'

PJ blushed. 'Yes. I had a good time too.'

They grinned at each other and PJ was startled to find himself getting slightly aroused. Almost to remind himself, he blurted out, 'It was very unprofessional of me. If anyone found out . . . '

'Oh, don't worry — your secret is safe with me.' Then, with a slight smirk, she added, 'I'd hate for the sergeant to lose his job.'

'The sergeant wouldn't like that either,' he replied with a little chuckle. Both of them wondered if this was what flirting felt like.

'What brings you up here anyway, Brid?'

'I just needed to get away for a while.'

'Away?'

'You know. Anthony, the fridge.'

'Anthony's a fridge?'

Brid smiled. 'You could say that, but no, I

132

meant wine. I'm trying not to drink and it's hard with everything that's going on. Don't tell me you're the only person in Duneen who doesn't know my reputation!'

'I had heard a whisper or two.'

He wanted to hold her in that moment. To fall to the ground with her and shelter together against the wind rushing in off the ocean, but he knew that mustn't happen. He had unfinished business. He cleared his throat.

'Brid. This is awkward, but I do still need to ask you a few questions about Tommy Burke's disappearance. I'm sorry. I don't want to upset you.'

It was still a shock for Brid to hear Tommy's name again after all these years, and it took her a moment to reply.

'Of course, of course. Do you want to sit in the car?'

PJ looked at the little Honda.

'I think we might be more comfortable in the squad car, if you're all right.'

Brid glanced between the two vehicles and back at PJ. 'Of course.'

They took the few paces back to the Garda car and got inside. PJ started the engine and fiddled with the plastic controls by the radio.

'This should thaw us out.'

'Lovely,' and Brid meant it.

PJ stretched across to open the glove compartment and took out his notebook and pen.

'Very formal,' Brid remarked

'It's the head honcho up in Cork. He needs it

all done by the book,' PJ offered apologetically. 'So. You were engaged to Tommy Burke?'

'I was.'

'And when did you last see him?'

'It was the night before he vanished. He came up for his dinner.' Brid turned in her seat and put her hand on PJ's arm. 'I can't tell you how strange all of this is.'

'Strange? What do you mean?'

'Well it's just that . . . I was such a child. I've always thought of Tommy Burke as the love of my life. I've blamed everything — you know, my life — on him. Ridiculous. He never loved me. I knew that even then. Jesus, I was more like one of those girls that wins a competition to go on a date with their pop idol than an actual fiancée. I thought I'd lose my mind when I was told they'd found his body, and here I am a few days later laughing at the very idea of being in love with Tommy Burke. Nearly losing the children, Anthony, you, this is reality. This is the life I have to try and figure out.' She glanced across at PJ. He wasn't taking notes. 'Does any of this make sense?'

'Oh God, yes, yes, I understand, but . . . ' he hesitated, 'but I've still got to interview the woman who was engaged to the man who disappeared. You know Evelyn Ross thinks you killed him?'

Brid let out a hoot of laughter. 'Evelyn Ross! Sure I thought she had driven him away, and then when I heard about the body I did wonder if she might have done something crazy. You don't know that woman. I've seen her like a

134

creature possessed. She looks so serene as she wafts through the village, everything just so, but mark my words, she is unhinged. I'd say they all are. I mean, really, three spinster sisters living up there all alone, it's not right.'

PJ wasn't sure how to respond. He found himself agreeing with Brid but felt that it would be somehow disloyal to Evelyn to say so. He decided on another question.

'Excuse me for asking this, but were you sleeping with Tommy Burke?'

A little snort. 'No. No I was not.'

'And do you think that he and Evelyn Ross were having some sort of affair?'

'Are you serious?' Brid's voice was raised. 'That woman screams virgin! I doubt she's even been kissed, never mind anything else.'

PJ shifted uncomfortably in his seat. 'All right.' He decided to end that line of questioning.

Brid raised an eyebrow and gave him a sideways glance as she recalled the two of them stood together outside the chapel. Maybe . . . No. No, that wasn't possible.

'Have you ever heard from Tommy again?'

'I haven't.'

'Heard of anyone seeing him?'

'No. Well, my mother heard people had seen him getting on the bus to Cork. Quite a few people had that story.'

'Who told your mother?'

'As far as I remember, she had it from Cormac Byrne in the pub.' PJ made a note.

'Weren't people surprised that he just disappeared?'

'Not that I remember. Sure, I suppose people could understand him making himself scarce after the fight in the street.'

PJ decided to feign ignorance. He wondered how Brid's version of events would differ from Evelyn's.

'What fight?'

Brid groaned inwardly. He didn't know about the fight. She was so embarrassed to recount what had happened that morning outside O'Driscoll's.

There was an electronic ringing sound, and PJ started slapping his various pockets trying to locate his phone. Brid silently gave thanks for the interruption.

'Hello.' PJ's face was scrunched in concentration as he listened to the voice at the other end of the line. 'Yes.'

There was a long silence, with PJ just holding the phone to his ear. His face relaxed and his mouth formed a small pink circle. Eventually he spoke.

'Right. Well thank you for letting me know. Of course. Of course. Yes, I will. Thanks again. Goodbye.'

He hit the small red button to hang up and stared down at the steering wheel. Brid sat in silence, looking at him expectantly. After a moment or two PJ turned to her.

'Well that was the results of the DNA. Whoever was buried up there, it wasn't Tommy Burke.'

Outside, a lone seagull was battling against the wind, suspended in the moment.

Part Two

1

Four months had passed. Four long, dark months, but now finally some tight green buds had appeared and a few clumps of daffodils hinted at the bright yellow blankets that were to follow. Some days the clouds would part and tease the good people of Duneen with a patch of blue. The children returning from school stayed out after the bus dropped them off, and their thin, high voices could be heard until it was dark. Cormac Byrne spent one whole Sunday sanding and oiling the picnic tables before taking them out of the shed and placing them in a neat row along the front of the pub. It was hardly café society, but it gave the smokers an air of respectability rather than standing huddled against the wall like some very unappetising prostitutes.

Time never went quickly for the residents of the village, but after the news broke about Tommy Burke it seemed to stop completely. Everyone had enjoyed putting forward their theories about what had happened to Big Tom's son, but when it came to light that the discovery was really just some bones in a field that would probably never be identified, it was harder to get involved. The people of Duneen felt they had been cheated. The wind had been taken out of their sails, their lives robbed of excitement.

Susan Hickey had distracted herself by

deciding that what the village needed more than anything else was a ride-on lawn mower for the cemetery. So far she had raised less than two hundred euros. She understood. Her heart wasn't really in it either.

Over at the shop and post office, business was ticking over as usual. All the faces were once again familiar. There were no more journalists sniffing around or gardaí from Cork standing by their unmarked cars trying to look important. Mrs O'Driscoll had recently noticed some of the builders coming back into the shop looking for cigarettes or cartons of milk. Work must have resumed up at the site. Life truly had returned to normal.

Brid and Anthony existed in an artificial calm. There were no raised voices and she made an effort to go up to bed at more or less the same time as he did. She often lay there beside him, awake and sober, going over things. Sometimes she thought about Tommy; on other nights she saw herself sprawled on the stairs with PJ, and occasionally she imagined herself smartly dressed in an office somewhere, with friends to see after work and a broad, unforced smile on her face.

Brid had decided that not rocking the boat was the best course of action at the moment, but she hadn't given up. With sobriety came more time for thinking and coming up with ideas, ones she could remember the next day. There would be a time once the kids were older when she would step off the leaking boat of her life and walk alone into the unknown. The thought of it scared her but also kept her going through each monotonous sober day.

She had deliberately not thrown any of her wine away. The bottles still stood in the fridge, and she took pleasure in staring back at their glossy labels. Every time she closed the fridge without finding a glass in her hand made her feel like somebody who had been granted supernatural strength.

Things had changed at Ard Carraig in the last four months too. One night, about a week after it had been revealed that Tommy Burke was still missing, Abigail came into the kitchen carrying a shallow cardboard box with crudely drawn tomatoes printed on the side. Evelyn was at the sink peeling the paper off some tin cans to get them ready for the recycling. She turned to look over her shoulder at her sister.

'What have you got there?'

Abigail stepped back from the table.

'It's for you. Well, all of us, but especially you.' She gave a little flourish towards the box.

Evelyn wiped her hands on a tea towel and crossed the room to the table. Looking into the box, she found an old towel, which she pulled back tentatively.

'Oh Abigail!' she gasped. 'I don't believe it.'

Lying on the bottom of the box fast asleep was a plump blonde puppy. Its eyes were squeezed shut, a hint of pink tongue at the mouth, and the rest of the body seemed made up of a silky belly softly moving up and down with steady careless breaths.

Evelyn reached her hand into the box and touched the warm softness, and with that the

141

eyes opened and the puppy struggled to its feet like an old drunk that had fallen asleep at the bus stop.

'It's a little boy,' said Abigail. 'What will you call him?'

Of course the first name that leapt into Evelyn's head was Tommy, but she instantly dismissed it.

'What about . . . what about Bobby? He looks like a little Bobby.'

Abigail said nothing.

'What?'

'Well, it's just that's what Mammy used to call our father.'

'I know.'

'Isn't that a bit, I don't know, strange?'

'Would it bother you? I think it would be nice.'

'I suppose it would.' Abigail smiled. 'Bobby it is.'

'Will Florence mind, do you think?'

'It's a puppy! She wouldn't care if you called it Adolf. She's going to adore him!'

The two women laughed and Evelyn picked up little Bobby.

'Let's give you a bowl of water.'

Bobby twisted his head from side to side, seeming to be surprised to find he had ears.

It was strange the effect something so small could have on a household. A little creature predisposed to happiness, with no sense of what had come before, Bobby transformed the sad old house. Even the piss stains on the threadbare hall carpet seemed a cheerful sign. Life where there had been none.

As the months passed, he grew bigger and more confident. Abigail had acquired him from some of her gardening friends just outside Bandon on the way to Cork. His mother was a pedigree retriever, while the father was an overly friendly collie neighbour. It was clear from his wide paws that he was going to be a large dog, and sure enough after four months he had outgrown two dog beds and was already on his third collar. Most of the time he just ran wild in the garden or in the field that sloped down to the river, but a couple of times a week Evelyn would attach a lead to him and walk him into the village. Cars slowed down to peer at the curious sight of poised, collected Evelyn Ross wrestling with a very wilful dog along the side of the road. No cowboy breaking in a bucking bronco had struggled harder than Evelyn, as she found herself either being pulled towards her destination at a breakneck speed or dragging a surprisingly heavy recalcitrant dog straining against the direction she had intended.

After a couple of months she decided that Bobby was a good excuse to visit PJ, so one Friday morning she and the dog had arrived at the door of the Garda barracks, Evelyn covered in sweat and Bobby bouncing with excitement at the idea of going inside another house. As it happened, the sergeant was out, but Mrs Meany took the message to say they had called. As they headed back down the short drive, at more of a jog than a walk, Evelyn wondered why the housekeeper hadn't even remarked on Bobby. You mightn't want him yourself, but he was a beautiful big pup that nearly everyone they met took the time to admire. Mind you, Evelyn thought, the woman didn't look well. Not well at all.

If Ard Carraig had found new life, then the Garda barracks had surely lost it. Mrs Meany still cleaned and chronically over-catered meals for one, but she did so in near silence. Where once her monologues of chatter and gossip played like department store muzak constantly in the background, now there was just the hum of a hoover or the hollow clang of lids being put on pots.

PJ sat at his desk staring at a computer screen, wishing life was different. He wished they had never found the human remains. A crime that couldn't be solved was worse than no crime at all. He wished that Brid and Evelyn had never shone their light on him. The brief flurry and excitement of his love triangle had soon flatlined. He felt more alone than ever. For the first time in twenty-five years he wondered about leaving the police force. When word got out that the body wasn't Tommy Burke and it became clear that the murder hunt had hit a dead end, he had felt the way people looked at him. For a few weeks there he had sensed respect and interest, but now it was closer to pity. Walking down the main street in his uniform, he knew eyes were at windows thinking to themselves, 'Would you look at that big fool, all dressed up with nowhere to go.'

If he had seen her through the window of the shop he would never have gone into O'Driscoll's, but by the time he noticed Evelyn squeezing the loaves of bread with her long, cool fingers it was too late.

'Sergeant Collins!'

He could feel himself blushing and in that moment loathed himself completely. A woman was saying hello to him in a shop. Why did he always have to feel so awkward? He managed to look her in the eye. Her face held no secrets, just the happy smile of a woman who seemed genuinely pleased to see him. He relaxed a little. 'Hello.' Evelyn stepped towards him and then the two of them were trapped in the narrow aisle. PJ felt uncomfortable again. This was far too close for comfort.

'I thought you might have come up to see us.'

PJ squinted at her, puzzled.

'Did Mrs Meany not tell you I called around with Bobby the pup?'

'Oh yes. Yes, she did,' PJ lied. Mrs Meany had never mentioned any such visit.

'He is such a dote. Do you like dogs, Sergeant?'

'I do.'

'Well you must come up and see him. What are you doing now?'

PJ's mouth hinged open and shut like a fish.

'Nothing.' There it was. He had said it.

'Great.' Evelyn smiled. 'Come up now,' she said. 'And selfishly, you can give me a lift!' A little laugh.

PJ nodded his agreement, but in his head he was wondering what had happened to the awkward, distant Evelyn he had met just a few months earlier. He thought she might be on some sort of medication. Surely just being high on puppy love couldn't have this strong an effect?

Out on the street it was still light and a few cars were going through the village on various stages of the school run. PJ walked around to open the passenger door for Evelyn. She tucked her coat beneath her and slipped into the seat as if she were getting into a limo outside a five-star hotel, then put her basket on her lap. PJ eased himself in behind the wheel and shut the door. He had just started the engine when there was a tap on his window. Slightly annoyed, he glanced to his right. There was no mistaking that it was one of the builders from the site.

Window down, he poked his head towards the pavement.

'What is it?' He tried to sound busy, but he felt it was probably obvious that he was just a bored guard who was literally going to see a woman about a dog.

The builder cleared his throat and glanced at Evelyn. PJ looked at her too. She was sat very still staring straight ahead with both hands on the top of her basket.

'You're all right. Spit it out.'

'Well it's just that . . . well, we think we're after finding some more bones up above.' He paused. 'Little bones.'

Evelyn let out a squeak like a puppy dreaming of rabbits.

2

PJ couldn't believe it. He didn't consider himself to be a religious man, but this did seem like the answer to prayers he didn't remember saying. After the DNA results from the old bones, he had desperately tried to keep interest in the case alive. They could continue the search for Tommy Burke, and besides, whoever the body might turn out to be, there was still a murderer to find. When the DNA failed to match any names on the system, though, Cork lost interest, and the lads in Ballytorne treated him the way he himself dealt with old Miss Baxter, who every summer was convinced that someone was stealing the blackberries from the hedgerow outside her bungalow. Finally he took the hint and let it drop, but now everyone was going to have to listen. New remains!

The village was soon filled once more with Garda cars and press. A second body meant this story had legs. It might be a serial killer, or some bizarre suicide pact. Long fluttering ribbons of police tape flapped in the breeze and the white overalls of the technical team picked their way carefully across the muddy crime scene. It also meant the return of Detective Superintendent Linus Dunne.

The last four months had brought great change to the detective's life. One evening (it had been a Thursday, he knew, because he had

147

met some of the uniforms who played five-a-side in the pub for a pint or two after their practice), he had got home, not late, ten at the latest, to find the house in darkness. He remembered he had breathed a sigh of relief: how lovely to walk into a quiet house, no baby screaming, no wife with greasy hair who seemed to live in sweat pants haranguing him to do things. The note had just said, *At mum's. Call me.*

He had assumed the baby was sick so he made himself a cheese sandwich and watched the news before ringing. With any luck his wife might have gone to bed. Sure enough his mother-in-law answered the phone. She sounded even more hostile than usual. Linus began to suspect something was seriously wrong. The voice on the other end of the line told him that his wife was too upset to come to the phone. She'd had enough of being a single mother, so she and the baby had moved out. If Linus wanted to see them, he could call round in the morning.

When he hung up the phone, he was shocked, of course. He'd had no idea that June was so unhappy. For some reason, because the situation had been making him miserable, he had assumed she was happy. If they both hated this new life with a baby, why were they bothering?

As he sat on the sofa with the flickering light from the TV throwing shadows against the curtains, he asked himself if he was some sort of monster. His wife and child had left him, and if he was being totally honest, he didn't really care.

Life with June had been great to start with. He'd put on a fresh shirt after work and meet her somewhere for cocktails or dinner, often both. He had enjoyed having her on his arm. She was beautiful and flirty, and once they finally had sex, things had been very close to perfect for him. That was the life he wanted back. A girlfriend when he wanted one. Getting married had been a mistake, and what on earth had he been thinking when he had agreed to the baby idea? He supposed he had imagined a child would distract June and keep her occupied so that he could reclaim some of his own life. Of course it hadn't worked out like that, but now the solution to everything had simply fallen into his lap. There was nobody moving around upstairs; the hallway wasn't blocked with a buggy the size of a small car. He was alone in his own house and he liked it. If that made him a bad person, then so be it.

When Sergeant Sumo's name had come up on his phone a couple of months later, Linus had been tempted to ignore it. Since the bones in Duneen had proved impossible to identify, he just wanted to get on with other cases, but Sumo wouldn't let it go. Linus understood. Duneen was hardly a crime hotspot, and he could sense the sergeant's loneliness, but neither of those things was his problem.

He had been busy dealing with an awful abduction case that hadn't ended well. A French chef from a restaurant in Cork had taken a custody battle into his own hands and got on the ferry to Roscoff with his seven-month-old son in the boot of his car. Linus was the one who had to park outside the house of the baby's grandparents.

Inside, the mother was sat on a sofa still in her waitress's uniform. She was just a child herself, he had thought as he sat opposite her and explained that the French police had stopped the car somewhere on the road from Morlaix to Rennes. Her hope was so great, she couldn't read his expression or the tone of his voice. 'Did they find Killian? Have they got my baby?'

Linus stared into her face, willing her to understand telepathically what was coming next. Nothing. Her eyes wet with tears, she looked at him expectantly. 'They recovered the body of an infant,' he told her. 'They think it had suffocated.' He could still hear her crying as he sat in the car outside. Sergeant fucking Sumo didn't know how lucky he had it.

★ ★ ★

When the silver Mercedes came to a halt in the rutted area of mud that served as a car park, neither PJ or Linus would have admitted it, but they were quite happy to see each other. The sergeant walked down towards the car and they greeted each other with the sort of overpumped handshake two men who had been friends years before might give each other at a school reunion. PJ led the way up a small incline to the edge of the site. Protruding over the brow of the hill were the white hoods of the forensics team. The sergeant took great pleasure in being able to bring Linus up to speed with the case.

'The lads were saying that if it hadn't been buried in some sort of metal box, there would have been nothing left after all this time. Their guess would be that it's been here at least thirty years, maybe longer. They'll know more after the proper tests, obviously.'

'Of course.' They were right at the edge of the excavation now, and Linus peered down into the chocolate-brown soil. A few rusty fragments were dotted in a loose rectangle, and there in the middle were the small, dull bones. To a casual observer it might have been the remains of an ancient picnic or discarded Sunday roast, except for the tiny skull lying on its side staring into the ditch for eternity. Linus thought of his own baby. How big was he now? He thought of the waitress and her howling tears. Who had wept for this little mite? Who had placed the tiny frame into that box and buried it up here away from the house?

Over to his right a blackthorn tree was heavy with noisy birds. Were they chaffinches? He wished they would shut the fuck up. Despite the blue sky, the wind still had some chill in it, and he pulled his coat around himself as he turned without speaking and headed back down towards the car. He could hear PJ's heavy breathing following him. 'Are they sure it's only one body up there? It's not some weird burial ground for unwanted babies, is it?'

'They can't be sure yet, but it's unlikely. The local place for those babies is in the old famine graveyard beyond the creamery. There was one found there as recently as about four years ago. It turned out it belonged to this little one from Ballytorne. She — '

'Right,' Linus announced, interrupting PJ. 'Once we get a timeline, I want you talking to anyone who would be the right age to remember. Babies come from somewhere. Who was pregnant? Who lost their kid?'

'Will do. I've already established it wasn't Mrs Burke herself. She was only pregnant the once, and that was with Tommy.'

At the mention of his name, the two men looked at each other. Tommy Burke. Where was he? Was he even now walking past them in a hi-vis jacket, smirking with pleasure because of his well-kept secret?

'Do you think there's a connection between — '

'I don't think anything,' Linus snapped. 'I don't know anything.' He opened his car door. As he got in, he turned back towards PJ. 'We'll know more soon.' Raising his eyebrows as some sort of apology for his short temper, he closed the door and slowly navigated his way across the churned-up surface towards the road.

PJ watched the silver car go and then, squinting against the sun, looked back up towards the baby's burial site. He was not a man who got feelings, or acted on hunches, but there had to be a link, he thought. Two bodies on one farm. They had to be connected somehow. He balled his hands into fists as he headed towards his own car. He was enjoying this.

★   ★   ★

Back at the bungalow, there was silence. PJ stuck his head around the kitchen door, but there was no sign of Mrs Meany. He considered going down to the pub for a sandwich. People wanted to talk to him again, and he knew that the solution to this case had to be in the collective memory of Duneen. It might only take one person to remember something very simple for everything to become clear. In his office a small corner of paper was on his desk with Mrs Meany's writing on it. *Back soon* was all it said. He wondered if he should wait. No, he'd go to the pub.

Byrne's was the only pub that did food beyond crisps or packets of nuts, so he parked outside and went in. It took his eyes a moment or two to adjust to the gloom, and when they did, it appeared he was the only customer. A radio phone-in was coming through the speakers. A woman was berating the lazy mothers of Ireland for childhood obesity. PJ rolled his eyes. This was the last thing he wanted to listen to. He considered sitting up at the bar but in the end opted for a small table behind the door just under the dartboard. Even after more than a decade there was still a smell of stale cigarettes. Behind the bar was also deserted, so PJ just sat and waited. He was in no hurry.

'If you loved your kids you would. Sure it's no effort to peel a couple of spuds.'

'When I come home from work I've only got the energy to put something in the microwave, and sure that's all they'll eat. They wouldn't thank me for a potato.'

Behind the frosted amber glass of the window PJ saw a couple of ghostly passers-by probably heading into O'Driscoll's. A large truck trundled past, plunging the bar into momentary night.

He wasn't in a rush, but this waiting was making the sergeant anxious. What if he was some sort of criminal? He could have carried the whole till out to the car by now. He stood up and went to stand by the bar. From somewhere came the noise of bottles being moved. At least he wasn't alone.

'Hello?' he called, his voice sounding flat and tinny in the hollow air.

'Be with you in a second,' came the muffled reply from somewhere behind the door at the back of the bar. It was Cormac Byrne's voice.

Another few minutes ticked by and then Cormac burst through the door rubbing his hands on an old rag.

'Sorry about that. The deliveries were late.'

'No problem, Cormac.'

'Ah, it's yourself, Sergeant!' as if he only knew him by the sound of his voice and had been unaware who the very large man in the Garda uniform was. 'What can I get you?'

'I'll just have a ham and cheese sandwich on brown bread if you have it, and a glass of 7Up. Thanks.'

Cormac walked back towards the door and called out PJ's sandwich order to a nameless helper in an unseen kitchen. Then he got a green bottle out of one of the fridges.

'Ice?'

'Yes please.'

'Actually, you're the very man I wanted to see.'

154

'Oh?'

'Did you know that my mother is in the nursing home over near Schull?'

'I didn't. I'm sorry to hear that. Is she all right?'

'Ah, she's fine. Not too steady on her feet and her memory is going, so I didn't like leaving her here on her own. I said I'd bring her home again if she didn't like it, but she's happy out there. I get over to visit a few times a week; normally it would be midweek because it can be busy here at the weekends.'

'Of course.' PJ nodded and took a sip of his drink. He wondered where this was going.

'The thing is, it's very hard to think of things to talk about. She'd know me, but that's about it. I find if I talk about things long ago she sometimes has more of a clue. That's why the Tommy Burke excitement was great. She could remember his parents, and the girls scrapping in the street and all of that.'

'Right.' PJ was becoming more interested.

'Well I remember you were in a few months ago asking about Tommy getting on the bus to Cork and I told you that I'd heard it from my mother but that I'd no clue who told her. Last night I was telling her about the baby bones and she was asking about Tommy. I had to tell her he was gone a long time ago and then she said, and this may or may not be true, but what she said last night was 'Oh that's right. Abigail Ross saw him getting on the bus.''

'Abigail?'

'That's what she said. It might be nonsense. I

mean, this is a woman who thinks Maggie Thatcher is in the room next to hers, but when she's talking about the past she gets it right more often than not.'

'Abigail Ross.' PJ thought back to the conversations that had taken place at Ard Carraig. He couldn't remember asking directly, but surely one of the sisters would have said something if Abigail had actually seen Tommy Burke getting on the bus.

A small, thin girl with greasy black hair scraped into a ponytail came from behind the bar and plonked a plate in front of PJ.

'Your sandwich. There's salt and pepper on the tables.' She turned and disappeared from view.

The sergeant looked down. It was on white bread and there didn't appear to be any cheese in it. He decided not to make a fuss. Picking up the plate and his glass, he headed back to his small table.

'Thanks for that, Cormac. I'll check it out, and if your mother has any bright ideas about the mother of the dead baby, be sure to let us know.'

The two men laughed, and then the only sound that remained was the voice bemoaning the low price of chicken nuggets.

3

A dark shadow moved slowly against the black outline of the hedgerow. It might have been a ghost, but then the crunch of a heel against some loose grit on the road betrayed that it was a living soul. Someone was walking with a steady confidence through the darkness up the hill past the primary school. One foot in front of the other, both hands clutching the collar of their coat to their throat even though it was a mild, windless night.

Nothing had changed since Mrs Meany was a young girl who had walked this road every day for nearly a year. She knew exactly where she was. She paused by the old gate lost in a jungle of briars and weeds, then kept going till she found the wide gash that had been opened as the entrance to the building site. She hesitated and then ventured forward. She was moving slower now, unsure of the terrain. Following the tracks left by the various cars and vans that used the site, she made her way up the slope. When she came across the plastic tape hanging limply, she knew that she had found the right place. Turning around, she could just make out the glow of lights from the village below. Yes, this was the spot.

Mrs Meany didn't know why she had come here, but it seemed like the right thing to do. A pilgrimage of sorts. She squeezed her eyes shut and hugged her bony frame tightly. Anyone can keep a secret when nobody suspects anything, but now it was unbearable. Until a few days ago, only four people had known about the baby buried up here, and three of them were dead. She knew that soon she would have to tell someone, and then everything would unravel. A vision drifted into her mind where she was nailed to the big cross that sat behind the altar. She saw her grey-haired head slumped to one side, the blood from the crown of thorns trickling down her face, her body draped in a silky dressing gown. All the people of the village she had ever known, alive or dead, sat in the pews and glared at her, their eyes full of unforgiving judgement.

Mrs Meany opened her eyes and stared into the darkness. Almost fifty years had passed since she had stood here shivering under a starry sky, reciting the rosary. Old Tommy Burke had asked her to say some prayers, but she had only ever been to her grandmother's funeral and could hardly remember it, she'd been that young, so wasn't sure what was appropriate. At first she hadn't cried. Just stood there pointing the big heavy torch while the shovel scraped against stones in the soil under the hedge. She had wondered why they hadn't chosen a spot in the pretty little kitchen garden behind the house, but Big Tommy had explained that too much digging went on there and it might be discovered. She had nodded her head as if she understood, but her mind swarmed with unanswered questions. Why not call the priest? Should there be a doctor? If this was so wrong, then where would the little soul end up? Was there no way to have it baptised? Somehow she knew that the answers to all these questions had something to do with trying to protect her, so she stayed silent.

Tears only came when Big Tommy had picked up the tin chest that until a few hours earlier had contained a random selection of tools. It looked so small and light in his big dark hands. She thought of the empty cot with its neatly folded blankets, and then looked down at the cold, dank hole where this tiny child would sleep forever. Her shoulders shook with sobs.

'Hold the torch still, girl,' Big Tommy had hissed at her as she tried to control her juddering chest. The tin box disappeared from view and the scoops of earth fell on the lid like heavy rain.

Mrs Meany peered around her and tried to get her bearings. It was useless. With the house gone and trees felled, there was nothing to help her figure out where the other body had been found. Her head ached from all the thinking, all the secrets. Soon, she thought, they must escape. Like a lanced boil, the poison of the past had to be released.

Picking her way carefully back to the road, she remembered the last time she had left the farm. It had been so quiet after all the noise and commotion. Her throat was still sore from the screaming, her body felt unfamiliar, and every step had made her flinch. She hadn't been back at home for long before her mother had got her the job up at the priest's house. Had Mam known? She went to her grave never having said anything. Mrs Meany had desperately wanted to tell her, but by the time she was standing by her narrow bed in the nursing home, it had seemed too cruel to upset her.

It didn't matter. Nothing mattered any more. Going to work for the priest was as good as becoming a nun in her mind, and she had simply chosen to ignore her own pleasure or enjoyment. Back then, just living was enough; just knowing gave her all the comfort she needed. Then the comfort had turned to heartbreak, and as the house slowly vanished under its shroud of branches and weeds, so did she. She had chosen not to exist. That was weak and selfish of her and had led to all the trouble. It had led to this moment fifty years later, as she made her way home through the empty night.

In the morning, she was surprised to see two cars outside the Garda barracks. It turned out that the detective from Cork was down early, so she made two full breakfasts. It was more work but it was nice to have the sound of voices in the kitchen after the months of silence. As she wiped down the counters and left the pan to soak for a few minutes, she listened to snatches of conversation. They were going to question Brid Riordan and the Ross girl again. The theory was that the baby had probably belonged to one of them and was linked to Tommy's disappearance. The other body could have been a jealous boyfriend or . . . Their scenarios ground to a halt.

Mrs Meany wondered if she was acting suspiciously. Was it possible to tell by looking at her that she could solve their mystery, or at least some of it? She could have pulled out a chair and told them everything. Instead she made a fresh pot of tea and poured the two men a mug each. They were talking now about Abigail Ross being the last person to have seen Tommy. The old lady folded a damp cloth carefully and hung it over the taps. Abigail? Something about that didn't ring true. The detective fellow was explaining to PJ how they needed to collect DNA from the women to help identify the baby. DNA? Mrs Meany had seen enough episodes of *CSI* to know that stuff could tell you everything. Soon they would unearth the truth.

4

It was Abigail herself who opened the front door at Ard Carraig. She looked pale and drawn and PJ wondered if she was ill. She offered no greeting and seemed perfectly comfortable for the three of them to just stare at each other. Linus broke the silence.

'Good morning. I'm Detective Superintendent Dunne, and I'm sure you know the sergeant here.'

PJ gave a weak smile of acknowledgement and Abigail simply nodded. She clearly was in no mood for this intrusion. Linus cleared his throat and tried to take control.

'There have been further developments up at the building site and I would like to ask you a few questions.'

'This is Abigail Ross,' PJ interjected. 'It's really Evelyn we're after.'

'My sister is out at the moment but I'm sure she'll be happy . . . Oh.' Abigail stopped herself in mid-sentence as a long-limbed golden dog came bounding around the side of the house and threw himself against Linus and PJ as if they were long-lost family members returning from war.

'Bobby! Down! Bad boy!' Abigail commanded without much conviction. 'He's a bit wild, I'm afraid. He'll calm down in a minute.'

Linus was not a fan of dogs at the best of

times, and he certainly did not appreciate struggling with this writhing mass of hair and saliva while trying to conduct an investigation. PJ was secretly pleased at the detective's discomfort. He rubbed his hands along Bobby's back, enjoying the sheen of his coat and the crazed energy of the young dog with its warm squirming body that didn't seem to contain a single bone.

'I'm so sorry!' It was Evelyn, slightly out of breath, rushing from the side of the house. 'He heard voices and was off like a shot. He loves new people. He'll calm down in a minute.'

'So we hear,' muttered Linus.

Bobby, oblivious to any sense of calm, seemed even more excited now that Evelyn had joined the group. The pack was complete!

Evelyn spread her arms as if she were herding small children. 'Shall we head inside?'

Abigail turned on her heel and went into the darkened hallway, followed by Linus and PJ. As Evelyn closed the door behind them, Bobby decided it was a race to see who could get to the kitchen door first. He won.

PJ was struck by how different Ard Carraig seemed. No lamps were lit to dispel the gloom, and the previously pristine kitchen had small collections of dirty crockery scattered on the counters, while the floor was covered with a patchwork of old newspapers stained yellow from what he assumed was dog piss. There was a strong smell, and it wasn't of baking.

'Forgive the mess,' Evelyn said as she walked over to the sink. 'Bobby hasn't quite got the hang of where to do his business. Have you, Bobby?'

163

She leaned down to the dog and rubbed his ears. 'You don't know where to do your business, do you?' Bobby wagged his thick tail furiously from side to side, as if he thought 'business' might be some sort of chicken drumstick.

The gardaí looked at each other, unsure how to react. PJ felt oddly wrong-footed by this display from Evelyn. There was something not right in this house. He glanced over and saw that Abigail was still standing silently by the door, her expressionless face giving nothing away. She couldn't approve of her house being turned into a kennel, thought PJ.

Linus decided it was time to try and regain his professional authority. 'Is now a good time to talk? We have a few questions.'

'Yes, yes, of course,' Evelyn replied. 'Let me just get Bobby some more water.'

PJ raised an eyebrow. God forbid that Bobby ran out of piss, he thought.

Abigail opened the door a little. 'I'm going out to the garden. Will you be all right, Evelyn?'

Evelyn turned from the running tap. 'Of course. See you later. Lunch might be a little late. Florence said they're doing school photographs today.'

'Fine.'

'Oh, just before you go.' It was PJ. 'I've been told that you actually saw Tommy Burke getting on the bus that last day he was seen?'

A stillness settled on the room. Evelyn stood holding the brimming dog bowl, and even Bobby seemed to sense that all eyes were on Abigail. She turned slowly.

164

'Me? No. I heard people down in the village talking about it, that's all.'

'You don't remember who told you, do you? It could be important.'

'I'm not sure. Doubtless it was one of the sources of village news. It might have been old Mrs Byrne from the pub . . . Yes, I'm fairly sure that's who told me.' Abigail stretched her lips into a tight smile. The subject was closed.

PJ spoke slowly. 'Well, isn't that a strange thing? That's the very person who said you were the one who saw him go.'

If the room had been still before, now it was frozen. Three sets of eyes transfixed by the grey-haired statue by the door. A moment passed, and then another. PJ held his breath.

A muscle twitched in Abigail's jaw and then she spoke.

'Isn't that woman in a home, Sergeant?' She glared at PJ, but he steeled himself to hold her gaze.

'Yes. She is.'

'Well I think that explains that. She must be confused.' A beat. 'Now I've got work to do. Excuse me.' She turned to leave but then changed her mind. Deliberately not looking in Evelyn's direction, she addressed the two men. 'But if I had seen that boy getting on the bus, I would have happily waved him on his way. He had caused enough upset around here. As far as I'm concerned, it's good riddance. He's gone, he's still gone and I'm glad.' She paused, then turned to Evelyn. 'If you need me, I'm just down in the far greenhouse.'

165

Evelyn nodded. 'OK.'

Throwing one more look at PJ and Linus, Abigail left the kitchen, closing the door carefully behind her.

The silence she left was broken by Bobby, who got up from behind the kitchen table and rushed over to Evelyn as if an imaginary barman had just rung the bell for last orders.

'Good boy!' she cried and set the water down next to a second empty bowl sat amongst the debris of stained sheets of newspaper.

PJ cleared his throat. 'Is your sister all right? She didn't look herself, I thought.'

Evelyn shrugged. 'I think she's fine. She was complaining about an upset stomach. Maybe she didn't sleep very well. Will I put the kettle on?'

The men looked at each other and then Linus took the lead. 'Yes, a cup of tea might be nice. Thank you very much.'

'I'll make a pot. Please, take a seat. I'm afraid it will just be tea. There's precious little baking gets done these days.' She pointed to Bobby, who was now lying on the floor licking one of his front paws.

'I'd say it's made a big difference to you all having him around.' PJ thought it best to keep the conversation general till they were all sat down. He wasn't sure why Linus had asked for tea. Maybe he just fancied a cup. Odd, though, because he'd had about three mugs of it up at the barracks. Was he trying to endear himself to Evelyn for some reason?

I'm overthinking this, he thought, and stopped. Evelyn was speaking rapidly.

'I'd forgotten how much work they are. I mean, we had dogs when we were kids, but I suppose Mammy and Daddy or the older girls did most of the looking after and cleaning. I'm not complaining. I love having him around. You know, a bit of life about the place, instead of just three old spinsters gathering dust!' She laughed.

PJ and Linus, both unsure of how to react to her referring to herself as a spinster, just smiled.

'How old is he now?' Linus asked, reasoning that he should feign some sort of interest in the beast.

Evelyn was putting the teapot and mugs on a small metal tray. 'He's only six months. We're hoping he might stop growing soon.'

'Big paws,' PJ chipped in, like an old farmer sizing up a cow for sale at the mart.

'Don't! That's what everyone says!' Evelyn put the tray on the table and sat down. She started pouring the tea. 'So what can I do for you?' It suddenly struck her that she didn't know exactly why these men were here. She felt a vague sense of unease creep over her.

PJ turned to Linus, who began to speak. 'The discovery of the infant remains has cast a new light on the body that was found at the end of last year. We just wanted to ask you some more questions. They are a little personal in nature, so I hope I don't embarrass you.'

Evelyn raised an eyebrow and brushed some non-existent crumbs from her lap. She was listening intently.

'When you were first interviewed a few months ago, you said you hadn't been sexually

167

active with Tommy Burke.'

'That's right.'

'And is that still your answer?'

'What? Yes. I mean, I wasn't lying, if that's what you mean.'

'Nobody is suggesting that, but at the time you might have wanted to keep some things private that didn't appear to be relevant. The dead baby makes a great deal of difference to the investigation.'

'I understand.'

'Were you aware of Tommy Burke being involved with anyone else?' Then before Evelyn could speak he added, 'Apart from Brid Riordan, of course.'

Evelyn wrapped both her hands around her mug and stared at the steam gently rising. 'No. No, I never saw or heard anything, and I was in that house almost every day. To be honest, I can't imagine he and Brid ever . . . Well, that was no love match.'

'And what about other girls at the time? Were there rumours at school? Did anyone suddenly drop out or disappear for a few weeks?'

She rolled her eyes. 'I really can't remember. I don't think so. Certainly there were no stories about anyone that stuck.'

As if prompted by all this talk of sexual activity, Bobby sprawled himself wide on the floor and started noisily lapping at his nether regions. All three humans glanced down at the dog and then back at their tea. No one considered this the right time to make a comment.

Linus was frustrated. Normally he could read people. He prided himself in interviews on getting a feel for who was telling the truth and who was just playing for time. Evelyn gave nothing away. She just sat there with the hint of a smile playing across her lips.

'How did you hear that Tommy had disappeared?'

'Abigail. Probably Florence as well. They'd have heard it down in the village.'

'And you never tried to contact him?'

'I told Sergeant Collins all this months ago.'

'I know. I'm sorry. I just wanted to be certain. Sometimes memories can be jogged.'

'Even if I'd wanted to, I couldn't. It was a different world. I sometimes walked past the house to see if there was any sign of life, but there never was. After a few years even the house had disappeared.'

'Fallen down?'

'No, not exactly. The garden just took over until the place was completely hidden.'

'It was fierce creepy,' PJ added, trying to sound authoritative.

Linus and Evelyn turned to look at him, as if they were surprised he was still there.

Linus sighed. He had other questions in his head but he could tell he was going to get nowhere. He folded his notebook.

'Well thank you for your time. And the tea,' he added as he picked up his mug and drained it.

'Yes. Thank you,' PJ repeated and smiled at Evelyn.

They all got up and walked towards the door.

As they left the room, PJ glanced back and saw Bobby squatting by the back door while a puddle of piss spread out around him. He wondered if he should say something but suddenly felt very tired. Fuck it, she'll find out soon enough.

★ ★ ★

PJ didn't enjoy being a passenger, and to make matters worse he had hardly fastened his seat belt when he realised that he should have taken the hint from Bobby and gone to the toilet in Ard Carraig. He would have to hold it until they got to the Riordan farm.

He told Linus to head back down to the village, before giving him more detailed directions. As they drove, the silence hung between the two men in the car. PJ decided to try and recover the slightly easier rapport they had had that morning back at the barracks.

'How's the baby?'

There was a tiny pause before Linus answered. 'Fine. Fine.'

'And your wife?'

A longer pause. 'She's well.'

'I suppose the baby's sleeping through now, is he?'

'Yes. Yes, he is.'

Realising that PJ wasn't going to let the subject drop, Linus exhaled slowly and said as casually as he could muster, 'To tell you the truth, myself and June are on a bit of a break.'

PJ froze. This was not how this conversation was supposed to be going. How had his

170

half-hearted attempt to make small talk ended up here? He rubbed his slightly sweaty palms on his thighs and wondered what the appropriate response might be. 'Oh. I'm sorry to hear that' seemed to do the job.

Linus paused before he said quietly, 'Actually that's not the truth. June wants us to tell people that for the time being, but it's over.' Before PJ could speak, he continued, 'It's for the best. This job, it's . . . well, it's hard.'

PJ was really struggling to think of something to say, but he knew he couldn't just let the car return to silence. 'Yes, I suppose it is.'

Linus threw him a look. 'Have you ever been married yourself, Sergeant?'

PJ was horrified. He hated talking about himself in any circumstances, but the thought of having to discuss his romantic history with Dunne was too awful to contemplate.

'No. No, I never got round to it.' He gave a half-smile and hoped that would be an end to the subject.

'Do you not get lonely out here all by yourself?'

Why was Linus asking these questions? He couldn't really want to know about the emotional well-being of Duneen's sergeant.

'Sometimes.' PJ stopped.

'I sort of envy you. Out here by yourself. I love the job but I can get very cheesed off with the shower I have to work with. What's that phrase? 'Hell is other people', or something like that.'

PJ felt a rush of recognition. 'I know what you mean. I was in Thurles for about ten years before

171

here, and that was the hardest part. Duneen might have been going a bit too far in the other direction, though.' He gave a little laugh.

'Did you always want to be a guard?'

PJ had to think for a moment. 'No. Not really. I did the bank exam after the Leaving and got into AIB. I stuck it for a couple of years thinking it might get better, but I hated it. I've never known boredom like it. I had thought about the guards but I just thought I couldn't because of, well, you know.' He patted his stomach. 'I've always been on the heavy side. Anyway, there was this guard used to come into the bank and he was nearly my size, so I began to think about it. Then one night I'd had a few and I saw him in the pub, so I just walked over and asked him straight how he managed.' He laughed, and so did Linus. 'I was lucky he didn't punch me.'

'You were.'

'It turned out the fitness requirements were a bit of a joke. Not like now. You know yourself.'

'I do.'

'I was never the top trainee,' PJ thought back to the self-defence classes he had endured, red-faced and struggling to catch his breath, 'but I managed to graduate. And do you know what? It was all worth it for the look on my parents' faces that day. I don't think they had ever been proud of me before. The picture of me in my uniform standing in between them was on the sideboard alongside my sisters' wedding photographs till the day my mother died.'

PJ was suddenly aware that he had been talking for quite a long time, so he stopped.

Speaking in a dry monotone, Linus volunteered, 'My parents didn't come to my graduation. My father was a doctor and they never forgave me for becoming a guard.'

PJ glanced at Linus's face but it gave nothing away. He was looking straight ahead with his neat hair slicked back and the knot of his tie tight against his throat. He was obviously still pained, but there was nothing PJ could say. He wasn't capable of tending that sort of wound. He waited to see if Linus was going to say anything else, but he didn't, so the conversational shutters slowly slid down.

Looking out the window PJ became aware of where they were on the road. 'You want to take the next right after that cream bungalow.' The indicator began to click.

★　★　★

It was the little fist. Brid couldn't get the image of it out of her mind. She remembered so vividly holding Cathal in the hospital and being mesmerised by his tiny hands. The shine of each perfect pink nail, each one like a delicate exotic seashell. That was her overwhelming memory of both births. Just smelling and kissing their fingers. Anthony had arrived at the bedside and Brid had been horrified by the sight of his huge rough weathered hand touching the baby. How was it possible that her little boy's silky flawless skin would one day become as leathery and calloused as the flesh of the hand that was stroking his chubby little leg?

173

She kept thinking of the person who had placed that tiny body with its miniature limbs and unblemished skin into the ground. How could you shovel dirt on top of something so clean and pure? Not for the first time she felt herself well up. Who was the mother of that child? How was it possible that nobody knew? And where was Tommy Burke? She had liked the thought that he was dead and buried up on the farm. Well, not liked exactly, but the finality of it helped her. It had closed a chapter of her life that she hadn't fully realised was still open. Now there was a strange uncertainty that left her feeling unsettled. What if Tommy got wind of everything that had happened? Might he come back to explain himself? Christ, what would Anthony do then?

She could recall vividly how she'd felt sitting in the car with PJ up on the headland. Her focus trained on her life with Anthony and the kids. She had felt cut free from the past but now it was as bad as ever, maybe worse. For some reason she still associated Tommy Burke with a happy time in her life, which she knew was nonsense. Even all those years ago it had been a form of torture, but for a few months people had treated her differently, looked at her as if she had won a competition, and that was the feeling she couldn't shake. Tommy himself was just some stupid boy and what she had felt was nothing more than a crush. She had often imagined what would have happened if the wedding had gone ahead: in every projected scenario, the marriage was a disaster. Sometimes he left her for Evelyn;

174

in other versions he got drunk and abusive, and occasionally she fell in love with a Greek god who had somehow ended up as a labourer on the farm and they eloped up the country to live happily ever after.

Brid was baking. It was a part of her new life. She had resolved to get more involved in school activities and make the teachers respect her, so she was breaking up nuts to add to her coffee and walnut cake for a fundraising sale. There was something comforting about measuring the ingredients out on the old-fashioned weighing scales that her mother had used before her. She liked the familiarity of the chipped cream enamel, and the smooth cold weights mottled with age.

Despite her best efforts to fit in at school, she still felt like an outsider. She would stand awkwardly near the table laden with cups and saucers watching the other mothers chatting and laughing. Sometimes she would see faces she recognised having coffee together on one of the small tables at the front of the hotel in the square. They were clearly friends, and while Brid knew what that meant, she no longer had any idea how to go about it. She wasn't shy, but whenever she approached a small group of women at one of the school events, after some smiling introductions she found her mind wandering as the others discussed the new parking scheme or some politician who had made a fool of themselves on *The Late Late Show* last Friday. If being lonely meant not having to talk about shit like that, then she would choose it every time over having coffee dates and ladies' lunches.

The noise of a car engine brought her back to the kitchen table. She wiped her hands on a tea towel and walked to the back door. Anthony hadn't said he was coming back for his lunch. A silver Merc. She didn't know anyone who drove a car like that, but then both doors were opened and PJ eased himself from the passenger seat. She hadn't seen the driver before. Early forties, a beige mac, hair that had clearly been styled using a mirror. They were walking towards the front of the house. Her heart beating faster, she opened the back door and called out, 'PJ! I'm back here.'

The sergeant turned towards her voice and smiled. 'Hello!'

The two men started walking towards Brid. Linus leaned in and whispered, 'PJ, is it? I didn't realise you were such good friends, Sergeant.'

PJ blushed and they walked to the door in silence.

'Come in, come in.' Brid ushered them into the kitchen, her breathing now fast and shallow. What had they come to tell her? Was Tommy back? Did the baby have a mother?

'Mrs Riordan, I'm Detective Superintendent Dunne, and I see you know Sergeant Collins.' Linus smiled and held out his hand. Brid shook it, her eyes glancing nervously at both men.

'Please have a seat. Can I get you a cup of tea or coffee?'

'I'm grand, thanks,' Linus said as he sat down and took out a notebook.

PJ had planned to say, 'Nothing for me,

thanks,' but what actually emerged was a dry cough. He cleared his throat and tried again. 'No thank you.' It felt strange to be back in this room. Everywhere his glance fell caused vivid flashbacks to crowd his mind: himself and Brid crashing against the furniture or rolling on the floor. Over the months he had thought about that night often. He had turned it into a sort of erotic fantasy, and to be back sitting in the brightly lit reality made him feel grubby and small. The room felt warmer, more lived in. The weighing scales along with the bags of flour and sugar surprised him. He hadn't thought Brid was the sort of woman to bake, but then he didn't actually know her at all. A sadness crept over him and he slumped into his chair. Linus was staring intently at his notebook.

Brid couldn't stand the silence. 'What can I do for you?' she asked. 'If it's some sort of bad news, please just tell me.' By now she had added the safety of the kids to her list of concerns.

'Oh no, Mrs Riordan. Sorry if we worried you. It's nothing like that. We just have a few more questions for you, that's all.' Linus smiled in an attempt to reassure her.

PJ couldn't wait any longer. 'Would you mind if I used your bathroom?'

Brid, relieved that all was well, smiled at him. 'Of course.'

PJ headed towards the door, but before he escaped to the toilet, he clocked the expression on Linus's face. Shit. He shouldn't have made it so obvious that he was familiar with the house. Oh well. Too late now, and besides, nothing mattered quite as much as his full bladder.

Once he returned, the interview began, playing out in a similar fashion to the one they had conducted in Ard Carraig. Brid knew nothing about a baby, and had no idea who might have been the mother. Tommy had simply vanished into thin air.

This time Linus felt confident that the woman in front of him was telling the truth. He decided he liked Brid. There was something open and warm about her. This was a woman who had got on with her life, or perhaps it was just that it was a life he recognised. The strange domestic arrangement of the Ross sisters made him feel uneasy. Maybe it was because they reminded him of nuns. Linus hated nuns.

5

What a difference a day made. Twenty-four hours earlier, PJ had been sitting in on interviews with people connected to a murder inquiry; now, here he was directing traffic.

The Church of Ireland fete happened every spring, but this year, what with the distractions of the discovery, PJ had managed to forget all about it. His job was to prevent people parking on the narrow tree-lined road that led up past the church towards the entrance to the old rectory, where all the stalls were erected in the large gardens. Instead they were encouraged to park up in the GAA grounds or, if they could find a space in the village, to just walk to the main attraction.

The crowds of people who came every year suggested to PJ that this fete must be something very special indeed, but when he finally made his way inside he discovered it was just like every other fete he had ever been to. Small white marquees stood on the lawn at various drunken angles while crowds milled around peering at trestle tables laden with home-made jams, piles of unread books and dusty bits of broken bric-a-brac. At the front of the rectory several plastic garden tables were provided for those in need of tea and cakes. People sold raffle tickets; children queued impatiently for their turn on the small bouncy castle. Everyone shuffled.

Knowing what was going on behind the high hedges made PJ's job even more difficult. There was important police work to be done, but no, he had to stand out in the street in a high-vis jacket that was too big even for him. Jesus, he thought as he unpacked it from the boot of the car, it could be one of the marquees. What made it worse — if this menial task could ever be considered worse — was that this year the weather had not favoured the Protestants. Easter had failed to deliver any spring sunshine and a fine misty rain hung in the air, while a chill wind slapped at the tents. PJ desperately wanted to leave the job to the few volunteers from the church but knew that he couldn't. The organisers had made their application for traffic control and paid their fee. He belonged to them till five o'clock that afternoon.

Most of the morning had been taken up with getting various vans on and off the site, and letting the cars drop off their precious cargoes of unwanted jumble at the rectory gates. At twelve the high-pitched howling sound of the precariously erected public address system informed people that the fete was now officially open. Let the fun and fundraising commence!

A steady stream of traffic came and went, but PJ left the volunteers to do most of the directing. He stood back from the road slightly, sheltering from the weather under an old horse chestnut tree that leaned out, heavy and weary, over the wall. He kept checking his phone to see if there were any updates from Linus, but he didn't have a signal. Fucking Duneen! He turned it off and on again and stared hopefully at the small screen, but nothing. He shoved it angrily back into one of the giant patch pockets on the side of his jacket. The raindrops landing on his cap sounded loud and dull. He gave a long sigh.

An orange umbrella sailed in front of his face and was lifted high.

'Hello, Sergeant!'

PJ controlled the groan that threatened to escape his mouth. It was Susan Hickey and another woman he didn't know. They were both dressed in an odd assortment of heavy-duty rain gear and brightly patterned headscarves, as if they were going to do a little gardening up a mountain.

'Nice to see you. Shame about the day,' he said in a tone of voice he hoped came across as both polite and off-putting.

Susan Hickey was not skilled at picking up on tone.

'This is my little sister, Vera. She's back from the big smoke to see us.'

'London,' said the other woman. 'Well, a bit outside. Do you know England at all?'

PJ's inner voice wondered why she thought a rain-soaked guard at the side of a road in Duneen would give a flying fuck where she lived, but he managed to say through slightly gritted teeth, 'Where it is, that's about it for me. Well, enjoy your stay.'

The umbrella didn't move.

'Exciting times in Duneen! It was never like this when I was a girl.'

'Now, Vera, there was always plenty going on in the village. Any news, Sergeant, about the . . . '

Susan paused, wondering how to express it. She lowered her voice and her mouth formed the words as if she was discussing a venereal disease. 'Dead baby?'

PJ used his professional voice. 'The investigation is ongoing. Forensics should shed some light on the matter shortly.'

'Yes. Yes, of course. Terrible to think of a little — '

'Susan,' interjected Vera, 'I'm sure the guard is very busy. We should go.' She smiled at PJ and nudged her sister in the direction of the rectory gates.

'Goodbye, Sergeant!' their voices called from beneath the orange umbrella that had lowered to envelop them both.

PJ took out his phone. Still nothing.

Across the road three familiar figures approached carrying small cardboard boxes filled with pot plants. They walked in single file like the three wise men bearing gifts. PJ knew at once despite the large rain hoods that covered each head that it was the Ross sisters. As the others continued on to the rectory, the sister bringing up the rear crossed the road towards him. It was Evelyn.

'Sergeant Collins.' She looked out from under the dripping fabric of her hood and smiled. 'PJ. I just wanted to apologise for yesterday.'

'Apologise? For what?' PJ was struck by the scent she was wearing. She smelled like summer. There was a thin strand of damp hair clinging to her cheek. She really was a very attractive woman.

'I didn't want you to think I was being

182

unfriendly. I just found that other policeman a little off-putting, that's all.'

PJ gave a small grin. 'I know what you mean, but he's not the worst. He's good at his job, I think.'

'Well I consider you a friend, PJ.'

Their eyes met for a moment and neither of them was sure what would happen next. PJ's heart was beating a little faster.

'Can I help you with that box?' he asked.

'No, I'm fine. It's light. They're just a few cuttings that Abigail grew for the plant stall. We should have been here much earlier but Abigail wasn't feeling well. I'd better try and catch them up. Will you be popping into the fete later?'

PJ was surprised to find that not only did he say yes, but he was actually looking forward to it.

6

It was too much. The absurdly high heels, the dyed hair swept up into a sort of loose bun, the lipstick, the white blouse revealing a generous amount of cleavage. Linus understood that she was trying to make a point — it was a man's world and she was a woman — but surely a simple pair of earrings would have had the desired effect?

Norma Casey was indeed the only woman working in the technical bureau, and at the age of forty-nine she was now the most senior member of the team. She had decided early on in her career to embrace her femininity. The heels and high hair made her feel strong. She towered over her colleagues, and as she strode along corridors with her unbuttoned lab coat flapping behind her like a flag-bearer heading into battle, she somehow knew that she was destined to be in charge.

Linus and Norma had only met a handful of times, and there was a mutual sense of distrust. Today, however, there was also an air of irritation. Linus had insisted that Norma come to his office to go over the DNA results from Duneen face to face.

'I just thought it was easier,' he was saying, 'rather than try to figure all this out.' He brandished her meticulously prepared report.

Norma bit her lip. Easier for who? If he was

too thick to interpret data, how was that her fault? She sighed.

'Right, what do you want to know?'

'Well, the baby's DNA is a match for the Burke parents, right?'

'Yes.' That was detailed in the opening paragraph of her report, but Norma had resolved not to snap at the superintendent.

'So does that mean Tommy Burke could have been the father of the baby?'

'The younger Tommy?'

'Yes.'

'No. He's not the father.'

'How can you be so sure?'

'Because the DNA is a precise match to the bodies that were exhumed. If Tommy was the father, that would only be half of the make-up. Besides which, the timeline makes no sense. The infant remains had been buried far longer than those of the young male. This is Tommy Burke's brother. We can't be exact, but he was certainly only a year or two older or younger. It might even be his twin.'

'Twin? Is there any way of knowing that for certain?'

'Only if you get me Tommy's DNA, and even then it wouldn't be definitive if they were only fraternal and not identical.'

'OK. So just to be completely clear: Mrs Burke had two babies?'

'Yes!' Norma found she had snapped after all. She stood up. 'Look, if that's everything, I've got things to do.'

'Of course. Thanks for coming down to see

me. I'm not the brightest when it comes to this stuff.'

'You're welcome.' She smiled. He was forgiven.

Once Norma was gone, he left the door of his office open to let the residue of her perfume escape, and got on the phone.

Sergeant Sumo didn't answer. He left a voicemail message.

'Hello, it's Dunne here. I want you to see how far back the medical records go for Mrs Burke. Try the hospital in Ballytorne, local doctors, that sort of thing. Let me know how you get on.'

He hung up and bowed his head low over his desk. He turned his wedding ring round and round. I should really take this thing off, he thought. But he liked how it felt.

He forced his mind back to the case. A stillborn twin. It could be as simple as that. It would shed no light on the other body after all. But then why was the baby buried in a field? The priest would surely have come and it could have been placed in the cemetery. The Burkes were a married couple. There was no cause for secrecy or scandal. It made no sense.

The wedding ring went round and round.

7

She had never felt pain like it. A small crowd had gathered around her where she had fallen to her knees, her face pressed against the wet grass. The damp earth felt good against her cheek and yet the intense shooting pain continued to claw at her back.

She could hear voices.

'Are you all right, Miss Ross?'

'Would you like a glass of water?'

'Should we phone for an ambulance?'

Suddenly she was aware of Florence kneeling beside her.

'Oh Abigail! What is it?' Her voice seemed to come from far away, small and frightened.

Abigail tried to answer but another sharp pain meant all she could do was groan.

Florence stood up. 'Evelyn! Has anyone seen my sister Evelyn? Evelyn!' She was shrieking now.

'She was down having tea with the guard.'

'Get her, can you? Please go and get her!'

A young woman in Wellington boots ran awkwardly in the direction of the plastic tables and Florence rubbed her sister's back, making soothing sounds as if she was tending a sick animal at the side of the road.

Evelyn and PJ had finished their tea and she was showing him pictures of Bobby on her phone. It was hard not to smile at the images of the puppy in various cute poses, and PJ was also enjoying how their fingers touched as they shared the small handset.

Evelyn noticed the anxious-faced young woman running around the side of the rectory and wondered what was wrong. Then she realised the woman was heading straight for their table. She just had time to say, 'PJ . . . ' because she assumed the emergency had something to do with the policeman, when the woman cried out, 'Evelyn Ross! Your sister is very sick. She needs help.'

'Oh God. Oh God.' Evelyn jumped to her feet and looked left and right as if searching for some explanation for what this woman was saying.

The young messenger was leading the way. 'She's round the front.' Evelyn and PJ jogged behind her.

When they got to the group of people standing in front of the bottle stall, Evelyn could see both her sisters on the ground. She felt sick. PJ held back, trying to disguise his panting. He didn't like the look of this.

Florence jumped to her feet. 'Oh Evelyn. It's Abigail. She's in awful pain. We must get her an ambulance.' Evelyn turned to look at PJ. She felt confident he would know what to do.

The way she looked at him was how he had once thought being a guard would be all the time. He put his cap back on, ready for action.

'Are you sure you want to wait for an ambulance? It could take a long time. The squad car is just down by the bridge and with the siren we could have her at the hospital in about twenty minutes.'

Evelyn looked back at Florence. 'Oh Sergeant Collins, that would be marvellous. Thank you so much.'

'Thank you, PJ,' added Evelyn. He felt as if she had just cooed 'My hero!' into his ear.

He peered down at Abigail. She was trying to take long, slow breaths. 'Miss Ross, would you prefer to wait for the ambulance?'

Abigail stuck her arm up in the air and waved her fingers from side to side as if an invisible sock puppet was saying 'no'.

'Right.' He turned back to her sisters. 'Keep her warm and I'll be back in five minutes.'

★ ★ ★

The journey was a blur, but PJ did as he had promised and got them into the hospital in under twenty minutes. He was now sitting with Evelyn and Florence on a row of orange plastic chairs outside the small A&E department where Abigail was being examined. Three Styrofoam cups of milky tea had been produced. Evelyn and her sister worried over the warning signs they had missed when Abigail had first mentioned feeling ill; if only she'd seen the doctor, they said. They talked in circles of concern while PJ looked around.

The corridor where they sat was cut in two by a pair of swinging green doors that didn't appear to serve any purpose. The cream walls were mostly bare apart from one or two paintings that he assumed had been donated by grateful patients. Plastic bilingual signs indicated the

189

direction of the various departments. Occasionally a nurse walked by, her shoes squeaking against the light green lino. The only voices that could be heard were hushed and very far away. The whole building seemed like it was waiting for the other shoe to drop.

The tension was abruptly interrupted by a loud electronic beep. PJ realised it was his phone and wondered if the hospital was like a plane. Could his handset have interfered with life-saving equipment? Glancing at the screen, he saw he had a new voicemail. He listened to the message as he looked across at the two sisters. They had stopped speaking. Evelyn was staring at her shoes, while Florence had her eyes fixed on the door to the A&E department. She looked like a dog that had been tied up outside a shop.

When he heard what Linus wanted, he couldn't quite believe it. So little in his life went according to plan; he wasn't used to smooth coincidences like this. He needed medical records and he was sitting in the hospital. He leaned over to Evelyn and whispered, 'I've got a little bit of work to do. It shouldn't take long. I'll see you back here.' She nodded and he made his way back to reception, the squeaking of his shoes announcing his progress.

He was directed to a small suite of offices on the first floor. Slightly out of breath from the stairs, he opened the door cautiously. A lady in her early sixties with glasses that took up most of her face was sitting behind a desk, tapping furiously at her keyboard. PJ cleared his throat and she looked up, giving him a perfunctory smile.

'How can I help you?'

'I'm looking for some medical records in connection with a case and wondered if you could help me.'

'Right. Well I should be able to, but it all depends what sort of years you're looking for. Some of it's online, then there is the microfiche over there,' she indicated two large filing cabinets, 'and for further back it's in the basement.'

'Well this would be . . . ' PJ fumbled for his notebook. 'Is it all right if I sit down?'

'Of course. Please.' The woman gestured to a squat chair with wooden arms just to the side of her desk.

'Thank you.' He sat and leafed through the pages covered with notes, muttering to himself, 'Twenty-nine when he disappeared. He was born in . . . 1966.' He addressed the woman directly. 'I'm looking for 1966. A woman who lived out in Duneen. A Mrs Burke.' He turned a few pages of his notebook. 'Patricia Burke.'

The lady stood. 'Well, if we have anything, it'll be in the basement.'

'Sorry to disturb you.'

'It's not a problem.' She grabbed a large bunch of keys from the windowsill behind her and leaned into the doorway of the adjoining office. 'I'm just nipping down to records, Trish. Can you get the phones?'

'Yes!' replied a disembodied woman's voice.

PJ followed her back into the corridor and down two flights of stairs. She moved quickly, her leather heels beating out a rapid staccato on the steps. PJ lumbered behind trying to keep pace.

The records store was larger than he had expected, all four walls covered by shelves laden with box files. The room was split in two by another set of storage units. Fearing he might not fit between the shelves, he waited by the door. He wished he knew the woman's name, but it was too late for introductions now. She had gone without hesitation to the far right corner and was running a finger along the boxes. Now she stopped and, holding her large glasses, peered closely at the label in front of her.

'If we have her, she'll be in here.'

She slid the box from the shelf and dropped it heavily to the floor. After lifting off the lid, she knelt down and began to flick through the individual files. PJ waited awkwardly, faintly embarrassed that this woman was now on her hands and knees doing his bidding. After a few minutes she produced a file from the box with a flourish.

'Got her!'

'Amazing!' and PJ really was amazed. This case had become a series of dead ends, so to actually find something was a real novelty.

'I can't let you take it away, but you can make copies upstairs if you need them.'

'Thanks,' he said, taking the file from her outstretched hand. As he opened it, the woman busied herself putting the box back on the shelf.

He didn't know what he was looking for, so he turned to the last few pages in the file. There were various numbers, which he presumed were blood pressure or weight. The writing was indecipherable. At the bottom of the page was a large stamp in red ink. *Copies sent*, it read.

'What does this mean?' he asked, holding out the file.

'Let me see.' She took it and moved to stand directly under one of the bare light bulbs that hung from the ceiling.

'So this just means that the original file was copied. I wonder why?' She held up the page to get a better look. 'She was seeing Dr Murphy here, pregnant, but it looks like she transferred to a doctor up in Cork. A Dr Phelan, I think that says, at the Bons on College Road.'

PJ took out his pen and started to make a note.

'Dr Phelan from the Bon Secours Hospital?'

'Yes, the maternity department.'

'That's great. Thank you so much for all your help.' He went to hold out his hand to shake hers but thought better of it. Unfortunately she had noticed and started to hold out her own. The aborted handshake became a strange waist-height wave.

'Sorry.'

'Sorry.'

'I'd better . . . '

'Yes, of course.'

PJ opened the door and with a final 'Thanks again' closed it behind him.

Back in the corridor outside A&E he found the Ross sisters waiting for him. Abigail had been moved on to a ward. The doctor thought it was most likely kidney stones, so they were going to keep her in to see if she passed them naturally. Failing that, they would have to operate. The women seemed relieved to know it wasn't anything worse. They smiled at PJ and teased each other about which of them would have to help out in the garden.

The three of them walked slowly through the hospital, retracing their steps towards the car park. It reminded PJ of being back in school. They left through a side door that was a short cut to where he had left the Garda car. It was the opposite of the scenic route, as they passed the oil tanks and some sort of rubbish compactor.

Up ahead, at the edge of the milky pebble-dashed wall, a young couple were kissing. She was clearly a nurse, with long dark hair that had fallen free. The man was pushing her against the wall and running his hands up and down her back. As PJ got closer, he noticed that in fact the man wasn't that young. His hair was receding and there were lines around his eyes. Neither of the lovers seemed to notice the trio as they passed.

As he got the keys of the car out of his pocket, PJ turned back to look again at the couple kissing. That man. He looked familiar. Who was he? It would come to him in a minute . . . and then, all at once, it did. He knew exactly who it was pressing that young nurse into the back wall of the Ballytorne Hospital. It was Anthony Riordan.

8

The fete had finished hours ago. The cars and crowds were long gone, the abandoned marquees still visible in the gloom as if the rectory garden had been put under dust sheets. The low grey cloud of the afternoon had given way to a clear night sky that glittered with stars. The moon was nearly full and shone so bright and close it looked like it had been sprinkled with sugar. PJ pointed it out to Evelyn and Florence as he drove them down the hill into Duneen.

He parked outside O'Driscoll's, where the sisters had left their car. Once the engine was turned off and the car doors opened, the stillness of the night engulfed them. For a moment nobody moved, then Florence said quietly, 'Thank you so much, Sergeant Collins. You were a life-saver.' She gave a small laugh. 'Actually you really were.' She got out of the car and shut her door.

Evelyn was still sitting in the passenger seat next to PJ.

'We really do appreciate everything.' She touched his arm. 'Thank you.'

PJ looked down at her pale hand on the dark sleeve of his uniform. When he raised his eyes, Evelyn's face was coming towards his. A quick kiss on his cheek. He felt it all. The slight stickiness of her now faded lipstick, the smooth skin of her nose against his cheek, the light touch of her hair to the side of his eye. She pulled back and smiled. 'Goodnight, PJ.' Quickly she slipped from the car and followed her sister into the night.

He sat for a moment, not sure of how to react. Perhaps she was just being friendly, or had he been supposed to grab her and shove his tongue into her mouth like that Riordan guy with the nurse? No. Whatever he should have done, that would have been wrong. She was too delicate, too fine for that sort of behaviour. Maybe he should have reached out and stroked her face, or touched her hair? He sighed heavily. Some other man could have done that. Not him.

Using the steering wheel as leverage, he manoeuvred his way out of the car and stood up. He needed milk and he couldn't rely on Mrs Meany any more. She really was losing it. Whatever was wrong with her, he hoped she decided to retire before he had to fire her.

O'Driscoll's was bright and empty. He nodded to acknowledge the girl — why couldn't he remember her name? — sitting behind the till, and made his way to the chiller cabinets at the back of the shop. He surveyed the bright orange blocks of cheese and plastic envelopes of pale pink ham. No, just milk. If Mrs Meany hadn't left any dinner, he knew there were eggs and bread. He wouldn't starve. A litre of milk in his hand, he headed back to . . . Petra! That was it.

When he got there, a woman was paying for two packets of biscuits. Too late to take evasive action, he realised it was Brid Riordan. She smiled broadly at him, but he suspected she might have taken cover behind the cleaning products and toilet paper aisle if she had seen him first.

'PJ.'

'Brid.'

'Everything all right? Any progress?' she asked as she held out her hand for change from Petra.

All PJ could think about was her husband grinding his hips against that young nurse. Should he say something? Surely she had a right to know. He opened his mouth to speak. 'No. No.' He paused. 'How's Anthony?'

The words hung in the air and he knew they had been a mistake. What had he been thinking? She stared at him, clearly taken aback. Why was he asking about her husband?

'He's . . . fine.'

'And the kids?' PJ thought that might have made this awkward exchange a little better, but it hadn't. Brid snatched up her biscuits and stepped back from the till.

'They're fine too.' Had she rolled her eyes?

PJ put the milk on the counter. 'That's good. Good.'

As Brid turned to leave, she gave him a cold stare.

'You have a bit of lipstick on your face, by the way.'

Like an overweight chameleon in a Garda uniform, his whole face turned the same shade as the phantom red lips on his cheek.

★　★　★

197

Back at the barracks it looked as if no one was home, but when he opened the front door he could see a small glow of light coming from the kitchen. Strange. Mrs Meany must have left something on. Her days really were numbered. He walked down the hall and pushed open the kitchen door.

'Jesus Christ!'

A small figure was hunched at the table, the only light coming from the small bulb above the hob of the cooker.

'Sorry, Sergeant. It's only me.'

'Jesus, Mrs Meany, you gave me a terrible fright.'

'Sorry. I was waiting for you. I need to talk to you.' Her voice was low and serious.

'Right. Of course.' PJ pulled one of the wooden chairs back from the table and sat down. Whatever she wanted to talk about, he was certain it wasn't good news. Cancer maybe? Dementia? 'What is it?'

Mrs Meany looked up. Even in the half-light from the cooker he could see that she had been crying. 'I should have told you this before but I . . . I just couldn't.'

'All right.' PJ put his hands on the table and prepared to listen to whatever she had to say.

Mrs Meany was ready to tell her story.

★　★　★

She had been christened Elizabeth, but since she was just a few hours old, everybody had called her Lizzie.

198

'Look at her. Lizzie, our gift from God.' The Meanys had believed they were not going to be blessed with a child, and Lizzie was nearly taken back several times when she was an infant. She found it hard to keep food down and was small and sickly. Somehow she survived and grew into a diminutive but healthy girl. She was an only child and lived with her parents in a rented two-bedroomed cottage just to the west of the village. Her father was a well digger and his father had been one before him. Her mother did everything else.

Making friends didn't come easily to Lizzie, but by the time she was attending the convent in Ballytorne she had two best friends: Fiona and Angela. Fiona was the prettiest of the trio, Angela the dumpy one and Lizzie the runt. The sort of girl whose nostrils were permanently red and raw from the cold she was just getting or the one she was recovering from.

The three girls sat next to each other in class, ate lunch side by side on a bench under the shelter of the bicycle sheds and shared all their secrets. They combed each other's hair and made scrapbooks full of pictures of horses. As puberty nudged them towards womanhood, they compared their burgeoning breasts, showed each other the various bras their mothers had bought them and, when the dreaded periods struck, helped each other with their Kotex pads. They were closer than any sisters and promised to be best true friends for ever and ever.

But that was not to be. Fiona, of course, got a boyfriend. Angela and Lizzie were appalled. He was a tall, skinny boy from the Christian Brothers who, with his pimpled skin and greasy ginger hair, bore no relation to Paul Newman, the previous love of Fiona's life. The end of their triumvirate came when Fiona called the other two babies and stormed off to join her beloved 'Ger' and the other couples in the short alley that ran along the back of the library. Everyone knew people went up there to 'shift' each other. Lizzie sneered at the very mention of it, though in reality she had no idea what it meant.

The sixties were an odd and unsettling time for teenage girls in Ballytorne: magazines and films showed them a world full of long-haired boys with skinny jeans, and rock 'n' roll was a special sort of music meant just for them, yet there was no sign of either in their town. Of course there was the Stella Ballroom on the other side of Ballytorne, but that was full of old farmers who came down from the hills on their bikes to listen to country and western bands with names like the Haymakers or the Country Cousins. Angela and Lizzie made do with making more scrapbooks but with the pictures of horses now replaced by ones cut from newspapers and magazines of the Beatles and Cliff Richard. Lizzie really liked the look of Cliff. Sometimes she imagined his smooth, pillowy lips were kissing hers.

It was Angela who discovered Brian Bello and the Diamond Dust showband. Her older sister, Alison, worked in the bank up in Cork and she had seen them in the Majestic one Saturday night. Afterwards she had bought their LP and brought it home to show Angela, who begged to borrow it so she could show it to Lizzie. One look at the picture of Brian on the album sleeve and they were in love. It was a close-up of his face, framed by his dark curls, with his blue eyes staring straight out at you. 'I wish I had eyelashes like that!' they squealed, and then Angela pointed at the small tuft of dark chest hair just visible where the button on his white shirt was undone. They took turns kissing his beautiful mouth, then rolled around Lizzie's bed shrieking with laughter at the silliness of it all. The music was irrelevant, because they knew that no matter what it sounded like, they would love it.

It was Lizzie who stumbled upon the heart-stoppingly amazing news that Brian Bello along with his Diamond Dust would be performing in the Stella Ballroom. The sight of Brian's beautiful face looking out at her from a poster in the window of the hotel in Ballytorne had stopped her in her tracks. She had to read all the information at least twice before she understood fully what was going to happen. Brian Bello, the actual flesh-and-blood Brian Bello, was coming to Ballytorne!

Lizzie ran as fast as she could back to the convent. She found Angela in the toilets getting changed for camogie.

'No! It's true. Not this Saturday, but the next one!'

'We have to go. We have to!' They whooped and hugged each other tightly. They were going to breathe the same air as Brian Bello.

This was easier said than done. They needed

tickets, and for that they needed money, plus they had to get out to the Stella Ballroom so would have to organise a lift, and all of this relied on them getting permission from their parents.

Lizzie's mother and father were seeing their little girl in a whole new light. She was so excited and enthusiastic, and desperate to do something with her friend Angela. The Brian Bello chap looked like a right queer one, but it was for the youngsters. The tickets were bought as an early sixteenth birthday present and it was arranged that, because Angela lived nearer to Ballytorne, Lizzie would stay with her and they would get a lift there and back with Angela's father.

For two weeks the girls were incapable of talking about anything else. Blouses were looked at and rejected, skirts tried on and set aside. Pictures of hairstyles were considered and they giggled at the idea of make-up. It became harder and harder to get to sleep, until on the Friday it was almost impossible.

When Saturday afternoon finally came, Lizzie arrived at Angela's ready to meet her idol. She was wearing a black skirt and a new short-sleeved lemon blouse, and over her shoulders she had a white mohair cardigan that she had borrowed from another girl in her year. At the last minute her mother had relented and lent her a pair of black patent high heels. When Angela's mother opened the front door, she smiled at the sight of the little woman before her. Her own daughter was wearing a dress she had bought that afternoon. It was a full-skirted navy affair covered in an abstract pattern of red and white triangles. It had been on sale and Angela loved it. Her mother chose not to reveal her suspicions that the low price had something to do with it looking like a cut-up Union Jack flag. Angela's mother took pity on Lizzie before she left and let her borrow a little bit of red lipstick and a quick spritz from her bottle of Shalimar. Photographs were taken on the big heavy camera that lived in the bottom of the sideboard, and then off they went.

There was already quite a crowd outside the Stella when they arrived. Angela's father turned round to address the two girls in the back seat. Lizzie liked the smell of his hair oil.

'Now, young ladies. Here's a pound each to get you some soft drinks and crisps or whatever. Mind your change. Don't be talking to any strangers, there'll be all sorts in there, and I'll be waiting for you out here from half ten.'

'Ah Dad . . . ' Angela pleaded.

'Half past ten. I know it'll still be going on, but there will be lads with drink taken and I don't want you staying any later. Understood?'

The girls nodded their heads.

'What would Mr and Mrs Meany say if they thought I wasn't looking after their precious daughter?' He smiled widely. 'Have fun, girls. You both look smashing!'

Angela and Lizzie grinned with pride and clambered out of the car. They stood and watched their last link to everything they were familiar with drive off.

Groups of boys in dark suits were standing around smoking. Occasionally a small scuffle broke out or they started jeering at each other. The girls who were already there looked very grown up. They were smoking too and talking earnestly, though intermittently one of them would sneak a glance over to the boys to see if they were looking back at them. They weren't. Music could be heard coming from inside.

'That'll be the Markers,' Angela announced authoritatively. 'They're on first. Will we go in?'

Lizzie just nodded. Her excitement had turned to dread. She didn't like the look of any of these people standing around. She clutched her mohair cardigan to her throat and followed Angela to the large wooden porch that had been stuck on to the front of the long low ballroom as an afterthought. A woman with scraped-back hair and ruddy cheeks who Lizzie recognised from the bakery tore their tickets without smiling, and then they approached the large double wooden framed doors. Coloured lights could be seen through the frosted glass.

Opening the doors, the girls were completely overwhelmed by what met them. A thick layer of cigarette smoke hung over the small crowd that stood in clumps on the dance floor. People were shifting slightly from side to side but no one had progressed to what might have been described as dancing. The music was much louder than either of them had ever heard before, and they couldn't even make out who was on the stage at the other end of the hall because of the flashing red and blue lights mixed in with the heavy cloud of smoke. The largest crowd was to their right. This was the bar. Angela pointed towards it and started walking. Lizzie followed.

They stood together by the wall halfway down the hall, each holding a bottle of Deasy's red lemonade with a straw sticking out of it. Wide-eyed, they just stared at the people walking back and forth, too overawed to speak. It was only twenty past eight, and the woman behind the bar had told them that Brian Bello, not forgetting his Diamond Dust, wouldn't be on stage until half past nine. The Markers had by now run out of new material and were making their way through a selection of popular songs by British and American bands. Hearing the familiar tunes relaxed the girls, and they began to sway a little and smile at each other. This might be all right after all. It might even be fun. Lizzie felt extremely brave when she made her way back to the bar all by herself to get them two more lemonades.

When the Markers finished, a very tall, thin man with a long face made even longer by large bushy sideburns clambered on stage to announce the raffle. The prizes were a dried flower arrangement provided by Ballytorne Blooms and a cooked ham from O'Keefe's. It wasn't clear which of them was the top prize. A woman standing close to Lizzie and Angela won the large basket of what appeared to be mostly dried grasses. When she brought it back and shoved it behind her on one of the high, narrow windowsills, the girls nudged each other and sniggered. Lizzie blew bubbles in her lemonade with her straw.

By nine thirty the crowd had increased threefold and the place was packed. The smell of sweat and cheap perfume mixed with cigarettes filled the air. Realising that Brian would be on soon and they couldn't see the stage at all, Angela grabbed Lizzie by the hand and dragged her through the throng towards the stage. They stopped about three people back from the front. The stage was surrounded by a group of girls who clearly weren't from Ballytorne. Their hair was backcombed and lacquered, their dresses were sleeveless and they sounded like they might be from the city. Angela and Lizzie silently agreed that they had come as far as they were going to.

Within minutes the main lights were turned off and the beams of blue and red began pulsing through the smoke. The women at the very front began to scream like the girls Lizzie had seen in films. Through the dense fog on the stage they could make out bodies taking up their positions behind the drums and at the microphones on either side. The Diamond Dust had arrived. The dull thump of the drums started, closely followed by the deafening twang of the electric guitars. Lizzie could feel the music vibrating in her bones. The girls' screeching had increased in volume and pitch. Angela squeezed Lizzie's hand. This was it!

A flash of white light bathed the stage and then there he was, standing just feet from them. They gasped and found themselves joining in with the screaming. It was the only way they could express their excitement. He was even more beautiful than he appeared in pictures. Yes, he was shorter than they'd expected, but so slim.

He was wearing a pale grey suit that had narrow tapered trousers. His shirt was white and his skinny tie was red. He pushed his hair back from a forehead already bathed in sweat, and then with a single smooth gesture unbuttoned his jacket, revealing a thin leather belt the same colour as his tie. The crowd of girls were jumping up and down now with excitement, and Angela and Lizzie joined them. It felt wonderful. So wild and exciting. Neither of them had ever experienced anything like this.

After three songs Lizzie felt herself getting hoarse, but she didn't care. She drained the last of her lemonade and, with only a moment's hesitation, let the bottle fall to the floor. This was mad and brilliant and she had never been so happy in her entire life.

The whole crowd was dancing now and she was aware of being pushed nearer to the stage. She was pressed right into the group of girls and felt very hot. She felt too hot. Her vision was becoming a little blurry and she felt . . . she wasn't sure. Was she dizzy? Was she going to be sick? Too late she realised she was going to fall to the ground. She reached out for Angela's hand but it wasn't there. The lights and music disappeared into a small white dot and then vanished completely.

When she came to, she found herself sitting on a wooden chair with her head between her knees. A wide hand was stroking her back and she heard a woman's voice.

'You're all right. You're all right. Big breaths, love. That's it. Good girl.'

She looked sideways and recognised the woman from the bakery who had been taking the tickets at the door. She heard a door open and a wave of music came rushing in followed by a man's voice.

'How is she?'

'She'll be grand. Won't you, pet?'

'I'm fine,' Lizzie managed to say.

The woman's veiny red face loomed in front of hers.

'There you are. Welcome back to us.'

'Where am I?'

'You fainted, love. We brought you in here to the side office till you were feeling better.'

Lizzie nodded her head. 'Thank you.' Her throat felt sore and dry. 'Can I have a drink, please?'

'Of course. I got you a little brandy there. It'll make you feel better.'

Lizzie either didn't hear her properly or hadn't understood, because she took the glass and downed its golden contents in a single swig. Her throat was on fire and her stomach was heaving. She spluttered and coughed and spat on the concrete floor.

The man was laughing! 'Jesus. She likes a drop!'

'Ah, it'll do her no harm,' the woman replied, and then, turning to Lizzie, she said, 'Wait there till you're feeling strong enough to get up.'

After the brandy Lizzie doubted that she would ever want to get up again. She leaned into the bony bentwood back of the chair. She saw her cardigan draped over piles of messy paperwork on the desk beside her. Reaching out for it, she could see that the milky-white mohair was now streaked with cigarette ash and mystery stains from the dance floor. She presumed it had happened when she fell. She gave a weary sigh. All she wanted to do was go home. Where was Angela?

The door opened, letting in another blast of music. The woman from the bakery was carrying a cup of tea perched on a saucer. She handed the steaming cup to Lizzie.

'There you go, love.'

'Thank you.' She held the saucer with both hands and blew at the steam. 'What time is it?'

The woman glanced at the tiny gold watch that pinched into the flesh around her wrist.

'Nearly eleven. Not long now.'

Lizzie jumped to her feet, slopping tea into the saucer. She put it down on the desk and then leaned on the back of the chair to steady herself.

'I have to go. My friend will be waiting. Her father got here ages ago.'

'Oh, right. You can get out just here.' She indicated a second door with a Yale lock and two small panes of glass. 'Put your cardigan on.'

'It's all dirty,' Lizzie said and realised she sounded pathetic.

'That'll wash out. Everything will be better in the morning. You go home and have a good sleep.'

The gust of chilled air that hit Lizzie's face felt refreshing. She stepped out into the night.

'Thanks for taking care of me.'

'Not a problem. Safe home now, love.'

Lizzie walked down the side of the building and found the wide gravel area at the front where Angela's father had dropped them. A few cars were loitering with their lights on. She got closer and peered at them, but none of them were the right car. Maybe he was late. She looked around at the people smoking and laughing. A few couples were standing in the shadows kissing. Where was Angela? Could she have met someone? Trying to look casual as her heart began beating faster, she walked back and forth inspecting the dresses of the girls. No Angela. However, with a sickening jolt she realised that one of the couples was Fiona and Ger. Fiona mustn't see her like this. Lost and alone, like the little baby she had accused her of being. She dashed back to hide behind the side of the porch. She would see the car from there.

The welcome chill had turned to cold night air. What had been in that drink? She rested the back of her head against the wall and felt a little better. She looked up into the stars and watched her breath float upwards.

Time passed and various cars arrived and left. Each time she looked up full of hope, only to be disappointed. He must be really late now. She was beginning to get worried. What if he never came? What would she do then? She suddenly remembered that there was a phone box just beyond the Stella Ballroom on the side of the road. She had no change because she'd given it all to Angela, but surely she could reverse the charges. This was an emergency.

When she got to the phone box, the smell of

piss hit her before she had even opened the door. She pulled her cardigan up over her nose and stepped inside. The cord fell limply down to the side of the phone. Some idiot had ripped out the receiver. She could feel herself getting close to tears. She stumbled out of the phone box and headed back to the Stella. Something must have happened, but she was sure he'd come for her. They wouldn't just leave her here at the side of the road.

Back at the ballroom, streams of people were coming out and getting into waiting cars. Clearly the show was over. She ran the last few yards expectantly. With so many cars, surely one of them contained Angela and her father. Was that him? No. Over there? Different colour. Car after car was not her golden carriage. Soon the front of the ballroom was deserted. Even the chip van had shut up shop and driven away. Lizzie wrapped her arms around herself and whimpered. She had no idea what she was going to do. She realised she had been a fool. Why had she let all the cars drive away? One of them would have given her a lift back into town. But then what if Angela's father did come? He'd be looking for her and she'd get in trouble for going off with strangers.

The lights in the porch had been switched off, but Lizzie could see a glow coming from the back of the building. He'd never be back there, she reasoned, but with nothing to lose, she decided to go and check. When she got there, she found a van with its back doors open. Before she could investigate any further, a man came out of the building carrying a large electric speaker. After it had been stowed in the van he turned and noticed Lizzie.

'Hello, missy.' His voice was deep and it sounded like he was from up the country. Dublin maybe.

'I can't find my friend.'

'A girl, is it?'

'Yes. Angela.'

'Well I'd say we know where your Angela is.'

'Really?' Lizzie's eyes widened. 'Where?'

'She's getting a ride somewhere.'

'Well her father was supposed to give us a lift.'

'I don't mean that sort of . . . ' He laughed until he made himself cough. 'Where are you trying to get to, missy?'

'Back into Ballytorne.'

'Well if you can wait ten minutes I can drop you off in the van. I'm heading back to Cork with the equipment.'

'Really? Thank you so much.' A wave of relief swept over her. Everything was going to be all right. Wasn't God wonderful? Wasn't he looking after her tonight?

'Sit in there.' He indicated the passenger door. 'I won't be long.'

Lizzie opened the door with a creak and a clunk. She lifted her skirt a little and stepped up into the van. It stank of cigarettes and the ashtray on the dashboard was overflowing with extinguished butts. She pulled the door shut and waited in the darkness.

It wasn't long before the other door opened and the man slid behind the steering wheel. With the cab light on she got her first good look at him. He wasn't as old as she had first thought. His hair was curly and dark and nearly touched the collar of his leather jacket.

'I'm Barry,' he said and smiled at her. His teeth looked white against his dark stubble.

'I'm Lizzie.'

'Dizzy Miss Lizzie.'

'What?'

'The Beatles, love. Have you heard of them?' He chuckled and started the engine.

'Of course. I know that song, I just didn't . . .' Her voice trailed off. She giggled too. She felt warm inside. Maybe it was the brandy. 'Are you in the band?'

'Me? Jesus, no. They're all in the minibus. I'm the roadie. I just follow them around with all the kit. Do you like them, Dizzy Miss Lizzie?'

Lizzie felt herself blush. 'I like Brian Bello. That's who we came to see.'

'Well I reckon Angela saw some fellow she liked more.'

'No. Angela would never . . . ' Lizzie wasn't sure what Angela wouldn't do, but she knew that she wouldn't.

'Mark my words, we'll see Angela's arse sticking out of a bush somewhere along here.' Barry laughed.

Lizzie was shocked. She had overheard boys saying things like that before, but nobody had ever talked like that to her.

'The joke of it is, all you young ones love Brian, and he's a big fairy.'

'A fairy?' Lizzie thought she knew what that

213

meant, but it must mean something else, because there was no way that Brian Bello could be one of those sorts of men. 'Are you sure?'

'Well I've never actually seen him with a dong in his mouth, but no girlfriend? Come on. All those girls throwing themselves at him, and nothing. Not one girl in the three years I've been working with them. If that isn't a fairy, then I don't know what is.'

Silently Lizzie thought that just made Brian Bello sound like a very nice man, but she imagined Barry might not agree and said nothing.

Soon the lights of Ballytorne came into view. Lizzie had never imagined that the sight of some street lights outside the ESB offices could make her so happy.

'Nearly home,' she said.

'You just tell me where.'

They drove on past the cinema and down into the main square. Lizzie thought she would get Barry to drop her at O'Keefe's corner and then she could walk up the hill to Angela's house. She hoped they wouldn't all be in bed.

'Just here, please. This is fine.'

Barry pulled the van up to the deserted footpath and turned off the engine.

'There you are now.'

'Thank you so much.' Lizzie was struggling with the handle.

'Sorry. It sometimes does that. I'll come round and let you out.'

Barry jumped from his side of the van and then walked around to open Lizzie's door. As she

214

turned to get out, he grabbed her waist and lifted her up before placing her on the pavement. He slammed the van door shut behind her and looked down into her face expectantly. Lizzie pushed her hair behind her ears, but it immediately fell forward again.

'Thanks again. Thank you so much.'

Barry cocked his head to one side and grinned.

'Have you no little thank-you kiss for me?'

Lizzie froze. She didn't know what to say. Of course she shouldn't kiss this man, but he had been very nice to her, so she knew he wasn't bad.

Barry leaned down. 'Just one kiss,' he whispered. His left hand was back on her waist. Lizzie could feel her heart beating frantically.

'I . . . I don't know.'

He put his other hand gently under her chin so that she was gazing up at him. He leaned in even closer and spoke in a soft growl. 'A little goodnight kiss.' And then his lips were on hers and he pulled her whole body against him.

Lizzie knew this was all very wrong, but she liked the feel of his strong arm around her back and the pressure of his lips. He was nuzzling her hair now, and the roughness of his stubble scraped against her cheek. She winced but made no sound. She felt herself being pushed backwards by the weight of his body. She took a couple of steps back but he kept hold of her and steered them both into the deep doorway of O'Keefe's butchers. She wriggled and tried to speak but his mouth was on hers again. She felt the wetness of his tongue probing her lips and she decided she didn't like this kissing. His breath smelt strong and acrid and he was making low grunting sounds. His left hand slipped down and grabbed her bum. She raised both her hands and pressed against his chest, but he was leaning heavily down on her.

'Shhh.' His hot breath was in her ear. 'You're a good girl.' He moved his mouth down to her neck and started to kiss it.

Lizzie felt sick. This was such a very bad, bad thing, but she couldn't stop it. His legs straddled hers and she was pinned against the shop door. His hand ran down the back of her leg and then was travelling up underneath her skirt, rubbing her bare skin.

'Please . . . please. I have to go home.' But even as she said the words, she knew that he wasn't going to release her.

He put his right hand around her throat. 'Good girl. Good girl.' Then he pressed his face against hers, his big hot wet tongue going everywhere, and moved both his hands underneath her skirt, where they grabbed at her knickers and started to pull them down. Lizzie leaned her head back as far as she could and twisted her body from side to side, but it was useless.

'Please God, no. Please let me go home. Dear God. Please stop.' She whispered her prayers over and over again, while Barry began to rub himself against her.

'Good girl. Good girl.'

Her tears had started to fall. She felt his

fingers between her legs, doing things, awful things. The glass of the shop door was cold against her buttocks, then there was the sound of a zip and she could feel his thing against her thigh. It was clammy and warm. She shuddered but made no sound. It became more difficult to know what he was doing. She could feel the knuckles of the hand holding his penis moving back and forth against her skin. He centred himself and moved it between her legs, still pumping furiously. His breathing was fast. 'You're all right, love, I'm not going to . . . ' He pushed his face very hard into the side of her head and let out a series of little gasps followed by a groan. Lizzie could feel a warm stickiness between her legs. Barry had stopped moving. His full weight was against her and he was breathing heavily. She began to shiver violently.

Barry stepped back and turned away. He bent down to fumble with his flies. She stared at him but he wouldn't look at her. Not raising his eyes from the ground he just said, 'You got me all hot and bothered, didn't you?'

Lizzie didn't answer. Her legs felt weak and she found herself sliding down the door till she was crouched on the ground. After a moment or two, Barry just walked around the van, got in and drove off.

As the sound of the engine faded away, Lizzie thought about God looking down at her. Was he floating high above the market square, with the lights from the shops spilling out on to the deserted streets? Could he see the frail little girl with messed hair and lipstick smeared across her

217

face slumped in the doorway? Her skirt was rolled up around her waist and her knickers stretched between her knees. She squeezed her eyes shut. She wasn't sure what had just happened to her, but she was in no doubt that it was the worst sort of sin.

She stood up. She had to get back to Angela's. She took off her knickers and wiped herself as clean as she could with them, though she could still feel the damp stickiness between her legs as she walked up the hill. She shoved her underwear in a bin, making sure the pale blue cotton was hidden beneath some old newspapers.

There were lights on in the house. Thank God. She paused to make one final effort to look more presentable before she rang the bell, but the expression on Angela's mother's face when she opened the door suggested it had not been enough.

'Lizzie! We've been worried sick. What happened to you?' She found herself being pulled into a hug, her face nestled in the ample bosom of Angela's mother, and the relief at being warm and safe brought on another wave of muffled sobbing tears.

'There, there. You're home now. John, put the kettle on!'

'Lizzie!' It was Angela in a pink and white nightdress at the top of the stairs. Making her way down as quickly as she could, she tried to hug her friend from the other side. Through her sobs, Lizzie wondered if they could smell Barry on her. Could they tell what had happened?

The four of them gathered in the front room and Lizzie drank a cup of sweet tea. It transpired that Angela had been told by someone at the Stella that Lizzie had left, so she and her father had expected to come home to find her waiting. When she wasn't there, they decided they would wait to hear something. There was no point driving round half the night. Lizzie was sensible and would phone them. When she hadn't, they had got very concerned and Angela's father had been all set to go out looking for her when she had rung the bell.

Lizzie told her side of the story without mentioning the doorway of O'Keefe's, and everyone went to bed relieved and happy. Everyone apart from Lizzie. She lay under the covers and touched her skin where his hands had been. She still had the metallic taste of his tongue in her mouth. She spat into the candlewick bedspread.

★   ★   ★

The next few weeks were hard. Life returned to normal and yet Lizzie knew that for her, things could never be the same again. She thought about that night all the time. The graze of his stubble, the heat of his hands, the animal noises pressed against her ear. What could she have done differently? Should she have called out, bitten him, run away? She longed to have that night to live again so that none of it would have happened. She couldn't concentrate on any-thing; her schoolwork suffered, and of course the nuns just assumed she had fallen in love with some lad. They had seen it all before.

It was about a month later that she had started to feel sick. On more than one occasion she was forced to run out of the classroom, and once she hadn't made it to the toilets and was just sick in a waste-paper bin she found in a corridor. Of course her mother noticed and encouraged her to see the doctor, but Lizzie refused. She didn't know exactly how, but somehow this illness had to be something to do with what had happened the night of Brian Bello and the Diamond Dust.

A few weeks later, she found she couldn't zip up her school uniform skirt, and counting back to her last period she realised that she had missed one. She couldn't be sure, but she had a horrible dread that somehow she had become pregnant. She knew she should talk to someone, but who? Angela would probably just panic and tell the whole convent, so she was useless. Her mother would kill her because she had been so stupid. The doctor would tell her mother and that would just lead to her being killed a little later. In the end, Lizzie decided that the only person who could help her was the priest.

She sat in the confessional, breathing in the familiar smell of dusty wood and wax polish. Father Mulcahy listened patiently behind the screen as she spoke. A list of minor sins went on at length while she tried desperately to summon up the courage to say what she needed to. Finally she blurted out her confession.

'A man did things to me.'

It was such a relief to at last tell another living

person what had happened to her, to speak the words out loud. She gave him a version of events that she felt was suitable for a priest to hear, and finished by explaining why she was there. 'I think I'm going to have a baby, Father.' The words hung in the air and she lowered her head in the darkness of the confessional and began to cry. 'What am I going to do?' she asked between sobs.

Father Mulcahy was a man of the world. He had worked with the missions and had even spent six months as a young deacon in north London. He had talked to girls like Lizzie before. He tried to calm her down. He asked her simple questions, leading her through what exactly had happened, but even after she had described to him in as much detail as she could the events of that night in Ballytorne, he still wasn't clear if it was a possibility that she was expecting a child. Erring on the side of caution, he arranged for her to see a doctor he knew up in Cork. The girl on the other side of the grille from him did not deserve to have her reputation ruined by local tittle-tattle.

Lizzie's worst fears were proven to be correct, and she found herself sitting on a hard leather chair opposite Father Mulcahy up in the priest's house. Her world had ended and she sat with her head bowed, twisting a hankie soaked with her tears between her thin, trembling fingers.

Father Mulcahy had an idea. Did she know Mr and Mrs Burke? She didn't. The priest explained that Mrs Burke was having a very difficult pregnancy. She had been confined to bed and they needed help around the house. He would speak to them, but if they agreed, Lizzie would go and live on their farm. When the time came, he would take the baby from her and find it a home. Lizzie began to consider the possibility that she might get her life back. The end of the world had been postponed.

Father Mulcahy was wonderful. He arranged everything. With his help she left the convent, though it was agreed that it was only temporary; she could go back. Her parents were surprised, but accepted the priest's explanation. Lizzie was doing her Christian duty by going to help Mrs Burke for a few months. Had they guessed what was really happening? Afterwards they had never spoken about her returning to the convent. It was as if they knew their little girl was damaged goods. She didn't like to think about it, but she had to admit that it seemed likely they had seen through the priest's plan and just been relieved that they didn't have to deal with any of it. In just a couple of weeks she was sitting beside Mr Burke with a small suitcase on her lap, being driven up the hill to the farm, where her life would change in ways she could not know.

★   ★   ★

Mrs Meany stopped speaking. By now PJ had reached over and was holding the old lady's hands. Her skin felt like waxy brown paper, and her tears had formed a shallow puddle on the surface of the table.

'So that's your baby buried up there?' he asked

tentatively, his voice little more than a whisper.

The old woman looked up, her brow creased.

'No. No, that's Mrs Burke's baby. They found Patricia Burke's little boy. He only lived for a couple of days before he was taken. It was such an awful time. I kept looking at Mrs Burke howling into her pillow and I thought about how I'd feel when the priest came to take my baby. I suppose that's why I went along with the plan.'

'Plan? What plan?'

'My baby was due in a few weeks, though no one from the village knew, of course. Mr Burke sat me down the afternoon their little boy died and explained that my baby could stay on the farm with them. Nobody would know it was mine, because nobody knew yet that they had lost their own baby. I remember I was nervous because of what Father Mulcahy would say, but at the same time I was so happy because my baby would be staying. Not with me, but in Duneen.'

'And is that what happened?'

'Yes. I had an easy birth, thank God, and Mrs Burke just wrapped my little boy in a blanket and carried him back to their bedroom.'

'But what about birth certificates? Health visitors? Did no one notice that the baby was still so small?'

'Mr Burke thought of that. He changed doctors and the new midwife helped fill in the forms, and that was that.'

PJ's mind was working fast.

'So your baby . . .'

'My baby is Tommy Burke.'

9

A heavy grey mist lay low over the whole valley. Brid could hardly see the trees at the other end of the yard. She decided that they had better leave soon. Crossing the kitchen to get the packed lunches out of the fridge, she shouted through the open door into the hall to tell the children to hurry up.

'You won't get much done today,' she commented to Anthony, who was sat at the table with his second mug of tea and his iPad.

'Sure it might lift, and I'm only planning to put out a bit of top dressing. I'd say I'll get it all done.'

'I thought you did the top dressing yesterday,' Brid said distractedly as she tried to scrub a stubborn piece of porridge from a spoon.

Anthony didn't speak. Brid turned to find him staring intently at the screen of his iPad.

'Anthony?'

He looked up.

'I was supposed to, but I ended up having to go out to Maher's for a few more sacks . . . '

A pair of anoraks and heavy schoolbags burst into the room. Between them they were carrying a large square of plywood, with various model houses and cars stuck to the surface.

'What in God's name have you got there?' asked Brid.

'It's my geography project,' said Carmel. 'The

one about the farm. It's due today.'

'Look! The tractor is bigger than the barn!' Cathal said laughing.

'Shut your face.'

'All right, you two. We don't have time for that. Are you planning to bring that thing now, because I'm telling you, it won't fit in my car.'

'I have to bring it. It has to be handed in today or I'll lose marks.'

Brid approached the plywood square that was now resting against one end of the kitchen table and measured it with her arms.

'No. There's no way. Anthony, do you need your car, or could I use it to get this thing into school?'

Anthony looked up as if he hadn't been listening to any of the conversation. 'The car? Sure. I can use yours and we can swap back at lunchtime. The keys are on the hook.'

'Great. Thanks. Right, come on, you two.'

'Bye, Dad,' the children chimed in unison.

'Goodbye,' he called without looking up from the small screen in front of him on the table.

The fog wasn't lifting, so after Brid had dropped off the children and what remained of the plywood farm, she thought she'd get a bit of shopping done. She drove the mile or so outside the town to where they had built the new supermarket. It had been open for about seven years, but everyone still referred to it as new. The car park was fairly empty, so she got a space near the door. She was about to climb out of the car when she remembered that she'd need a euro for the trolley. Impatiently she grabbed her handbag off the passenger seat and went through the various pockets and zipped pouches where she normally kept her change. A few coins, but no euros. She wondered if Anthony kept any change in the car: nothing in the little well beside the gearstick or in the bottom of the door, but the glove compartment maybe?

Leaning across, she pressed the small chrome button and the flap fell forward. Dozens of white squares of paper were stuffed in the compartment. She pulled one out and examined it. It was a parking ticket from the hospital car park. She reached in and took another one. The hospital car park. She grabbed a handful of them. All for the hospital car park.

Her mouth was dry. What was wrong with him? What terrible disease did Anthony have that meant he couldn't tell her? She noticed the date on the ticket she was still holding. Yesterday. She sat perfectly still, trying to decide what to do next. She'd have to say something. It wasn't as if she'd been snooping, and whatever it was, surely it was better she knew. She suddenly felt a huge surge of affection for Anthony. That poor man, suffering all alone, trying to protect her feelings.

★   ★   ★

Bobby's barking sounded muted and distant through the fog, making Evelyn feel nervous. She couldn't afford to waste time this morning tramping across fields looking for him. Abigail was going into the operating theatre at three and both the sisters wanted to see her before then.

They had been warned that afterwards she would probably be groggy or asleep till the next morning. Evelyn had made a list of personal things she was going to pack in a small weekend bag to take into the hospital for her.

'Bobby! Bobby, come! Good boy . . . ' She peered into the thick milky air. Nothing. She sighed. She would have to go back into the house and change her shoes if she was going to go looking for him. She debated how long to wait for him to appear of his own volition. She tried calling again: 'Bobby, come!' She thought she heard something moving through the foliage, and then there he was, like a shadow set free moving along the fence back up towards the house. 'Good boy!' As he drew closer, however, Evelyn realised that any praise was premature. His golden fur was caked in dark, wet mud.

Once he was close enough, she grabbed the dog by his collar and, bristling with anger, frogmarched him up into the yard. As they approached the hose, Bobby realised what was going to happen and began to wriggle and pull away. Evelyn struggled to keep hold of him while also trying to turn on the outside tap. Her grey and white tartan skirt was now nearly as dirty as the dog, and the water from the hose splashed up off the concrete on to her legs.

As she pleaded with Bobby to stand still, she was overcome by a profound loneliness. There was something pathetic-seeming about a woman struggling by herself to wash a dog that had no interest in being clean. She allowed herself to imagine for a moment that PJ was here with her, helping to hold Bobby still. They would both be laughing as they got drenched by the unruly hose. Ridiculous, she chided herself. She got the feeling that PJ wasn't that keen on Bobby, and besides, he might have a heart attack attempting to wrestle a big wet dog. She let go of the collar.

'Fuck it,' she said out loud. 'Fuck you.' And even she wasn't sure if she was addressing the dog, PJ or herself, but there was a certain satisfaction in saying the words. She turned off the tap and watched Bobby doing a victory lap of the yard before stopping beside her and shaking himself vigorously. She felt utterly defeated.

Leaving Bobby locked in the yard to dry off, she headed upstairs to collect Abigail's things. In the bathroom she picked out some toiletries, then headed across the landing into her sister's room. It felt strange being in here alone. The bed was neatly made and a half-drunk glass of water sat on the bedside table next to a brightly coloured seed catalogue. She took the dressing gown off the back of the door and then went over to the chest of drawers. As she slid open the top drawer, the smell of lavender and wood polish reminded her of when she had come to visit her sick mother in this room. She took a few pairs of underwear and tried to remember the rest of her list. No bra — Abigail could wear the one she'd had on — but a clean top for when she was discharged; something nice and warm. She opened the bottom drawer, thinking it was the most likely place to find her sister's knitwear, but the contents were not what she was expecting. On one side were plain grey blankets and on the other a stack of photo albums.

Without picking it up, Evelyn opened the album on top of the pile. There was a black and white photograph she never remembered seeing before. It was her mother and father, very young and smiling up at her. They were standing on a bridge — was that Patrick's Bridge in Cork? — with their arms linked against the breeze that was whipping her mother's coat out to one side. She turned the page. Her father as a young man on a tractor. Another page. Her parents and another couple sitting on a blanket in some sand dunes. Her father had taken off his shoes and socks and all four of them seemed to be finding it hilarious. It was their life before the three girls came along, but why was it hidden away here? Did Abigail think these photographs would have upset herself and Florence?

She shut the album and was about to close the drawer when something else caught her eye. It was a small corner of material sticking out from under the stack of books. Evelyn froze. She slowly reached out her hand and tugged at the fabric. It was really nothing more than a tattered rag, stained black by what looked like oil. She smoothed it out on the floor. In one corner, where the oil stain was lightest, she could make out the faint remains of a pink rose. Her heart was thumping and her mind swirled in a confusion of unanswered questions, but one thing was certain. She was holding the remains of Tommy's scarf.

Brid had made some cheese and pickle sandwiches and put them on a plate in the middle of the table. Two empty mugs sat opposite each other. The kettle was boiled but she was waiting for Anthony before she made the tea. She darted around the kitchen like a goldfish in a bowl, wiping a mark on the counter top, tearing up an old envelope, folding a tea towel. Finally she heard her own car drive into the yard. She took deep breaths.

It had been her intention that when he got back, she would immediately ask him what was wrong. She wanted to unburden him of his secret as soon as possible. She had a small speech prepared in her mind, but when he walked in and threw his cap on the dresser, there was something about him. A twinkle in his eye? A bounce in his step? She couldn't put her finger on it, but in that moment she knew with complete certainty that this was not an ill man. She switched on the kettle.

Lunch was eaten in the usual manner, Brid asking a few questions about the farm and letting Anthony know about some parents' evening up at the school. He mostly communicated in grunts as he scrolled down the screen on his iPad. About half an hour after he had sat down, he wiped his mouth with a bit of paper towel, pushed away from the table and announced, 'Right.' This was his signal that lunch was over and he was going back out to work.

'Do you still need my car?'

'No.'

'Right. I'll see you about seven, so.'

She watched him go to the back door and put his boots on. Out of the kitchen window she saw him stride towards his car in his dirty blue overalls. All through lunch she had been looking at him surreptitiously and asking herself a question: if this man wasn't ill, what the hell was he doing at the hospital every day? She flung a wet dishcloth into the sink and grabbed her coat off the hook by the door. She was going to follow him.

Brid had never followed anyone before, but she had seen enough movies to know the basics. Don't get too close. She saw that he had turned left out of the gates, so she did the same. At the bottom of the hill she just caught a glimpse of his car turning left again. He was heading on to the main Ballytorne road. She felt almost relieved. This was not just the product of her imagination. Whatever he was doing, it wasn't top dressing. Something was up.

Keeping her distance, she followed him into Ballytorne. He made his way slowly around the main square and took a right up the side of the hotel. When Brid took the same turning, the car had disappeared. She slowed down before spotting it again — he had pulled into the car park at the back of the hotel and was getting out. There was nothing behind her, so she sat for a moment and watched as he took a bag out of the boot of his car and headed towards the hotel. He didn't go into the main entrance; instead, he

231

took the metal stairs off to one side.

Brid drove further up the street and found a parking space. Then she walked back to the car park and went over to the metal steps. A small sign with an arrow pointing upwards said *Health Centre*. Brid was puzzled. There was nothing up there but the gym. What the hell was going on? She certainly hadn't noticed him getting any fitter. His small, neat belly was the same size it had been for years.

Feeling like a spy, she pulled up her collar and went to stand opposite the entrance to the car park, where she could keep an eye on things. There was a bookshop on that side of the street and whenever a car passed by, she endeavoured to look like the sort of woman who had a keen interest in local history or Neven Maguire's new healthy recipes. Her heart was beating fast, and she had to admit that she was enjoying all this. It was exhilarating and strange.

She had only been waiting twenty minutes or so when she heard loud footsteps clanging on the metal steps. She sneaked a look over her shoulder. It took her a second to realise it was Anthony. He was transformed. He had changed out of his old overalls into his good navy trousers and the nice blue-and-white-striped shirt she had given him at Christmas. He'd clearly had a shower, and what hair he had left was slicked back. She had to admit that he looked quite good. She hurried back to her car and sat watching in the rear-view mirror as he nosed out of the car park and turned left. She slid low in her seat as he drove past, then rushed to get into gear so that she could continue her pursuit.

Within a few minutes it was clear that he was heading for the hospital. Brid began to feel uneasy. What if she was wrong and he really was here being treated for something? Not only was he lovely for trying to protect his family, but she was an awful human being for doubting him. She watched him drive to the end of the car park nearest the hospital, while she pulled into a space down by the road. He bought his ticket and put it in the car before setting off towards the back of the hospital.

She jumped from her car and half walked, half skipped along the wall towards the hospital building. As she rounded the corner at the back, she stopped and threw herself into reverse. Anthony was standing by himself, leaning against the railing alongside the wheelchair ramp. She risked another look. He was still there, picking at his nails. Clearly he hadn't spotted her. Brid realised how ridiculous she must look hunched against the wall like some overgrown schoolgirl playing hide-and-seek, so she stood up straight and tried to give off the air of someone waiting for a friend or a lift. She heard voices and warily poked her head around the corner once more.

This time Anthony was not alone. A young nurse with dark hair was standing at the top of the wheelchair ramp. Brid noticed that her uniform was slightly too small, catching her under the arms and pressing her breasts together. The nurse made her way down the ramp and threw herself against Anthony, who wrapped his arms around her and began kissing her in a way he had never once in all their years together kissed Brid. Whatever attention Anthony was getting at the hospital, it certainly wasn't medical.

*   *   *

Was Florence deliberately trying to annoy her? It didn't seem to matter what Evelyn said, her sister had some opinion to add or a fact to correct. The leaves weren't early this year. Town was no busier than usual. She was such a teacher. Evelyn gripped the handles of the small overnight case on her lap a little tighter and stared out of the car window as the hedges blurred past.

Abigail was in much better spirits and almost seemed to be looking forward to the surgery. She and Florence chatted happily, but Evelyn sat mute. All she could think about was the silk scarf, and the last time she had seen it, neatly folded on the table up at the farm the day Tommy went missing. She was desperate to ask Abigail how she came to have it; there had to be a good reason why she had kept its existence a secret from her all these years. Evelyn felt she needed in some way to respect that and not bring it up in front of Florence. She sat willing her sister to leave the room till she could bear it no longer.

'Florence, why don't you go and get us all some tea and I can unpack Abigail's things?'

Florence stood up and Evelyn let out a sigh of relief, but then Abigail spoke.

'I'm not allowed anything before the operation.'

Florence hesitated. 'Do *you* want anything?' she asked Evelyn.

'Oh yes please. A cup of tea would be lovely, thanks.'

'Right, two teas coming up. I'll be back in a minute.'

Evelyn smiled and gave a little wave goodbye. The moment her sister had gone out the door, she pulled her chair to the edge of the bed and clutched Abigail's arm.

'What is it, you silly girl?'

Evelyn spoke quickly and in a whisper.

'Abigail. I wasn't snooping. I was just packing the bits and pieces that you needed and I found . . . I found the old photo albums.'

'Photo albums?'

'Pictures of Mam and Dad.'

The clouds of confusion passed from Abigail's face as she realised what her sister was talking about. 'Oh, the old albums in the bottom drawer. I haven't looked at them in years. I hid them there to get them away from Florence. After Daddy died she became obsessed with them. It wasn't healthy. But we should get them out. Maybe frame a few of them.'

Evelyn said nothing but squeezed Abigail's arm a little tighter.

'What is it?' she asked uneasily.

Evelyn swallowed hard. 'At the bottom of the drawer I found . . . I found a bit of Tommy's scarf. The scarf he gave me.'

Abigail's face froze. She turned and looked at

the wall for a beat, and then back to Evelyn.

'Oh God.'

Evelyn waited for her to say more, but she remained silent.

'How? How do you have it?'

'Evelyn, I never wanted to upset you. I did see Tommy Burke getting on the bus to Cork. It was Tommy. He gave me the scarf.'

Evelyn tried to process what she was hearing. Her sister, this woman she had been with every day for the last twenty-five years, had seen Tommy. She had spoken to him and never said anything to her.

'What did he say?' she implored. This was no distant memory to her. She felt it all as urgently as if it had happened only days ago.

'He . . . he wanted you to have it. He said it was his gift to you and that you should have it.'

'Is that all he said?'

'Yes. He wasn't exactly my favourite person that day, if you recall. I was hardly going to engage him in conversation.'

'But why . . . why didn't you give it to me?'

'I thought it was for the best. I wanted you to get over him.' Abigail reached out and stroked Evelyn's cheek. 'I didn't want you moping around the house holding that scarf like some sort of holy relic.'

'What happened to it? Why is it — '

'Two teas! The finest Ballytorne Hospital has to offer.'

The three Ross sisters were reunited.

*　*　*

236

Brid felt like she was drowning. She stood behind her car, gasping for air. One hand steadied her against the roof of the car and her head was bowed. Every detail of the tarmac was unnaturally vivid. The green of a weed. The yellow of a discarded chewing gum wrapper. The shades of black in the tarmac itself. The material world was making itself so clear just as her inner feelings were collapsing into a jumbled mess. There was rage, but there was also fear. A sort of panic gripped her and she had no idea what she should do next. Part of her wanted to run at Anthony and his nurse like a deranged warrior, screaming and pounding them with her fists till they both lay on the ground in a bleeding, broken heap. But more than that, she wanted her children.

She stood back from the car, still struggling to get enough air. She couldn't drive like this. She'd crash. A clanging sound made her look up. It was the rope slapping against the flag pole standing at the entrance to the car park. A blue and white flag announced that this was Ballytorne Hospital. The material flapped carelessly around in the breeze. Stupid fucking flag. What did it have to be so happy about? She put her hands in her hair and pulled hard. She needed to feel something, anything, that she could understand. That bastard. That sanctimonious prick. Judging her. Making her feel like a piece of shit on his shoe and all the time . . . all the time he was fucking some floozy in a nurse's uniform. A nurse? Could it be any more tawdry or pathetic? Her husband was Benny fucking Hill.

She began to walk back towards the hospital. She wasn't clear in her own mind why, but it felt good to be walking. Her breathing came easier. She was about fifty feet from the corner when she stopped. Were they still there? Was he still rubbing his hands across her? Was his tongue still deep in her mouth? She decided she didn't want to know and was about to turn back to her car when a figure emerged from behind the wall.

No. Not her. Anyone but Evelyn Ross. Brid imagined how she must look with her wild hair and dishevelled clothes.

The moment Evelyn spotted her, she stopped. Her face was wet with tears and in her hand a dirty rag fluttered in the breeze.

The two women stared at each other, neither of them knowing what to do, both wondering how they had ended up face to face like unwilling time travellers.

Brid suddenly felt weary. So very tired. She wanted to sink to her knees and sleep. The years. All those years. All that time had passed by, and for what? Here she was once more standing beneath a wide-open sky confronted by Evelyn Ross, and for the second time in her life it appeared that she had lost a husband.

10

It felt strange, Mrs Meany sitting at the kitchen table and PJ putting the mug of tea down in front of her. He was embarrassed to admit that he had no idea if she took milk or sugar, so he just nudged the jug and sugar bowl towards her. He glanced at the clock. He'd be here soon.

After Mrs Meany had shared her story, PJ had promised her that he would try to keep her secret for as long as he could, but he did warn her that if there was ever a trial then it might come out. Mrs Meany had shaken her head. It didn't matter. And that was the truth. After all those years of secrecy, it seemed so pointless. Fifty years of fear had come to an end in an hour sat in the darkened kitchen. She felt hollow and so light she thought she might float away. After PJ had driven her back to her cottage, she had slipped between the cold sheets of her bed and fallen into a deep, dreamless sleep.

The next morning she had stepped outside to walk to the Garda barracks as she did every day. She looked left and right as if expecting the world to seem different, but no. She wondered if the people driving past or out walking their dogs could tell that she was utterly changed. She felt transparent without the dark cloud of the past trapped inside her. She prepared breakfast as normal. The left side of the pan was hotter than the right. She had to press the toaster down twice. It seemed her emotional earthquake had not created a single ripple. The world was the same.

PJ explained that he would need to tell Detective Superintendent Dunne what she had revealed and he'd probably want to ask her a few questions. They'd also want to take a sample of her DNA so that they could find out if the remains were those of Tommy Burke. She nodded. Whatever happened over the next few days, she knew she had relinquished control. Things would unfold; she felt very calm.

Sitting with her tea, though, everything felt unfamiliar. This was where she worked, but now she was here as somebody else. A woman helping the guards with their enquiries. PJ saw her differently too. The night before, he had watched her slight frame get out of his car and walk down the path at the side of her cottage, and he had felt ashamed. So much for his enquiring mind. He realised that he had known almost nothing about Mrs Meany before that evening. Discovering what she had gone through and what she had lived with for all those years made him admire her as much as it made him sad.

When Linus arrived, PJ had to admit he was impressed with how he handled Mrs Meany. He could be quite brusque and businesslike in interviews, but this time he lowered his voice and only took occasional notes. Mrs Meany didn't have much to add to her tale of the night before. She explained how she had gone to work for Father Mulcahy because it became too difficult to be around the baby. Watching Mrs Burke pick him up when he was crying, or handing her the bottle to feed him when she longed to reach out and hold him herself was all too much for her. She left the farm and, without ever deciding to, walked away from life as well. She had tried it and it hadn't agreed with her. The years that followed were lived as a sort of penance for her one monumental mistake.

Listening to her speak, PJ began to understand what a torment her life must have been. To see Tommy holding Mrs Burke's hand, to watch him grow into a man, trying not to stare at him in mass. All those years of not being allowed to be the only thing she actually was: somebody's mother. He felt the urge to give her a hug, but of course he didn't. He just sat on the far side of the room watching this familiar woman turning into someone he didn't recognise at all.

When Linus was finished, he fetched a small plastic pack out of his briefcase and explained that he was going to take a sample of DNA. He put on some thin rubber gloves and took a swab from inside Mrs Meany's mouth. She sat passively with her mouth open. It reminded her of taking communion.

PJ showed Linus to the door.

'Why do you think she's telling us all this now?' the superintendent asked.

'I don't really know. The baby? She can't know who the other body is, but she knew exactly who the child was, so I suppose she felt it was her duty to help.'

'I'm not saying I don't, but do you think we can believe her?'

PJ was taken aback. It hadn't crossed his mind that Mrs Meany was lying.

'Definitely. There'd be no reason for her to lie. Not about this.'

'Right.' Linus held up his sample kit. 'Well I'll put this in and then we wait.'

*   *   *

Brid and Evelyn's agony had ended when Florence appeared round the corner of the hospital.

'Mrs Riordan!' she had called cheerfully, and Evelyn had simply followed her away. Brid decided not to move. If she turned to go back to her car, it looked as if she was following the Ross women, and if she went forward, she might have to confront the nurse situation. She waited until she heard an engine starting up, and then turned to watch the sisters' car pulling out into the street.

Back in her own car, she considered her options. Leave him? Kick him out? Forgive him? Ignore the whole thing? She had dreamed of change for so long, but not like this. She glanced at her watch. The kids. It was time to pick them up. She smoothed her hair down in the rear-view mirror, plastered on a calm smile and turned the key in the ignition.

*   *   *

Evelyn was sitting in her room. The oil-stained material was draped across the end of her bed.

She had been holding it against her cheek and stroking it, but then she had caught a glimpse of her reflection in the wardrobe door mirror and realised how foolish she looked. She reached out and traced the outline of a rose with her forefinger.

A message. She had been given a message from Tommy. He did have feelings for her. She wondered where he was at that very moment. Was he sitting on a bed thinking about her? The discovery of the body had stopped her pointless games, but now she found her mind was playing them again. He was driving a taxi in New York. Maybe he was working on an oil rig in the North Sea. On a horse doing something on a sheep ranch in Australia. Sometimes when she was feeling very low she would populate his life with a wife and children. The marriages were never very happy but he was a wonderful father. One of her favourite scenarios was where he was a widower raising three small children by himself.

These fantasies had begun about a year after he had disappeared. With her hopes of his return fading, she had created places where she could find him but somehow had never managed to go and look. There had been times when she had seriously considered it, but in the end she knew it was pointless. Like a person lost in the woods, she had decided to stay where she was so he wouldn't miss her when he came back to find her. If he could, he would, of that Evelyn was certain.

Now here was his love token on the bed. He had sent it to her and finally she had received it.

She knew she was being ridiculous. She felt like the princess in the stories her mother had read to her as a little girl. The prince was battling through swamps and walls of thorns to find her. She touched the silky material again and wondered if maybe, just maybe, this was the beginning of her happy ending.

★ ★ ★

Alone now that the children had gone upstairs to do their homework, Brid moved swiftly. She took a can of Coke from the fridge, opened it and poured its contents into the sink. Returning to the fridge, she removed a bottle of white wine, twisting the lid open with a satisfying crack before carefully pouring the pale yellow liquid into the can. Her hand was shaking slightly and wine slopped on to the counter top. Once the can was full, she put the bottle down. She stared at the wet can in her hand and hesitated before taking a couple of deep breaths and putting it down beside the wine bottle. With a few sheets of kitchen roll she wiped up the wine that had spilled. Paper in the bin, she returned to the kitchen counter and wrapped her hand around the cold can. She held it to her nose and took a long sniff of the sweet aroma. What did it matter? Nobody could deny she deserved this drink. It didn't mean she was back to her old ways. This was a special . . . not a special occasion . . . special circumstances.

She held the opening of the can to her lips. The brief gap between before and after, and then she shut her eyes and drank. It was cold, and it tasted so very familiar. It was like putting on her favourite blouse. The navy one with the white collar. God, it was good. She took another long slurp. She wiped her mouth with the back of her hand. This was the right thing to do. She was going to cope with all of this. She was going to get through it.

Back to the fridge, where she returned the bottle to the door shelf and took out a ham in its thick plastic bag. It was the easiest thing to cook for dinner. She could have made this in her sleep. A pan of water was on the stove. The ham was in. That's that, she thought, and sat heavily on one of the kitchen chairs. She pressed the Coke can to her lips. The clock said six. One hour. In sixty minutes he would walk through that door.

Looking around the kitchen, she took in every detail. These were her final moments in her old life. She had no idea what might come next, but Anthony had given her a gift. He had handed her the key to a future without him. She took a couple of small sips from her can. Spuds. She got up, went over to the vegetable rack and filled a colander with a couple of handfuls of potatoes, enjoying the slight fog of the wine swirling around her brain after so long with no drink. Peeled and chopped, the potatoes went in the pan of boiling water. Two more sips of wine. Christ, she had missed it.

Like a domestic robot she went through the motions of peeling and slicing carrots, and then making a thick white parsley sauce. The potatoes were done, so she mashed them in the saucepan, the steam billowing up into her face. She breathed in all the smells. This was her favourite dinner. She smiled. The last supper.

The table was laid and the plates were in the warming drawer when the lights from Anthony's car made the steamed-up kitchen window glow bright white. A slightly bigger gulp of her wine.

The back door opened and Anthony came in wearing his dirty overalls; she assumed the other outfit was now neatly folded in the boot of the car. His sparse hair was no longer slicked back but looked almost deliberately ruffled.

'That smells great!'

'I'm doing a ham.'

'Lovely. I'll just go wash up.'

She watched him walk across the kitchen in his stockinged feet and go out the door into the hall. She heard him turn the light on in the downstairs toilet. The sound of the running tap. What was he washing away? Where had he been for the last few hours? What exactly had he been doing? Images of pink flesh being scooped out of the crisp white uniform flashed into her head. She hurried over to the fridge and topped up the Coke can.

The dinner was like any other. Carmel and Cathal told their parents about their day at school, the really funny thing their friend had said, the rumours about the school trip, the window no one would admit to breaking. Anthony spoke about what he had to do the next day. Apparently the top dressing wasn't finished. It was a longer job than he'd thought. Brid smiled and nodded. She sliced ham and handed around parsley sauce. She cleared the plates and stacked them in the dishwasher. Carmel and Cathal were offered a scoop of ice cream each. The minute it was finished, they both scraped back their chairs to return upstairs to their rooms. They shut the kitchen door behind them and a stillness descended on Brid and Anthony.

Her finger was resting on the top of the Coke can, and she looked at Anthony, who was once more busy scrolling the screen on his iPad. She wondered how long she would let the silence continue. After a few minutes, he glanced up and caught her gaze. He raised his eyebrows in a silent 'What?'

Brid blinked slowly and then said, 'Are you all right?'

'Me? Yes. I'm fine. Why?'

'Well, with you visiting the hospital, I just wondered how you were.'

Anthony put the iPad down on the table.

'The hospital?'

'Yes. Where you were today.'

'Who saw me at the hospital?'

'I don't think it really matters who saw you there, does it? You and little nursey so caught up in your own lovely world.'

'What are you talking about, Brid?'

'Seriously? You're going to try and deny it? Don't waste any more of my time, Anthony. You're having an affair with some little nurse.'

Anthony stared at her.

'Well? That's true, isn't it? Isn't it?'

'She's . . . a friend. That's all.'

'Christ. I wish I had friends like that. Fierce friendly, isn't she?' Brid spat the words out.

'Look, I don't know what people have been telling you . . . '

'Nobody has been telling me a fucking thing,' she said, getting to her feet. 'I saw you. I saw you with that bitch of a nurse. And don't you dare try to tell me that little whore is your friend.'

Anthony got to his feet and reached out towards his wife. 'Shush, will you. The kids can hear you.' He continued in a hoarse whisper. 'Look. Nothing has happened. I'm sorry. It was stupid. I'll stop it.'

Brid spoke in a low growl. 'Oh it was stupid all right, just not as stupid as me. I've been such a fucking fool. Trying to please you. Trying to be the wife you wanted. You never wanted me. You never loved me.'

'Brid, that's not true.' His right arm was stretched out, his hand patting the air, trying to calm the beast that had come between them. 'I'm so very fond of you.'

'Fond? Fond? You giant fuck! The only thing you ever loved was my farm. Well it *is* my farm. Mine! And you can fuck off.'

'Brid. You're overreacting. We can work this out.'

'Oh I've worked it out. You're leaving here. Thank you. Thanks for opening my eyes to what a moron I've been. I felt guilty that I wasn't a better wife when all the time you were off fucking someone else. Just get out!'

She gestured towards the door with her hand and knocked over the Coca-Cola can. A thin

248

puddle of pale liquid spread across the table. They both looked at it. Anthony dipped a finger in the wet pool and tasted it.

'Of course you are. Of course you're drinking! You really are pathetic.'

'No. No, no, no. You don't get to judge me. You left the moral high ground when you decided to stick your cock in that nurse. Yes, I'm drinking. I'm drinking because of you, and you will not make me feel bad about it. Now get out.'

'No, Brid. I won't leave you in this state with the children.'

'Then I'm leaving.' She lunged for her coat that was hung by the door. 'I'm going, but when I come back, I want you out of here. This is my family home. My farm. You don't want me, then you don't get to have this land. This land. This fucking land!' She buried her head in the other coats and began to cry. 'Why could nobody love me? Me? Just me?' She looked over at Anthony. 'Am I really that hideous?'

'You're drunk, Brid, and every single thing about you disgusts me.'

Brid felt as if he'd punched her. She opened her mouth, but no words came. Her hand flailed at the handle of the door and then she was outside, running towards her car.

The headlights lit up the back of the house and she could see the dark silhouette of Anthony standing in the kitchen window. Soon he would be gone. She would rip that dark stain from the house and it would be hers once more. The car took off with a shudder and then she was hurtling down the hill.

Duneen was deserted. The lights were out in O'Driscoll's and both the pubs only had a couple of cars outside. She drove down to the bridge and parked. Standing leaning against the rough stone of the wall, she could hear the water rushing by in the darkness below. She stared into the blackness and shakily breathed in. The sour, earthy smell of the hogweed reminded her of being a little girl. She would pick the broad, flat white flowers and squeeze them together to form a makeshift bouquet. Sometimes she draped the grey cardigan from her school uniform over her head and pretended she was walking down the aisle. A car drove by. The wine had made her restless. She didn't want to stand.

Back in her car, she didn't know where she was going. Stupid notions struck her. Ard Carraig. The Burke farm. The cliffs beyond Ballytorne. But no, she'd had enough drama for one night. Without ever deciding that it was her final destination, she found her car sliding to a halt outside the Garda barracks. A light glowed through the dimpled glass of the front door. With the slow, steady pace of a sleepwalker, she approached the porch. Before she had even reached it, PJ was standing by the open door. Brid stood before him. Neither one of them felt the need to speak. He stepped back and she squeezed past him into the hall.

11

A missed call and a voicemail. PJ groaned. It was Linus. He picked up the phone and listened to the message.

'Dunne here. Just wanted to let you know, we have a victim. The DNA was a match. Tommy Burke is our man. I'll be down before lunchtime. I want to interview the other Ross sisters and anyone else you think is worth another stab at.'

PJ rolled on to his back and stared up at the ceiling. For a moment he felt as if the case was solved, then he remembered that this was just the beginning. The blow to the skull. Someone had killed Tommy Burke.

He turned his head to the right and looked at Tommy's former fiancée sleeping peacefully. Her lips were slightly apart and in the half-light he studied her face. The delicate eyelashes, the broken veins, the single hair on her chin. He leaned over and kissed her softly. Brid opened her eyes and gave a half-smile.

They had not made love the night before. When she came into the house, they sat and had a glass of whiskey each while Brid told him about Anthony and what had happened up at the farm. PJ debated telling her that he already knew about the nurse but decided it was simpler not to. There was no point upsetting her further. He had held her in his arms as she had stretched out on the little sofa and rested her head on his belly.

251

He'd stroked her hair and Brid had wondered aloud about what the future would hold. He reassured her that everything would be all right, but he was worried for her. A divorce and a custody battle could leave her with nothing.

He'd led her to his bedroom and undressed her, but not in a sexual way. As she sat on the edge of the bed, it was more like caring for a sick child. He lifted back the covers and she lay down. Once he had stripped down to his T-shirt and underpants he got in beside her and let her fall asleep in his arms. He took deep breaths, drinking in the smell and heat of another human being in his bed.

Brid asked him what time it was. It was nearly a quarter to eight.

'I must go. I want to make sure the kids get off to school.'

PJ didn't envy her going back to that house. Who knew what Anthony had told the children.

'Promise me you'll see a solicitor.'

'I will.' She reached across and pinched his ear lobe.

'You have to be sensible. You have a lot at stake.'

Brid was out of bed now and putting on her clothes.

'I know.' She smiled.

'It turns out it was Tommy Burke's body up above.'

'What?' Brid's head sprung around, her eyes wide.

PJ silently cursed himself. Why had he told her that? She was bound to be upset, and besides, he

252

was sure that he shouldn't be giving details of the case to a woman who was still on a list of suspects. He decided not to be so forthcoming with the rest of the facts.

'We've identified the body and it turns out it was Tommy Burke after all.'

'How can that be? I thought . . .'

'It's a long story. Look, the prick from Cork's coming down and . . . well, he may want to come out to the farm and ask some more questions.'

'Right.' She sounded hesitant. She suspected that she mightn't like this long story that the prick from Cork was going to tell her.

PJ propped himself up on his elbows. 'It's just that I think we should . . . you know?'

Brid smiled. 'Don't worry. This is our secret.'

There was a noise in the hall and the sound of a door closing. 'Good morning, Sergeant!' It was the voice of Mrs Meany.

Brid sniggered and PJ let out a long, low groan. This was all too much for this hour of the morning. He pushed himself off the bed.

'Good morning, Mrs Meany!' he called through the closed door. Christ, he thought, in a moment I'm going to have to break it to her that her son is dead. He raised his index finger to his mouth and made a shushing sound towards Brid. He could hear Mrs Meany going into the kitchen.

'Who owns that car outside?'

The car! They might as well have hung up a sign by the roadside.

He hastily pulled on his trousers and went to the door. Opening it a fraction, he peered outside to check if Mrs Meany was still in the kitchen. She was. He opened the door fully and encouraged Brid towards the hall. Once there, he suddenly spoke in a loud, clear voice.

'Well thank you very much, Mrs Riordan. That was very useful. Thanks for popping in.'

Brid's shoulders shook with a silent laugh. 'You're very welcome, Sergeant. Goodbye now.'

She went out the front door and PJ closed it behind her. Going back down the hall towards his bedroom, he called out to Mrs Meany, 'Early visitor there. Mrs Riordan had remembered a few more facts'

'Oh, I see.' Mrs Meany appeared at the kitchen door holding the two used whiskey glasses. As PJ stared at them and then at her, unsure how to react, the doorbell rang, breaking the tension. That couldn't be Dunne already. He hadn't even cleaned his teeth!

There were two figures waiting. PJ could hardly mask his look of dismay when he opened the door and discovered them to be Susan Hickey and her sister. What was her name? God, his memory.

'You remember my sister Vera.'

'Of course, of course. Are you enjoying your stay?'

Before Vera could speak, her sister interjected. 'She's leaving today. I'm just driving her up to Cork airport, but we were talking last night and she told me something you should know.'

'Oh, right. Will you come in?'

Vera looked at Susan, who made the decision for them.

254

'No, we really ought to be on the road already, but I remembered that you had been asking around about the people who had seen Tommy Burke. Well, Vera has something to tell you.'

PJ's mind began to whir. If this woman had seen Burke in London, then that meant he must have left and come back.

'When was this?' he asked Vera.

'When was what?'

'How many years ago did you see Tommy Burke in London?'

'Oh no!' Susan practically shrieked. 'She didn't see him in London. Tell the sergeant what you told me.'

Vera looked at her sister to check if she was really giving her permission to speak.

'Susan mentioned you'd been asking who had seen him leave, and I remembered who it was told me that they had seen him getting on the bus.'

'It was Abigail Ross!' Susan couldn't hide her excitement.

'Abigail Ross? You're sure? It was a long time ago.'

'It was definitely her,' Vera said. 'I remember because it was so strange that she chose to speak to me. She's older than me and we were never friends, but she made a point of crossing the road just to talk to me.'

'I still can't believe you didn't tell me!' Susan obviously felt the slight keenly even all these years later.

'She made it sound like a secret, so I didn't tell anyone.' Vera was clearly trying to justify

255

herself; not for the first time, PJ was guessing.

'Well thank you very much,' he said. 'I appreciate you coming to tell me.'

'Not at all. I immediately understood how keen you would be to hear what she had to say.' Susan slipped her arm around her sister, and the two women turned to walk back to their car.

PJ shut the door and rubbed his eyes. If Abigail had seen Tommy getting on the bus, then why would she deny it now? If you told the landlady of the pub and the sister of the biggest gossip in Duneen, it was as if you wanted everyone to know. And if Tommy had left, why had nobody seen him come back? Something didn't add up.

'Breakfast is on the table!'

Sometimes he felt himself just going through the motions of eating Mrs Meany's cooked breakfast, but this morning PJ relished every bite. Things were beginning to shift. It was like undoing a very tight knot and sensing a tiny amount of movement. Soon they were going to unravel this mess.

After breakfast he had a shower and then sat at his desk reading and deleting emails. He wondered how Brid was getting on and why she had come to find him last night. He liked her and was happy to see her when he had opened the door, but that wasn't enough. He couldn't be with someone simply because they were willing to be with him. Besides, her life was in turmoil and was about to get even worse. Did he really want to take on all of that? He thought about Linus and his marriage woes. There were no

256

happy endings in this life, he decided, so why bother looking for one?

He checked the clock. Half past ten. Should he wait for Dunne or head up to Ard Carraig by himself? He was impatient to have a showdown with Abigail Ross. The attitude she had given him the last time he was up there! Well, Vera Hickey was not suffering from dementia. It would be harder to dismiss this bit of information. He felt the key this time was to talk to her away from Evelyn; he couldn't pinpoint it, but there was something strange about the Ross sisters when they were together. He had seen it in the hospital the other day. A closeness but at the same time an awkwardness, a resentment between them.

He grabbed his coat off the chair. He was going to head up to Ard Carraig now. In the hall he called to Mrs Meany. 'I'm just going out. If the detective superintendent from Cork shows up, tell him I'm at Ard Carraig.'

'Oh, Sergeant Collins!'

PJ turned to see the old woman's grey-haired head poking out from the kitchen.

'Yes?' He hoped his voice didn't sound as impatient as he felt.

'I was just wondering if you'd heard anything about the NDA?'

'The . . . Oh, Mrs Meany.' He dropped his arms to his sides and looked at the little face in the doorway. He was ashamed of himself. This poor woman was waiting to find out the fate of her only child and all he could think about was charging around the country being the big cop who solved the crime.

He walked slowly down the hall and led Mrs Meany back into the kitchen.

'Well I did get some news, but I wasn't sure if you'd prefer to hear it from Detective Dunne.'

She looked up at PJ and a flicker of fear danced across her face.

'Oh no, Sergeant. I want you to tell me.'

'All right then.' He pulled out a chair for the old lady. 'The tests we carried out prove that the remains found on the old farm are . . . ' He hated how this was coming out. Surely there were kinder words, softer ones to tell this woman the fate of her baby? He ploughed on. ' . . . are those of your child.'

Mrs Meany slowly raised her right hand to her mouth and lightly drummed her fingers on her upper lip.

'Poor Tommy.'

'I'm very sorry, but I suppose it is better to know.'

Her faded blue eyes filled with tears.

'Yes. Yes. Of course.' Her cheeks were wet now. She wiped the tears away with the back of her hand. PJ handed her a roll of kitchen paper and she tore off a couple of sheets to dab her eyes.

She sighed. 'It was a bad business. I should never have agreed to any of it.'

'You did what you thought was best.'

'I knew it was wrong. We all knew. If it was right, why did those two babies both end up buried on that farm, without a prayer, without a flower?'

PJ didn't know what to say. How could anyone

explain why bad things happened? He looked across the table at the little old lady wiping her eyes and thought about Lizzie Meany all those years ago. Why had evil been visited on that small defenceless girl? Why had she spent her whole life punishing herself for a sin she didn't even commit? He felt utterly useless and at the same time a strange affinity with Mrs Meany. Somehow life had conspired against them both. If, as it seemed to PJ, the world was divided into winners and losers, he knew which group the two people sat across from each other at this kitchen table were in. He spoke softly. 'It's not fair. That's what it is. Not fair. But it was a different time and at least you saw him grow up into a man. Not many girls like you got to do that.'

Mrs Meany pushed her hair back from her face.

'You're a good man, Sergeant, but if you don't mind I'm going to go home now.'

'Of course. Can I give you a lift?'

'No. No, the walk will do me good.'

12

Brid wasn't surprised. The wide grey expanse of the deserted yard was exactly as she'd expected to find it. Inside, there was no note, just three washed cereal bowls leaning against each other in the dish rack. They were still wet. Brid pulled the door of the dishwasher open. Last night's dinner dishes, still dirty. She took one of the detergent tablets from under the sink, slid it into place and slammed the door shut. The familiar sloshing and whirring sound that she heard nearly every day began. She felt very calm.

Upstairs she laid a suitcase on the bed and started packing a small selection of clothes. Where was she going? For how long? She didn't know. Suddenly she froze. No. She mustn't do this. Some shadowy corner of her brain was telling her that she shouldn't abandon the family home. Why? She couldn't remember that, but she was fairly certain she should stay. She thought of PJ. He was right. She really should see a solicitor.

The sun was high and bright as Brid drove towards Ballytorne. It felt good to see the unbroken blue sky and feel the warmth of the light hitting her face through the windscreen. Everything seemed possible. After she checked that Carmel and Cathal were in school — they were; Anthony hadn't done anything crazy — she drove through the town and up the long, slow hill that led to the coast road. Bungalows and detached houses sat in their neat gardens. Each one had something that made the person who lived there think it was truly special. The dormer window, the cut-stone facade, the hacienda arch that joined the house to the garage. She thought of Anthony and of driving as a family through the countryside. Every new house they passed sitting squat and square in the middle of a bare field prompted him to say, 'Somebody's pride and joy.' The words were meaningless, a simple verbal tic, but today Brid wondered if they could be true. Could bricks and mortar piled up in a field really bring someone pride and joy? She imagined that for Anthony they actually could. Brid wondered if she had ever in her whole life felt like that. Of course she had. Carmel and Cathal. Holding their small, wriggling bodies had filled her with pride and joy. She could feel like that again. She was sure of it.

She began to slow down and checked the driveway on the right. She was almost disappointed that it had been so easy. There, sitting outside her mother-in-law's own slice of bungalow bliss, was Anthony's car. She parked on the street and walked up the short drive. A small cherry tree sat in the middle of the blanket of lawn bursting with eager pink blossom against the wash of blue. Brid felt a little jolt of confidence. She had a plan.

Her mother-in-law opened the door and stared at her. Her face wore the expression she reserved for buskers and the groups of schoolgirls shrieking at the bus stop at four

261

o'clock each afternoon. She raised an eyebrow. Brid swallowed. She would not rise to the bait.

'No,' she said firmly.

'No? What do you mean?'

'I'm saying no to your attitude today. I want to speak to your son.'

A silence. Brid wondered if she was about to get a door slammed in her face, then, 'Anthony, your wife is at the front door.' With that her mother-in-law turned and walked back into the house, leaving Brid to wait on the narrow concrete path. High above her a jet heading out towards the Atlantic had left a long white arch smudged across the sky. She heard a door open and close, followed by whispering, and then Anthony stepped forward.

'So you're alive then.'

'Yes.'

'We were all very worried about you.'

'Well I'm sorry about that, but quite honestly, you are not the injured party here. I only left because you refused to.'

Anthony lowered his voice. 'I was not going to leave you in that state, not with the kids.'

Brid felt herself becoming irritated. She didn't want to get bogged down in all of this. This was the past. She didn't want to waste time with the same tired squabbles. She had a plan. She must stick to it. Raising both her palms in front of her to signal a full stop, she decided to start again.

'Look, Anthony. Can I come in? I want to talk to you. I have a proposal.'

Anthony stepped back in a silent invitation to enter the house. Brid walked down the short hall and then to the right towards the front room. She knew it would be empty. Anthony followed. He shut the door behind them. They stood looking at each other, both remembering the last time they had been in this room. The tears. The begging. Brid had a twinge of regret that this was where they were going to have this conversation.

'Shall we sit?' she said.

He nodded and they took either end of the stiff sofa. Brid smoothed her skirt and then looked Anthony in the face.

'This is over.'

'Brid, I — '

'Anthony, please. I don't want to argue. We don't need to fight any more. Here's what I want to happen. Let me finish and then you can tell me what you think. Agreed?'

He gave a small nod.

'Right. I think our marriage is over. I know it is. We both know that. And that can be a good thing. I suggest that we don't try and get divorced — not yet, anyway. If we go to court, it'll be lawyers and judges and money and custody. OK. So what's really important to us? You want the farm, and you'd like it if Cathal could farm it after you, if that's what he wants. I want to keep the house and the children together. So my plan is that we sell a few sites — maybe the bottom half of the lower paddock — to raise some cash. We use that to build you somewhere to live on the farm. The four of us can sort out some sort of rota for when the children stay with you, and I'll draw an allowance from the farm income.

We both get what we want, and if the kids don't want the farm, then we can think again when you retire.' She folded her hands in her lap. 'What do you think?'

Anthony rubbed the back of his neck and squeezed his eyes shut. A long sigh and then he looked at her. 'I don't know what to think. It seems so final. Should we not be talking about trying to make things work? I don't know, Brid. This is going to be so hard on the kids.'

'It's going to be hard on all of us, but not as bad as a divorce. If you want to fight me on this, then we will fight, and surely that's worse. This way they sleep in their own beds and they still have a mammy and a daddy who at least pretend to like each other.'

'What about your drinking?'

'What about it? It is just that — my drinking. I've shown you I can control it. I don't want to throw myself some pity party or try to blame you, but when I need a drink it's because I'm unhappy. I'm not happy. You're not happy. That's why something has to change.'

Anthony held his head in his hands, breathing deeply.

'What would we tell people?'

'Tell people?'

'You know. People will ask questions. What would we say?'

So much of the plan was very clear to Brid, but she hadn't considered this. It surprised her that this was the first thing that concerned Anthony.

'Well, we'd tell them that we're separated,

because that would be the truth. An amicable separation.' She liked the sound of that.

'It just feels so strange.'

'People break up all the time, Anthony. I don't want to start a slagging match, I really don't, but if you were happy in this marriage, you wouldn't be off fucking some nurse.'

'Ah Brid. I never even . . . It was a mistake. I felt flattered, and one thing led to another.'

'I don't care, Anthony, I really don't, but if you refuse to agree to what I'm proposing, then I will go ahead and divorce you.'

He looked at her blankly.

'And if we get divorced, the farm, the house, it will all have to be sold.'

'Not necessarily. I might be able to raise the money.'

'And what? Send me packing into the night with a suitcase full of cash? It's my family home, where I'm raising our children. If anyone is sent packing, it'll be you. All that work for nothing. No inheritance for the kids. My plan is a good one. It's the best offer you're going to get, Anthony Riordan.'

Brid felt pleased. She hadn't become emotional, and looking over at Anthony, she could see that he looked frightened. He knew that these were not idle threats. She was surprised by how detached she felt; this was just some man she was negotiating with. She couldn't imagine that this person had ever touched her or licked her neck or stroked her breasts, and yet she knew he had. This was the father of her children.

'I'm going to give you some time to think

things over. I'll pick up the kids and I think it's best if you stay here for the next couple of nights.' She stood up.

Anthony clearly hadn't thought this far ahead. 'But why don't I just sleep in — '

Brid was at the door. 'Stay here, Anthony' As she stepped into the corridor, she turned. 'What have you told the children, by the way?'

'I said you were sick. I said you'd gone to stay with a friend.'

'Right.'

He stood and quickly called after her, 'Where *did* you go last night, Brid?'

'Goodbye, Anthony.'

The sound of the front door shutting, and then silence.

13

The house looked different today. It was the first time PJ had seen it in sunshine, and somehow the bland grey exterior seemed to rise to the occasion. The small panes of glass flashed, the door looked wide and effusive, and the dark slate roof had a sheen to it that he hadn't noticed before.

He could hear the bell jangling deep inside the house, but nobody came to the door. He tried again. Nothing, just the jaded caws of a few crows perched in the trees that lined the driveway. There was no car, but PJ knew that didn't mean that nobody was at home. He crunched his way across the gravel to the door in the low wall that led away from the house to the left. He let himself into the yard and was greeted by Bobby the dog. PJ wrestled him away, trying to avoid muddy paw prints on his uniform. 'Good dog. Down, boy. Down, boy.'

He edged forward and checked to his right. There were no lights on in the kitchen. He decided to look behind the outhouses where he had first found Evelyn all those months earlier. In the far corner of the yard one door was slightly ajar. For some reason it made PJ wary. He walked across the cobbles and gave it a small push. 'Hello?' The door swung open fully and the morning sunshine flooded in to reveal a figure sitting on some old wooden pallets in the corner.

'Evelyn?' PJ felt compelled to speak in a whisper.

She looked up and gave him a weak smile. 'PJ. Hello.'

'Are you all right? What are you doing out here?'

She ran her hand through her hair and shook her head.

'I really don't know. Just being a sentimental fool, I suppose.'

'Right.' PJ stood awkwardly, unsure of how to respond. Bobby was sniffing at his feet.

'This is where I found Daddy, you know.'

'Oh.' PJ had heard the story. Was there something appropriate to say to a woman sitting in the room where her father had hanged himself? 'That must have been a very hard time for you all' was the best he could muster.

'Yes. Yes it was.' She sounded distracted, as if her mind was on something else. 'Why am I like this, PJ? Do you think I'm half mad?'

Finding her sitting alone in the gloom made PJ consider that maybe she was, but he reassured her with 'No. You're bound to be finding this very upsetting.'

'Things happen to everyone, don't they? Everyone. Bad, awful things, but people get over things. They manage to move on.' Evelyn spoke slowly, stressing each word like a teacher explaining the key points of her lesson. 'Why can't I? Why am I still sat here?'

PJ knew better than to try and answer that question, so he just stood and looked around the old storeroom. The cobweb-covered stone walls, the rough rafters overhead with old hooks and pulleys, their purpose long forgotten.

'Daddy left. Tommy left. I just don't think I could . . . You know, this morning I beat the poor dog.'

'Bobby?'

'He ran away I don't know, rabbits or a fox or something, but he just ignored me calling his name. It was like he had forgotten my existence. Everything in the world was more important to him than me. When I finally caught him, I was so angry and upset I frightened myself. I beat him with my fists. I felt awful afterwards. He's just a dog being a dog.'

PJ felt uneasy. He didn't really know how he could respond to any of this. He inched backwards towards the brightness of the yard. 'Is Abigail around?'

'No. No, they kept her in for an extra night. She should be back after lunch.'

'Great. Thanks.'

'She did see Tommy, you know.'

PJ froze.

'What? She told you that?'

'She had to. I found this.' Evelyn held up a small pile of material that had been bunched in her hands. 'It's a scarf. Tommy gave it to me.'

'Sorry. I don't understand. Where did you find it?'

'Abigail had it. I left it at the Burkes', but Tommy wanted me to have it, so he gave it to her when she saw him in Ballytorne.'

PJ hesitated before he spoke.

'Why did she never say that she'd seen him that day?'

'She didn't want to upset me. She was just trying to protect me, that's all. I'm sure she'll tell you everything now when you ask her.' Evelyn looked up at him and slowly balled the piece of material into her fist.

PJ looked down at her. He didn't want to upset her either. He wanted to protect her, but he knew he couldn't.

'Evelyn, there's something you should know.'

'Yes?' There was something in the way she had leaned forward on the pallets that made her seem much younger. She looked like a girl.

'The body. The first body that was found has now been identified as Tommy Burke's.'

Her face went blank and then a look of horror crept over it.

'How? You told us that it wasn't.'

PJ thought of how best to explain it to her. 'More tests were carried out and . . . it's definitely Tommy.'

Evelyn sprang to her feet.

'But if he came back, then surely he would have . . . Why didn't he . . . '

She sank back down on the pallets and pressed what remained of the scarf to her mouth to muffle her sobs. PJ wondered if he should try to give her a hug or even place a hand on her shoulder, but the figure hunched in the corner seemed beyond any comfort. He opened his mouth to say something but thought better of it. Instead he slipped away silently, knowing it was the right thing to do but still feeling like a coward. Halfway across the yard, he noticed Bobby at his heels. PJ glanced back at the door

270

of the outbuilding. Evelyn was all alone.

Back in his car, he looked at his watch. It was nearly twelve. He knew he should probably wait for Linus, but he wanted to speak to Abigail before she was discharged. He liked the idea of her being confined to bed. It made her seem weak and vulnerable. He felt that if he waited till she got back to Ard Carraig she would have regained her strength and would be able to bat away his questions with her familiar haughtiness. He really did not like that woman.

*   *   *

At Ballytorne Hospital, PJ was just going up the steps to the main entrance when Abigail herself appeared at the doors holding a small overnight bag.

'The very woman I was coming to see!' he called. Abigail looked down at him with a confused expression on her face, almost as if she didn't recognise him, or, if she did, couldn't fathom why he had chosen to address her. PJ climbed the last couple of steps so that he was standing beside her.

'I needed to ask you some more questions about Tommy Burke now that we know it was him buried on the site.'

Abigail's eyebrows arched, opening her eyes wide and literally gave PJ a sideways glance. 'Really? Are you sure this time?'

'Yes, Miss Ross, we're certain.'

'Well what a pity you didn't figure that out months ago. It might have saved a great deal of upset. I wonder who messed that up?' Abigail asked in a tone that suggested she knew exactly whose incompetence it had been.

PJ took a deep breath. 'Are you heading back to Ard Carraig? I can give you a lift in the Garda car.'

'Thank you but I have my own car. One of the Lyons boys dropped it in for me last night.' She took a step down as if the subject was now closed. PJ put a hand on her arm and she stopped sharply. 'Sergeant?' She glared at him.

'I think it's best if you come with me. One of the Ballytorne uniformed lads can drop your car out later.'

Their eyes were locked and PJ wondered what his next move would be if she refused, but then Abigail broke her stare and said with a studied nonchalance, 'Well, if you insist.' She continued down the steps and PJ followed her.

Once they were in his car, she began to rummage through her bag with increasing agitation.

'Anything wrong?' PJ enquired.

'They must be here somewhere. My keys.'

PJ watched her churning through the contents of the small bag.

'Isn't that infuriating? I don't think I have them. Sergeant, I wonder, could you run in to the reception desk and ask someone to check the little bedside locker?' She turned and gave him a warm smile. It struck him that he had never seen her actually smile before. It didn't suit her.

'I'll be back in a minute,' he said.

The nurse behind the desk looked familiar.

Was she the one he'd seen with Anthony Riordan? He couldn't be certain; they all looked the same to him really. A call was made to the ward and instructions were given for the search. PJ waited, leaning on the reception desk, idly glancing at the small piles of leaflets. Cancer support groups. Montessori schools. Sponsored runs for the hospice. So many people trying to make the world a better place; it made him feel weary. The nurse was talking to him. No sign of the keys.

'Well, thanks for looking.'

He made his way back to the car, wondering how this news would go down with Abigail. He imagined that he wouldn't be seeing her smile again any time soon, but as he got to the door, he could see that that was precisely what she was doing. He sat behind the wheel and she held up a little key ring and rattled it in front of his face. 'I'm a fool. They were here the whole time. I'd put them in the little zip pocket and forgotten.'

'Great.'

PJ put his own key into the ignition to start the engine, but it didn't respond. He checked he was in neutral and pressed the clutch, but still there was nothing.

'That's odd.'

'What?'

'The car doesn't want to start.' He jiggled the key and made sure the steering wheel wasn't locked. No response. He could feel Abigail staring at him. Of course this would happen with her in the car. He considered getting out and looking at the engine, but what was the point?

He would have no idea what he was looking at, and it would just give his passenger more opportunity to think less of him.

'Sorry about this. I'm going to phone the barracks here in town and see if they can lend me a car. It shouldn't take too long.'

'All right. Though of course I do have the solution right here.' Abigail held up her key ring. 'We could go in my car.'

PJ hesitated. That would be the quickest way out. He had visions of a very impatient Linus waiting at Ard Carraig.

'What's the matter? Are you too nervous to let me drive you?' Abigail was smiling again. God, it was unsettling.

'Fine. We'll take yours.'

PJ would never have admitted it to her face, but he was quietly impressed by Abigail's driving. She was confident behind the wheel and responded well in the traffic as they made their way through the busy lunchtime streets of Ballytorne.

He felt he should ease into his enquiries, so he began by asking her how she was feeling.

'Much better. It's a very simple procedure. It's all done with some sort of scope. I was a little uncomfortable afterwards, but really I'm fine.'

'Good. Good.'

They drove in silence for a mile or so, and then Abigail spoke.

'So have you been talking to Evelyn?'

'I have, yes.' PJ wondered what direction this conversation was going to take.

'Did you tell her your new theory that it was

Tommy that was found after all?'

'I did.'

'And how did that go? She was upset, I imagine.'

'A little, yes. She told me about you seeing him getting on the bus.'

'Yes. Sorry about that, Sergeant. I just didn't think it was that important, and she must have explained why I didn't tell her back then.'

'Yes. Yes she did.'

More silence. They were coming down the hill into Duneen now. PJ spoke.

'It seems odd that we can't find anyone else who saw him leaving that day.'

'Really? It was a long time ago. Why would anyone remember?'

'What's stranger still is that not one person mentioned that he came back.'

'Came back? What do you mean?'

'You saw him go, but his remains were found here in Duneen, so at some point he must have returned.'

'Oh yes. I see. Yes, that must be what happened.'

'And nobody noticed. Even though the whole village must have been talking about him running off.'

The entrance to Ard Carraig was coming up on the left-hand side. PJ waited for Abigail to slow down, but instead she pressed her foot against the accelerator and drove straight past the old grey walls and narrow gates.

'What?' PJ looked helplessly out of the window. 'Where are you going?'

'Sorry, Sergeant. It's just that if we're going to talk about this, I'd prefer to do it in the car. I don't want Evelyn having to hear it all again.'

PJ didn't like this turn of events, but nor was he sure what he should do. Insisting that she turn the car around or stop seemed somewhat heavy-handed, and if she refused, he'd be in an even worse situation than he was already in.

'What were you saying, Sergeant?'

'I was wondering why nobody saw Burke's big homecoming.'

'I know that, Sergeant, but what is it you're really saying?' The atmosphere in the car had changed. Abigail's voice had an icy tone. PJ looked at her. A small muscle was twitching in her jaw and her eyes were staring straight ahead.

'I'm saying that maybe Tommy Burke never went anywhere. You must admit, everything makes more sense if he never got on that bus.'

Abigail didn't respond. The road had become steeper as it climbed to the top of the headland.

PJ felt as if he finally had the upper hand. 'It would make complete sense if you had invented his departure in order to protect your sister. A lot of people would have done the same.'

'Evelyn?' She shot him a look. 'You think Evelyn was capable of dispatching Tommy Burke?'

'At first I didn't, but she is very . . . ' he had to choose his words carefully, 'emotional. It's not hard to imagine her having an extreme response to something or someone.'

'Oh for God's sake. Evelyn didn't kill Tommy Burke.'

'You sound very sure.'

'I am very sure, Sergeant. I know for a fact that my sister didn't kill that arrogant boy.'

PJ's heart was beating fast and he was aware of a dryness in his mouth.

'So who are you covering for? If you know who committed the murder, you . . . well you must, you have to tell us.' He hated how weak and ineffectual he sounded.

'You're really not a very clever man, are you? Waddling up and down the village meddling in things that are best left alone. There was no need for any of this. None.' She hit the steering wheel with her right hand to emphasise her frustration. 'You stupid, fat, sweaty fool. No need. There was absolutely no need.'

PJ clutched the sides of his seat to stop himself from slapping her across the face. He hadn't been spoken to like that for years, and even then it was only by drunks he was taking into the station to sleep it off on a Saturday night. He took a deep breath. 'Insult me all you want, Miss Ross, but if you know what happened to Tommy Burke, you are going to have to tell us.'

Abigail threw her head back and barked out a single laugh.

'You want to know what happened? All right, I'll tell you what happened. That day the engagement was in the paper . . . well, I hadn't fully realised how deeply Evelyn felt for the boy. I had just assumed it was a silly schoolgirl crush. Then when she came back from Burke's she was so distraught. I hated it. I hated to see her crying. After our parents died I was forced to

277

take charge, and seeing her like that I just felt like it was my fault, my failure. I was furious with that little Burke boy. We had rented our land to him and it had been my idea for Evelyn to help him in the house, and after all that, this was how he was repaying us.

'I went up to the farm to confront him. There was no way he was still going to rent our land, and I wanted to tell him myself. When I got to the house, the door was open. I called out a few times but eventually just went in. There on the table was the scarf that had made Evelyn so happy. I remembered the sobbing mess back at Ard Carraig and my blood was boiling. I grabbed the scarf and went around the back of the house to see if he was in the yard. He wasn't, but I heard a tractor up the hill so I decided to head up there to see if it was him. It was. Not a bother on him, just sat up straight on the tractor seat, pulling a harrow across the ploughed field. It was business as usual for him. I remember looking at the back of his head as he drove away from me down the field, and how unconcerned he seemed. He had broken a girl's heart that morning and he was harrowing. I was shaking with anger.

'He was about halfway back up the field when he saw me. He waved, but I stood my ground inside the gate. He tried talking to me from the seat of the tractor but I was having none of it. I called him down. I don't remember exactly what I said. I shouted at him. I told him about the farm and I thrust Evelyn's scarf into his hand. He looked at it as if he didn't even recognise it.

He blustered and began to explain that Evelyn was just a young girl and he'd done nothing to encourage her, and then . . . '

PJ sat perfectly still. He felt as if Abigail had almost forgotten that he was still in the car with her. She was telling this story to herself.

'And then the wind caught the end of the scarf. It wasn't even a windy day. A breeze, that's all it was. The scarf furled out behind him like a long, thin flame. It was all so fast. The power drive on the back of the tractor was still spinning around and in just one moment it had caught the scarf. Tommy was yanked back off his feet and smashed his head against the side of the harrow. I'll never forget that sound: a loud, wet crack. He lay completely still and the scarf, now he'd let it go, just flapped harmlessly around the power drive. It was all so sudden. I had been so angry and now this horrible scene lay before me. It was as if I'd made it happen but I knew that wasn't true. I checked the body, but he was dead. It's strange to think back and remember how calm I was. I stepped up on the tractor and turned off the engine, and then I dragged Tommy away from the harrow.'

Abigail stopped speaking. Her lips formed a small grin. PJ wondered if she was going to laugh.

'I know what you're thinking, Sergeant.'

PJ felt strangely uneasy now that she had acknowledged his presence once more.

'What?' he asked quietly. He wasn't sure how he should be handling this woman. The mood in the car felt brittle and dangerous. They were moving quite fast now, coming down the hill, and as the car sped around each tight bend, PJ caught glimpses of Aikeen Bay, all piebald blues and shimmering beneath the sun.

'You're wondering why I didn't come straight down to the village and tell someone what had happened. Of course I considered it, but then I thought about Evelyn. You know it was her who found our father's body? I thought that the news of Tommy's death might have killed her. Everyone would be talking about her. She was already one of the tragic Ross sisters; I couldn't heap this misery on her as well.

'Everything seemed very clear and simple to me then. I went down to the yard and found a shovel. The ground was ploughed, so it wasn't that difficult. I rolled him in and I remember he fell face down and for some reason that bothered me, so I turned him over to face skywards. After he was buried, I drove the tractor down to the barn and cleaned the blood off the side of the harrow with a bit of straw. What remained of the scarf I picked out of the power drive, and then I was done. I used the keys from the tractor to lock up the house and went home. Tommy had run away.

'That night I went down to the village and told a few people about the bus. It was as simple as that, Sergeant. And for twenty-five years everything was fine. Nobody cared and Evelyn got her life back.'

PJ stared at her. Was she serious? Did she really think her sister had got on with the rest of her life? Didn't she realise that she might as well

280

have buried Evelyn along with Tommy? The woman was probably still sobbing into that fucking scarf up at Ard Carraig.

'I do wish — God, how I wish — that the builders' JCB had just angled its bucket to the left or right, then none of this would have had to happen.'

PJ didn't like her tone as she spoke. It was as if she still knew more than he did. Was there more to her story? He opened his mouth and found that he just told her the truth.

'I don't know what to say. I'm shocked.'

'Why? Because I'm a woman?'

'No. Not at all. I expected it to be a crime of passion, not a simple accident that for some reason you saw fit to make look like a murder. Did you not think about confessing after a day or two?'

'It was a good plan. A solid plan. It worked for twenty-five years. It's not like anyone cared about him.'

PJ thought of Mrs Meany with her head bowed over his kitchen table.

'Why tell me everything now? Why not just brazen it out? You must know that we could never get any sort of conviction with the evidence we have.'

'Why now? Because, Sergeant, it doesn't matter.'

'Doesn't matter?'

'Nothing matters any more.'

The car took a sharp right on to a small road with thick hedges and a ridge of grass ripping through the tarmac in the centre of the lane.

'I don't understand.'

'I'm a dead woman, Sergeant. Tumours. That's what they found when they went in. Stage Four. As one nurse with not the best bedside manner put it, I'm riddled with it. I have weeks, months at most. Like mother like daughter. I'm the chosen one.'

The hedges were whipping past now in a green blur, and PJ realised that they were heading down to Dromore Pier. The car was going far too fast and he was gripped by an awful fear.

'I'm sure there must be something they can do.'

Silence. He glanced across at her. She was staring straight ahead, her hands pressing on the steering wheel so that her body was pushed back against her seat.

'Miss Ross. Where are we going?'

She didn't reply.

'Don't do anything stupid, Miss Ross.'

Abigail reached over and switched the radio on, turning the volume high. Lyric FM blared out some jaunty light operetta. Gilbert and Sullivan maybe? PJ undid his seat belt. The car had cleared the hedges and was hurtling towards the pier.

'For the love of God, woman!' PJ shouted above the music and reached across to grab the steering wheel. Abigail fought back, stronger than he had expected. The low wall of the pier was just feet away. He yanked the steering wheel as hard as he could to the left, and the car veered away from the pier, bouncing across the rough grass. Desperate, he seized the handbrake and pulled. The car spun once, twice, and then on the third turn everything went eerily quiet as they flew off the edge of the cliff into the air above the churning sea below.

As PJ clawed at the door handle, time seemed to stop. Moments from his life flashed into his mind. Emma Fitzmaurice's laughing face in the darkness of the cinema. His mother crying with pride the first time he put on his uniform. The sweat falling from his face on to Brid's pale skin. Then he was engulfed by a sudden deafening roar as the car hit the waves.

The cliff was deserted. There was no one to see the car being swallowed whole by the ocean. No one to hear the strains of 'The Queen of the Night' coming from beneath the waves that slapped the cold rocks at the foot of the cliff.

14

Two funerals in one week. The weather had turned and a dark gloom had descended on Duneen. Petra looked at the digital clock on her till. They'd all be up there now, she thought. So strange that the whole village wanted to pay their last respects to that woman. She was a killer. Maybe that was why Mrs O'Driscoll had decided not to shut the shop. Petra chewed the end of her long bleached hair. Ireland was a mysterious country.

Up in the cemetery, Evelyn leaned against Florence as the priest finished his prayers. Both women remembered the last time they had stood by this grave. Then it had been their father and his death by misadventure. Abigail had stood between them, her arms like angels' wings draped over their shoulders to shelter them from the large crowd of mourners that surrounded the grave. Now it was Abigail who lay before them. Florence had wondered if the village would come given the circumstances, but she needn't have doubted them. A funeral was always going to be more important than the person who was being buried.

Mrs O'Driscoll joined the long line of mourners. When it was her turn, she shook hands with the sisters. 'Sorry for your loss.' Florence gave her a small smile and mouthed 'thank you', but Evelyn didn't even raise her head. As she turned away from the two women and began to descend the steps, she wondered what they'd do now. Sell up? She knew that was what she would have done. Ard Carraig was cursed. They'd find no happiness there.

★   ★   ★

Back at Ard Carraig, the ticking of a clock and the motor in the fridge suddenly starting up were the only sounds. Florence fussed around Evelyn, making her cups of tea that went undrunk and meals that went uneaten. She read or marked exercise books, stealing glances at her sister. Evelyn just sat with her hands in her lap, sometimes staring at the floor, at other times into the middle distance. Bobby had quickly learnt that crying or pawing at her leg no longer resulted in a treat or even a stroking of his ears. He transferred his affection to Florence and curled up beside her, his chin resting on her foot.

Evelyn felt numb and defeated. What was the point in caring or trying or believing or loving when the odds were so clearly stacked against her? All of this couldn't have just randomly happened to her; somehow, she reasoned, it must be her fault. To try was to fail. To care was to get hurt.

The darkness of early evening had crept over them and Florence put down her book and walked across to switch on a light. Evelyn didn't flinch. It was as if she hadn't seen it.

★   ★   ★

Linus wasn't sure why he was here. There were heaps of paperwork on his desk and he had hoped he would never have to see Ballytorne again, and yet here he was driving into the hospital car park.

He walked up the steps carrying the small bag of green grapes he had bought in the SuperValu on the square. Why did sick people get grapes? He felt like a fool. At least he had stopped short of bringing a bottle of Lucozade as well. He approached the nurse at reception.

'I'm looking for Sergeant PJ Collins.'

There was something about the hospital bed with its side rails and high mound of pillows that made PJ look even more enormous than usual. Linus was reminded of those nature documentaries where they had to transport giant mammals under sedation back to their natural habitat.

PJ's head was thrown back and his eyes were closed. Linus hesitated, not sure what to do. Should he wake him? He decided to sit on the high-backed chair by the bed and wait. He picked absent-mindedly at the grapes.

After about ten minutes PJ raised his head and didn't seem at all surprised to see the detective superintendent sitting beside his bed.

'Hello.'

'Hello, Sergeant. How are you feeling?'

'Not too bad. I should be out soon. It's good of you to come.'

'Don't be mad. We're just glad that you're alive. I brought you a few grapes.' He held out the bag.

PJ peered down at the mixture of grapes and bare stalks.

'Sorry. I had a few of them there when I was

waiting for you to wake up.'

Both men chuckled. There was an easiness between them that had been absent before.

Linus had been genuinely happy when he found out that PJ had survived the crash. The alarm had been raised by a trawler that saw the car come off the cliff, but by the time the coastguard had arrived, PJ was already sitting in a shivering heap on the rocks. He had managed to open the door just before impact and been half out of the car as it sank to the bottom of the bay. He had broken his collarbone against the frame of the car and cracked three ribs. He now had a plate and screws holding his clavicle together.

During his days in hospital, as he drifted in and out of sleep induced by painkillers and the after-effects of his general anaesthetic, he thought a great deal about the accident. He wondered if he should have tried harder to save Abigail from the car. In fact he had made no effort whatsoever to return to the vehicle. He had sat huddled, his flesh stinging from the glacial salt water, grateful to be alive and cursing the woman who had tried so hard to kill him. It didn't cross his mind at the time that he should risk his life to try and rescue her.

He wondered too what he had done wrong. How as a guard he might have seen the warning signs; was there a way he could have avoided the situation? When the Ballytorne boys had recovered his car from the hospital car park, they had discovered that every wire below and around the steering wheel had been neatly cut. They guessed that someone had used something small

287

like nail scissors. It shocked him to recall how long it was before he realised he was in real danger. Clearly she had been planning his demise from the moment they left the hospital.

'When do you think you'll be back at work?'

'I don't know.' This was something else that PJ had spent a long time considering. 'To be honest, I don't know if I'll be going back at all.'

Linus was taken aback. 'Really? Why? I thought you liked the job.'

'I do. I did. All of this has done my head in a bit, to be honest.'

'The accident?'

'No. No, the whole investigation really. I've been lying here thinking and remembering why I wanted to join the gardai. I thought I could help. You know, be of service. The whole village thing appealed to me back then. I liked the idea that I'd be part of the community. Helping. Like I say, providing a service. But then I just got on with the job and somehow over the years didn't notice that what I was doing day to day wasn't like that at all. I just issue licences and check tax discs. A monkey could do it. Having you around — the technical guys — it made me realise what the job could be. I really don't think I can go back to setting up checkpoints for speeding or getting people out of the pub. I'd lose my mind. Do you understand?'

'Of course. I couldn't stick all that when I joined first. Still, think about it. We'd be sorry to lose you.'

'I will,' PJ said, though he had in fact already made up his mind.

Linus stood. 'Well, I should be getting back. Good to see you in one piece.'

'Thanks for coming. I do appreciate it.'

'Take care.'

Linus had his hand on the door when he turned.

'What about Cork?'

'What?'

'If I put in a word for you, would you consider moving up to Cork?'

PJ didn't know what to say, but Linus was warming to his plan.

'You've got the skills. I'd say you'd make detective without much bother.'

PJ flicked through the pages of a life not yet lived. He thought he liked the sound of this chapter.

'Really? You could do that?'

'No promises, like, but I could give it a shot. Do you want me to try?'

'Yes. Yes please.' PJ was beaming.

★ ★ ★

The second funeral had three mourners. Three women. Each one stood slightly apart from the others. Nearest the grave was Mrs Meany. She had borrowed a black coat from a neighbour. It was slightly too big for her, and just the tips of her fingers poked from the sleeves as she stood with her head bowed. Little Lizzie Meany was finally putting her baby to bed.

At the end of the prayers she approached the graveside and threw a handful of the dark red soil on to the coffin lid. In her mind's eye she saw Mrs Burke holding a gurgling bundle. This coffin seemed so big and cold.

Behind her, standing about ten feet apart, were Evelyn and Brid. As the old lady stood looking into the grave, Brid went over to Evelyn and gave her a hug. She felt she had enough going on in her life without holding on to her teenage anger at Evelyn Ross. Immediately she regretted it. Evelyn's arms remained hanging limply at her sides and Brid had to force herself to maintain her hold for a second or two before stepping back. Evelyn looked awful. Her eyes had dark bags under them and she stared back at Brid with no flicker of recognition.

'Are you all right?'

'Yes.' Her voice was a whisper.

'Can I give you a lift home or anything?'

Before Evelyn could answer, Florence had come around the side of the chapel.

'Hello, Mrs Riordan. I'll take her. Don't worry.' She put her arm around Evelyn's shoulders and began to lead her away. 'Such a sad day.'

Mrs Meany was at Brid's side now.

'Oh, are the Ross girls leaving?'

'Yes. I don't think Evelyn is feeling very well.'

'Oh. I see.'

The two women stood in silence, neither sure what to say next. The mother he never knew. The bride he never wed.

'I don't know if it's the right thing, but if you wanted to come back to the house, I made a few sandwiches.'

'Oh, thank you very much, but I've got to pick

290

up the children now.'

'Of course. Of course.'

Brid decided against attempting another hug so just shook the old lady's hand.

Back in her cottage, Mrs Meany took off her borrowed coat and hung it carefully on the wooden hanger that was waiting on the back of the kitchen door. She stood and looked at the table. Her best china was laid out. Six cups and saucers, a small stack of plates. Beside them a damp tea towel was draped over two plates of sandwiches, and on the kitchen counter by the bread bin was a tin with a freshly iced carrot cake in it.

She sat heavily in a chair by the table and peeled back the corner of the tea towel. She retrieved a small triangular sandwich with the crusts removed. It was ham. She nibbled at the corner, then put it down. With a deep sigh she stood and took the plates over to the bin. What a waste, she thought.

★   ★   ★

One large green suitcase and two small canvas bags was all he took with him. He looked at them squashed into the boot of his car. They were the same cases he had packed when he had headed off to training at Templemore all those years before. That was a lifetime ago. PJ wondered if he had done enough. Had he lived a life in those intervening years? He suspected that he hadn't, but it didn't matter because he was starting one now. He slammed the lid shut. It felt good to finally be leaving after the months of waiting.

At first the delay was because they were looking for someone to replace him, but eventually it was decided that the Garda barracks in Duneen would be closed and the village and surrounding townlands would be covered by the officers in Ballytorne. PJ had raised his eyebrows when he heard. It turned out he was irreplaceable, or else, he thought, trying to suppress any feelings of bitterness or regret, the job he had been doing for the last fifteen years had been pointless. He decided he was being too harsh on himself. Certainly the way people had spoken to him when the news of his transfer got out convinced him that his job had been worthwhile. He felt he would be missed. Would he miss them? He thought he might.

He locked the front door of the bungalow and got into his car. Every silly thing had taken on a ponderous sense of history; it didn't matter what he did that day — brushing his teeth, boiling the kettle, lacing his shoes — everything was accompanied by a running commentary of 'This is the last time I will . . . '

The leaves had already begun to turn, but there was still some heat in the sun that meant Duneen was looking its best for his departure. He drove slowly down Main Street, taking it all in.

Will I ever be back here? he wondered.

Mrs O'Driscoll was outside her shop. He waved at her. She looked a bit puzzled and raised her hand in return. PJ smiled to himself. Clearly

292

she had forgotten that today was the day. To his left was the hill that led up to the old Burke farm. The development was finished now and, in a move that had surprised many, Florence and Evelyn had sold Ard Carraig and bought one of the new houses. Of course it was very handy for the primary school, but people still questioned if it was the best place for them to be. PJ had called up the week before to tell the sisters that he was leaving, but Florence had said Evelyn wasn't well so he hadn't seen her to say goodbye. In fact very few people saw Evelyn any more.

Florence had almost taken on the role of carer. Each evening she picked up a few things in O'Driscoll's and headed back to the new house. She liked how clean everything was. The kitchen, the bathroom, the windows: nothing was covered in a thick layer of memories. She wasn't sure what to do about Evelyn. Clearly she needed help, but she refused to go and see a specialist. The local doctor had called out a few times and prescribed some anti-anxiety medication, but it didn't seem to make much difference. Occasionally someone would report having seen Evelyn out walking the dog either very early in the morning or after dark, but other than that she had vanished from village life. Her sister was no longer Florence. She was, and would remain, 'poor Florence'.

Once through the village, PJ sped up and thought about his new life in Cork. He had rented a small one-bedroomed flat in a new development on the outskirts of the city. He was looking forward to having a home that was separate from where he worked. He wondered if he would maybe lose a bit of weight without Mrs Meany cooking all his meals. He hoped so.

He passed the turning that led up to Brid Riordan's farm. He had wanted to go and say his farewells, but he knew that things weren't easy for her. It would be just his luck that he would arrive at the same time as Anthony.

Anthony had been staying with his mother for a while, but once the work building him a small house on the farm was under way, Brid had relented and let him move back into the farmhouse. The children seemed happier with everyone under the one roof, even though they knew their father was sleeping in the spare bedroom.

Brid had been surprised by their reaction at first. She had thought Cathal would be the most upset, but in fact it was Carmel who had taken it hardest. Brid and Anthony had told them together. Cathal had just nodded. Brid could tell he was trying very hard not to cry. She hated that she was doing something that hurt him. Carmel had decided that her father was leaving because her mother was so awful. She had screamed at Brid. Called her a bitch and a drunk. Anthony had tried to reprimand her and tell her that it was what Mummy and Daddy had both agreed, but she was having none of it. Mummy had driven her daddy away.

Over the months things had calmed down, and she was at least civil to Brid now. Sometimes it was tempting to tell her about Daddy and the nurse, but Brid knew she would probably blame her for that as well.

Another big change was that Brid was earning money. Apparently she had inherited her mother's flair for baking, and after a few of the other mothers had asked her for her recipes, one of them offered to pay her to make a cake for a birthday. Other requests followed, and with her confidence riding high, Brid had gone into the little deli in Ballytorne called the Coffee Nook and showed them samples of muffins and cakes. She now had a regular order. It wasn't enough money to live on, but she could tell Anthony was impressed and she liked the feeling of being busy.

Once, quite soon after he had moved back in, Anthony had tried to kiss her. Brid had come out of the bathroom ready for bed and found him standing on the landing. She wasn't sure if it was planned or if he had just been waiting to brush his teeth and then the physical proximity had prompted him to lean in and plant his lips on hers. Brid hadn't pushed him away, but somehow they had both just sensed that it was not the right thing to do. He drew back from her, closed the bathroom door and had never tried again.

The road curved around the side of the valley and left Duneen behind. The sun was getting lower in the sky and long shadows draped themselves across the fields. PJ felt strangely self-conscious. It was as if he was being watched guiding the car around the bends. He leaned back and spaced his hands evenly on the steering wheel. It felt like he was in a movie, but he couldn't be sure if this was the beginning or the end.

Epilogue

PJ hated this. Sitting alone in a restaurant was something he tried to avoid. The way the other diners looked at him when he walked in. They didn't even try to disguise their amusement and disgust. What did this man want with any more food?

Then there was trying to manoeuvre his way into his chair. There was never enough room and someone always had to shuffle their seat forward. Outwardly they assured him it was no trouble, but he knew they resented all the space he was taking up.

The waiter approached him and asked if he'd like any bread and butter. Had PJ imagined the young man was smirking?

'Yes please.' This was even worse than he had been expecting. The thick carpet and starched tablecloths gave the room a hushed atmosphere. Was anybody speaking? All he could hear was the echo of cutlery on plates and his own breathing, which seemed to have been amplified somehow. He could feel a sheen of sweat forming on his brow. Could he use the napkin to wipe it away?

The bread basket with a small ramekin of butter was delivered. That waiter was definitely laughing at him. PJ waited till he had gone and then picked up a piece of bread and spread some of the butter on it. God, it was good. He allowed himself one more piece. Then another. Only one slice of bread remained. He would not have it. He wouldn't give the smart-arse waiter the satisfaction of coming back to find the basket stripped of its contents. He stared straight ahead at a series of abstract paintings. How long had he been here? He looked at his watch. Five minutes. That was nothing.

Whenever the door opened he had to strain to see who it was; his table was just to the side of an alcove, so he could only see the bar area. An elderly pair obviously celebrating something, a group of three businessmen, a nervous young couple. PJ watched them hand their coats to the girl by the bar and then follow the waiter to their various tables. The place was almost full.

He heard the door open and saw the back of a woman wearing a camel-coloured coat. PJ didn't recognise it. She slipped it off and revealed a navy blouse with a neat white collar. The woman touched her hair as she spoke to the maître d'. When she turned to follow him into the restaurant, her eyes found PJ's. Brid Riordan gave him a small wave and smiled.

The last piece of bread was forgotten.

Acknowledgements

Writing a novel has been a long held ambition of mine, but the fact that you are actually holding this finished book in your hands is due to the encouragement, tenacity, support and general cheer leading of a great many people.

I couldn't have asked for a better publishing house. Carolyn Mays made me feel like a fully-fledged member of the Hodder family and my editor Hannah Black worked tirelessly to make this book a reality. Her notes and suggestions were always wise and welcome, but perhaps most importantly she made me feel like a writer. Other members of the Hodder family that I must thank are Lucy Hale, Alice Morley and Louise Swannell for alerting the world to the fact I had written a novel. Alasdair Oliver and Kate Brunt for making it look so beautiful. Claudette Morris, Liz Caraffi, and Emma Herdman for all your expertise, help and patience!

Melanie Rockcliffe and Dylan Hearne and everyone at Troika Talent for cheering me on to the finish line.

My early readers for their enthusiasm and eagle eyed notes, Gill Sheppard, Niall Macmonagle, Rhoda Walker, Paula Walker, Becky Nicholass and Maria McErlane.

To my friends and neighbours in Bantry and on the Sheep's Head in West Cork for making me feel at home and providing the inspiration for some of the locations (but none of the characters!) in the novel.

I am indebted to all my friends for feigning interest in this book for over a year and I am of course, supremely grateful to you for choosing to read my story. I hope you enjoyed it.

We do hope that you have enjoyed reading this large print book.

Did you know that all of our titles are available for purchase?

We publish a wide range of high quality large print books including:
Romances, Mysteries, Classics
General Fiction
Non Fiction and Westerns

Special interest titles available in large print are:
The Little Oxford Dictionary
Music Book
Song Book
Hymn Book
Service Book

Also available from us courtesy of Oxford University Press:
Young Readers' Dictionary
(large print edition)
Young Readers' Thesaurus
(large print edition)

For further information or a free brochure, please contact us at:
Ulverscroft Large Print Books Ltd.,
The Green, Bradgate Road, Anstey,
Leicester, LE7 7FU, England.
Tel: (00 44) **0116 236 4325**
Fax: (00 44) **0116 234 0205**

Other titles published by Ulverscroft:

THE LIFE AND LOVES
OF A HE DEVIL

Graham Norton

From his varied career to his beloved dogs to Ireland, once a place that felt stifling but that now is home, Graham Norton shows how life isn't simply a series of dates and events: it is who and what we love. And so he tells of the men he has loved and lost; the booze that has flowed freely — sometimes with startling results; of his love affair with New York, and the divas who have awed him with their power and imperfections. Here, he shares an amazing variety of experiences, from the mundane (falling asleep on the night bus), to the grotesque (vomit-covered socks), to the sublime (floating down the river singing with Dolly Parton) — a plateful of life stories, along with a dollop of 'Graham Nortonness' on the side.

THE ST. TROPEZ LONELY HEARTS CLUB

Joan Collins

Contessa Carlotta Di Ponti, stunningly beautiful and sole heir to a vast fortune, has finally escaped her abusive marriage and is looking to find true love in Saint-Tropez. She soon meets the colourful jetsetters and hangers-on who populate the Mediterranean paradise every summer, including Fabrizio Bricconni, gigolo and long-suffering toyboy of an ageing socialite. The party season kicks off with a spectacular bash at billionaire Harry Silver's palatial mansion, but tragedy soon strikes and, amid the social glitz and the parties, a series of bizarre and increasingly dangerous incidents occurs. Could seemingly innocuous events — a bad oyster, a fatal wasp sting, a faulty funicular — mean something more sinister? It is up to glamorous detective Gabrielle Poulpe to solve the mystery, or life in Saint-Tropez could be over for ever . . .

THE KEEPER OF LOST THINGS

Ruth Hogan

Anthony Peardew is the Keeper of Lost Things. Forty years ago he carelessly lost a keepsake from his beloved Therese. That very same day, she died unexpectedly. Broken-hearted, Anthony sought consolation in rescuing lost objects — the things others have dropped, misplaced, or accidently left behind — and writing stories about them. Now, in the twilight of his life, he worries that he has not fully discharged his duty to reconcile all the lost things with their owners. As the end nears, he bequeaths his secret life's mission to his unsuspecting housekeeper Laura, the one person he can trust to fulfil his legacy. But the final wishes of the Keeper of Lost Things have unforeseen repercussions that trigger a most serendipitous series of encounters . . .

MILLER'S VALLEY

Anna Quindlen

For generations, the Millers have lived in Miller's Valley, a small American town on the verge of enormous change. Mimi Miller describes her life, from the 1960s to the present, with intimacy and honesty, as though revealing it to the best friend she never had. As Mimi eavesdrops on her parents and quietly observes the people around her, she discovers more and more about the toxicity of family secrets, the dangers of gossip, the flaws of marriage, the inequalities of friendship, the risks of passion, loyalty and love. Home, as Mimi begins to realize, can be a place where it's just as easy to feel lost as it is to feel contented . . .

SLEEPING DOGS

SLEEPING DOGS

ED GORMAN

THORNDIKE
CHIVERS

This Large Print edition is published by Thorndike Press, Waterville, Maine, USA and by BBC Audiobooks Ltd, Bath, England.
Thorndike Press, a part of Gale, Cengage Learning.
The text of this Large Print edition is unabridged.
Other aspects of the book may vary from the original edition.
Set in 16 pt. Plantin.
Printed on permanent paper.

LIBRARY OF CONGRESS CATALOGING-IN-PUBLICATION DATA

Gorman, Edward.
    Sleeping dogs / by Ed Gorman.
      p. cm. — (Thorndike Press large print mystery)
    ISBN-13: 978-1-4104-0866-2 (hardcover : alk. paper)
    ISBN-10: 1-4104-0866-3 (hardcover : alk. paper)
    1. Large type books. 2. Political fiction. I. Title.
PS3557.O759S63 2008b
813'.54—dc22   2008015034

BRITISH LIBRARY CATALOGUING-IN-PUBLICATION DATA AVAILABLE

Published in 2008 in the U.S. by arrangement with St. Martin's Press, LLC.
Published in 2009 in the U.K. by arrangement with the Author.

U.K. Hardcover: 978 1 408 41259 6 (Chivers Large Print)
U.K. Softcover: 978 1 408 41260 2 (Camden Large Print)

Printed in the United States of America
1 2 3 4 5 6 7 12 11 10 09 08

To Kevin and Kate McCarthy

Every morning, to earn my bread,
I go to the market where lies are bought.
Hopefully
I take up my place among the sellers.

— BERTOLT BRECHT

Politics is a form of high entertainment and low comedy. It has everything. It's melo-dramatic, it's sinister and it has wonderful villains.

— RICHARD CONDON

ACKNOWLEDGMENTS

Thanks to Julie Hyzy for her help with the Chicago material.

And, as always, thanks to Linda Siebels for her tireless work on my manuscript.

CHAPTER 1

That morning two things happened right away. Chicago had a freak October snowstorm, and Phil Wylie, the man I'd replaced, was in the news. He'd committed suicide the night before.

The staffers up front were gathered in small groups. This was the headquarters for Reelect Senator Nichols, usually a busy and happy place.

It was obvious that Wylie had had a lot of friends here. The mourning, among men and women alike, charged the air with grief.

The staffers closest to the senator had joined him along with Mayor Daley for a breakfast saluting five men and women who'd once been drug addicts but who had managed to go three years without hitting up. Noble as it was, this kind of tribute always strikes me as cynical. This is exactly the kind of presentation politicians, even the good ones, choose for photo ops, as if it

11

were something they did that lent these people the courage and determination they needed to handle their new lives so well.

I was happy to be here, in the private office reserved for the chief staffers. I was the paid bogeyman, as the media had come to privately call all political consultants. That is one reason we stay away from cameras and microphones. Our presence just reminds reporters of how much campaign cash flows to various kinds of advisers, gurus, visionaries, and snake charmers. We've come a long way from Abe Lincoln, who wrote his own speeches on the backs of envelopes, no doubt about that.

I read the *Trib* and the *Sun-Times* on my computer. I also checked the log to see if we'd been mentioned on any of the local or regional TV or radio newscasts the previous evening. We had, but it was routine stuff — as were the mentions in the newspapers — so I went right on to see how the fund-raising was going.

The race was tightening. Jim Lake, our opponent, had once been dismissed as a histrionic nut job. But apparently he'd gone to sanity school recently. He'd gone more mainstream lately — he no longer demanded that teachers carry guns in inner-city schools — and that had no doubt helped him. But more than anything, he was a powerful presence on the stump and on TV. He was a damned good speaker. Senator Nichols, for all that I believed in his politics if not in him personally, was an efficient but uninspiring politician. It was a problem for us. Phil Wylie had handled Nichols's two congressional campaigns as well as his first senatorial one. I still had no real idea why they'd split so bitterly six months earlier. That was when my own consultant firm had been brought in.

I was just finishing up my third cup of coffee for the morning — thank God for McDonald's drive-thru — when Doris Baines, one of the local staffers who'd been with Warren since the days when he was an alderman here in Chicago, drifted back and said, "I wish you could have known him. Phil Wylie, I mean. He was one of the nicest, sweetest people I've ever known." Her nose and eyes were red. She tamped them occasionally with a Kleenex. "Everybody loved him."

She wanted to talk. I pushed back from my desk. "Anybody have any idea why he might have killed himself?"

She shook her head obstinately. "That's the thing. We kept in touch — everybody here with him, I mean. Every few weeks

13

we'd have dinner with him. He had a lot of friends — especially girlfriends — but lately he'd seemed pretty lonely. He had so much — he was so good-looking and so wealthy and he was always in the society pages for being at this gallery opening or this opera —" She started crying again. "But I guess it wasn't enough."

"I'm sorry I never got a chance to know him."

She started picking at her hands. Then smiled bitterly. "I remember what we all thought of him when Warren first brought him on. We thought he was this spoiled rich man. He drove a Maserati in those days and sometimes a Town Car would bring him to work. Those were in his drinking days. But once he got serious about working here, all that went away. He was just like the rest of us then —"

"With the exception of several million dollars."

A teary laugh. "Well, I guess you could say that. But you know what I mean. He worked harder than anybody else. He really believed in Warren."

"I don't think I ever got that story straight. Why'd he quit the campaign, anyway?"

Working her Kleenex around her eyes again. "You know, I've never been sure. The

14

official reason was that they'd disagreed on some political issue. But they'd disagreed so many times before — they'd really argue. I have two brothers and they were like that growing up. Argue all the time. But there was never any doubt about how much they loved each other. And Warren and Phil were like that. So I'm not sure we ever got the straight story. All that mattered was that Phil was gone. Everybody always turned to him. He was like our older brother. He always knew what to do."

"Nobody tried to patch things up between them?"

"Teresa did. She'd gone to college with Phil back east. They were great friends. In fact, Phil introduced her to Warren one summer when they were all home from college. That's how far back they went."

Teresa was the senator's wife. Unlike many spouses of important people, she was not one who envied her mate the spotlight. An elegant woman who was nimble in public as well, she was much better on the stump than Warren. And there was a sweetness about her that I always drew on when the day had gone on too long or too angrily. A good woman.

"He was a lot like you, Dev. Sort of a disillusioned idealist. He still wanted to believe that people would come to their senses and do the right thing. Even the bastards, if you just fought them hard enough."

Kenny Lane, another staffer, knocked on the window that let us look over the entire front part of the onetime supermarket that was our official campaign headquarters. He waved for Doris to come out.

"Well, I need to get to it. We'll all be a little slow this morning, Dev. It's really a blow."

By now, and even though I'd never spoken to the guy, I was starting to get a little dejected about his death, too.

CHAPTER 2

I put a gleaming silver fork into my rich red spaghetti. After my first bite, I hoisted my scotch and soda and said, "Raeburn, we're going to kick Lake's ass around the block tonight."

"My poor deluded friend. You'll be getting thirty sessions of electroshock after tonight. You'll be desperate to forget how bad old Nichols does. Did I ever tell you that he once put an entire stadium to sleep?"

"Uh-huh. Will these shock treatments come before or after your man withdraws from the race?"

"And why would he withdraw?"

"Because he can't take the shame of being on the stage with a man as superior as Nichols."

The place was the Italian Village in the Loop. My lunch buddy was Tom Raeburn, campaign manager for Jim Lake, our opponent. In high school we'd played basketball against each other. Only six months ago we had met up again when Raeburn, then a lobbyist for electric companies, had resigned his post to take on Lake's campaign.

Give Raeburn five thousand dollars to buy himself a custom-tailored suit and then watch the magical transformation that takes place. The moment Raeburn puts the suit on, it looks like something he bought at Sears for a hundred dollars. He's got the magic touch in reverse. He looks sweaty, disheveled, even a bit of a hayseed. Hard to imagine him in a room of sleek, gold-cuff-linked, tough-ass lobbyists trying to figure out how to slip the party in power a couple of mil under the table in the next year or so.

But I've always wondered if the seemingly guileless blue eyes, the almost juvenile way he laughs and tells jokes, and those moments when he just doesn't seem to understand something that's obvious to everybody else — I've always wondered if that's not part of a minutely constructed persona meant to deceive people into thinking that here's a rube they can run over at will.

Maybe the joke's on us.

"So how do you like living in a hotel, Dev?"

"I miss not having my books and my CDs,

but other than that, it's not bad at all. Room service up until midnight. Maid makes my bed every morning and cleans up really well. I don't have to live in my usual hovel."

"And speaking of hovels, my friend, our internals are looking mighty good. While yours are more hovel-like."

"Hovel-like?"

"I don't suppose your internal polls show you how badly you're slipping, do they?" He said this ostensibly as a joke, but we both knew better.

"Shows us holding steady. Six, seven points."

"I have to remind you what that lead was less than a month ago?"

"That's because you muzzled your man. He hasn't mentioned being abducted by aliens lately. He was bound to pick up."

"I admit he can get a little out there once in a while, but at least he only takes his pee-pee out to screw his wife and to piss. He doesn't cast his seed over half the country."

"Warren's changed."

"Sure he has."

"I'm serious."

"I know you are and that's what's so sad. You can't admit to yourself that he's a serial fornicator. Does the name Bill Clinton sound familiar? You know, if Nichols

19

could've kept his dick in his pants, he might have been your presidential nominee four years ago."

There was no disputing it. Despite the fact that he wasn't a great speaker, Warren Nichols was both handsome and imposing on the stump and in front of the camera. He had a manly charm that women loved and men were able to accept. Plus, he had, or so I believed anyway, a true sympathy for the people our system had long ago tossed aside. He'd come from great wealth, but his mother had managed to give him a social conscience. The summer right before the last national nominating convention, the two leading candidates had had the same number of delegates pledged to them. Warren was considered the alternative to both of them should the convention dead-lock. But forty-eight hours after the press dubbed him a serious spoiler, his own chances were spoiled when a sixth-grade teacher's husband came forward and said that Warren had slept with his wife and that he had subsequently divorced her. Warren was lucky to be elected to his Senate seat. His presidential dreams were over.

"People change."

"You know, I believe that, Dev. I really do. I have a brother who used to have the worst temper I ever saw. His wife told him to do something about it or she'd leave him. He started seeing a counselor. He isn't perfect but he's cut it back sixty, seventy percent. People do change. I just don't happen to think Nichols has."

"You're ruining my lunch."

He smiled at me. "You think I spoiled *this* meal, wait'll you try to eat breakfast tomorrow morning. Lake's going to do so well tonight, you won't be able to eat for days."

CHAPTER 3

I'd spent most of the afternoon in meetings. I needed to be alone. The light flurries that had swept into Chicago via Lake Michigan in the morning were now, by seven o'clock, heavy and relentless.

I was enjoying a one-person pizza and a beer in the parking lot of Wellington University, the Chicago college that tries hard to live down its previous rep for dumb rich kids drinking their way through four years of sex and mayhem. New dean, many new associate profs, several new endowments, and a public relations woman who was so good I was thinking of offering her a job in my political consulting firm.

I'd left the army after eight years of serving in the intelligence section, where I'd basically been a gumshoe reporting on suspicious people who seemed to have undue interest in various domestic military installations. Because my father had been a four-term congressman before his death, and because I had an uncle in the consulting business, I signed on as a copartner in a political shop. In four years we'd won five seats, two in the Senate and three in the House. We were attracting national notice these days.

Even back in my army days, I'd learned that if you wanted to be left absolutely alone, turn off your cell, park your car in the center of a huge empty lot, and enjoy your solitude.

I sat in my car in the parking lot near the building where tonight's televised debate would be held. Right now, with an hour to go before the stage was lit and the candidates took their places, the lot was almost completely empty except for a truck moving back and forth, with a rack of evil yellow headlights shining on its roof and a snowplow on its front.

Warren's campaign manager, Kate Bishop, had called earlier and said that there was something she wanted to tell me tonight. I was of course curious.

As the truck scraped the snow away, I reached over and took the small silver flask from the glove compartment. I'd been needing a lot more of this stuff lately.

Eventually the plow deserted this particular lot and I was left in the darkness, two drinks down and with the kind of pinpoint headache just above my right eye I always get when I have this kind of anxiety. Performance anxiety — Warren's performance tonight. It needed to be good.

I put the flask back in the glove compartment, I shut off the engine, I slid out of the car, locked the door, and stood for a minute, letting the snowflakes snap at my face like so many mosquitoes. The cold air redeemed me, chased a lot of my fear and most of my headache away. I felt one of those movie bursts of confidence where the hero shakes his fist at the heavens and shouts in triumph. Warren was going to kick Congressman Jim Lake's ass tonight in the debate. For one wonderful moment I was sure of it. Absolutely sure of it.

Backstage was crowded with technicians, makeup people, and the staffers who'd come with the three newspeople who'd ask questions in the final segment. All of them on the move at one time. We'd been in the auditorium twice in the past thirty-six hours. I'd wanted Warren to get used to the feel of the stage, to his physical relationship to the seats where the audience would sit.

Lake was a crooked bastard and the errand boy for every mercenary corporation in the state, but he had the kind of table-pounding, self-righteous, easy-solution bravado that, kept under control, came off well on the tube. A man who knew his own mindlessness, as one pundit had recently noted. And Warren was going to expose all that tonight. The overnights would show that we'd picked up a few points.

Yesterday afternoon we'd spent two hours here, just Nichols and myself, going over the points that would most likely be raised in the debate. Instead of nerves, I noticed a kind of distracted quality in both his eye contact and his delivery. As if his mind was on something else.

A scent of sandalwood. A gentle hand on my arm. A whisper in my ear: "If I wasn't so beautiful, I just might let you sleep with me."

I kissed Kate Bishop on the cheek. She hadn't been kidding about her beauty. Hitchcock's gleaming blonde, that Grace Kelly upper-crust attitude that just missed arrogance. Tonight she wore a black sheath. Her golden hair was drawn back into a chignon. She was the world's most elegant single mom. She had a three-year-old daughter whom she kept under a nanny's lock and key. She'd been with Warren one

25

term in Congress and during his first term in the Senate.

We were buffeted, jostled, bumped by streams of people rushing to get everything ready in the remaining forty-two minutes before airtime.

She was knocked against me. My arm went automatically around her waist to steady her and draw her near.

"Well, I guess we've both had our thrill for the evening," she laughed. "I'm going through the vapors right now."

"Me, too." Then, "So what were you going to tell me tonight?"

She put her soft lips to my ear, the scent of sandalwood arousing me not only to lust but to a strange kind of melancholy, and whispered, "I'm getting worried about Laura. The last couple days I caught her in the ladies' room really crying."

"Got any idea what's wrong?"

"No. But I think we both better keep an eye on her."

Then she took my hand and said, "Let's go see the lord and master."

Senator Warren Douglas Nichols had what looked like a lobster bib stuffed in his shirt collar. It was a piece of crinkly paper fitted so that none of the makeup being applied would get on his clothes.

His eyes were closed as the young makeup woman finished dabbing around his cheeks and eyebrows. He was a trim, good-looking man of fifty-six with the kind of Harvard virility Jack and Bobby Kennedy had. He was old Illinois money, the kind that made his great-grandfather a close friend of the most prominent men of his time, including the Wrigleys, the McCormicks, and the Searses.

"It'd help if you sat still," the makeup woman said gently. She was very young, very slender, pretty in a wan, wounded sort of way, a bit nervous and uncertain of herself when she had to give Warren an order. She wore an emerald-green sweater that set off her dark hair perfectly. And dark jeans that showed her slender body to be rich with soft curves.

Billy Hannigan, our chief speechwriter, and Laura Wu, our communications director, sat in canvas-backed director's chairs talking to Warren as we came in. Billy was one of the best speechwriters I'd ever worked with. He'd been able to give Warren a voice he'd never had before, a way of improving the presentation by choosing simpler and stronger words for Warren to speak. He was invaluable. And you could

27

send him out to fix problems in the field.

Warren faked a frown and said in a mock unhappy voice, and more to himself than to us, "They're supposed to be calming me down, but all they're doing is making me more nervous. And now she wants me to sit still."

"We told him no sex jokes onstage tonight," Billy said. A black Irishman of twenty-seven, Billy was a Rutgers man and proud of it, as you could tell by all the T-shirts, sweatshirts, hats, and scarves he wore bearing the Rutgers logo.

"We also told him not to refer to Lake as 'my asshole opponent' for the first five minutes," Laura joked. She was a slender Asian beauty, usually confined in designer suits. She'd done undergraduate work at Dartmouth and graduate work at George Washington. Laura and Billy were both critical to the success Nichols had had in his first term.

Nichols raised a glass of Diet Pepsi to his lips, forcing the makeup woman to take a step back. Apparently she didn't want to get drenched if he got too wild with his drink. I wondered what she'd say to her friends about *us*. Probably that we were a bunch of overpaid wusses. And she wouldn't be wrong.

"Never get between him and his Diet Pepsi," Kate said.

Warren puckered his lips. Made a face. "The ice cubes have all melted down in this glass. Tastes like hell."

"See all the traumas he faces every day?" Laura said to the makeup woman.

Gabe Colby came in just then. Gabe was the policy wonk and second-best speechwriter we had. Given the long graying hair he wore in a ponytail, the collarless shirts, and the vests and the jeans that were his daily attire, you might guess correctly that he longed for the days of takin' it to the streets. He was one of those men of the sixties generation who believed that they'd never had a fair chance of turning our government into a utopia of acid with Jimi Hendrix images plastered on public buildings. He always smelled of cigarettes and sweat. It was easy to dismiss him as an angry, aging hippie, but the sorrow in his dark eyes was too vivid for tossing him overboard that way. I had no idea what the source of his grief was, only that it was a terrible burden for him.

"Hey, Gabe," Billy said. "Ready to see Lake get his ass kicked around the block tonight?"

Gabe wasn't a cheerleader. He just

shrugged and said, "Sure hope so."

Kate and Laura patted him. One on the back, one on the arm. You couldn't watch him without wanting to help him in some way. But he sure was up on the issues. He could probably give Google a good run.

Warren set the glass down on the table next to him, then assessed himself in the large round mirror that road show actors made themselves up in. "God, I'm looking old. That's another thing that bothers me. Lake's ten years younger."

"Yes," Kate said, "but you're thirty years smarter. Once he gets off the subject of his support for the NRA, the antigay groups, and the talk-radio fascists, he won't have much to say."

"Do you suppose he'll be wearing his Nazi armband tonight?" Billy quipped.

"The senator here still won't go for my idea," I said. "When he walks out he breaks into a rap song and then lights up a joint. Get the eighteen- to thirty-five-year-olds."

"Hey, that'd be great," Laura said. "And every time he looks at Lake, he says, 'Hey, you my bitch.' "

Nichols smiled. "I appreciate you people trying to cheer me up, but I have to admit I'm scared as hell. I just wish I was a better speaker."

"You don't have to go out there and wave the flag, Warren," I said. "Just be yourself. You've got a good record, we're ahead in the run-up to the election, and Lake always overplays everything. That's why he scares so many people."

He sighed, waving his hand to silence me. "Lake's gotten better on the stump. You can't deny that." His gaze touched on every one of us. "None of you will say it, but that's what's going on here. Even if we're ahead, I have to be damned good tonight."

"You've got to forget everything but the debate tonight, Warren," Kate said. "We didn't have this conversation. Nothing negative even entered your mind tonight. You're a handsome, articulate, manly, caring person who has a genuine need to help people who need help. And you know what's in this country's best interests and aren't afraid to stand up and say it. That's what you've got to remember tonight."

A sad smile. "I wish I could send you out there, Kate. You made me want to stand up and salute just then."

"All done," the makeup woman said.

"I should've introduced you," Nichols said. "This is Megan Caine, everybody. Billy tells me Megan is a registered member of our party and does work on commercials."

31

"Megan, you tell him he's going to do a great job tonight," Kate said.

Megan looked surprised that she'd been brought into the conversation. She even seemed a bit embarrassed. "Well, *I'm* sure going to vote for him. I don't trust Lake at all."

"That's what we need to hear," Billy said.

Megan opened her makeup kit and put away the pieces she'd needed to get Nichols ready for the lights and camera. "Well," she said, still sounding a little embarrassed, "good night, everybody."

We all said our good-byes as we watched her leave the small room, closing the door quietly behind her.

"Very nice woman," Nichols said. "I think she actually calmed me down a little."

He stood up in his starched white shirt with red-and-blue rep tie, blue suspenders, and blue suit pants. He walked over to the hangers and took his suit coat down.

"Ravishing as always?" he said.

"The ladies will be rushing the stage," Laura said.

"Well, as long as that includes my wife," he said. "I always feel better with her in the audience." He paused. Thought of something. "You know, I haven't had a cigarette in fifteen years but right now I'd sure as

32

hell like one."

"You do good tonight," Kate said, "and we'll buy you a carton of Camels."

"Oh, God no," Warren said. "I know that if I smoked even one cigarette, my nicotine habit would come roaring back. I'd be up to a pack and a half a day in no time."

The knock. It could have been anybody at the door but we all knew better. Billy was closest, so he opened it. A man with a headset on said, "We need the senator on-stage so we can get the final lighting set."

"Thanks," Billy said, closing the door again.

Nichols went into his breathing exercises. Deep inhalations, deep exhalations. He insisted that these helped, and if they did, I was all for them.

Laura stepped over and gave his suit coat a close inspection. Dandruff, dust, bird shit — who knew what she was looking for. But whatever it was, she brought her steely focus to the task.

Kate worked on his tie. There was a gap between the top of his shirt and the knot. She wanted to make the gap disappear and apparently it took some doing. He made a joke about her trying to strangle him but she didn't laugh. When work was at hand, Laura and Kate were heat-seeking missiles.

All you could do was get out of their way.

"There," she said.

Warren directed his next words to me. "I don't make any weird faces this time, right, Dev?"

"Right. No matter what he says, you don't mug. You just stand there straight and tall. You're the adult. Leave all the drama to him." Lake was one of those pols who enjoyed eye-rolling, forehead-slapping, and premeditated frowning. All the time his opponent was giving his response, Lake was doing his version of a Three Stooges episode. Unfortunately, Warren had started doing some of the same thing during the last debate.

"And I never use the phrase 'average American.'"

"Right again. Because that's a phrase he uses all the time. What I want you to do tonight is wait for him to use it and then say that there's no such thing as an 'average American.' That each man and woman in our society is an individual and should be treated as such. And that's why his proposal to suspend certain constitutional rights we have is so dangerous. Because we have the right to act as individuals, think the way we want to, express ourselves the way we want to, and he wants to take that away from us

34

while pretending it's because of terrorism."

"You could knock him dead with that one," Billy said. "Even if he doesn't wear his Nazi armband, people will know what you're talking about."

"That's enough tutoring," Kate said. "Information overload. Now he just needs to get out there and relax and do what comes naturally."

"I love it when people talk about me in the third person — when I'm standing right next to them."

Kate stuck her tongue out at him. They exchanged smirks.

Laura took his arm and said, "I'll walk out with you, Senator."

"Well, I can't go wrong there, a pretty woman like you on my arm."

"I'll go with you," Billy said.

And Gabe said, "Me, too."

They left.

Naturally, I turned to Kate and said, "So you don't have any idea what's bothering Laura?"

"Not really. Laura keeps everything to herself."

"Well, I'll keep a closer watch on her. See if I can figure anything out." I glanced at my watch. "We better get to the auditorium."

She took my hand. Squeezed it. "God, I hope he doesn't fuck it up tonight."

CHAPTER 4

I once had a congressional client who thought I should pick out a comely maiden in the crowd and bring her backstage after the speech was over. You know, the way Elvis used to have his Memphis boys do it. I gave him a choice. I could function as his consultant or his pimp, but I couldn't do both such taxing jobs at the same time. He took my point but he wasn't happy about it. One day after he won the election he fired me.

I once had a senatorial client who took so many personal flights on corporate jets that his own staffers joked that he needed to register as a lobbyist.

I once had a congressional client who was a virulent supporter of civil rights but would not eat in a place where black people worked in the kitchen and would not shake hands with gay men for fear of AIDS.

They come in all shapes, sizes, and degrees

of greed, lust, megalomania, pettiness, treachery, and — never underestimate this factor — plain stupidity. In other words, they're pretty much like the rest of us. Sometimes you're amazed that a pol you've always thought of as a dreadful hack on the other side of the aisle will do something so noble it's breathtaking. Likewise, you'll see one of your own do something so cynical and underhanded, you're genuinely shocked and wonder if you know this man or woman at all.

Part of my job as a consultant is to simply babysit and hand-hold. The congressional staffs do the same thing. The more focused the public event, the more danger there is. Tonight I was wishing I'd brought a cyanide capsule along to put under my tongue in case things went badly. One tiny little bite on the capsule and I'd be out of my misery.

We were seated in the front seats, aisle right. Lake's people were seated aisle left. We all waved and smiled at each other, of course, resisting the impulse to flip each other off and then rush across the aisle and beat the holy shit out of each other.

Both groups were well-dressed, excited. They didn't hope to learn anything. They just wanted to see a career destroyed. The other fellow's. Of course. They wanted that single slip of the tongue that would forever paint the candidate as a clown. Fodder for comedians, pundits, and editorial writers. These were political gladiators up onstage tonight and they'd damned well better make it bloody.

A few of Lake's staffers glanced over at me and made faces insinuating that they felt sorry for me. That Warren was doomed. Not if he just stuck to the prep we'd given him. Staff and consultants alike spend hundreds of hours sifting through information from many sources trying to define a few issues that their man or woman can base a campaign on. Some of the time the issues are obvious. Other times you have to manufacture an issue. The other side is generally better at this because their voters like bombast. They can plug in to talk radio and pick up two or three issues a day. Our side likes to think of itself as more noble and sophisticated. Even if this is true, and it certainly isn't true all the time, noble and sophisticated can easily translate into boring. Think of our last four or five presidential candidates.

For all the prep we did with him, Warren was actually better when he didn't stick to the prep. When he spoke simply and directly and passionately about his beliefs. The

39

problem was, once he got away from the talking points, he tended to wander and sometimes get lost. Time was a big factor — a sixty-second response in many instances — so he had to be concise.

I wanted to get up and pace. Sort of tough to do when you're sitting in a theater chair. I had a bad feeling about tonight. But then I had a bad feeling about every night. I suppose it's the consultant's version of flop sweat.

The debate was only a few minutes away, the audience packing the seats, the three journalists in place onstage and ready with their questions, and the microphones being tested and tested again. The atmosphere was that of a prizefight.

Kate leaned in and said, "I wish I'd gotten drunk for this." She was feeling the pressure, too.

"Just smoke a couple of joints."

She smiled and socked me in the arm. "Can you imagine what the press would do if I lit up a joint now?"

"They're just as worried as we are," I said, indicating the row where the upper echelon of Lake's staffers sat.

"If they are, they're hiding it better."

And that was true. Our half row of people was decidedly reserved, where the Lake

people were laughing and grinning and jab-
bering away at people around them. They
were treating this like party time.

Gabe was staring off. If he was interested
in anything around us, he wasn't letting on.

The woman representing the university
then walked to center stage with a hand
microphone. She offered a pleasant, studied
smile to the anxious audience and then went
to work.

"I'm very happy to see that we have a full
house for this very important debate tonight. I'd first like to thank the Wellington
people for letting us use this beautiful new
auditorium and for helping us bring this
event to the public. They went above and
beyond in making sure that we got everything we requested. And the same for state
public television. They sent some of their
best people here for three full days to give
the candidates a chance to get used to the
stage and the lighting and standing at the
lecterns. The two gentlemen we're bringing
you tonight are under a lot of pressure to
do well this evening, so having the opportunity to be familiar with the physical
setup is a blessing for all of us, not just the
crew."

She moved downstage to where the three
reporters were sitting at a long desk. Be-

cause they faced the stage, we could see them only by watching the big monitors suspended from the ceiling on both sides of the apron.

She introduced each journalist with abundant praise and then said, "Now let me present our guests for this evening."

They appeared quickly, resolutely, both of them swollen with fake confidence and toothy swagger, both blue-suited, hair-spray neat, red-white-and-blue happy to be here among the voters. They'd both likely peed their pants twice already.

The walk to the lectern went fine until Nichols stumbled when he was about three feet away from it. The audience gasped when it looked as if he might fall, then laughed when he not only righted himself but risked a courtly bow. He'd saved the moment. No need to put the cyanide capsule under my tongue just yet.

"That was really nice," Laura whispered to me.

"Oh, yeah," I said, "you can't underestimate the value of a good stumble."

"Oh, you."

The hostess kept the bios brief. Each man got fulsome applause from his side of the aisle. They stood firm accepting it, gripping the lecterns as if they were guiding a ship through turbulent waters. They knew better than to smile as their applause peaked. It would look too Hollywood.

The debate, though it really wasn't a debate at all, just a Q&A, began with the downstate reporter asking Warren if he regretted cosponsoring a bill that would have lessened mandatory prison terms for first-time drug users. "No regrets at all. If it's proved that they were merely using and not selling, then confining them to prison is a waste of their lives and taxpayer money. The prison population is too big now because of mandatory sentencing. Even the ABA has come to question the fairness of five-year terms for possessing a small amount of pot or crack."

Jim Lake, guardian of all that was right and holy, was quick to respond. "I have one question for my friend Warren Nichols. How can we be sure that a person is simply a user? Maybe all the police could *find* was a small amount. But maybe somewhere this person has a lot more than that. Maybe this person, unbeknownst to the justice system, is a major dealer. And maybe this person that Warren is so concerned for — maybe this is the same person who, allowed to walk the streets, will be the one who gets your son or daughter hooked on narcotics for life.

I don't have to tell you what a miserable life it is for every family member when one of their own becomes an addict. I have good friends who are going through this very thing right now."

The fucker. I was against mandatory sentencing in most applications. But his answer had been much more dynamic and dramatic than Warren's.

And so it went.

The military, foreign policy, tax cuts, sex education classes in public schools, the influence of big business on Congress — you're always waiting for one of the journalists to lay your client out with a question so unexpected that you see, depending on how he answers it, a career hanging in the balance.

In the first twenty of fifty-five minutes, nothing extraordinary was asked or answered. They both were being given time to settle in, get more comfortable, so that as the hour progressed, they'd be better prepared to start laying the heavy-duty accusations and smears on their opponent.

The audience had been instructed not to applaud, so the candidates' voices were clear and distinct in the auditorium. The twenty-minute mark was reached, several more familiar questions asked, several more

44

familiar responses given. Lake, a five-ten former Purdue running back and, unlike Warren, a very physical man, writhed under the constraints of politeness. His consultants had told him, as I'd told Warren, to start doing the drive-by shooting just about now. Lake was ready to blow up an orphanage if need be. All I could hope for was that his "opposition research" people hadn't come up with anything we didn't already know about.

Then I noticed Warren weaving as he stood at the lectern. At first I assumed his back was sore from standing so rigidly and he was just trying to loosen up when the camera was off him. But very soon not only was the weaving more pronounced, so was the way his head was angling to the right. He seemed groggy, like a prizefighter suddenly stunned by a punch from nowhere. He'd been hurt and maybe badly.

I don't know if I was the first to notice it or simply the first to make note of it out loud. The swaying got more pronounced. Whispers from the audience. Now he wasn't merely placing his hands on either side of the lectern — he appeared to be gripping it desperately in an attempt to stay upright. If I didn't know better, I'd say he was drunk.

"Something's wrong," I muttered to Kate.

And then another problem: He started slurring his words. Now he not only appeared drunk, he sounded it, too.

"What the hell's wrong with him?" Laura said.

"Shit," Billy said.

"Dev, you've got to do something," Kate said. And then she shook her elegant head and said, "Sorry. That was stupid. There isn't anything any one of us can do."

By now the entire audience was aware of Warren's problems. Not only was there whispering, there were also sniggers and the occasional outright laugh. Everybody was remembering the way he'd stumbled on his way to the lectern.

Lake started glancing over at Nichols with a kind of gentlemanly concern. He was playing it just right. Not scorn, not mocking, but alarmed that there might be something wrong with Nichols. *What a good and decent man this Lake is,* you hear Mom and Pop at home saying. *He looks like he's genuinely concerned.* No need for *his* consultant to pop a cyanide capsule in his mouth.

Stage left I could see the hostess appear for a closer look at Warren. Her body language said that she was as worried as we were. She glanced at the journalists.

"Senator," the Chicago newspaperman

46

said, "when you first ran for this seat four years ago, you promised the voters that you would make certain that funding for special-needs students would be doubled if not tripled. But in fact in the projected presidential budget, it's been cut by twenty-five percent. Is that a major disappointment to you? And if so, what do you plan to do about it?"

There are moments in prizefights when you see that one man has no idea where he is or maybe even *who* he is. That was Warren at this point. His head was rolling around on his shoulders cartoon-style, his eyes were fighting to stay open, and one of his hands slid off the edge of the lectern so that he seemed to lose balance.

"Did he have a stroke maybe?" Laura said. I think we were all wondering the same thing.

The woman from the university reappeared and rushed over to him. And just in time. He seemed ready to collapse.

And here came the cavalry.

Lake quickly crossed the distance between lecterns and got his arm around Warren, lowering him gently to the floor. The consultant part of me thought: *This'll be on the Internet within fifteen minutes. And it'll generate thousands and thousands of hits within the first hour it appears.*

Lake played doctor, checking Warren's pulse, neck and wrist, putting an ear to Warren's heart, feeling Warren's forehead, apparently for fever.

People in the audience were standing now, trying to see what was going on up onstage. The monitors had been killed. There was no more laughter; instead, fear filled both sides of the theater. Death is something we all have in common. And right now everybody in the audience was terrified by its sudden dominion. Maybe he wasn't drunk, after all. Maybe he'd really had a heart attack.

Lake had never had a better moment. Even I had to approve of the way he whipped off his suit coat and balled it up to serve as a pillow for Warren's head. Even I had to approve of the way he gently raised Warren's arm for a second time and checked for a pulse again. Even I had to approve of the way he got Warren's shirt open and tossed away the necktie.

But my admiration was short-lived. I couldn't afford it. The man on the floor was my client. And no matter what it was that had felled him, the heretofore mad-dog opponent had gone out there tonight an also-ran and come back a star.

I tried to estimate in my rattled way how many points in the polls he was picking up. Two? Three? God, could he pick up five? And then when I saw what he was about to do, I had to wonder if he could possibly pick up seven.

Because he was about to perform — right on TV, right in everybody's home, right in front of God — CPR on Senator Warren Nichols.

No, he's not some full-mooner lunatic. He's a strong and compassionate man we can trust and have confidence in. No, I don't agree with some of his positions, but that doesn't matter when I've just seen what he's made of. He's the kind of guy you'd want for your next-door neighbor.

The only thing we were spared was the CPR. By then a real live doctor had run up the four steps on the west side of the stage and was tending to Warren. Was that a brief hint of disappointment on Lake's face?

Probably.

CHAPTER 5

Ambulance.

Teresa Nichols rushed backstage from the audience, joining Kate, Laura, Gabe, and Billy as they stood next to the techs loading the gurney bearing the senator into the rear of the vehicle. Red emergency lights gleaming, stink of medicines from inside the ambulance, exhaust pipe propelling snowflakes into the darkness. Nose-freezing temperature. Winds that had already knocked down a lot of freestanding signage. Sand trucks now joining snowplows.

From what I could see when I got out there, Warren was either asleep or comatose. He showed few signs of life.

Teresa Nichols, a shining blonde who vaguely resembled an older Kate in certain ways, huddled under her fashionable blue winter coat and said, "I want to go with him."

The female driver nodded. "Sure thing,

Mrs. Nichols. Let me help you up here."

Teresa glimpsed me over her shoulder. "I have your cell number, Dev. I'll keep you informed from the hospital. I know you'll be busy here." Then she disappeared inside.

Kate, Laura, Gabe, and Billy escaped. I made a couple phone calls on my cell. By the time I reached the hall, a small lynch mob of reporters had gathered. They wouldn't bother to find Kate when I was at hand. I put up my hands as if surrendering and let their questions rip and tear and rend me with their imbecility. It wouldn't do any good to point out that they'd seen exactly what I had and thus knew exactly as much as I did. They insisted that I knew something I didn't.

"Have you been keeping any of the senator's health secrets from the public?"

"No."

"Does the senator like to take a drink once in a while?"

"That's not the question you're asking. You want to know if the senator has a problem with alcohol. The answer is no. And I'll save you some time — he doesn't have a problem with any kind of drug dependency. Period."

"Did you see him before the debate tonight?"

"Yes. And he acted fine."

"Do you have any idea what happened to him?"

"None."

"Would you agree that Congressman Lake showed people that he's not the crackpot your campaign has implied?"

" 'Crackpot' is your term, not ours. We've had and will continue to have disagreements over policy with Congressman Lake, but right here and now I want to thank him for all he did for Senator Nichols tonight. It shows that he's a man of great character."

I wanted to puke, of course. But that probably wouldn't have looked good to the folks at home.

Finally, the police got there and broke it up. This press conference, that was up to us. But it would have to be in another part of the building. For now, move along.

Twenty minutes later I was standing outside the back door of the auditorium letting the cold and the snow have at me. Once again the elements revived me. So much had happened in so little time that I hadn't had the chance to sort through it. The cyanide capsule was sounding better all the time.

The doc from the audience had been under the impression that the senator had suffered a stroke or heart attack. That was his first judgment. But as his examination continued he said he wasn't sure. He obviously regretted his first assessment. He'd not only looked foolish, he might even have left himself open to some kind of lawsuit. I felt sorry for him.

I thought through his second judgment, that he was no longer sure. But if it hadn't been a heart attack or stroke, what *had* it been? An aneurysm? I wasn't a doctor, I didn't even play one on TV. So my speculation was useless.

But being the cynic I am, my thoughts shifted from medicine back to politics. Not much doubt about who'd looked best tonight. There would be worry and sympathy for Nichols — despite the closeness of the race, he was a respected man in Illinois — but it would be Jim Lake who got the coveted John Wayne Award for the evening. The manly way he'd strode across the stage to grab Warren and keep him from toppling. The heroic way he'd helped the incapacitated man to the floor. And then — the sonofabitch — the way he'd returned to the stage (the cameras on him of course) and said, "I think we need to say a prayer here for a very good man we all have a lot of respect for. This isn't a time for politics, this is a time for joining together in asking God to spare the life of a true patriot and an honest politician."

The Internet. The cable nets. All the major newspapers. Slots very near the top on the evening news. And editorials across the land commending Congressman Jim Lake — who was happy to let pollution, global warming, racial discrimination, hate crimes against gays, ridiculous bank loan rates, and much more prosper on and on indefinitely — for being an example of what Jefferson and John Adams and whatever other boozers had in mind when they first got together to write the Constitution.

Tonight, a star was born. Phony as hell, most likely, but tricked up as it was, it had played beautifully for the camera.

Then I looked at it the way an army intelligence officer would in gathering facts for a report. Had it all been coincidence? If the audience doc wasn't sure it had been a heart attack or stroke, what had it been? What if what we saw onstage hadn't been an accident? This was politics, after all, and in the era of Karl Rove, just about anything you could get away with was the order of the day. (And the Clinton machine of personal destruction had been a good warm-up act to Rove.) So you had motive

— to sideline your opponent and make it look accidental. And who stood to gain? Why, the John Wayne Award winner himself, Jim Lake.

Image: Warren in the dressing room making a face when he swallowed the Pepsi. He'd complained that it tasted bad.

Image: The young makeup woman dabbing makeup on Warren's cheeks, his glass of Pepsi very near her elbow.

Image: Chic Kate saying, "God, I hope he doesn't fuck it up tonight."

Behind me, her voice ragged with the cold and snow, Laura said, "We're going back inside, Dev. It's too cold out here."

Laura said to Billy, "People survive heart attacks all the time, Billy."

But something about the heart attack scenario bothered me. Bothered me a lot.

CHAPTER 6

I'd asked Billy, Kate, Gabe, and Laura to wait in the hall while I worked alone in the makeup room. Occupational paranoia had set in. You couldn't trust anybody, not even your closest staff members. They were privy to everything — our stands on issues, our media buys, our schedule, who we had waiting in the wings to endorse us, how the money flow was going, and, most important of all, if there was some whisper of scandal we were trying to cover up. And each of them had had the opportunity to be in here alone earlier in the evening. I wanted to check things out myself. But my search was a waste of time.

When I came out of the dressing room, I said, "Did any of you happen to catch the last name of the makeup woman?"

They each took a turn at saying no.

"Which of you got to the room first?"

Billy shrugged. "I guess I did. Why?"

"Was she there when you got there?"

"Uh-huh."

"Are you going to tell us what's going on, Dev?"

"Who was there, Billy?"

"Just her. The senator got there a few minutes later."

"How did she introduce herself to you?"

"Just said she was the makeup lady."

"Nothing else?"

He paused. "Uh, let's see . . . Oh, she said she was a big fan of the senator's and that she'd voted for him before and wanted to vote for him this time, too."

"And nothing else? You're sure?"

"I'm sure."

"We should be going to the hospital," Kate said.

"Good idea. You folks get over there. I'll be about twenty minutes or so behind you."

"I wish you'd tell us what's going on," Kate said. "Obviously you suspect something."

"I don't want to say anything until I've got a little more information."

One of the crew members walked halfway down the hall and said, "There are two detectives out here who'd like to talk to you."

"Thanks," I said. "Kate, why don't you

talk to them?"

"They'll want to know about today. How he was acting and everything. You saw him a lot more than I did."

"I need to talk to somebody else. You saw what I saw. You saw more, in fact, since you were in the makeup room longer. And you're the campaign manager. You're the public face. And Laura's the communications director."

"We're going to lose this argument, Kate. We may as well give in."

"Thanks for speaking up for me, Laura. We all want to get to the hospital as soon as possible. Teresa has my cell number. You heard her. She'll keep in touch."

"Yeah," Billy said, "but that doesn't mean that you'll tell us anything she said."

"Let's get going," I said.

I walked to the opposite end of the hall and took a short staircase down to the main floor. I was looking for the woman who'd seemed to be in charge of the event. I remembered seeing a line of glassed-in offices to the right of the stage.

She was on the phone when I walked in. She was saying, with strained patience, "I don't know anything more than I've told you. I don't want to be quoted as saying it was a stroke or heart attack, because I don't know for sure what it was." She signaled for me to take a chair in front of her desk. "Of course he wasn't drunk." Pause. "Everybody saw what happened onstage. He obviously had some kind of medical problem that I can't speak to. If you want that kind of information, you should call the hospital." Pause. "It's not my problem that the hospital won't release information. He's probably only been there for ten minutes or so. Now, I'm really busy, all right?"

As she hung up, she said, "God. I'm beginning to wonder if the idea of a free press isn't better in theory than in practice." Then she laughed. "Don't quote me on that. I'm all for a free press, of course. It's just when they start moving in on you —"

Her oblong name plaque on the desk read PAULINE DOYLE. She was probably forty or so, a few pounds overweight, with wonderful little teeth that gleamed when her full lips parted. In her dramatic dark blue dress with a slash of lighter blue stretching from the left shoulder to the right hip, she was definitely in the desirable category.

After I introduced myself, she said, "Any word on the senator?"

"Not yet."

"I couldn't believe it. No matter how you prepare for these things, you never quite know how to respond."

"You can't prepare for anything like this. I just hope he's all right."

"Would you like some coffee?" she asked, inclining her head in the direction of a Mr. Coffee.

"No, thanks. I just wanted to ask you about the makeup woman we used."

"Oh, yes. Megan, uh, Caine."

"Do you use her regularly here?"

"I guess I'm confused about that."

"Oh? Why?"

"First of all, I'd never heard of her before. But second, somebody in your office called me yesterday and said that you wanted your own makeup person and that this Megan Caine would be here tonight promptly at six-thirty."

"Does that happen very often? That people bring their own makeup person?"

"Depends. Some do, some don't. I wouldn't say it's common, but it's not unusual, either."

"And my office called."

She leaned toward me, her eyes apprehensive. "I hope I didn't do anything wrong."

"I don't suppose the person who called gave you a name."

"Uh, Frank something, as I recall. I didn't see any reason to write it down. I'm sorry."

"You don't have anything to be sorry for."

Her phone bleated. "Oh, Lord, it'll be another reporter."

I stood up and smiled. "I wish I could help you. And thanks."

Near the back door a couple of undergrads, girl and boy, clipboards in hand, worked along two racks of costumes from the theater department. Apparently they were cataloging what they had. I watched them as I approached. Before they wrote anything on the clipboards, they examined the particular garment extensively. Whoever had ordered the catalog wanted a lot of information about each entry. There must have been thirty costumes each on the long racks. They were both about halfway done.

"Excuse me," I said, "I wondered if you saw our makeup lady leave here a while ago." I told them who I was and said that she'd left some of her things in the dressing room and I wanted to get them to her before she left. I described her to them.

The boy, wearing a crew cut that would have marked him a BMOC back in '58, hadn't seen her, but the girl, an attractive but awfully thin twenty-something, said, "I saw her. She had some trouble getting her car started. She parked right behind the door out here, which, technically, she wasn't supposed to do."

"Fast getaway," the boy said, not knowing how right he was.

"Did you happen to look out the door and actually see her car?"

"Oh, sure. Rob here went to get us a snack. So while he was gone I went out on the steps and asked her if I could help her. She looked like a nice woman, actually. Very pretty. Probably just a few years older than I am."

"Did you notice anything special about her car?"

"Well, it was an old clunker," the girl said. "Really pitted out. The car was brown but the door on the driver's side didn't match. It was gray."

"Would you happen to mean primer?"

"I guess I don't know what that is," she said.

I explained primer to her.

"Oh, I see. Sure, it could've been that. Like it was ready to be painted. Though I sure wouldn't waste any money on a clunker like that."

"You notice anything else about her or the car?"

"Hey," the boy said. I'd pushed too hard and suddenly all three of us realized it.

"Why're you asking so many questions?" the girl said.

"I'd like to see some ID," the boy said.

I obliged him. "In case I'm a Russian spy?"

He scanned my license and then showed it to the girl. "How do we know you're really with Senator Nichols?"

"Pauline Doyle is just down the hall. You can go ask her."

Both of them lost their confidence now. I must have offered the right name.

Girl looked at boy, boy looked at girl. Girl said, "Well, she had a big sack in the front seat from a store named the Daily Double Discount. It's this kind of tacky little store over by Riverdale."

She surprised me. The makeup girl was very white, very middle-class. Riverdale was a grim place for someone like her. "I worked with an outreach program our class did last summer with poor black kids. The store was nearby."

This was about all I was going to get. I thanked them and started off to the lot where I'd parked my car.

Just as I opened the door and stepped outside into the whipping snow, my cell beeped.

Kate said, "They've got Warren in an examination room now. This place is a zoo with reporters. But one of the doctors in the ER told me that they were checking for a heart attack or stroke. But he also said they run tests looking for every possibility."

"I'm on my way," I said.

CHAPTER 7

Kate hadn't been exaggerating about the press. I had to push, shove, even kidney punch my way through the pack to get to the ER registration desk, where a surly nurse said, after I'd introduced myself, "You better be who you say you are. Two of them —" Her eyes took in the phalanx of reporters, videocams, recorders, and still cameras that I'd just escaped. The only thing that stopped them from overrunning and sacking the ER was the lone and nervous-looking uniformed security guard. "Two of them tried to pass themselves off as interns. They were so stupid they couldn't answer the first question I asked them."

Now I understood why she was so surly. The press can be a juggernaut that can unhinge the strongest of people. They'd descended on this poor woman and undone her. Her face gleamed with sweat and her gaze was jittery and bitter.

Billy rescued me. He'd wandered here from somewhere down the hall. When he saw me he came over. The nurse looked relieved. "So he is who he says he is?"

"Yes. He sure is." Billy looked at the press mob now calling his name. They knew who he was. I guess they thought he was going to say, *Aw, let them come back and hang with the senator awhile.* Instead, he said to the nurse, "You'll have nightmares for six months about this."

She managed a smile. "This isn't quite as bad as when that alderman got shot. But close."

As we walked down the corridor to the room where Warren was, the hospital smells began to bring out my Irish fatalism. Irishmen (I wonder about Irish*women*) have two obsessions, sex and death, and not necessarily in that order. Maybe it's because we spring from the loins of certifiable maniacs, the Celts, those merry fellows who painted themselves with blood before charging naked into battle. Their war cries, this being documented by historical accounts, were said to be so terrifying that the Celts could take villages without lifting a sword. Their screams alone sent villagers running into the forest.

The hospital smells didn't create images

of the Celts, but they did create images of what lay behind all those ER curtains. And the sounds augmented the aromas. The little girl whose temperature had soared to a dangerous number, crying out now in sweaty delirium, and her tormented parents standing next to her gurney, imploring the young ER doc to save her. The old man lifting spidery fingers to receive the hand of his middle-aged daughter, who knew he would never leave the hospital alive. The teenage boy sobbing through the fog of drugs and drink, not knowing yet that his reckless driving had killed his best friend.

Sharp stench of meds. Muffled words of nurses. The stray cry, piercing as a bullet. The quick ratcheting clamor of curtains being ripped back along metal rods.

Two security guards stood outside Warren's door. They'd already dealt with Billy, so all they did was nod as we went into the room.

Warren lay, eyes closed, pale and damp on a gurney. He was hooked up to two different monitors that beeped quietly and frequently. His wife, Teresa, leaned over the bed, gently touching the back of her hand to his cheek. On the other side stood Kate and Laura. Kate's lips moved in silent prayer. Gabe sat alone in a corner, his eyes downcast.

When Teresa saw me, she offered me her free hand. I took it and moved closer to her. "So far the tests they've given him don't indicate a heart attack or a stroke. They're doing more tests. But one of the older doctors stopped in and asked if he'd been throwing up. Which Warren did twice in the ambulance."

A young doc came into the room just then. Indian, almost delicate, pretty. She walked toward Teresa. I stood aside. She introduced herself as Dr. Ajeet.

"I consulted with two other doctors, Mrs. Nichols. They wanted to know what he's had to eat in the last eight hours. We've already got the blood we need for a test. It's in the lab now."

"I'm afraid I wouldn't know, Doctor. Kate might know."

Kate raised her head as if scanning the ceiling. "Let's see — we had lunch brought in to campaign headquarters from a deli down the block. He either had corned beef or ham on rye."

"He had one of those energy drinks around four o'clock," Billy said. "I was alone with him going over a speech for tomorrow."

"He guns Diet Pepsi all day," Laura said.

"It's pretty much a joke with the staff that when the senator dies, he wants heaven to be one big vending machine with Diet Pepsi in every slot." She was smiling until she realized the implications of what she'd said. "Oh, God, I'm sorry, Teresa."

"Oh, c'mon, Laura, I know you didn't mean anything by that," she said, looking down fondly at the face of her husband. Teresa was one of those trophy wives who'd surprised everybody by being a woman of intelligence and compassion. And a valuable political asset. The men of Washington wanted to jump her and their wives wanted to count her as a friend.

"I'm wondering about the Pepsi that tasted funny," I said. "Right before the debate."

"So am I," Kate said.

We told Dr. Ajeet about the incident that Warren had put down to melted ice.

"That's very interesting," the doctor said. "We're already working on the possibility that he ingested something harmful in his food or drink. But we're considering many possibilities. From what we can see so far, Senator Nichols is in a deep sleep. His vitals are all normal."

"He's asleep?" Laura said.

"Yes. The same kind of sleep you'd get if

you took too many sleeping pills. Not enough to kill you or do any permanent damage — hopefully not anyway — but enough to put you to sleep for a long time and then to wake up with a pretty bad hangover." She turned to Teresa. "Remember, when we first examined him, Mrs. Nichols, we were able to get him to open his eyes and talk a little. That's certainly something we can do with cardiac patients, too. But it's also symptomatic in some cases of drug overdoses."

"Then he'll be all right?" Teresa said, hope making her voice sound much younger, stronger.

"Well, we're more confident now that that's what we're dealing with, anyway," the doctor said. "We still want to run some more cardiac tests on him, but at this point I think we're going to be able to eliminate cardio pretty soon now."

Billy said, "He's snoring!"

And so he was.

We all fixed our eyes on Warren's face. The waxen look was receding. The eyelids fluttered, though they remained closed. And through his lips came a wet nasal blast that was almost violent. He was a master snorer, no doubt about it.

"Oh, thank God," Teresa said, clutching

my hand again.

At this point I assumed that Warren was going to be all right, so my mind shifted back to the mysterious makeup woman. And to a man named R. D. Greaves, the dirty-tricks man Jim Lake had employed in all three of his congressional elections. And had most likely employed for this one, too. Tampering with the drink sounded like something Greaves would do. Lake was, after all, running behind with only three weeks to go.

"Are you leaving, Dev?" Teresa said. She seemed frightened by the possibility.

"I'm afraid I have to, Teresa. There's a lot to handle now."

"Me, too," Laura said. "I need to go out there and face down that pack of jackals. Kate had her turn, now it's mine."

"You want me to write something for you?" Billy said.

"Thanks, Billy. But I'm going to give them so little information we won't need to write it down." A sly smile as she said this.

"I'll stay with Teresa," Kate said. The two women had always been friendly, something you don't always see in political relationships. The wife threatened by the beautiful staffer. The staffer gloating over the long hours she got to spend with the candidate alone. But these two women actually hung out together, with Teresa, who could not have children, even frequently babysitting Kate's daughter.

"So you won't need me?" Kate said.

"No. But maybe R. D. Greaves will."

She knew what I meant by that. Billy and Laura were already walking through the door and hadn't heard me. Gabe stood up, silent as usual.

"Oh, yes," Kate said. "I hope you can find him and pay him a visit."

Teresa wasn't paying us any attention. She was too busy touching Warren's face with her hand.

"I'll call you later," I said to Kate and then went looking for Greaves, though I didn't get far. In my search for a side exit door, not wanting the press to see me leave, I was approached by a long, lean black man in a tan Burberry and a brown snap-brim fedora. He approached me with his ID in hand and a large public smile in place.

"Detective Richard Sayers. And I believe you're Dev Conrad."

"That's right."

"I just missed you over at the auditorium. I talked to the campaign manager, Kate. Very nice, bright lady. But I wanted to talk to you, too. See if you had any ideas."

"I'm not sure what you mean." But I did know what he meant. He wanted my opinion. He obviously knew there was a possibility that Warren had been drugged.

"I'm looking to see if there's any criminal angle here. Maybe the senator had a heart attack or a stroke or an aneurysm. But then there's the possibility that a bad guy slipped something into his drink. That would make this a criminal act. A lot of people thought he was drunk. I imagine that's just what the bad guy *wanted* them to think. If there was a bad guy."

"I can't disagree with you there."

He studied me with dark eyes that held no compassion for anybody unfortunate enough to belong to the human species. "You're a little rattled right now. And I don't blame you. But we need to have a sit-down and very soon. You know everybody who was in that makeup room tonight."

"I don't like the sound of that. You mean that bad guy is one of the staffers?"

"I'm not saying that. Not yet, anyway. But that's as good a place to start as any." He smiled with those big white perfect teeth. "I'll be seeing you around. You probably need to relax a little right now."

He nodded and walked past me, toward the front of the hospital.

CHAPTER 8

"Freshen that up for you, friend?" the bartender asked.

"Please," I said.

As he mixed me another scotch and soda, he said, "Hope you don't have far to go tonight. That damned snow doesn't want to quit. I told the wife I might wind up staying here. We've got a cot in the back. Of course she thinks I'm hitting on the two waitresses." He was sixtyish, balding, and saddled with the kind of smile that would remind younger women of uncles and granddads. I doubted his wife had too much to worry about.

The Parrot Cage lounge sat across the street from a new three-story hotel, a hotel that offered suites pretty much like small apartments for travelers who planned to be in the city awhile. I was here because two of the newspapermen I'd called said that, so far as they knew, Greaves was staying at the hotel and doing a lot of his drinking at the Parrot Cage. I knew he had an apartment somewhere in the city but was told that when he wanted to celebrate something, he took a hotel room for a week or two. I'd checked the hotel. Not there. I was hoping he would end up here for a couple of quick ones before he went across the street to get into his jammies for the night.

"Well, I'm going to stick around for a little while longer, anyway. Hoping to run into an old friend of mine. Man name of Greaves."

The bartender's face cracked wide open with a grandpop smile. "R.D.? He's some character, isn't he?"

"Oh, you know him?"

"Well, not know him, know him. But he's been coming in here the last three weeks. He likes it when the gal comes in to play the piano onstage. Always giving her money to play songs he can sing along with. He's got a hell of a good voice, you know that?"

"No. I guess I didn't."

The stage was not much bigger than a walk-in closet, and even that space was halved by the shiny new electric piano. The bar was on the west wall, small tables on the left. There were only three other customers, a black man in a gray suit five stools away from me and a thirtyish couple who laughed a lot. It was a middle-class bar for salespeople who traveled and imbibed. I couldn't find a single physical reference to parrots. Maybe the urinals were shaped like them.

"Plus he'll buy two, three rounds a night for people. Usually scores with the ladies, too. Of course, they're not the little chickadees we'd all like to score with. He gets the middle-aged ones. But nice middle-aged if you know what I mean."

The black gentleman raised his empty glass. The bartender went to fill it.

A good singing voice, rounds for everybody, a better class of women in his lonely bed. This was unfortunate information to have because it gave R.D., the prick, a humanity I didn't think he deserved.

Where did you start with R.D.? There were some who insisted that he didn't exist. The reasoning went that nobody that corrupt and mercenary could possibly avoid prison as long as R.D. had. Then there were those who half-believed that R.D. was some kind of supernatural force. Nobody human could be as devious, as ruthless, as merciless as R.D. Just wasn't possible, the human genome being what it was. He had to be some kind of satanic being.

Item: Two election cycles back, Greaves

paid sixty elderly black people to help pass out flyers that claimed that the sitting candidate had once been arrested for beating a black man so severely the man had been in the hospital for three weeks. Greaves had one of his techies Photoshop an arrest warrant that detailed the charge. He repeated this in four different cities and towns in the congressional district. This, along with equally dishonest direct mail pieces and truly inflammatory radio spots, helped suppress the black vote and contributed significantly to the incumbent's loss.

Item: The somewhat mannish wife of a sitting governor became the focal point of flyers that claimed that, as a NOW member, she saw nothing wrong with lesbians being gym teachers and touching girls and even watching them shower. The wife was Photoshopped holding hands with another unidentified woman. This was another candidate who lost his seat partly due to Greaves's cunning. His wife, heterosexual from all accounts, was said to still be suffering from acute depression, blaming herself for her husband's loss.

Item: Greaves hired a hacker to obtain the private medical records of an opponent. The senatorial candidate had suffered a severe breakdown following the death of his younger brother in a boating accident. This had been back in the Vietnam era. According to Greaves, the candidate used his brother's death and his own depression (which included shock treatments) to get out of being drafted, "the way too many rich boys were able to avoid that terrible war." The candidate broke down one night at a press conference trying to explain what the loss of his brother had meant to him. The raw emotional display helped lose him the election. Too unstable.

Probably the most explosive charge Greaves had ever concocted dealt with a congressman who'd developed a rare blood disease and lost thirty pounds in a five-month period. Sounds like AIDS to me, the flyers said.

And the push calls, too, those phone calls that start out by claiming they're doing an independent survey and need only about sixty seconds of your time. In this case the second or third question of four was: Would you vote for a congressman if you knew he had contracted the AIDS virus? Hundreds of these calls were made in the final two weeks of that election cycle. And they worked perfectly.

Make no mistake. Neither side can claim virtue. Just about any election you can point to is dirty on both sides in some way, from teenagers tearing down the yard signs of your opponent to shouting down the man or woman who is trying to speak to a crowd. It's a matter of degree. Both sides, at the congressional level all the way up to the White House, have their election assassins. And both sides have done a lot of sleazy and unforgivable things to the election process. But only one side ever fielded anybody like R. D. Greaves.

"I'm going to be closing up pretty quick here," the bartender said after walking to the front window and taking a look at the parking lot. "Doesn't show any signs of letting up."

"Give me one more while I visit the john."

"Sure thing."

And when I got back, he was there. R. D. Greaves himself. Sitting at the far end of the bar where the black gentleman had been.

He didn't recognize me. I took my seat and started working on my fresh drink. During my brief sojourn in the john, the other customers had left. Now it was just the three of us.

The bartender looked confused. He must have thought that I'd be sitting up close to Greaves, since I'd told him we were old friends. He finally said, as he wiped out a glass with a towel he should have tossed about twenty glasses ago, "R.D., man down there's been asking about you."

I suppose the bartender thought that this introduction would end in some kind of beer commercial backslapping by two big manly men. *Hey, shit, I didn't recognize you! How the hell you been, man? Let's us have a brewski!*

But all that happened was that Greaves turned a bit on his stool and glared down the bar at me and said, "Is that right? He tell you *why* he's been asking about me?"

Greaves and I are both shaggy mastodons. Six-four or thereabouts, noses broken a few times by those snobs who found us less than charming, waistlines that had to be carefully watched, and the ready anger that shrinks would probably call paranoia. He wasn't physically afraid of me and I wasn't physically afraid of him. The bartender clearly sensed this and as a result started looking nervous.

"So why're you asking the barkeep so many questions?"

"I thought maybe he could tell me if you were really as big a prick as people say you are."

Now in your standard cop or cowboy

movie, those would be fightin' words. The stuntmen would double the actors and a furniture-bustin' brawl would ensue. But this, alas, was reality, and men our age and our size had to be careful about brawls. Even in your early forties, you didn't recover from physical violence the way you once might have.

He laughed. Or rather, bellowed. "Hell, yes, I'm a big prick. Probably more than you even heard. So who the fuck are you?"

"Campaign consultant to Senator Nichols."

All he said was, "Figures." Then he turned around and faced the mirror again. He shoved his empty glass at the bartender. "Hit me again, Mike."

I slid off my stool and slowly made my way up the bar. Mike looked to be quietly hyperventilating.

"I suppose you heard about tonight. The debate?"

He didn't turn to look at me. "Was there a debate tonight? Guess I didn't hear about it."

"Somebody put something in my client's drink. Something that made him so groggy he passed out onstage."

"Man, sounds like I missed something. Maybe I can pick it up on a news show.

That'd be some footage I'd bet."

"Sounds like something Jim Lake would hire somebody to do."

He angled around to face me. "I don't know anybody who'd do anything like that, Sport. We all have too much respect for our system of government. The whole election process is a sacred right. A lot of people have fought and died for it."

I didn't do it. Somebody else did. Somebody who looked an awful lot like me. I just stood back and watched as this doppelgänger smashed a right hand into the side of Greaves's head. Hard enough to knock him off his stool and onto the floor, where he cracked his head on landing.

Mike pulled a sawed-off from behind the bar and started shouting at me. "You freeze right where you are, mister! I ain't putting up with this kind of shit from anybody!"

Carefully keeping both barrels pointed in my direction, Mike came out from around the bar to see how Greaves was doing.

Greaves was doing just fine. Picking himself up, straightening his clothes, touching his fingers tentatively to the spot where my fist had collided with his face.

"You want me to call the cops, Mr. Greaves?"

"Hell no, Mike. I was actually going to

look this creep up anyway. He just saved me some time is all." He lifted his drink, draining it, "C'mon, creep, I'll buy you some food."

So that was how I met the one, the only, R. D. Greaves.

"You know, Leno and Letterman are always making jokes about Denny's, but I like this place. The food's good and pretty cheap. I've never found anything in my food. You know, a finger or anything like that. And the booths are comfortable. You take Burger King, those are the most uncomfortable fucking booths I've ever sat in. You ever eat at Burger King?"

"Not unless my kidnappers forced me to."

He was shoveling ketchup-drenched french fries into his mouth one by bloody one as he talked. He had red streaks across his upper lip and on the left side of his mouth.

"So how'd you ever get into the political racket?"

"My father was a congressman. He got tired of seeing people like you working for people in Congress."

He winked at me. It was obscene. "Not to brag, but there's never been and never will be anybody 'like me.' Look it up. Nobody's got my track record."

"I'll bet your mother's proud of you."

"As a matter of fact, she's *very* proud of me. Brags about me to everybody in the old neighborhood."

"Figures."

He seemed to bring me into focus for the first time. He had the kind of Gene Hackman looks that could turn easily into good guy or bad guy. "You're a sanctimonious bastard."

"One of my many failings." And it was.

He ate some more french fries. He'd obliterated his cheeseburger in four Olympian bites. I was almost afraid to see what he'd do to the three-scoop chocolate sundae he'd ordered right along with his meal. It had been sitting here long enough to melt. "So you think I did in Nichols tonight, huh?"

"Pretty sure you did."

"What makes you think so?"

"(A) It's your MO. You get creative when you're down this close to Election Day. (B) The woman who actually dropped the drug in the drink gave a phony name and lied about being part of the Nichols campaign."

He snorted. Now he had ketchup all over his fingers, too. "You think a grand jury would buy that?"

"Probably not."

"But you're gonna go ahead and try to nail me for it anyway, right?"

"Don't have time. Maybe after the election. Sooner if I can find the woman."

He held a single french fry that drooped under the weight of the ketchup. Then he opened wide as if I were his dentist and shoved it into the darkness between his teeth. "It's funny, I don't even know who she is, never met her, never saw her, but I've got this feeling about her. Sort of a psychic kind of thing."

"Sure. Psychic kind of thing."

"I just have this feeling she got on a plane right after this thing at the auditorium tonight — she got on this plane and flew bye-bye. If she's any kind of pro, that is."

He was having some fun with me. Scatting. Seeming to pretend he knew something about the drugging while denying it when asked directly. He was good at confusing you.

"You think so, huh?" I said.

"I know so."

"Funny, I had the impression she was local talent."

"You never heard of local talent flying away somewhere till things cool off?"

"More coffee?" the waitress said.

We both said no but Greaves pointed to his sundae. "I didn't get to this as fast as I thought. How about throwing this one away — or giving it to somebody in the kitchen — and getting me a new one. I'll pay for it of course." He patted her hip. "Or you can eat it for yourself, darling."

She smiled. "I think I'll take you up on that. It looks good."

When she was gone, he said, "Nice ass but no tits."

"She should be killed for not measuring up to your high standards."

His last french fry got swished around through a large dollop of ketchup remaining on the platter. "You're an owly son of a bitch."

"The nuns always told me that, too."

"You went to Catholic school?"

"Yeah."

"Hey, so did I. But then one day it hit me."

"What hit you?"

"All this God shit. It's all a crock. When we die, we die. Same as when you see a dog or a cat that's been run over by a car. It's all they get and that's all we get, too."

"So why follow the rules when this is it right here on earth, right?"

"You're getting sanctimonious again but, yeah, that's right. I mean, what the fuck,

86

may as well enjoy ourselves. You only go around once in life."

"That's a line from a beer commercial."

He winked at me again. "I take my wisdom where I find it, Sport."

The waitress brought his sundae. She stood away from him this time. She didn't want to be patted again. She dropped the check on the table and left.

He laughed. "Don't think I'll be waking up with her in the morning." He then proceeded to demolish his sundae in six skilled attacks. He had whipped cream on the tip of his nose. I didn't tell him. I liked him better as a clown. He made a big "Aaaaahhhh!" sound as if he'd just finished a feast so impossibly wonderful, complete words couldn't describe it. He crossed his eyes and peered down his nose. "Hey, I got something on my nose?"

"Yeah. Whipped cream."

"Why didn't you tell me?"

"Guess I didn't notice."

"You are some kind of asshole, Sport." He napkined off the whipped cream and then sat back in the booth, spreading his arms out on either side. Something had changed in the eyes. They appeared to be a much deeper brown, almost black. And the jaw muscles were bunched now. This was the political assassin I'd heard about.

"Sport, you got much bigger problems than what happened tonight."

"I do, huh?"

"Yeah, you do. And you're sitting there thinking you're such a superior shit — smarter than me, slicker than me, marginally better-looking than me — the kind of guy who gets invited to all the parties with the pretty people. The ones who hire me but don't want me around afterward. You know, I've never been invited to a single inaugural ball? Or to a single congressman's office. Or to a single governor's mansion. And it was me who helped put most of these motherfuckers where they are today."

I didn't say anything. I wasn't sure *what* to say. His cold anger had the force of a punch.

"But I'm getting off the subject here. We were talking about you."

"Right. And that I've got a much bigger problem than what happened tonight."

He went right at it. "I have a videotape of your senator fucking the brains out of a hotel maid. Nobody knows I have it."

My response was lame and we both knew it. "The kind of technology today, you can fake anything."

"I hired the girl myself and now she's my

88

witness. So don't give me any bullshit about the tape being fake. You know I've got the real deal."

"If you've got it, why not give it to Lake and let him leak it to the press?"

He tapped his right temple. "You really are a babe in the woods, Sport. I give it to Lake, he just considers it part of my job. He might give me a little bonus or something. I did this on my own time. I want a big payday. So I'm offering it to you first."

"How much is this big payday you want?"

The smile was novel length. He had dreamed of saying these three words all his life. "One million bucks." And then he said, "By noon, day after tomorrow."

CHAPTER 9

"You don't look so hot," Billy said the next morning when he found me in the coffee shop.

"Thanks. I needed to hear that."

As he opened his menu, he said, "What's that bruise on the side of your head?"

"I slipped and fell last night in the snow. A lot of people slipped and fell in the snow last night, Billy. It's no big deal."

I'd slipped and fallen in the snow after R. D. Greaves had punched me from behind as I was getting into my car. He not only wanted a million dollars, he also wanted revenge for me knocking him off his stool in the Parrot Cage.

"How we going to handle this, you know yet?"

I ate the last bite of my cheese omelet and said, "I need to get with Kate and Laura. If you mean are we going to charge Lake with putting something in Warren's Diet Pepsi, I don't know. This is the last thing you folks ever want to hear, but I want to see some overnight polling, see how people view Warren. That debate probably had a very big audience. Haven't seen any figures yet. But that would be my guess."

"I guess I don't understand. If Lake did it —"

Waitress. Billy was in a decisive mood this morning. "What'd you have, Dev?"

"Cheese omelet, orange juice, unbuttered toast, and coffee."

"Same except butter the toast."

When she went away, he said, "But we know Lake did it."

"We don't *know*. We *think* we know. There's a difference. Our only lead is that makeup woman, and the only thing I've been told about her is that she shops at Daily Double Discount."

"Never heard of it. And I grew up here."

"I've never heard of it, either. And I don't even know if it's a true lead. One of the college kids working backstage told me she saw a Daily Double Discount sack in the woman's front seat."

"Well, that's something."

"Maybe and maybe not. What if she'd borrowed the car or stolen it? And even if it was her sack, why would anybody at the store remember her? Presumably they've got a lot of customers or they wouldn't stay open long in the discount business."

"Oh, yeah, I see. But I still don't see why we can't call a press conference and sort of imply that Lake hired somebody to take down the senator last night."

Waitress with Billy's coffee.

"Because you can never be sure where an accusation like that will lead. It might look like desperation on our part."

"But we're ahead in the polls."

"We *were* ahead in the polls as of last night when Warren walked out onstage. I'm not sure where we stand this morning, though. And again, you and I are sure Lake is behind it all. But we don't have proof. And without it, it could all backfire on us very quickly. These are the three most dangerous weeks in a tight campaign."

"That's for sure."

"So what I'm going to recommend to Warren and Kate is that we hold a press conference sometime today when Warren is up to it and all we say is that Warren ingested some kind of contaminated food or drink last night. We'll have one of the hospital docs standing next to him when we say this."

"What if the press wants to know more?"

"We'll just say that we need to have more lab tests done before we can say for sure what it was he took into his system last night."

"You know they're going to be all over this story. He used to have a woman problem, but way back when, he had a drinking problem, too."

"Not much of one. He got into a couple of fights when he was in the National Guard. That's not much of a drinking problem."

"Yeah, but he was arrested once for public intoxication."

I'd thought the same thing during my long and sleepless night in bed. But by dawn I'd dismissed the "drinking problem" angle. The public-intox arrest was made when he and four other recent college grads set up their garage band out on the lawn of a vacated manse in the Gold Coast area. The movers and shakers of such a neighborhood were not at all amused by being awakened at four-thirty a.m. But he was twenty-one at the time and, as seen through the voters' eyes, who among us wouldn't want to cost those rich, selfish bastards some sleep? I still couldn't see the "drinking problem" angle that worried Billy.

"The staff's over at headquarters this

morning," I said. "As soon as I finish up here, I'll be going over there."

"They did a great job on the streets during the night," Billy said. "At least we can get around everywhere this morning. Most of the snow is already melting. No Michael Bilandic moment."

Bilandic had been a briefly popular mayor who'd lost all his support when he failed to deal competently with a snow emergency. His administration's response was so lame that he lost to the then-unknown Jane Byrne in the mayoral primary.

"Warren's got three stops on his schedule today. He's going to keep every one of them."

"You really think he's strong enough, Dev?"

"He doesn't have any choice. We need to show that he's strong and can bounce back right away. That's another reason I don't want to make any accusations. It's more important to show that he's in charge of the situation than to put blame on somebody. They thought they could queer his drink and put him on his back for several days? Not our man. He's hitting the bricks the very next day. That's the signal we have to send."

Billy giggled. "It's like you're playing with

toy soldiers, man. All you consultants are like that."

"That isn't a compliment. Not to me, anyway."

"But it's true."

"We want to win, Billy. And part of the reason we want to win is because we believe in what a given candidate stands for. I know that sounds like bullshit, but it isn't. I get pitched all the time by candidates I have no faith in and I say no. Elect these guys and they'll be in the pockets of every big-money lobby in Washington. Nobody's pure, Billy, but there are degrees of dirty. Our man Warren is pretty clean, considering."

Billy was smirking now. "Wow, I'm surprised. You actually do give a shit."

"Yeah," I said, "sometimes I even surprise myself."

I first started working in local politics when I was a sophomore in college. I did so for a simple reason. The pol I volunteered to help had some really fine-looking college girls working out of his campaign headquarters. I was hoping to get laid. While that didn't happen, my fascination with the political world took serious and lasting hold, mostly because of my father then being in Congress. I admired the pol I worked for because, even though he was a machine man, he didn't hesitate to veer from the party line when he felt it necessary. Pretty damned cool, I thought. And so did a lot of others. He got elected. And he singled me out for some suggestions I'd made to one of his paid staffers.

My reward was that I became a paid staffer when he was up again two years later. I did my work after my college day at Northwestern was done. Where before I'd done mostly phone answering, Xerox copying, pizza getting, and so on, this time I worked under the campaign manager, who was in charge of the finance director, the field director, the communications director, the scheduler, and the consultants. That summer I worked full-time, and it was better than a graduate program in politics. I learned the game and the game's most important rule: The first thing a pol generally does when he or she takes a mortal hit from the opponent is to fire the campaign manager. Announce that he or she is really sorry that such a mistake could happen (some real PR screwup most often) and that the campaign manager has been canned and a new one is on board and a fresh start begins right now. Campaign managers are well aware that they can and will be dumped at any moment when necessary. That's why they're paid well.

The second most important rule: Stay out of all the palace intrigue you find in campaign headquarters. There are endless rivalries for the candidate's approval and face time, hurt feelings, jealousies, even plots to get others fired. Human nature. The smart pol operative — which I already knew I wanted to be — keeps as far away from these follies as he can.

The Senator Nichols campaign headquarters was the standard battle zone you found everywhere with three weeks to go. Phones, faxes, copying machines, TV sets, cell phones, and iPods created a relentless electronic annoyance that you either adapted to or fled from. Some people can't handle it and quit. There were too many people despite the spacious floor plan of what had once been a supermarket. That was because the press was here today, en masse it appeared. They knew that Warren was in his office in the back of the headquarters. They were waiting to attack him.

I got myself a cup of coffee and headed back there, smiling, nodding, waving to people who smiled, nodded, and waved to me. The younger ones didn't much like me. Their poly sci profs had warned them about political consultants. People like me, they said, were responsible for candidates being prepackaged and bland and focus-grouped and polled to death. And unwilling to take any kind of stand that polls indicated might not be popular. And worst of all, their finale went, in the old days consultant services at least ended when the pol went to Washington. But now many pols kept their consultants on the payroll and wouldn't cast a ballot in the House or Senate unless the consultant approved it.

It always surprised people when I said that I generally agreed with these objections. And that I was guilty of some of those sins myself. What I didn't say was that the average consultant was much smarter than the average candidate.

"I think Dev's right," Senator Nichols said half an hour later, after Kate and Laura had argued that we should at least hint that we believed Congressman Lake was behind last night's incident. He looked better than I'd expected he would and his voice was strong and persuasive. "Number one, we don't have any hard evidence. And number two, we don't know where an accusation like that would lead. Like Dev said, it might take over the whole election. The Chicago TV boys wouldn't let go of it. And the cable news people would go after it twenty-four/seven. Our message would get lost in all the drama. We don't even know where we stand today. I'm like Dev. I want to see some polling from last night before I do anything except stick my head out and say that I'm feeling fine, thank you very much."

Billy frowned. "Polls."

"Polls help pay your fee, Billy," Warren said gently. The top campaign slots offered some very attractive salaries. "And speaking of which, Kate tells me that we can expect a lot more money from the national party committee because of last night. They'll be getting it to us right away. They've suggested that we need two new thirty-second spots that show me strong and vital."

"I wrote them in the middle of the night," I said. "I have a production company scouting indoor tracks, handball courts, places like that. We can cheat a lot of the shots." I smiled. "You won't have to run more than fifteen yards, but we can make it look like you're doing a marathon."

Everybody smiled at that one.

Warren clapped his hands together. That always signified that we were done. "So if that's it, I'll let you all get back to work and I'll do the same here myself. I need to make

99

some calls. And then about twenty minutes from now I'll go out there and face the jackals."

"You'd better," I said, "before they start bringing in blankets for the night. They might not want to leave."

Kate, Laura, Gabe, and Billy all said goodbye. Warren was expecting me to leave, too. He seemed surprised when I said, "There's a coffee shop down the street. It'll be busy right now, perfect for talking in private because everybody else'll be talking, too."

I tried to sound amiable but he caught the tension in my voice. "I have this place swept three times a week."

"I'd still feel better about us having coffee down the street." No matter how often you sweep an office, there's always the possibility that some new electronic spying gadget won't show up on your radar. If this office was bugged, all kinds of information would now be in Lake's hands. But nothing about blackmail and hotel maids.

"You're the boss," Nichols said. He tried to keep it light whenever he said that, but there was an edge of bitterness to it. We slipped out the back way and took the scenic route down the alley.

■ ■ ■ ■

Back booth. Place packed. Poor waitresses frantic.

I said, "Hotel maid. Married man who happens to be a United States senator. Sound familiar?"

At first he didn't seem to understand. But then every feature on his face was suddenly dragged down as if by gravity.

"I thought you gave that shit up, Warren."

He made a fist. "That was a slip."

"Some slip."

"How the hell did you hear about it?"

"Courtesy of R. D. Greaves. He wants one million dollars cash for the video he has."

"Are you fucking crazy?"

"He says you come from big money. As you do."

"Not that kind of money."

"We pay for our sins, Warren."

Waitress. All either of us wanted was coffee. There's something about blackmail that curbs the appetite. We gave her our order then resumed talking.

"God, last night and now this? R. D. Greaves is scum. He must've planted a camera in there."

"Yeah. He did. And the girl was a plant.

101

He has the tape, Warren. Adultery. Sleazy video."

"One million bucks. That bastard. I really think I'm going to start hyperventilating. No shit."

"Warren, we have to face this."

"I can't believe this." He shook his head three or four times. A fine sheen of sweat covered his face. "Have you seen the video?"

"No. But I will before we arrange for the money."

"How will you contact him?"

"He'll call me. He doesn't have any reason to hide."

"There's no way I can come up with a million. No way at all. Getting that much would cause so much suspicion we'd have the feds on us. And anyway, that kind of money is invested. Nobody would have it laying around in currency."

"He's given us till tomorrow afternoon."

"Well, I won't do it. I'd rather resign my office."

"No, you wouldn't."

"Shit." Then, "You're right. No, I wouldn't."

I said, "There's another angle here."

He smiled sadly. "With you there's always another angle. You work like a confidence man sometimes, Dev. Nobody knows quite what's going on except you."

"You'd know the same thing if you thought about it."

He shrugged. "Probably not. You've got street smarts, I don't. There's a downside to growing up privileged. You don't know jack shit about the real world."

The waitress gave us more coffee.

"I can tell I'm not going to like this," Warren said.

"You're right. You're not going to like this."

"You can be a real prick sometimes."

He'd spoken too loudly. The crowd had thinned considerably now that it was pushing nine o'clock. You could hear actual words instead of just noise. A couple of men in blue real-estate blazers looked over at us. They were surprised to see their senator. He usually had a bodyguard with him. Right now he was just another guy.

In a stage whisper, he said, "You can be a real prick sometimes, you know that?"

"Here's the other angle. It's called honesty. When I signed on with you, one of the first things we discussed were all the rumors about you chasing women around. You said you'd given it up. Bopping a maid doesn't sound like you were telling the truth."

"She was the only one."

"Bullshit."

He really hated me at that moment. Senators don't get pushed around the way regular folks do. Many of the laws that apply to us don't apply to them. And they don't take kindly to regular folk challenging them.

"The truth, Warren. I have to know what might be coming at us sometime. You know, like Clinton's 'bimbo eruptions.' "

He sat back and for a long moment closed his eyes. He wasn't a drama queen, so this kind of behavior told me that he had some serious fessing up to do.

"Six or seven others," he said when he returned to earth.

"In what period of time?"

"The last year, say."

"All one-night stands?"

"All but one. A stewardess. We got together three times."

"All in Washington?"

"No. All here. In Chicago. I have a small apartment absolutely nobody but me knows about."

"You said the last year. How about the last two years? How many would that be?"

"Probably about the same number. Six, seven a year."

"So we're talking twelve to fourteen

potential scandals."

"They won't talk. Hell, a few of them are married. They sure aren't going to risk their family life."

"How many are married?"

"What difference does it make?"

"How many?"

"Shit, I don't know. Say, uh, four."

"Four from twelve leaves eight. Eight potential bimbo eruptions."

"They haven't said anything so far."

"So far. But three weeks is a long, long time. And maybe one or two of them are mad because they wanted more than a one-night stand. It's not very often that a woman gets to sleep with a real senator. But you blew her off. So every time she sees your face on TV she gets mad and hurt and vengeful. Most women just ride with it. They don't want to humiliate themselves by getting caught up in a scandal. But there's always one who's like all those people you see on trash TV. 'Sure I'm having sex with my mother, but I'm on TV and that's all that matters.' Maybe one of these eight women you feel so confident about, Warren — maybe at this very moment she's picking up the phone and calling Lake headquarters and saying that she's got a piece of information that's so hot she'll only talk to Lake himself. Remember Paula Jones, Warren?"

"You're scaring the hell out of me, Dev. And I mean that."

"Well, you're scaring the hell out of me, too. Right now I want to punch your face in."

"I don't blame you."

"Oh, don't cheese this up with remorse, Warren. You lied to me and now we're all in trouble."

"Well, excuse me for saying I'm sorry. I guess that's a no-no with big bad Dev, huh?"

"We've got Greaves — or rather he's got us — and we've got to explain to the press about last night, and we've got a campaign to run. If we've got time to squeeze it in between everything else, that is. And then on top of it all we've got maybe one or two women who just might like to see you take a real hard fall."

By this time he was pale and sweaty and a familiar tic had started working on his left eye. The tic usually appeared when stress reached overload proportions for him. He was suffering and I was happy to see it. He'd lied to his wife, to his staff, and to me. Laura had told me soon after I'd signed on that he'd gathered them all together one day and told them in a very formal way, "I am changing my lifestyle. I want to become an adult instead of this compulsive teenager I've been all my life." He didn't have to elaborate. He didn't have to say that heretofore he couldn't seem to keep it in his pants. They knew what he was talking about.

"So now what, Dev?"

"Now we just go on and do our jobs and hope for the best. I want to see Greaves's video, and then I want to see if I can find that makeup woman."

"She doesn't matter anymore."

"Sure she does. If she'll admit that Greaves or somebody else from the Lake camp hired her, we can coast the rest of the way home. We'll wind up with a ten-point lead."

"But what about the tape?"

"Separate issue. I'll look at it and tell you if I think it's been altered in any way."

"But I'll never be able to come up with a million dollars."

"You won't have to. Get me three hundred thousand in cash. I'll bring that to him when we make the swap. He'll piss and moan, but the sight of all that green — he'll come around."

"God, I hope you're right."

"Yeah," I said, "I hope I'm right, too."

CHAPTER 10

Daily Double Discount was located in what had once been a two-story concrete block building belonging to the YMCA. The neighborhood had gotten too rough for the Y folks, so they'd sought safer digs.

The interior had the eternal smell of Salvation Army and Goodwill stores, that faint whiff of the grave that is actually an amalgam of fabrics, mustiness, and the inexplicable scent of decay.

The merchandise was thrown on long folding tables and displayed as was. No racks, no hangers, not even any signs directing you to clothes, housewares, appliances, and so on. I assumed the second floor was more of the same. I browsed the shirts while I waited for the two women up front wearing matching DDD blouses to finish talking to a customer.

Every shirt I picked up had some small thing wrong with it. A pocket had been stitched wrong. One sleeve was a few inches shorter than the other. Color was faded here and there. These kinds of factory rejects could be bought for a fraction of regular wholesale price and sold cheap. I wandered back to housewares and found that all the boxes the irons and mixers and lamps came in were pretty badly banged up. Some of the boxes were crushed, some were so worn on the edges that only the cardboard base was left. Presumably the appliances worked.

A Christian radio station filled the tinny speakers stationed on walls throughout the store. It used to be said that the devil got all the good music. These days it was the reverse. Christian music could claim lots of stars who were talented musicians and singers. My problem was the lyrics. I'd once heard a song where a young woman sang to Jesus as if he were her lover. It made me very uncomfortable. *Hey, Jesus, let's get it on, dude.*

The people were heartbreaking to watch. No matter how low the prices were, they were still too much for many of the customers, those being members of America's first official underclass — black, white, brown, red, physically challenged, mentally challenged, druggies, winos, the perpetually underemployed, people so old they didn't have to die to become ghosts, people possessed of rashes, scars, boils, walleyes, black teeth, yellow teeth, no teeth, the crippled, the insane, the grotesquely fat, the junkie thin — all these being things that a good job with a good health plan could cope with if not resolve, except for the junkies and the insane. Many of these minds would be focused on survival basics — what kind of grub they could scrounge up for dinner tonight. And the place was packed with them.

I went back up front. The black woman at the register said, "Help you, sir?"

"I hope so."

She had a sweet smile. "Well, I'll try, anyway."

The first thing I did was give her the physical description of the makeup woman. I didn't bother giving her the name, because the name was a phony. "She might be or have been a hairdresser who knew something about makeup. For TV. A lot of local newspeople get makeup advice when they get their hair cut."

She had a button with a photo of her granddaughter on it. Cute little two- or three-year-old. She touched it as she squinted her eyes, furrowed her brow, trying to shape all the words I'd given her into a picture.

She didn't address me. She called another cashier over. "Nikki, this gentleman is trying to find a woman he thinks may come in here. I can't place her, but you work nights half the time. Maybe she comes in then."

Nikki was white, thirty-something going on sixteen what with the nose ring, the tongue stud, the goth eye makeup, the spiky bottle-blond hair. If her face was hard, her body was soft in an extremely pleasing way.

She started shaking her head before I got halfway through my description. "That could be several of our customers. Is there anything weird about her?"

"Weird?"

"Yeah, you know. Like a sloe eye or big nose or a scar or something?"

"Not really."

"Hmm." Then, "You know who might know her? Janine in back. She's tried just about every hair place in the neighborhood. She's very, very picky. She probably knows everybody who works around here."

"Could I talk to her?"

"Sure. C'mon, I'll take you back."

"Thank you," I said to the black woman.

Janine was indeed a fan of hair salons. She had a cast-iron hairdo that had last been seen in the known universe around 1960, a kind of modified reddish hair helmet that was a perfect complement to the wild makeup that gave her the look of a sinister doll. I put her age at fifty-five or so.

Nikki did the introductions and left me alone with Janine, whose job, apparently, was going through the warehouse part of the store and matching the numbers on her clipboard with the numbers on the boxes stacked from floor to ceiling. They'd damned well better tally.

"Makeup, huh? Those are the hardest ones to find. Just because a gal knows hair don't mean she knows squat about makeup. And I've tried 'em all. And you know what? I do my own makeup now. I used to tell them how I wanted it to look — just the way it is now — and they'd try and talk me out of it. Every single time. Hey, who knows what I want better than I do? That's what I finally decided, anyway."

"So nobody comes to mind?"

"Sort of — vaguely, I mean. I mean, there was somebody who was supposed to be a real pro with makeup — and I'm sure I tried her, too — but right now I can't get a name or a face. You got a phone?"

"Why don't I give you my cell phone number?"

"You ever read those things can give you

brain cancer?"

"I've read that. Some studies say yes, some studies say no."

I wrote my number out and handed it to her.

"If I come up with anybody, I'll call you."

"I'd really appreciate it."

She patted her hair helmet. "I just wish my hair gal knew about makeup. If I had the time, I'd sit her down and explain it to her."

She was deranged but oddly likable. But then I realized that this description could probably apply to me, too. "I'm sure she'd appreciate that," I said and got out of there.

A breast, a thigh, a buttock, a young woman easing herself down on a man's penis. Breath coming in bursts, gasps. She has a fine, tight, lithe body. A couple very clear shots of her face. Surprisingly pretty.

The man — our own Senator Warren Nichols — is also seen very clearly at least three times in the eight-minute videotape. He looks a lot better with his clothes on. He is also less than an ardent lover. He just wants to get off. He could be having sex with an inflatable woman. He just keeps wrenching her into whatever position is best for him at any given moment. A few of the positions are obviously painful for her and she mutters protests. Not that he gives a damn. Not that he tries to be any more considerate. Not that he treats her like any kind of equal.

His cry is almost savage when he comes. Her expression is almost comic in the disgust and contempt it conveys as she watches him fall off her, sated and out of breath, flinging his arms out and lying on his back.

"You're quite the lover."

But he doesn't catch the sarcasm. Through gasps, he says, "Thank you. You're not bad yourself."

If he notices her slipping from the bed, tugging on her thong, combing her hair with her fingers, you can't tell it from what the camera eye sees. He still seems to be riding the wave of his orgasm.

"See you," she says, a slight figure moving swiftly to the door.

"You take care of yourself now," Warren says from the bed.

R. D. Greaves's laugh was harsh. "Your man is some lover. Shit, I've treated whores better than that. Even the ones that gave me crabs."

His hotel room apartment was a nice one. Too nice for somebody like good old R.D.

There were two Renoir prints, a massive TV, and a screened fireplace with an imposing natural stone hearth with rough edges. I would have been even more appreciative of the living room if I hadn't been brooding over the videotape.

"So, Sport, now you know I'm not bullshitting you, right?"

We sat in chairs side by side in front of the TV set. Curtains drawn. Day for night.

"I guess."

"You guess my ass. This is the real thing and you know it."

"A million dollars — we can't come up with it."

"Listen, man, I had my accountant check him out. That much cash is always a hassle, but it's there to be had. And if I don't get it by tomorrow noon —"

"I get sick of your threats."

"Well, I get sick of your bullshit."

"How about opening the drapes?"

"Scared of the dark?"

The sunlight was so stark it made me wince. This was one of those Midwestern turnaround days that would be unimaginable anywhere else. A near blizzard last night. Forty-two degrees this morning, the snow melting so fast it was flooding certain parts of the city.

I was thinking about tomorrow, about what I had planned for it when I came back to this room just before noon. It was crude but it would work. It had damned well *better* work, anyway.

"So what's it going to be?"

"We don't have much choice, do we? Tomorrow noon, you'll have your money. Where do I bring it?"

"Right here."

"There's no point in asking you if this is the only copy. I'm sure you've made several dupes of it. And I'm also sure you're going to come back for more."

"Not unless I blow through that million awful fast."

"That's reassuring."

"I don't get the full million tomorrow, asshole, I'm going to feed you to the rats. I don't like people who waste my time."

I walked over and picked up my coat and slid my arms into it. "What happens if Lake ever finds out that you didn't turn the tape over to him?"

"What happens? Nothing happens, because he'll never find out. You sure as hell won't tell him, because then he'll know your secret. And I sure as hell won't tell him, because then he'd tell everybody what I did, and that wouldn't exactly be good for my

116

business rep, now, would it?"

"Nothing's ever that easy, Greaves. You should know that by now. You've convinced yourself that this is the easiest money you've ever made. But you know how things can happen, things you don't expect at all."

A sneer. "If you're trying to scare me, man, it won't work. I want a million in hundred-dollar bills, just the way I told you. Then I'll worry about the rest."

At the door, I said, "I'm still going to nail your ass for drugging the senator's drink last night."

He smiled. "You never quit, do you?"

"Not when I'm after a scumbag like you."

"Aw, there you go again, Sport. Hurting my feelings. I guess you just don't know how sensitive I am. You get me?"

"Oh, yeah," I said, "I get you all right."

"I didn't have jack to do with putting anything in his drink. And neither did Lake. If he had, I would've known about it. He would've asked me to do it."

The sunlight highlighted the coarseness of his face. The old pockmarks, the furious redness of the booze over the years. Once again I didn't want to believe him, but I did. Nothing to do with rigging Warren's drink.

"You got some nice pussy working for you.

Don't suppose you'd line me up."

"Only way they'd ever go out with you, 'Sport,' is if they could wear biohazard suits."

"You're forgettin' how sensitive I am."

I got out of there without him winking at me. A small victory.

CHAPTER 11

When I got back to headquarters, I found Teresa Nichols, Kate, Laura, Gabe, and Billy sitting in Warren's office drinking coffee and looking glum. They were like seven-year-olds who'd just been told they couldn't go outside and play in the tornado.

Billy said, "Have you heard the radio in the last five minutes?"

"I just listen to the oldies station. The eighties was my decade. You know, when I was still innocent."

Laura dredged up a smile. "You were never innocent, Dev."

"All right, but I was at least *semi-*innocent."

"That I can live with."

"I'm afraid to ask, but what was on the radio?"

"Oh, Dev," Teresa said. "It was awful."

"Okay, which one of you is going to give me the first clue?"

"They didn't spend much time on Senator Nichols at all," Kate said. "Most of it was about how heroic and manly and family values Jim Lake looked walking across the stage last night to help his opponent."

"They of course mentioned that he led us in prayer?"

"Of course, Dev. They mentioned that twice, in fact."

Billy said, "They even mentioned the American flag he had stuck up his ass. Forgive my crudity, Teresa."

"Be my guest," Teresa said.

"God, can you imagine what the overnight polling is going to look like?" Laura said.

"Where's Warren?" I asked.

Laura said, "I got him another big radio interview."

They were all here. "He's down there alone?"

"I thought I'd leave pretty soon."

"You leave right now," I snapped at Laura. "Dammit, you're communications director, remember? Get going."

"There's no need for that, Dev," Teresa said. "I was planning on going with her. Sometimes you treat my husband like a helpless child."

"No offense, Teresa, but sometimes he *is* a helpless child. He gets overwhelmed and says the wrong thing. That's why he's hired all of us here. To save him."

She decided to let me live. She sighed and said, "I suppose Dev's right, Laura. We'd better get down there."

"It's only ten minutes on the Dan Ryan," Billy said helpfully.

Before the door closed, and spoken so loudly that I couldn't possibly miss it, Laura said, "I see Dev's on the rag again." And Teresa laughed, of course.

"You could have handled that a little better, Bunny," Kate said, standing up and walking over to get her coat from the rack. Bunny was her nickname for me. I'd never understood why exactly.

"I suppose I could have."

"Technically, you were right. I don't know what the hell Laura was thinking. She said she'd meet him at the studio. But I was starting to wonder when she was going to leave. But still — we don't need the stress of you losing your temper."

"You can't see it, but I'm actually groveling, Kate. I'll apologize to Laura first chance I get. And was the radio really that bad?"

"I've monitored five different stations," Billy said. "Every one of them leads with how noble Lake was before they even mention the senator's name. And since the senator is now up and around, the rest of the time is spent on how voters may now take a fresh look at Jim Lake, who the Nichols campaign and a lot of newspapers have tended to turn into a nut job who's in the pocket of every crooked corporation in the United States."

"The poor baby," Kate said as she left.

Gabe, pouring himself some coffee, said, "This too shall pass, Dev."

"I wish I could believe that."

"Look who we're dealing with here," Gabe went on. "The guy who said that any Catholic who votes Democrat should be excommunicated."

"Lake took it back."

"But it shows that he'll self-destruct. He probably would've done it at the debate the other night if somebody hadn't fixed Warren's Diet Pepsi."

"Maybe Gabe's right, Dev. Lake does tend to self-destruct."

"Yeah, Billy, and maybe Warren can fly without needing a plane."

"Lake always ends up saying the wrong thing," Gabe said.

"Will you guarantee that in writing?"

He appreciated the humor. "Sure. If I don't have to sign my real name."

■ ■ ■ ■

That afternoon, despite being pretty much drained from last night, I played handball for an hour. I was hoping to find a pickup opponent in the gym somewhere in the age range of eighty to ninety or who was legally blind. Unfortunately, the only guy I could find was about twenty-five and looked as if he bench-pressed Buicks to impress his girl-friends.

He did me the favor of reviving me. I forgot everything but the game. If I hadn't paid attention, he would have literally run over me. He saw what we were doing as mortal combat. He was a video-game star come to psychotic life. I don't think he chuckled the word "pussy" more than four or five times when I missed plays. I was about fifteen years and many muscle groups older than he was. Afterward he congratulated me in the manner of an invading general patting the loser on the back. "You gave it your best, man." I wondered how many times I could hit him in the face before he broke me in half. Well, "Pussy" was at least better than "Pops."

After showering, I found a deli that served Heineken and had myself a corned beef sandwich. I was playing hooky and I knew it. But finally the work ethic snuck up on me and dragged me back to headquarters. The press was gone. Phones, faxes, copiers, deliveries, minor crises — we were back to serious work again. And people of all ages, colors, religions, and degrees of power dreams ran about the place like the Japanese in those old Mothra monster movies cable can buy for cheap on Halloween.

"I think you need a cup of coffee," I said when I walked into the office in the back. Warren was alone, staring off with a frown making him look older than he was.

"I need a lot more than that, Dev. Friend of mine says the *Trib* is going to run a big piece on Jim Lake tomorrow. Family, friends, the whole nine yards. He's our new hero." He snorted and shook his head. "Let us now all bow our heads and pray. Shit, if I'da known it was that simple I woulda brought some holy water along and blessed everybody in the audience. I was an altar boy, you know — and, no, I didn't get bug-gered by a priest. You can't say you were an altar boy anymore without somebody ask-ing if some priest slipped you the sausage."

"Elegantly put. Now, c'mon. We're going down the street for coffee."

When the waitress brought us our Danish

along with our coffee, Warren said, "So you saw the video?"

"I saw the video." We had to speak much more softly this afternoon. The place was only half full. Words carried.

"It's legit?"

I nodded. "I'm done the day after the election."

I took some pleasure in his startled reaction. "What the hell's this all about?"

"Just what I said it was about. I'm quitting the day after the election. Win or lose."

"I see. You're getting sanctimonious on me. Thanks a lot. My ass is on the line here and you're leaving."

"Not till it's over."

"This is really bullshit, Dev."

"You lied to me. When I signed on, I said no lies."

"Well, you sleep around as much as I do and —" He stopped. "Before you give me a sermon, Monsignor Dev, let me correct that statement. When you sleep around as much as I *used to* —"

"It's all bullshit, Warren."

"What is?"

"You've never stopped sleeping around. You've just figured out a way to hide it better."

"Here comes the sanctimony."

125

"The tape is for real. And so is his demand."

"He wants a million in hundred-dollar bills. We're taking him the three hundred thousand. Right?"

"Right."

"What if he wants more?"

"He won't."

"But what if he *does*?"

"Don't worry. I can handle it. As much as I don't want to."

"And here I thought people in Congress were sleazy. This Greaves is something else, isn't he?"

"Both sides have got people like him."

"Oh, I forgot what you always say. That it's a matter of degrees. Well, thank God we don't have anybody as bad as Greaves."

"I need to know when the money will be ready."

"Tomorrow morning. I should be in the office by ten o'clock."

"Fine."

"Just don't do anything crazy, Dev. Sometimes you worry me. You've got a dark side, my friend. You need to watch yourself."

"Do something crazy like sleep around on camera when I'm up for reelection, you mean?"

"I was hungover. I've told you that. Dif-

ferent men react to being hungover in different ways. I always get this incredible
hard-on."

"You could always abuse yourself."

"When a little dolly like her walks in?
C'mon, not even a pious bastard like you
could resist."

"Maybe, maybe not."

"I wish you'd make me feel a little better
about all this, Dev. It wouldn't hurt you to
tell me this is going to work out all right."

I couldn't help myself. As much as I'd
come to despise him, I felt sorry for him for
just a millisecond here. "Warren, you're so
used to people propping you up, it's sort of
humorous. They forgive you everything and
when you're down they pump you back up
with bullshit. And that goes triple for when
you and the rest of them are in session. You
people in Washington are the most spoiled,
pampered, self-important group anywhere
in the world. And it just keeps on getting
worse. You vote yourself more and more
privileges every term. And that goes for both
sides as always. So when you're faced with
a serious crisis that you just happened to
cause yourself — you just assume that
somebody on your staff can make it all better. Well, I'm going to tell you that maybe

this will come out all right and maybe it won't."

"But you said —"

"I said I *think* he'll go for the three hundred thousand. But what if he doesn't? I could kill him and take the tape. You want me to kill him for you, Warren?"

"C'mon. That's crazy. That's what I meant about your dark side."

I leaned back in the booth. Stared right at him. "You love your Senate seat so much, Warren, that if it came right down to it — if the only way you could keep it was to have me kill Greaves for you —"

"Don't be ridiculous."

"I'm not being ridiculous. Maybe in the end you wouldn't be able to give me the order to off him. But I'll bet you'd have to think about it for a long time. And there're a lot of others in Congress just like you. It's just unthinkable that you'd give up power, isn't it?"

"I don't like you anymore, Dev. I really don't."

"Right now," I said, sliding out of the booth, "I could give a shit, Warren."

CHAPTER 12

Dinner that night was a rare delicacy known as a cheese-and-onion pizza that Laura and I shared as we discussed our next media buy. An internal poll had come in late this afternoon that I was seeing for the first time at headquarters. Our interpretation of it was that we were losing whatever gains we'd made downstate, which is more conservative than most people realize. We'd never planned on winning that area of the state, but we had to get a minimum of twenty percent of it to offset any sudden surge by Lake. One of our own pollsters faxed us an internal poll he'd conducted late yesterday. It showed that downstate we were running sixteen percent, down three since Lake had started playing Doc Savage. We'd been at twenty-one a week ago.

"I'd say it's time to unload number four on them. The nuke."

I'd said this with an air of bravado as a

joke. Laura had been anxious to drop the most negative commercial we'd ever done. The one that pointed out that if you were an average citizen, it didn't make any sense to vote for Lake.

But she didn't return my smile. Her brown eyes were fixed on a spot slightly to the right of me. She was gazing off into the middle distance, distracted by something that had been bothering her even before I'd walked in here twenty minutes earlier.

"The nuke, Laura. The one you've been waiting for."

"Oh, that'll be great," she said, forcing her attention back to me. The delicate bones of her face were as refined as ever. But in the eyes and in the voice there was a hint of agitation she was having a hard time controlling. "The big one."

"We've got plenty of money. We can saturate the whole area. We can force him to answer us point for point."

But she was staring off again. The temptation was to say something to her, but I decided to turn around and work on the computer for a while.

I called up the copy for the nuke spot. It was simple, and every charge it made was true. Each accusation was based on Lake's voting record.

Ask Jim Lake why he voted against
HEALTH CARE (for those who can't afford it)
EXTENDED UNEMPLOYMENT INSURANCE
TAX PENALTIES FOR COMPANIES OFFSHORE
STUDENT LOAN INTEREST REFORM
CAPS ON LOBBYIST SPENDING
MORE CONGRESSIONAL OVERSIGHT ON GOVERNMENT SPENDING
Ask Jim Lake. You won't believe what he's got to say.

Negative advertising has a bad name. A good deal of it is deceitful and excessive. But used properly, it's the best way to give the public an indication of what your opponent truly believes. This spot was aimed, as most negative ads are, at independent voters who might have started leaning toward Lake. We hoped we were raising at least one issue that would give each voter pause. A saturation campaign was our best hope of achieving that.

At first I didn't want to believe what I was hearing. The campaign was getting difficult enough. But when it didn't stop, I had no choice except to admit what I was hearing and then turn around and face it.

Laura, dutiful Laura, always reliable communications director Laura, was holding a Kleenex up to her eyes dabbing the tears gleaming down her cheeks. Her nose was red. The hand that held the tissue was trembling.

"Can I help, Laura?"

She shook her head and started crying again, snuffling into the Kleenex. I shoved the box of tissues closer to her. "Probably time to change that one, Laura."

She laughed raggedly, pitched the used tissue into the wastebasket, and then plucked a fresh one from the box.

"You don't think it'd help to talk about it?"

She shook her head again.

"Somebody sick in your family? Something like that?"

"I really can't talk about it, Dev," she managed to say.

"There's a bottle of bourbon in that desk over there. Would you like a shot of it?"

Another shake of the head.

And then she was on her feet, gathering up her coat and purse, clutching them to her as if she were afraid I'd take them away from her. "I just don't know how much longer I can do this," she said.

What the hell was "this"?

"You mean this job? Is that what you're saying, Laura?"

"I'm sorry, Dev. I really have to go. I wouldn't be able to concentrate tonight, anyway. I'll be here bright and early in the morning. I promise. But now —"

She stumbled as she walked to the door. I was afraid she was going to fall over. But she righted herself at the last moment. "I always told you I was a clumsy oaf."

"And I always told you you were crazy."

"I'm sorry to do this to you, Dev."

"Well, you're obviously in no shape to work, so don't worry about it. I just wish you'd let me help you with it, whatever it is."

"Sometimes you can be so sweet, Dev. We all appreciate it."

And then she was just footsteps heard out front in the public section of headquarters. She took the side door out so she wouldn't have to face the volunteers who'd been working late as the campaign hurried to Election Day.

Not a clue. "I don't know if I can do this much longer, Dev." Buy media? Sit in the same room with me? Associate with political people? Face an unhappy life every morning when she got up?

I wasn't worried about her as an employee. She was damned good, but so were others we could sign on quickly. I was worried about her as a friend. I'd never thought of her as being especially vulnerable. She liked to be tough to the point that it was sometimes comical. To see her break this way was shocking.

Fluffy scrambled eggs, warm toast with peach jam, two strips of crisp bacon, and a cup of rich, good coffee. Breakfast next morning.

I'd spent a half hour in the hotel gym. I needed to be as focused as possible for my confrontation with Greaves. He'd find out too late that I'd tape-recorded everything he'd said to me during our upcoming exchange at noon. Then I'd have a bartering tool as well. He might be able to sink the campaign with his video of Warren, but I'd be able to put him in prison for several years for extortion.

He'd come at me, of course, and I wanted to be sure I could take him out fast and sure. I even spent twenty minutes on the punching bag.

Now, after a shower and a change of clothes, I was enjoying my breakfast. Enjoying it right up to the point where one of the city's more prominent Lake supporters suggested in an op-ed piece that officials had conspired to cover up Warren's real problem at the debate the other night, that he'd been drunk.

The op-ed went on to remind voters that not that long ago there were many rumors about Warren in Washington. His girl chasing was one, but so was his excessive drinking.

Had police and hospital officials floated the "sedative" story to cover up his drinking? Nichols was, it went on, a powerful sitting senator and had enough influence to ask them to cover for him.

The charge was ridiculous — maybe you could get cops to cover up a story; hospital officials would never go along with it — but it sounded more convincing than our true story of something being put in his Diet Pepsi and vague hints of a conspiracy.

The lynch mob that listened to talk radio would be sexually excited by an allegation like this. By midafternoon they'd have painted Warren not only as a drunken philanderer but as a terrorist spy as well.

"I want to know what you and my husband are keeping from me."

I raised my head from the op-ed page, happy that somebody had distracted me, and saw a familiar and alluring face across the booth from me. Teresa Nichols was wearing a red ski sweater, her lustrous blond hair pulled back in a pert ponytail. Only the anxiety in her gleaming eyes spoiled the magazine-ad glamour of her patrician face.

"And good morning to you, Teresa."

She smiled. "I'm sorry. I should at least have said hello, shouldn't I? It's just I know he's hiding something. And since he doesn't have any secrets from you —"

"I'm not sure that's true, Teresa."

She had coffee only. Black. When we were alone, the hotel coffee shop starting to fill up with the last rush of the morning, she said, "He's been so distracted the last few days, it's like he isn't even there. And last night I was sure something was wrong."

"What happened last night?"

"Nightmares. He never has nightmares unless something terrible is wrong. He woke up twice shouting and covered in sweat."

"A lot of things could cause nightmares. It doesn't have to be a deep dark secret."

"How about a three a.m. phone call?"

"Now you might be on to something. Any idea who called?"

"No. It came on his cell. He grabbed it and took it down the hall in the den so I couldn't hear it."

"You didn't hear any of it?"

"He muttered a curse word when he answered it in our bedroom. I didn't hear any of the rest of it."

Now she had me curious, too. There was the possibility that the phone call had nothing to do with Greaves and his videotape. But three a.m. — it was difficult to believe that the call wasn't about the tape. There were always sudden campaign problems. But a three a.m. call made it unlikely that an aide had phoned him. He or she would have waited till morning.

"He said you're going to get together about ten at headquarters."

"That's the plan."

"Please do me a favor and see what you can find out. Tell him you had breakfast with me and that I was very concerned."

She still had a good wife's faith that her husband would tell the truth to a close friend and thus, eventually, to her. But Warren was a man of a thousand secrets. I knew only a few of them. I was assuming that this was about the tape. But possibly there was another secret I knew nothing about, something even more dire than R. D. Greaves's tape.

"I'll see what I can do."

She settled back into the booth, a shiny,

137

fine, middle-aged woman I'd had innumer-able fantasies about over the years. She was just so damned *clean* and sleek.

"I see you're reading that stupid op-ed."

"The one where he's an opium smoker and a pedophile?"

"I wish it *was* funny, Dev. But I know a certain percentage of people will believe it. He really has changed, Dev. No more chas-ing around. I'm sure of that."

"Truth doesn't matter to these people, Teresa." And it doesn't matter all that much to your husband, either.

"God knows Warren isn't perfect. But nobody is. For all his faults he's been a very good senator."

"Yes, he has."

"And I still think Jim Lake was behind putting something in his soda the other night."

"Maybe so."

She made a fist with her tiny hand. "Oh, this op-ed just makes me so mad, Dev."

She left the booth as quickly as she'd ap-peared in it. "I'm meeting Kate for coffee at Starbucks down the street. She's taking her morning break in about ten minutes."

Mention of Kate made me think of an-other staffer, Laura. And her strange break-down last night. Another secret I didn't know anything about? What had upset her so much that she couldn't stop herself from breaking down in front of me?

"Nice that you and Kate get along so well."

"God, people keep saying that. I guess they expect a catfight or something. But Kate's been working with us for six years now. We've always been good friends." She glanced at the slender gold watch on her left wrist. "Need to go, Dev. But please try and find out what's bothering him so much, will you?"

"I sure will, Teresa. You just relax and have a good time with Kate."

She leaned over and kissed me on the cheek, the touch of her lips and her perfume arousing me instantly.

I had more coffee and tried not to look at the op-ed page again. But of course I did. Maybe I could get the full-mooner who'd written this in a death cage match. We'd raise money for charity and I'd get to kill him legally.

I was about to leave the booth myself when I looked up from my newspaper and saw a familiar dark face. Detective Sayers.

He slid in across from me. "Sun's out. Glad to see it. You look tired, by the way."

"I wouldn't know why. I'm just rereading

the op-ed that says my client is a sleazy bum."

Sayers brushed his chin with a large hand. "And that's not the only problem you have."

I didn't say anything until after he'd ordered coffee and a bagel for himself. "So you brought me more bad news?"

"Not 'brought you.' You already had it. You're too smart not to have figured it out."

"I'm not sure what we're talking about here."

"We're talking about your man passing out onstage the other night. We're talking about who put the stuff in his drink. And we're talking about it probably being an inside job."

"Meaning?"

"Meaning somebody on your own staff."

I settled back. Whatever energy I'd managed to scrounge up at the gym was waning now. The weariness was back. Not only somebody on our own staff — what about the makeup woman?

"There were a lot of people backstage from four-thirty on. We canvassed everybody. Nobody reported seeing anybody who didn't belong there."

He hadn't taken off his tan Burberry. His brown fedora sat on the edge of the table.

"I'd like you to be my point man on the inside."

"I believe that's called 'ratting people out.'"

"TV talk. You need to know who you're dealing with and so do I. We want the same thing. The bad guy."

I couldn't disagree. Whoever had given Warren the drug deserved to be identified and punished. "I'm not going to name any names until I'm positive."

"Fair enough. I've got three other cases I'm working on. I'll let you figure out who we're talking about here and then I'll take over when it's appropriate."

"This won't be fun."

"You're friends with all of them?"

"We don't hang out together. Not that type of friends. But when you work as closely with people as I do — you want to see them happy. And succeed. You don't like to think of them as some kind of twisted nut jobs."

He smiled with big white teeth. "You should have my job. You get used to twisted nut jobs real fast."

Somebody at headquarters had blown up the op-ed piece to five times its normal size and made obscene comments in the margins. This would have to come down before a visiting reporter saw it. In the old days, Kennedy's babes and Nixon's innumerable lapses into insanity would never have been reported. (Thanks to Dr. Henry Strangelove Kissinger, we knew that Nixon prayed in his final days in office and urged Strangelove to do likewise; but why would Strangelove pray — when he was God himself?)

When I walked into the office and closed the door, Warren was swallowing two pills from a small brown prescription bottle. Because we were pros we'd moved past our bitter exchange yesterday. Nothing more needed to be said.

"Xanax."

"I thought they made you a little fuzzy."

"Maybe I need to be a little fuzzy."

"According to the schedule you've got four different stops today."

"Maybe you'd rather I come apart when I'm speaking to people."

"Pull a Jimmy Swaggart. There's still time to train that lower lip of yours to quiver the way his did. And then you can start sobbing and go into 'I have sinned.'"

He fixed me with an angry stare. He was lousy at self-pity, as most arrogant people are. "You don't give a shit about me personally, do you, Dev?"

I'd been wrong. He was back in his self-pity mode and seemed to have forgotten every single angry word I'd laid on him. He had the enviable ability of forgetting anything too painful to remember.

I gave him the short version. "I give a shit about what you believe politically. You want to accomplish the same things legislatively that I do. In your own patrician way you give a shit about the masses. And so do I, being one of them. But you personally? You told me a lot of lies to get me on board this time, the biggest one being that you were leaving the women alone. And that may not be all of it. I just had coffee with Teresa. She thinks you're hiding some other deep dark secret."

"Oh, God, she's been on my case since she got here the night of the debate. She's so fucking paranoid."

"Gosh, I wonder why."

"You a marriage counselor now, are you, Dev? That'd be funny for a guy who hasn't had anything but one-night stands for three years."

"I guess I'm being sanctimonious again, huh?"

"You want to know who called at three a.m.? It was Greaves. He just wanted to make sure I'd be ready with the money.

Sweet, huh? Three a.m."

"I'm sorry that happened to you, Warren. But we both know he's a creep."

I went over and got some coffee.

"You read that op-ed piece?"

"Yeah."

"Damage?"

"You're doing the radio interview in two hours. Dispute every point in the op-ed. Put it right up his ass."

"This is raw meat for those talk-radio bastards."

"Nothing new there. They already hated you. What I want to see is how much mileage Lake gets from the mainstream press. That's what we have to watch out for."

Once I was seated, he went over and got coffee for himself. He was careful about how he talked now. "I had this place swept again at seven this morning, but I'm still nervous about talking."

"Don't blame you."

He nodded to a brown leather valise on the table with the fax. He gave me a thumbs-up. Three hundred K.

"I'm still a little worried about afterward, Dev."

"So am I." I changed the subject quickly. In case the room was still bugged, I didn't want to say anything incriminating. "Laura's

144

having some personal problems."

He seemed surprised. "That's very interesting, but what the hell does it have to do with anything this morning?"

It wasn't the sort of thing I'd usually discuss on the morning I was going to drop off better than a quarter million dollars in cash to a blackmailer, but at least it got us talking about something other than the brown valise and the possibility that Greaves was going to keep on blackmailing us. I'd already ingested half a roll of Tums.

"Thought I'd mention it. I don't see her around this morning."

"She's under a lot of stress. She's a good woman. She'll pull out if it, Dev. And now can we talk about something else? Did anything good happen for our campaign today?"

But I wasn't up for making him feel better. Screw him.

"You go over your notes for the radio interview?"

"Three times. This Mindy Thomas, she's friendly to us, right?"

"She was last time around. Hard to believe she'd go for Lake, though she didn't go for our governor candidate last time."

"He was about as appealing as diarrhea."

"Be sure and mention that on the air."

He laughed. "I can't help it. Even when I'm pissed at you, I laugh at your stupid sarcasm."

"Oh, I forgot. You want to be universally loved."

"Am I that bad?"

"How many times have you studied yourself in the mirror today?" His Washington staffers told me he kept a mirror the size of a hardback book in his office drawer. Every major politician is a megalomaniac. There are no exceptions, not even the ones who look like parrots and advocate executing abortion doctors. Maybe they are megalomaniacs in particular. But so are the warm and fuzzy ones that everybody likes because they're for "the little guy," a bit of praise that stretches back to at least FDR, who saw just about everybody in America as his personal servant.

"Guess I'll go to the john," he said abruptly. He picked up the new *Time.* "Are we in here this week?"

"Yeah, you're on the cover and half the magazine is your biography."

"Someday that'll be the truth, Dev. You wait and see."

"You'll have to share it with Genghis Khan."

"I'm a lot better looking than he was," Warren said, trundling off.

CHAPTER 13

Laura got in around ten-thirty. I had the valise with the money pushed under my desk. I was trying to concentrate on a couple of niche print ads — one to labor; one to suburban women — that needed to be FedExed by late this afternoon. Either the copy was perfecto or I was so distracted I couldn't read English. I signed my name and initials in big looping letters. I even put an exclamation point on them, making the copywriters' day.

She didn't say anything. Despite the swank blue dress and the swank moussed hair, the dark circles under her eyes and the heavy, anxious sighs betrayed her agitation and sorrow. Sort of like me in the first months following my divorce.

I spoke first. "Mind if I ask how you're doing?"

"How the fuck you think I'm doing?"

"I guess that kind of answers it."

She sat at her desk, sipping coffee and checking her e-mails. I took a couple of inconsequential phone calls.

When I hung up, she said, "I shouldn't have said that."

"Can I be patronizing and say that I've hung from that cross you're on now?"

"Your divorce?"

"Yeah."

"I thought I was tougher than this."

"We all think we're tougher than this. Even professional wrestlers think they're tougher than this."

She giggled. "That was exactly the right thing to say. You are so weird sometimes, Dev, and it's almost always funny."

"I never told you I was a professional wrestler?"

"Billy used to brag about how you were a college boxer. And you were in the army, too?"

"Yeah. Did he add that I got my nose broken twice and had to be taken to the hospital once with a concussion?"

"Nah. He didn't tell me that. Makes a better story without it."

Then she took a deep breath and sighed it out. "For about forty-two seconds there you had me in a good mood. I think that's my record for the last twenty-four hours."

"I went as long as fifty-two seconds in the first month after I got dumped."

"Now I have a goal to shoot for. And please don't tell me that I'm going to feel better real, real, *real* soon. The next fucking person who says that to me is going to get their car blown up."

"I always figured you for a terrorist."

"Didn't you hate all the advice people gave you?"

"I wore those earplugs they wear on aircraft carriers." And I damned near had, too. Admit that you've got a broken heart and suddenly everybody you know turns into a grief counselor. I'm not even sure they mean well. It's a power position, and any number of them, it seemed to me, enjoyed being condescending.

"Tell me to focus."

"Focus, Laura."

"I've got so much to do."

"Focus or I'll beat the crap out of you. I was a boxer, remember."

"Yeah, but you got your nose broken twice."

"And don't forget the concussion. But I could still whip you."

"That did it. You scared me straight. Now I'm one hundred percent concentration."

"Good. So now you'll shut up so *I* can

concentrate."

"You sure put in long days," Laura said.

"The burdens of a role model."

"I'm going to the little girls' room and cry my eyes out."

"Really?"

"Really."

"Take plenty of Kleenex."

"Won't need it. Plenty of toilet paper there."

"Ah."

"I actually thought of calling you in the middle of the night."

"You know, I still don't know exactly what you're talking about here."

"Someday I'll be able to tell you."

"Call me anytime you want to, Laura. You know that."

She put her hand in mine. "I really did think I was tougher than this."

"Read Hemingway. He knew we were all cowards in all respects."

"Maybe I'll give him a try."

I was just settling in with my computer when Billy came into the office. "Good morning." He probably wasn't going to feel that way when I gave him some bad news. Billy hated to travel.

"We're having problems in Galesburg," I said. "Our man there had a heart attack, as you know. That was four days ago. In the interim the place has gone totally to shit. I need you to fly there and see if you can get things straightened out. You can be back on a late plane. We already bought you your ticket. You leave in two hours."

"Aw, shit, Dev. I've got things going on here."

"I'm sorry, Billy. You're good at this and you know it. All you have to do is figure out a new organizational chart. The woman who's number two is afraid to make any changes. You know, she'll hurt people's feelings and all that. So you be the bad guy for her."

"Hell, I could do that over the phone."

"Yeah, I suppose you could. But I'd rather you go there personally. Make it a little more official."

"Shit."

"I think you said that already."

The sun had turned Chicago into its usual road race. The streets were reasonably clear, tires could get traction, everybody was late or thought they were, and ordinarily calm, respectable drivers had suddenly begun trying out for the Daytona 500.

And what was Chicago without its sirens? Police, ambulance, firefighters. All day, all

152

night in some sections of the city. By the time I reached Greaves's hotel, I'd been slowed down by two fire trucks and an ambulance.

I knew this was the beginning of Greaves feeding off Warren. Right now I didn't care. Even if we got a monthlong respite from his greediness, it would be enough to work our way back up in the polls and have a good chance of winning by two or three points. It might not be the win we'd hoped for. But it would be a win. And while I didn't have much respect for him as a man, Warren and I did share the same view of what had to be done in this grotesquely unjust society the rich and shameless had turned it into since the early 1980s — Bush, Clinton, Bush — time for a serious new start. The only time I'd felt any support for Clinton after the first term was when the other side had tried to impeach him, talk radio's wet dream. I'd be afraid to impeach just about anybody. Once that door is opened, we'll become Italy within ten years, insurrections a monthly occurrence in the legislature.

The new siren wasn't any different from the ones I'd just passed. Not until I got within two blocks of Greaves's hotel did I see that his block had been cordoned off with yellow crime scene tape and that an ambulance and two police cars were standing in front of the hotel itself.

I knew then. I could have been wrong, of course. But I didn't think so. A man like Greaves lives the kind of life that was once said of the animal kingdom — short, nasty, and brutish.

I wish I could say something noble here. For whom the bell tolls and all that sort of bullshit. But Greaves was a predator, and we've got far too many of them in our society.

I found a parking spot a block and a half away and walked over to the crime scene. I've gotten to know a number of cops over the years. We've hired some of them to supply security for our various functions. We pay well. And over the years they become sergeants and then detectives. And we can call on them for information.

I didn't see a single cop I knew in front of the hotel. The first two print reporters were there by now, too. TV couldn't be far behind. "Hey!" one of the onlookers called. "Who says you can go up there?" And the woman he was with complained, "Who does he think he is?"

I was going to tell her I was Clark Kent, but she probably wouldn't know who that was.

I walked up to a uniformed woman and said, "My sister's staying here. I hadn't heard from her in a couple of days and —"

"Nothing to worry about, sir. This was a man."

I moved as close as I could get to the ambulance and still be on the public side of the crime scene tape. They brought him down on a gurney. Fortunately, there was enough wind to pick up the sheet over his face. I got a millisecond glimpse of him. It was Greaves all right.

A headache started over my right eye. Stress. Wouldn't last long. But for the moment it forced me to close my eyes.

My knees are always the first thing to shake when I lose control for a while. I'm not sure why. Maybe it's some kind of memory from my boxing days. My legs were my weakest point. Four, five rounds and they'd start to go on me. That accounted for the concussion that time. I started to fall into him and he did what any boxer would try to do, take my head off. All thanks to my legs. I walked, wobbly, away from the crime scene.

No problem now worrying if Greaves would take the three hundred thousand.

Now we had much bigger problems.

Who had the tape that he was going to sell us?

CHAPTER 14

The smells of corned beef, pizza, burgers with lots of onions — staff and volunteers were eating a late lunch when I got back to headquarters. None of them paid much attention to me. Maybe I didn't look as mean as I thought. I wanted to smash somebody up, exactly who or why I wasn't sure. Maybe I wanted to smash myself up. Maybe I'd mishandled this whole Greaves thing. We never like to think that we ourselves screwed something up, but this time maybe it really was me.

Laura was typing rapidly on her computer. Kate and Teresa judged as Warren held up various neckties for them to inspect. Gabe was reading a reference book that had to weigh fifty pounds.

"Tell him to keep the one he's wearing," Teresa said of Warren's tie.

"These others are god-awful," Kate said.

"This tie gives me bad vibes," Warren said.

"And he makes fun of astrology," Teresa said. "Bad vibes."

Warren knew the significance of me being back here with the valise still in my hand. He was the one who should be Clark Kent now. His eyes could penetrate the leather and tell which it held — the money or the tape.

"You up for a good Italian meatball sandwich?" Warren said to me. I could gauge his anxiety by him suggesting Italian. All the Tums he took a day even for bland food — Italian food meant he was desperate to get out of here. "We can just walk a block over. Won't need any guards or anything." Teresa was adamant about keeping his protection. He hated people hovering. It gets tiresome. You have to watch what you say. Bodyguards sell a lot of material to gossip columns.

"Sounds good. Lots of fat and cholesterol and maybe spill some of that sauce on me. What more could a guy ask for?"

Kate laughed. "When you first came in here, I thought you were in a real bad mood. But now that you're cracking jokes, I know I was wrong."

Fooled them again.

"You've got to talk to the veterans' group in two hours," Laura reminded him.

"We'll be gone thirty, forty minutes at the

158

most. Dev here will see to it that I'm on time."

"How was the radio interview?"

"One of His Majesty's finest hours," Teresa said. "Right, Kate?"

"We were like schoolgirls," she said, sliding her arm around Teresa's shoulder, "actually swooning, he was so good."

"He got through the questions about the debate very well and right up at the top. He spent the rest of the time contrasting his record with Lake's. You could tell the host was impressed. Off the air she said that he was much better on radio than Lake. She said Lake was too strident for radio. That he came over better on TV, where you could see him, and that helped cut down on what he sounds like."

"Too bad it isn't the other way around," Warren said. "TV is where the big numbers are. A lot more people watch TV than listen to radio at any time."

Kate said, "Never try to flatter our senator here. He reacts very badly."

"Thirty or forty minutes or we'll come and get you, right, Kate?"

"Absolutely."

Ten steps from headquarters, Warren said, "Well, did you get it?"

"No, but Greaves did."

"What's that supposed to mean?"

"It means somebody killed him in his hotel room."

He stopped walking. Stood on the sidewalk, paralyzed. All but the eyes that frogged out a bit. "What the hell are you talking about?"

"Just what I said. Now get a grip, Warren. We're out in public, remember?"

"Somebody fucking murdered him?"

"That's right."

"And we don't know who has the tape now?"

"We don't know one way or the other. Given Greaves's background, we can't be sure that this had anything to do with the tape. There were probably several other people who had reasons to kill him."

Once we were seated in the restaurant, speaking in lower voices, and after he'd waved to everybody who recognized him and a few who hadn't, he said, "What the hell are we going to do now? What if Lake has it?"

"I need to find the makeup woman. See what she knows. Maybe she worked with Greaves."

"And how do you plan to do that, for God's sake?"

"I've seen her. I know who I'm looking

for, anyway. There's at least a chance that she lives somewhere in the neighborhood I was in."

"Where would you even start?"

"Beauty shops, bars, dry cleaners. Everywhere."

"I don't like this." Petulant.

"Gosh, I'm sorry this is difficult for you, Warren. Myself, I'm having a great time."

"Don't mock me."

"Then quit feeling sorry for yourself."

"And don't give me any 'wages of sin' bullshit."

"That's your trouble, Warren. You think it *is* bullshit. But it isn't. You do something you shouldn't, you always run the risk of getting nailed. It's pretty simple."

"Thank you, Professor." Then: "We have to get that tape."

"I know, Warren. But you're forgetting the other possibility."

"I won't be able to eat anything now anyway. Tell me."

"Maybe the killer couldn't find the tape in Greaves's hotel room."

"So it's still there."

"So it's still there or the police got luckier than the killer and found it."

"The police." He'd spoken sharply. We both looked around to see if anybody was listening. The Italian music — Dean Martin, of course — covered a lot of sins. And we had a lot of sins to cover. "The police? And what would they do with it?"

"Hard to say. I don't know what the protocol is here. Who they turn it over to. Probably the Cook County State's Attorney's Office."

"Then what?"

"Then I don't know. Like I said. But the big thing right now is to find the makeup woman."

"You have her name?"

"Not really. She made it up. But I may be getting a lead from this store I checked with. I'm pretty sure I've got the right neighborhood for her anyway."

Warren visibly relaxed. "I'm glad you're handling this, Dev. Sorry I came unglued there."

"We just have to be careful here, Warren. We could create even more problems for ourselves if we do anything rash."

"Is there any way the police can link us to Greaves?"

"Depends on what he left behind. Did he keep notes? What's on his computer? Did he have an appointment book? The paper trail's going to figure in here. Not just for us but for the killer, too. The luckiest break we could have is if the paper trail leads the police to the right person right away."

We both passed on the wine. Coffee was what we needed.

He finally did eat his sandwich. I was hungry. I would have eaten half of his if he'd decided to leave it.

"You need to clear your head as much as possible now. And to calm down. No more Xanax, though. You need all the energy you can get. You did well on the radio interview. That's got a big metro audience. That'll help. Probably the interview'll get covered by TV and newspapers. So we're starting back the right way. We've still got the edge in the polls. We can build on that. Heroes don't last long. The press'll now be looking for some way to prove he *isn't* a hero. This is the fun part for them. Knocking somebody down they enshrined as nobility. Plus, when people start to think about it, what the hell did he do, anyway? He was courteous at best. He walked across the stage and gave you a little assistance. Most people, man or woman, would do that. So what? We've got his record to shoot down and we're doing it with our ads and with you on the stump. Once we get this tape thing under control — and I'm hoping that that'll be very quickly — we'll be able to relax a little. But for right now you have to do the old Bill Clinton bit of compartmentalizing. You need to look stronger and tougher than ever, Warren. You need to go out there and start talking about the way we've become such an elitist society. That's your strongest theme. And you've got the voting record to back it up."

He smiled. "I take it that was an official political consultant pep talk?"

But I didn't smile in return. "I'm just doing my job, Warren."

CHAPTER 15

I saw a documentary on a political campaign that mentioned everybody, including part-time volunteers, but never said anything about the scheduler. While it may not sound like a difficult job, it is. You not only have to decide — usually with the campaign manager's input — where the candidate will be in the next forty-eight to fifty-six hours, you have to be ready to make abrupt changes if the waters get dangerous.

Miriam Dobbs is a quiet grandmother who came out of the AFL-CIO political wing back when Walter Reuther was still running things. Ike and Jack Kennedy were presidents then, Elvis was in the army, and a tubby little man named Khrushchev was our country's main nemesis.

That Miriam was a black woman made her success even more remarkable. She's the best scheduler I've ever worked with. She pays attention to the news. She senses when one event will have to be bumped in favor of another. Today she was working out of our office across town, so we did our work by phone.

"I'm assuming we want max audience to show him off. Strong, sturdy, using his sleeve instead of a tissue when he sneezes."

She also makes jokes.

"I kind of like the sleeve thing. Distinguishes him from the rest of the pack."

"I thought he pretty much did that by eating with his hands."

"You may have a point there, Miriam."

After a few more gags, we settled into a review of the substitutes she'd come up with. All of them were excellent. All of them would attract the press. The previous appointments had been small towns reached by private plane. We could reschedule those for later. For now the city was where he needed to be.

"There's also a chance I can get him a good TV interview."

"Wow. How'd you swing that?"

"My son is a news producer."

"Nepotism, eh?"

"That sounds dirty."

"When will we know?"

"I'm hoping by late this afternoon."

"Let me know, will you?"

"Always."

My last call from the office was to a friend of mine at one of the big political action committees. PACs have an unseemly reputation, but there are PACs and there are PACs. This one was sponsored by a group of wealthy men who also happened to be hunters. While I'm not much for killing innocent animals, these people were at least enlightened enough to understand the connection between the environment and their favorite sport. We needed some extra money not only for downstate TV but for some massive radio buys the last week before the election.

I sweet-talked my contact there, a soft-spoken young woman named Heather whom I'd dated a few times in Washington. She'd decided that since I was still so hung up on my marriage, being with me was "like being with my brother." She probably wasn't far wrong.

"You're sounding a lot better these days, Dev."

"Feeling better."

"Good." She hesitated. "Now I'm the brokenhearted one."

"What's his name? Consider him rubbed out."

"I committed the single girl's ultimate sin."

"Married?"

"Not only married, three kids, too. I really felt like a home wrecker. I kept trying to break it off with him. I really did feel grubby about the whole thing. Finally he broke it off with me. He had the decency to feel guilty about what he was doing to his family. But I still haven't been able to get over him."

"I'm sorry, Heather."

"Well, my luck's bound to change. I'm sure I'll meet a closeted gay guy in the next week or so."

"There you go."

"Or a wanted fugitive. And speaking of wanted —"

"You could be a disc jockey with segues like that."

"— you of course want money."

"Lots of it and fast."

"What the hell happened to your man the other night?"

"Somebody probably dropped a sedative in his drink."

"Most likely one of the ladies he's been seeing on the side all these years."

"You're too cynical."

"You really don't believe he's changed, do you?"

"Hope springs eternal."

"So how much are we talking here, Dev?"

So I told her how much we were talking and I thought she might hang up on me. Luckily all she did was laugh and say, "It's a good thing we've got the same ideas politically."

"Yes," I said, "isn't it, though?"

CHAPTER 16

I was a suburban kid who grabbed every chance possible to get into the city. My main parental warnings fit into two categories: "strangers" and "neighborhoods." They weren't mutually exclusive, but the former could be anywhere and the latter you had to be lured into. I was on such guard against strangers that I didn't even trust police officers. I'd learned from many science fiction movies that even city officials could be aliens in disguise, which, when you think about it, just may be true.

On the days I took the bus in, I didn't see much in the way of neighborhoods. The route was a three-lane nonstop jaunt that wasn't even long enough to make you sleepy, the way bus trips always seemed to make me. Going in on the train, though, you got to see or at least glimpse a variety of neighborhoods. The rough ones always fascinated me. After all the warnings I'd gotten about them, they held a real interest for me. Scary, for sure. But also intriguing. What were the people like there? If I went in, could I get out alive? And — this was at the age of peak romantic notions — would I find my true love there and then carry her off to the land of three-car families and season tickets for all the Illini football and basketball games?

By now, though, my interest in poor neighborhoods had been trumped by reality. Working for various pols over the years, I'd spent many nights walking streets controlled by gangs and watching the sad, weary working poor try to stave off not only hunger but despair as well. They would listen to us but they wouldn't believe us. You can only hold out hope so many times.

And now, just as the sun began to slant downward in the cloudy sky, I was back in a place where most of the cars had taped windows and wired-shut doors and at least one tire that was nearly flat. Businesses had barred windows. The houses weren't much better. Taped windows, sagging doors, frost-staved sidewalks.

I passed three straight blocks of tiny shops so dusty and old they resembled something out of Dickens. Some of them didn't even identify what they had to offer. I counted four astrology readers on my way in. The taverns were narrow, dark except for the neon signage above the doors and just starting to fill up for the night, men from nearby factories entering in small and hearty groups.

Not even spreading dusk hid the wasteland here. Not even the deepest shadows could lie about the conditions of the houses, the stores, the people. I found the address I was looking for, thanks to the woman from Daily Double Discount. She'd given me the name of a Beth Wells. I slid into an open space along the curb, three car lengths down from where the two-story white house with the slanting side steps sat. I waited twenty minutes before I went up. If she came out I planned to follow her.

While I waited, I saw one of those heartbreaks you want to look away from as soon as you see it — an enormous woman in a cheap gray Goodwill coat came up the sidewalk toward my car, her limp so pronounced that she lurched violently to the left every time she stepped down on her right foot. She must have been three hundred pounds plus and even in the waning light her face showed the claw marks of a vicious skin disease. She kept her eyes downcast. Eye contact for her would be deadly. She wouldn't want to see people smirking or making disgusted faces at the sight of her. You try to think of lives like hers and they're incomprehensible. All the pain; life as the alien, the outcast. I wished I still believed in praying. It was all I could think of to offer her.

By this time of day, NPR was doing lighter stuff, which generally didn't interest me. The jazz station I listened to was doing Dixieland, which didn't interest me, either. I took these two omens as my call to action.

I'd brought along my Glock. I wasn't sure why. Security blanket I suppose.

Since the address listed ended in 1/2, I interpreted that as being the upstairs apartment. The wooden stairs were just beginning to gleam with frost as I made my way up them. I listened for any kind of sound. Nothing, neither downstairs nor up. No lights, either. Maybe Beth Wells wasn't home. I'd decided against calling her in advance. Didn't want to give her the chance to run away.

At the top of the stairs a voice. Then the door opened. I automatically touched the Glock in my overcoat pocket. And then one of those surprises that is so startling your first impression is that you're hallucinating. *This can't possibly be.* But it is.

He saw me now, too. But I already had the Glock pointed right at his chest. "Back inside."

"What the fuck is the gun for?" He couldn't decide whether to be scared or angry. He was a bit of both.

"Back inside, you bastard. I'll be asking the questions. Not you."

"What's wrong, Billy?" a female voice from inside said.

"Shit," Billy said, "I can't believe this."

I marched him back inside. I kept the gun in sight.

The makeup woman said, "Oh God. It's that guy from the other night."

"My boss," Billy said glumly, talking like a ten-year-old who's been caught stealing apples. "This is so totally fucked I can't believe it."

"Turn on a light," I said.

"God, please put that gun away. I had to live like this all my life with my father. He was always pulling guns on somebody."

"Lights," I repeated as I slammed the door shut behind me.

She clicked on a table lamp, bathing a sorry room of secondhand furniture in dusty gold. One of the end tables was missing a leg and supported by a stack of paperbacks. The couch was so swaybacked that a pair of throw pillows had been placed in the middle of it. Otherwise the sitter would sink out of sight forever. The wallpaper was stained grotesquely in the way of an X ray showing large patches of terminal cancer. Welcome home.

"Both of you on the couch."

"Don't I get to talk?" Billy whined.

"No. Now both of you on that couch."

"Or what? You'll kill us?" the Wells woman said. "I'm so damned sick of all you bullies." But she went over and sat on her side of the couch as Billy sat on his. Nobody wanted to sit in the middle.

I took the overstuffed chair with the ripped arm. Stuffing the color of urine climbed out of the tear. I opened my coat, set the Glock on the good arm of the chair, and said, "You talk first, Billy. How do you know this woman and what're you doing here?"

"You're going to fire me for sure."

Sometimes his naïveté gave me a migraine. He seemed to live in this dreamworld where no matter how badly you fucked up, people just slapped you on the back and said, "Just try and do better next time, Billy old salt, old pal, okay?"

"You're already fired."

Even for somebody who was an old master

175

at looking miserable, Billy gave me a peek at a terror I never want to experience for myself. His dreamworld had gone into nova at last.

"She's my friend."

"I'm his lover. He's just afraid to say it. And he doesn't have to tell you anything."

"The way you didn't have to tell us anything when you dropped that sedative into the senator's glass the other night?"

"Oh God. I should've known you'd accuse me of that. As soon as I heard it on the news, I said to Billy they'd try and put that on me." The shy, quiet girl who'd applied Warren's makeup was now street voluble and street tough. "I didn't have a damned thing to do with it and neither did Billy. Or my father, for that matter. And I never stick up for my father. You can ask Billy if you don't believe me."

"Who's this father you keep talking about?" I said.

"I guess I should tell you now, Dev. Her father is R. D. Greaves."

"Oh, man, what the hell is going on here, Billy?"

"It's not as bad as it sounds, Dev. I promise."

Beth Wells rubbed her fingers against her thumb. "Money. That's the only thing we were trying to get. I'm a beautician and I do makeup on the side. Billy helps me get hired for political things. He was just afraid of what you'd say if you knew who my father was, so we used a fake name and Billy pretended not to know me."

"Good old Billy."

"It's the truth, Dev. Neither of us had anything to do with putting anything in Nichols's glass. I swear."

"It's the truth," she said.

"You called Pauline Doyle at the auditorium and set it all up for Beth," I said to Billy.

"I thought it was pretty harmless."

"How long have you two been going out?" I said.

Their gazes met briefly. Billy said, "Since the last election. Her dad approached me back then. He wanted me to spy for him, spy on Warren, I mean. But I wouldn't do it. That's how I met Beth."

What I was thinking about now was the videotape. If my contact with the police had gotten the correct information, no videotape had been found among Greaves's belongings. Did these two know about the tape?

Beth brought me a glass half full of bourbon with ice cubes. I don't know what I expected, but the glass was clean and it came complete with a cocktail napkin. I'd marked her as being as uncivilized as her old man, but it wasn't a good fit. If her story was true, the worst thing she'd done was have Billy get her makeup jobs for politicians.

I could try to be coy or subtle, but I wasn't in the mood. "Your father contacted me about a videotape."

"What videotape?" she said.

"Please. I've had enough of your bullshit. You *know* what videotape."

Long, ragged sigh. "First you accuse me of putting whatever it was in Nichols's drink. And now you're accusing me of knowing something about a videotape."

"R.D. never told us much, Dev. He really didn't. And I mean about anything. He didn't trust us, I guess."

I didn't want to believe him. But I did.

Billy put a hand on her knee to comfort her.

She slid her hand over his. "He didn't trust anybody. He was even like that with my mom. After she died, I didn't want to live there without her. She was my best friend." Bitterness came into her voice. "He was drunk at her funeral. Made an ass of himself."

"But you kept up your relationship anyway?" I said.

"Yeah," she said, sounding both bitter and oddly wistful. "And you know what? If you asked me why, I couldn't tell you. I suppose because he was father and I was daughter and I just followed the script. I just played out the role. Thank God I met Billy."

I was done here. Such a wonderful, sinister lead — and such a pitifully believable explanation.

"I'm going to make a pizza if you'd like to stay," Beth said, and for some reason in that moment I liked her very much. There was something of my daughter in her.

"Thanks, Beth. But I need to get back to the office."

"Everything cool with us, Dev?" Billy said anxiously.

"Next time just tell me you want Beth to do the makeup, Billy. It'll be a whole lot simpler."

Then I was gone.

CHAPTER 17

Gabe was alone in the headquarters office. I could smell the whiskey as soon as I walked in. Out front, the place was packed with well-wishers and volunteers ready for their nightly assignments. Gabe, in his graying ponytail and granny glasses, sat at his desk with his feet up reading *The Rolling Stone Reader.* At least he wasn't doing any online gambling at the moment. The great Marxist who fell for the worst sucker game of all, gambling. Warren had had to loan him money several times. And as far as I knew, Gabe still owed him many thousands of dollars. He hated Warren for not taking more leftist stands. He hated him even more for having to beg him for money to replace what he'd lost online.

"I was just reading about the '68 Democratic Convention here in Chicago," he said after I'd settled in. "You should've been there. The American gestapo's finest hour.

Mayor Daley and his goons. Daley called one of the senators on the stage a fucking kike. You couldn't hear him, but you could see him say it. You could actually read his lips. Then he called out his pigs and his police dogs and it was a mess. I got six stitches in my head."

I'd noticed that left-wing people my father's age recalled even the worst moments of the sixties with a certain fondness. It had been, for many of them, as close to utopia as they would come here on Planet Earth. Yes, they'd been beaten, overdosed on drugs, suffered everything from scabies to incurable syphilis, broken bonds with families that had still not healed, and even been sentenced to prison. They'd had heroes as dubious as Timothy Leary, Bobby Seale, Abbie Hoffman, that only they could see the worth of. But even the worst of it all was cloaked in a nostalgia for that time when they — or so they saw themselves — bravely went up against the establishment that had contrived a war in Vietnam, persecuted blacks, let millions of their countrymen starve, and attempted to brainwash us with the Orwellian words of Nixon and Kissinger. For them these days, now approaching senior citizenship after all, there would never be a drug high, an orgasm, a guitar riff, or a speech as spiritually moving as the one they'd heard back in '66 or '68 or even '79. Those were the sacred days.

"Six stitches? Sounds like a lot of fun, Gabe."

"That's the trouble with you kids today. You came out of your momma's crotch with only one thought in mind. You wanted to get rich. No ideals."

"I think you're either overestimating your generation or underestimating mine." I couldn't look at him without wondering if he was still gambling on the sly. Addicted gamblers are like that.

"I'm hoping you all change. Not you personally, Dev. I mean you're like me, an idealist. You know it'll never happen, but you keep on working at it anyway. The other people around us — politics is a gig for them. They think it's exciting."

"It's probably more exciting than working for an ad agency or a brokerage house."

"But that's all it is — exciting. And most of the time it isn't even that. It's just slogging through to sell your candidate. Who'd sell out his country in a minute if he had to."

"I'm glad I dropped by for your nightly inspiration."

His laugh was bitter. "You know what I'm

saying is true. Warren only takes the position he does because that's his niche in politics. Remember, he was on the other side all through college. Was even an activist for them. He changed when he couldn't get the nomination for a seat in the state legislature."

Early in his career Warren had had to answer to that charge many times. There was no way short of a religious conversion that you could play the instant turnaround from one side to the other. And not look dishonest. But a scandal in the statehouse had squeaked him into office and he'd done so well in his first term in Springfield that even the press eventually began to see his conversion as real. Saint Paul on the Road to Damascus was frequently cited by way of explanation these days.

I wanted Gabe to shave the beard and cut the hair and quit wearing the crew necks and faded jeans. I wanted him to face the realities of the sixties and not live in the past. But mostly I wanted him to find peace for himself. There was such sadness in those faded blue eyes and in that cigarette-raspy voice these days. He was a wounded animal. For all his self-delusion, there was a saintliness about Gabe.

"I'm sorry, Gabe."

He'd been staring off. Now his eyes fixed on me. "Sorry about what, Dev?"

"Oh, you know. I'm always sanctimonious about something. Now it's the sixties I'm sanctimonious about. Your generation did a lot of good and the country is better for it."

He took his feet down from the desk, sat up straight. "Ah, who gives a shit anyway?" he said, reaching into his drawer for his pint. "You want a hit?"

"No thanks."

"Mind if I have one?"

"Not at all."

"You're a good man, Dev."

"But sanctimonious."

"Yeah," he smiled. "But sanctimonious."

I worked for about forty-five minutes, worked with enough intensity that I didn't quite realize that Gabe had slipped out and Teresa had slipped in, perching herself on the edge of Kate's desk.

When I paused to rub my eyes, she said, "In your own way, you're a good-looking man, Dev."

"I guess that's a compliment."

"It just means you're not conventionally handsome. You know, like my husband." She sighed. "I'm feeling very sorry for him to-night."

"Oh, right. That press association dinner."

184

"They're really going to lay it on about the debate."

Gabe came in just as she said that. "The cops doing anything about that by the way, Dev?"

"They claim to be." I hadn't mentioned the obvious to any of the staffers, that it was one of them. And now that I'd met Beth and believed her story, that fact was irrefutable. I had no idea what the police theory was at this point and it really didn't matter.

"How about a hug, Gabe?" Teresa said.

He went over and took her in his arms, careful not to pull her off her perch. Teresa was a collector of lost animals and lost souls. She'd long ago taken pity on Gabe, even when some of the midlevel staffers quietly questioned his value to the campaign. One of them had even drawn a business card that read:

GABE COLBY
Resident Hippie

After Gabe sat down, Teresa said, "Did you tell Dev the news?"

"I was going to but he got busy."

"Always the last to know." But there was something about the tone in her voice, a kind of remorse, that I didn't like.

"I got a book contract to edit a textbook about campaign politics over the last fifty years," Gabe said. "There's enough money for me to retire and do it full-time."

"Hey, that's great." But it wasn't great, because I didn't believe it. What the hell was going on here? I watched Teresa's face. She didn't seem happy.

"Who's the publisher, Gabe?"

"Oh, a — a new house. Small press. Rivington House is the name."

I was no expert on publishing, but I wondered if a small press, a start-up yet, could afford to pay the kind of money that would let Gabe retire.

"Yeah, I'm really excited about it," he said. "Something I've always wanted to do."

"So this'll be after the election I take it?" I said.

"Sure, Dev. Hell, the press would have all kinds of questions if I quit now."

Good old Gabe. Maybe he'd finally paid Warren off. Or maybe they were so sick of each other that Warren had agreed to forget the debt and just send him away.

Teresa went over to him and gave him another hug. "Warren and I are really going to miss you." So she didn't know. One thing this staff did was keep things from her. As they many times, apparently, kept things from me. I'd only been half-joking about being the last to know.

"And I know Dev's going to miss you, too."

"I sure am, Gabe. I'm glad you finally get to work on that book you've always talked about."

"Think of all the people I can libel." He laughed. "Especially the guy who wore a codpiece so he'd look bigger when he stood in front of female audiences."

Teresa grinned. "God, is that true?"

"It sure is."

"Who was it?"

"I don't know if I should tell you, Teresa. Might cut myself out of a book sale here. You have a credit card?"

She was delighted. "American Express Gold. Now tell me!"

"Okay." He nodded at me. "You know who it was, Dev?"

"Uh-uh. I'm as curious as she is."

"Downstate guy named Tim Aldrich. Real hot dog. I only worked for him because for some reason nobody could ever figure out he was against the war in Nam real early. Otherwise he was a reactionary bastard who thought half the population should be executed on general principle."

"And he really wore a codpiece?" Teresa said.

"He really did. But then so does Dev."

Teresa was in high spirits. "I doubt Dev needs one."

I made sure to give her a kiss on the cheek before I left.

Chapter 18

"You sound tired, Dad."

"Down to the wire, sweetheart. I'm always like this about now in the campaign." I almost said, "You remember." But of course she wouldn't remember. She was the first among her friends to have parents who divorced. She'd been ten. Sometimes four, five drinks down I could still hear her weeping, begging us not to split up. I once broke three knuckles smashing my fist into a hotel wall when those images came back to me one lonely night on the road. "How's school going?"

"I'm taking theater as a minor, I've decided."

"Well, at least you don't want to be a rock star."

She giggled. "Why? Is that the thing now?"

"I was sitting around with some pols downtown the other night and four out of five of them said they had college-age kids who told them they planned to be rock stars. Theater sounds like a sensible decision compared to that. At least you could teach."

"You're getting carried away, Dad. My major is still poly sci."

"Maybe you should make your major theater and poly sci your minor."

"You're really down tonight. Are you all right?"

"Tired, I guess."

"You need a woman."

"Believe it or not, I'm getting ready, I think. Finally."

"I have a beautiful English professor here. She'd love to meet you. I even showed her your picture. She thinks you look sad and that intrigues her."

"Wait'll she sees me if we lose the election."

"Lake really caught up after that debate. Did anybody ever figure out what happened?"

"The official chemical report is that somebody slipped something called flunitrazepam in his Diet Pepsi. It's one of those date-rape drugs. And they figured out how to time it so it hit about fifteen minutes into the debate."

"I haven't seen that on the news."

"We just got word late today."

Cupping the phone: "Hi, Lauren. I'm just talking to my dad."

Her roommate. When she took her hand away I said, "Listen, honey, I'm beat. I just wanted to call and see how you were doing."

"I love you, Dad."

"I sure love you, hon." It was one of those moments when I wanted to just sit there and sob and I wasn't even sure why.

Ten minutes later I was in my boxers with a Robert Ryan picture on TBS. Of all the noir men, Ryan's my favorite. Melancholy and crazy at the same time. Feelings not unknown to me on my worst nights.

When the phone rang I almost decided not to answer it. But I had to answer it. Otherwise I'd lie there for hours wondering what the message had been. If it was important they'd make any words they left on the machine as cryptic as possible in case one or both of us had our phones tapped. I picked up.

"I know how late this is." Kate.

"This couldn't possibly be good news could it?"

"No, Bunny." She loved pet names. "But not bad news, either. I just found out that Gabe is leaving us and I wondered if you

191

knew what it was all about."

"Who told you?"

"Gabe. On the phone. I called the office. He was still there. He was drunk but coherent. Some small press gave him a book deal?"

"Yeah, I know. Doesn't make sense to me, either."

Pause. "You know what I'm thinking . . ."

"Probably what I'm thinking."

"But I don't want to say it."

"Neither do I. But I may as well hang it out there. Maybe Gabe did the deed the other night."

"He had reason."

"He did indeed."

"And it wouldn't have been all that hard to do."

"No, it wouldn't."

"But it's not even good circumstantial evidence."

"I forgot you went to law school for a year."

"Two years."

"That's even worse."

She laughed. "You and lawyers."

"Can't live with 'em and can't live with 'em."

"Maybe we should just forget this call. I

just can't believe Gabe'd do something like that."

"You ever hear anything about him confronting Warren?"

"Gabe? Confronting Warren? That's impossible. Gabe doesn't have it in him."

"Yeah," I said. "He sure doesn't." I let go a sigh. It sounded weary even to my own ears.

"Sounds like you need some sleep, Dev."

"I sure need something. I'll talk to you in the morning."

CHAPTER 19

I worked from my hotel room the next morning. I got Beth's phone number from Billy and called her at home. He said she was working the noon-to-eight shift at the beauty salon.

She didn't sound unduly happy to hear from me. But then she had no reason to. She was struggling with her feelings about her father — whom she probably loved about twenty percent less than she hated — and I was forcing her to walk into a past fraught with proof of his sins.

"You want something. I can tell."

"I need your help, yes. I'll pay you to help me."

"I don't want any money, Dev."

"Well, I appreciate that," I said. "Did you ever do any work on the computer for your father?"

"Sometimes. He couldn't keep secretaries.

He always put the moves on them and they quit."

"I need to find his computer and his password."

"You want his computer?"

"I need to find out who he was working with the last couple of months. That may give us our killer."

"I guess I never thought of that."

"I know you have mixed feelings about him, but I'm sure you want to find his killer, don't you?"

"I guess I owe him that. He didn't deserve to die."

I was noble for once. I didn't tell her that there were a few hundred pols who might disagree with her on that. "No, he didn't. And that's why I need your help."

Long pause. "I have his laptop here in my apartment."

"Do you mind if I come over and get it?"

"I need to leave for work in an hour. Can you be here by then?"

I was there in forty-five minutes.

I went back to my hotel room and set off on a four-hour journey that took me through a list of Greaves's clients, which held several surprises. Some of the members of Congress who complained loudest about how corrupt and dirty politics had become had spent a lot of money, it seemed, with the wily Mr. Greaves. And from both parties. One page revealed a coding system that he used to hide various charges to his clients. They knew the code but were happy that nobody else did, the code hiding such items as escort services, gumshoes, even, in one case, a violent shakedown man well-known to the D.C. police. Greaves farmed out many of his smaller jobs. One of his principal tasks was collecting cash from firms that wanted favors from certain elected officials. This protected the client and the official alike. If a fall had to be taken, Greaves would take it.

Though no detail was given, there was an asterisked list of elected officials' names accompanied by specific dates and the names of cities. I was pretty sure that this was his private list of people he was blackmailing. He'd probably gotten to them the way he'd gotten to Warren. A man's opponent would hire him, in the course of his investigation Greaves would see an opportunity to do some blackmailing on his own, and he would keep everything from his client.

I was scouting names that recurred. Few did. You couldn't afford an association with Greaves. So you kept his employment brief.

You wanted to put a nasty on your opponent's head. Once you got the nasty, it was bye-bye, Greaves. He hadn't been exaggerating when he said that he'd never been invited to a governor's ball or to a party on the Hill. If he looked like a pal of yours, the press would have you for breakfast, lunch, and dinner. You would be handing your opponent a formidable campaign issue — your association with Greaves.

In the last hour I found one name that appeared three times. I cross-checked the name with the dates of Warren's travels. I was able to match the name and date to the young woman who played the hotel maid with Warren.

The full name was listed only once. It was coded SC for secretarial services. From then on she went by the initials DF. Dani Fame. Though I knew that I was probably being my old judgmental self, I suspected that anybody with a name like Dani Fame was not (a) a police commissioner, (b) a NASA spokeswoman, or (c) a nun. She was more than likely a stripper who might be doing a bit of hooking on the side. This last suggested by the fact that she'd gone in and bopped Warren with no apparent qualms.

Thus began the last of my journey. Going online and scanning through all the entertainment ads and strip club listings in the city. At any other time the names would have been fun to just sit and ponder. Mona Mountains. Candy Crevice. Bambi Big. But this was work, and about halfway through the listings I considered the real possibility that one Dani Fame might well have moved on to other cities and other pols, possibly even at Greaves's suggestion. A million-dollar score, even for him, had to be a very stressful hit. If she was in the city, there was always the possibility that she'd somehow be identified as his associate. Even worse, he had to know that there was also the possibility that she might start blackmailing *him.* The name Dani Fame didn't inspire confidence where virtue was concerned. If you'll pardon me being judgmental.

Then I got lucky. I not only found where she was appearing; I found her website. Only one nudie shot, breasts only. But a good number of suggestive poses — anal, oral, doggy style, missionary position, and a couple that would require the skills of a gymnast and superhero to respond to effectively. The surprise was that she had, if you scrubbed away all the bad makeup, a very pretty down-home face. And the lively blue eyes reflected a real humor, as if she knew that this was pretty hokey. I suspected she was intelligent and maybe even fun to be with out of bed as well as in.

I took a break, did push-ups and sit-ups to clear my mind for another round at the computer. I ordered a burger and fries for lunch as my reward for being such a computer whiz and then went back to work.

Detective Sayers's idea that one of the staff had drugged Warren's drink was worth following up on. I'd had the same idea, of course, and so had Kate. But as I worked through page after page, I didn't see any name or code or symbols that resembled any staff member. I spent a lot of time matching names with codes. But it led nowhere.

And then it was there. On a page by itself. At first I didn't understand its significance. I hadn't known him. His name wasn't familiar to me. I'd probably heard it only two or three times in my life.

PHIL WYLIE

I was just about to try the next page when the name's importance became clear.

Of course. The man who'd worked all those years for Warren. The man who'd been truly beloved by what seemed to be the entire staff. The man who'd committed suicide a few days ago.

PHIL WYLIE

The rest of the page was absolutely blank. No code. No indication of what their business had been. No hint of any time frame.

PHIL WYLIE

From the little I knew about the man, he'd been something of a highbrow. Opera. Theater. Galleries. And a lover of beautiful, wealthy women, any number of whom had gotten quite silly about him. The "silly" thing being nothing but envy on my part. He'd probably been the guy I'd always *wanted* to be. I still thought the Three Stooges were funny, and the last beautiful wealthy woman I'd known had been the wife of a rich client of mine. She always said that I scared her.

PHIL WYLIE

Suddenly he wasn't just a name. He was a mystery. He'd killed himself. And now his name was appearing in R. D. Greaves's computer.

It was amusing to imagine these two doing business — the handsome, sleek Wylie and the coarse, shaggy Greaves.

I spent the next half hour reading all the local news stories about his suicide. Not a hint of foul play was suggested in any one of them. An unidentified woman, said to be "a good friend," told a reporter that she'd noted a certain despondency in him lately.

"And he was almost never depressed. He was a pure pleasure to be with."

The stories confirmed my faded memories of his background. Moneyed family, Harvard Law, condo here, home in Aspen, political junkie who'd worked for Senator Nichols at one time. Twice married, twice divorced, a perennial on the local "Most Eligible Bachelors" list.

PHIL WYLIE

The Greaves connection just didn't make any sense. None at all.

And yet there his name was.

I poured myself a bourbon and drank it slowly, trying to think through all the angles the name presented. But by now I was too fatigued to puzzle them through. I even had to consider the possibility that the name meant nothing. That for some reason Greaves had decided to contact him but that the contact hadn't gotten him anything. The page was, after all, blank except for the name.

And then came the Edgar Allan Poe Hour and I nursed my familiar dusk depression for a time. Light a dirty city gray now in my windows. Roar of rush hour. Stream of limos disgorging people glittery or important enough to check into the hotel here. Voices of new guests in the hall. There would be fine food and finer sex for those lucky enough to indulge. Those insensitive swine. Did they think I *wanted* to be up here all alone? The only trouble with self-pity as a substitute for aerobics is that it doesn't do much for the waistline.

CHAPTER 20

Dani Fame's place of employment was the type of strip club where account executives took some of their best clients for a night out. Suits and ties everywhere, and the flashing of American Express Gold. Lap dances were discreetly limited to a large room off the main floor engulfing the runway. And even the strip music was reserved in its way, sexy but more artful in the way it enhanced the performances of the ladies.

And Dani Fame wasn't the only one of the ladies with a sweet face. In Leonard Cohen's *Beautiful Losers,* a character says that all he cares about is bodies: "I gave up fucking faces when I was fifteen." In college I thought that was a pretty nifty line. Maybe it's the glut of surgically altered features — whatever it is, I have a great appreciation for faces as well as for asses. Not great beauties necessarily. Just the nice, friendly girl-woman faces they were born with. And whoever chose these girls did, too. Their faces had youth, humor, intelligence. Like Dani Fame, they were in on the gag, too.

Purely as a matter of research, I sat slowly sipping a scotch and soda and watching the ladies for a half hour before I asked the waitress if Dani Fame would be performing tonight. "Gee, I'm not sure, I guess."

An obvious and awkward lie. I wondered what prompted it. This was between numbers. When the music hit she just shrugged her shoulders, tapped her ear as if she had been struck deaf by one of the dark gods, and walked away.

I finished my drink and walked back to the front door, where a Latin gentleman the size of a giant in a children's story was paid to decide who got in and who didn't — and who deserved punishment from his massive hands.

He didn't like me. Maybe he didn't like anybody. But for sure he didn't like me. I'd gotten no more than two words out when the bouncer said, "Not up for any bullshit tonight, man. You got a problem? Then that's *your* problem, not mine." He then pushed the door open for me, his expectation being that I would walk on out of there.

I decided to short-circuit the drama we were playing out, the drama that would likely end with him picking me up and hurling me out into the darkness.

"See this?"

"Yeah."

"One hundred dollars."

"I'm so stupid I don't know what I'm seeing?"

"I need to talk to Dani Fame."

"You and about a thousand other guys. She don't do lap dances and she don't go home with nobody afterwards."

"I just want to talk to her."

"And how would you do that, man?"

"That's where you and this hundred-dollar bill come in."

"Not enough, dude."

Oh, for those glorious days of film noir in the forties and fifties when a fiver would get you the secret to immortal life. Now a hundred dollars wouldn't buy you anything except the sneer of a bouncer.

"So what's the going rate?"

"Two hundred."

"And I get to talk to her?"

"And that's all you get to do. And you get ten minutes."

"I'd have to talk pretty fast."

"Make it three hundred and you get fifteen minutes."

He was running a business here.

"She happen to get any of this?"

"Half."

"She see a lot of men this way, does she?"

He shrugged. "Maybe."

If you were drunk enough and had cash enough in your wallet, this might be something to impress the client. Going backstage and talking to the stripper. Playing the man of the world. Oh, yeah, I know how to handle these situations. You'd likely have to keep the client on a short chain, otherwise he'd be trying to grope her. But after all the drinks and a lap dance or three, this would be an impressive evening capper for the right kind of client.

"You take the three hundred in pennies?"

"I don't know why you assholes think that's funny."

"You've heard it before?"

A sneering smile. "Ten times a month."

So much for my original and creative wit. I consulted my sacred wallet. I was down to four hundred-dollar bills. I pincered out two of them and lay them on the backside of the original hundred I'd shown him. "How's this?"

No magician ever made a stage prop disappear any faster. My three bills were long gone. He slipped his hand in the pocket of his extremely tight black jeans and dug out a cell phone. While he was punching in numbers, his biceps bulged in the narrow confines of his golden button-down shirt.

His near-twin appeared a few minutes later. They would have been twins except this guy was Caucasian. "Watch the door for me, Mickey. And make sure this dude don't wander back."

"Got ya. I owe ya anyway."

"I won't be long."

The bouncer and my three hundred dollars disappeared.

"He's a nice guy, ain't he?"

"Him? The bouncer?"

"Miguel is his name."

"You're talking about the bouncer?"

"Yeah. Miguel. What I just said, man. He's a nice guy. Why, you don't think so?"

"Well, I guess there are different ways of being nice." Maybe in Miguel's homeland, threats of violence are part of being nice. The same for shaking down rube customers when they ask to see one of the dancers. Nice.

Every once in a while, in the darkness redeemed only by the stage lights and the small bar on the far east wall, laughter would get so loud in the lap dance room it would drown out the music. Those had to be the right kind of lap dances.

Miguel came back. "Ten minutes."

"Hey, man, we agreed on three hundred for fifteen minutes."

"She's real busy tonight."

"I want a hundred back."

"You're gonna have to take it off me. And you try to put a hand on her, man, she calls me on my cell and I come back and break all your ribs."

"Your friend here was just telling me what a nice guy you are."

"He's young, man. He's never seen me in action. He won't be saying that after I get done with you, you step out of line tonight. And he can take you back there." He turned to the younger bouncer. "You take him back there, you hear?"

"Sure, Miguel."

"Get him out of my sight."

No doubt about it. There really are different kinds of nice. I just wasn't sensitive enough to pick up on Miguel's brand of it. There could be a whole new line of Valentine's Day cards. You bitch, you step out on me again I'll cut your fuckin' throat! Oh, yeah, and Happy Valentine's Day! (Be sure and make it a Miguel Masterpiece Greeting Card.)

The flashing runway lights. The conversations with the girls, the whistles and catcalls, all fell away after we closed the door behind us at the back of the place. Soundproofed. A long hallway with several doors on each side. Despite the claim that the girls weren't for sale, I wondered what was behind those doors. Could be a nice little hotel-style room. Not that I gave a damn. Or that I really gave a damn about most of the things that made me sanctimonious. I'd worn the label so long it was easiest to play to it.

Mickey knocked on a door at the far end of the hall. "Come in." Mickey pulled the door open for me then closed it after me.

I stood in a conventional dressing room. Three metal racks of various costumes, two plump overstuffed chairs, dozens of color photos on the walls of girls who'd appeared here. Some of them were likely dead now from drugs or beatings from boyfriends, husbands, or pimps. The dressing table was so long and wide you could play Ping-Pong on it. The folding chair, however, was slotted into a cut-out section close to the enormous round mirror where two spotlights from above gave the ladies maximum light. The rest of the table was cluttered with makeup bottles in dozens of sizes and colors.

Dani Fame wore a dark blue silk robe. She sat on the edge of one of the overstuffed chairs, a long white cigarette burning in the fingers of her right hand. She was innocent of makeup and looked as I had suspected she would, young and pretty in a simple but fetching way.

"Just so there's no misunderstanding, Mickey said you get ten minutes. I'm starting the clock right now."

"I saw a movie you made."

She knew what I was talking about. She didn't respond dramatically. But the mouth tightened with displeasure and the blue eyes showed unmistakable fear. "I've never made a movie."

"Oh, not the kind you see in a theater. Or even late at night on cable. But this was definitely a movie. Produced and directed by a Mr. R. D. Greaves."

She picked up an ashtray from the arm of her chair and obliterated her cigarette in it.

"You shouldn't smoke."

"I shouldn't do a lot of things."

"You shouldn't smoke and you shouldn't hang around R. D. Greaves."

"Maybe I should get Miguel back here. Tell him you grabbed me and tried to get me to do you."

"I'm carrying a Glock. If Miguel forced the issue, I'd shoot him and you'd be responsible because you told him a lie."

Now came the drama. She sprang up from the chair and clapped her hands together and said, "Fuck. He wanted me to do a bunch of them for him. With different men, you know. But that was the only one I did. And I felt real sleazy doing it. Prancing around here is different. When you come right down to it all it is is nudity. And there's nothing wrong with that. But ruining somebody's life . . ." She walked to the opposite chair. Sat on the arm. "How'd you find me?"

"Your name was in Greaves's computer."

Shaking her head. Looking up at me. "I suppose you're a cop."

"Uh-uh. I work for the man you were in bed with."

"The senator?"

"Yeah."

"As soon as it was over I started feeling sorry for him. I mean, he cheated on his wife with me, but a lot of men cheat. But they don't get blackmailed for doing it."

I sneezed. The powders, perfumes, and various kinds of makeup were shredding my sinuses. She got up and got me a few tissues from a box on the makeup table. When she turned around, her robe fell open. She was naked underneath. My kind of naked. Sweet little breasts and a modest crop of rust-colored pubic hair. "I guess it's working here. I'm not as modest as I should be."

"I appreciated the peek. I take it you don't have to have implants to work here."

"The two stars do. But the boss thinks it's a good gimmick to have the rest of us natural. I guess there're some guys who prefer us that way."

"Probably more than people realize."

But she was fully covered again as she sat down on the edge of the chair. "You ever really regret something you did?"

I smiled. "You mean when you're lying in bed at night alone and all the terrible things you did in your life come roaring back on you?"

She laughed. "Why don't we ever think of the good things in the middle of the night?"

"Maybe because we have consciences. A lot of people don't seem to these days." I hadn't been here five minutes and I'd just said something sanctimonious. "Of course I could be full of beans."

"You haven't asked me how I got hooked up with somebody like Greaves."

"You want me to?"

"Sure," she said. "I've got my excuse all ready."

"I'll bet I can guess. Money."

"I guess it wasn't that hard to figure out,

huh? My husband. He's a junkie. There's a place in Canada that's supposed to be real good. But it's expensive."

"Sorry to hear that."

"My first husband was a drunk and this one's a junkie. The problem is when I fall in love I can't break away. As much as I love him, sometimes I wish I could."

The important question: "Did you have any idea who Greaves was working for?"

"You mean who was paying him?"

"Right."

"No. He got a call on his cell right before I went into the senator's hotel room. It seemed to irritate him, whoever it was. He said he didn't need any advice and that he'd been doing this for years and that the suggestion was stupid."

"But no name at all."

"No. I'm sorry."

Knuckled knock: "Couple minutes and you're up, Dani."

"Thank you." She said, "I need to put on my makeup. I hate makeup. But anyway you'll have to excuse me."

"Thanks for everything, Dani. Would you mind writing down your home phone in case I have any more questions?"

"You're not going to the cops?"

"Right now I don't see any reason to."

"Oh, thank you. And don't ask for Dani when you call. My real name's Sharon Bagley. How'd that look on a marquee?"

If I ever write a book in my late years it'll naturally be about my time in politics. And the title will be *Always Bribe the Doorman.* I've never met one yet who wouldn't divulge the most dangerous of secrets if the money was up to his standards. Same with many cops, most corporate employees, at least half of all local pols, and — In other words, a good number of people will help you if the bribe is big enough. Shocking, isn't it?

The man with the red beard and the eye patch and the enormous nineteenth-century Austrian military coat that had spent at least one night in the shop of a Broadway costumer said, "That's very lower-class."

"A bribe is lower-class?"

"Do you have any idea who lives on these sixteen floors?"

"I know it isn't the pope. He's in the Vatican. And I know it isn't the president. They've got him in a psychiatric hospital now."

"Is your patter supposed to be funny?"

One of the clichés that's true is that the minions of the rich tend to be even snottier than the people who employ them. This six-

six warrior was well spoken, his ruddy cheeks as frosty as his blue eyes, and his loftiness sort of humorous for a man who probably earned a nice, comfortable middle-class living, had a couple of kids and a pleasant but modest home, and yet saw himself as belonging to the elite.

"Well, I guess you're not interested in four hundred dollars." (For people who keep track of such things, when last seen my wallet was empty but for a hundred bucks. Thank God for ATMs is all I can tell you.)

We were inside the marble lobby of the building where Phil Wylie had once lived. About ten feet away, on the street, was where his body had hit. The street was busy now. He'd had his moment in the spotlight. I had a kind thought about him. Anybody who could win the affections of so many disparate staffers had to have been a pretty decent guy.

"But I'm curious."

I turned my attention back to him. "Yes?"

"Would breaking any laws be a part of this?"

"Marginally. But not likely."

"You'd have to do better than that." Irritated.

"I want to get into Mr. Wylie's condo for about fifteen minutes or so."

"Why?"

"I can't tell you why. I just need to check something."

"You're not going to damage anything?"

"No."

"Or steal anything?"

"Nope."

"How can I be sure of that?"

"Well, I guess you can't where the damage thing is concerned. But why would I want to damage anything? Do I look like a thug to you?"

"Yes, as a matter of fact, you do."

"Ah."

"Nothing personal."

"It never is. But as for stealing anything, you can shake me down when I come back down."

"That might work. But I'd need six hundred dollars."

"I have five hundred in my wallet. And unless you take credit cards, that's the best I can do."

"I suppose that might suffice. But I'd need to see the money before I made any judgment."

"Aren't you afraid one of your tenants might see me handing you the money?"

"Most of them are in bed by now or coming back here so drunk they wouldn't know what they were seeing."

"How low-rent."

"Yes," he said without humor, "isn't it, though?"

CHAPTER 21

The condo had the feeling of a museum. Artwork from half a dozen centuries lined the walls like a historical parade; the shiny hardwood floors were covered with Persian rugs and many derivations thereof; a grand piano sat next to a long vertical window through which came a mix of moonlight and streetlight. The silence was utter thanks to the construction of the building. The smells in the living room were those of the fireplace, wine, and marijuana; in the kitchen of good meals well prepared. Seven rooms cluttered with objets d'art of every kind — religious paintings, wallpaper, tapestries, glassware, ceramics, and many other things I was too ignorant to recognize for what they were.

Only when I walked near the doors leading to the balcony did I notice the evidence of the police investigation. The scuffs on the floor. The lingering scents of chemicals.

Suicide investigations are also homicide investigations. Eliminate one and you have the other. The serology here is important. What were the contents of the victim's stomach, for one thing. Loaded up with drugs or alcohol may tell you something, for example. But there's always the possibility that the suicide was staged. A smart killer has been known to read a lot of material online looking for the best way to convince authorities that his man or woman did the deed themselves. I know of two cases where only after the medical examiner ruled suicide and the case closed was new evidence found that the person had actually been murdered. With as many friends and no doubt enemies as Wylie had had, the police would spend some time following up on any homicide leads no matter what the ME said.

I spent most of my time in the library because that was where his computer was. But that came to a quick dead end. The hard drive had been removed. I was assuming the police had taken it, but maybe not. The police or someone else had also emptied the desk drawers. I went to his videotape library, which didn't make sense. If he'd known anything about the blackmail tape, was he likely to leave it in full view on a shelf with his Fellini and David Lynch movies? I checked anyway.

I'd given the doorman my cell number. "It's been twenty-two minutes."

"I said 'or so.' "

"That's 'or so' to me."

"Five more."

"Two."

"Three."

"Two."

"All right. Two and a half."

"You've already used up the half."

I clicked off.

I know what you want here. The same thing I do. You want that last-second discovery where I shriek Zounds! And come bursting out of the condo like a madman, waving the blackmail tape and shouting the name of the person who'd not only hired Greaves but had also murdered him. And might have murdered Wylie in the process.

That happens in real life. Sometimes. This wasn't one of those times.

The final excitement for the long, long day and night awaited me back in my hotel room.

I'd been in just long enough to take off my coat when the phone rang. It was nearly eleven o'clock.

Billy said, half-hysterical, "Somebody broke into her place. It's a mess. Busted up all kinds of stuff."

He didn't have to say who he was talking about. Nor did he have to say why somebody had busted in. In fact he *couldn't* say why because, if he was telling the truth, he didn't know anything about the tape. Because presumably that's what the burglar had been after.

"Who the hell'd do something like this?"

"Nobody was hurt, Billy, right?"

"Well, no."

"It could've been a lot worse then."

"But what the hell would they expect to find here? In a neighborhood like this?"

"Junkies, Billy. They're desperate. They figure they can find a couple of things that'll help them make it through another day. Ask any cop."

"But then to go and trash the place on top of it. I just got here after work. They even left the door open."

"Maybe they heard somebody coming or something."

"Yeah, maybe. But you know this'll scare the hell out of Beth."

"It's up to you to convince her that she's safe there." And she would be. Tossing a place the way he or she had must have convinced them that no tape was to be found. Right now they'd be trying to figure where to put their skills to work next. They were working on a parallel course to mine. If Lake got it, the election was all over and Warren was finished forever. But there was the chance that it might come back to us via the blackmail route. Maybe they'd take Greaves's place in selling it to us.

I had all kinds of questions. Had they worked with Greaves? Were they freelancers who'd stumbled onto word of the tape? Or, the question I didn't want to ask myself, was one of our staffers involved?

"She said she grew up scared that somebody was going to kill her dad. And that they'd kill her, too. She said that when she was eight her dad and a guy opened fire on each other in their backyard. He got wounded pretty bad and the other guy got away. The weird thing is there's a part of her that still loves him even after all the crap he's done. I don't understand that, Dev. If my father was like him I'd never speak to him again. And even after her mother died, she stuck by him. But she was pretty pissed off at herself that she was at a movie when her mom passed away." He sighed. "I would've told R.D. to piss off a long time ago."

"Yeah," I said. "You'd think it'd work that way. But blood ties are hard to break sometimes. I always remember Jeffrey Dahmer's father showing up every day in court. Think of what he had to hear about his son. But he showed up anyway. I don't think I would've had that kind of nerve. Or love. Or whatever the hell it was. But he showed up anyway."

"I guess I'd never thought of it that way."

"I need some sleep, Billy. Just keep the doors locked."

"I bought a gun a couple weeks ago, Dev."

"Have you ever fired a gun, Billy?"

"I guess not."

"How about Beth?"

"I guess not, either."

"Then empty it out and put the bullets in one drawer and the gun in another."

"Maybe we'll need it."

"Trust me. In a panic you'll most likely shoot yourself or Beth."

"God, I was sort of looking forward to —"

"Bullets in one drawer. Gun in another. G'night, Billy."

CHAPTER 22

My mentor in the business was a former speechwriter for LBJ who quit over the Vietnam War early on and went into business looking for major pols who opposed the war as well. His name is Martin Steiner and he's still alive and well on his retirement farm on the coast of Maine.

As I sat in my office scanning the new internal polls, I thought of what Martin had told me about the situation I — and he, many, many times — was facing here.

Lake had the Big Mo right now. According to these internals he was two points behind. Which meant, all variables considered, that he was at least tied with us and maybe even ahead.

There are two kinds of TV spots you have to watch out for. One is when an issue breaks open suddenly. In Missouri a woman who'd been lagging opened fire in the last few weeks on her opponent's stand against stem cell research. The man had badly miscalculated the feelings of his state or he'd acted on principle. Whichever it was didn't matter. His stem cell stand cost him the election. Sometime issues work for you and sometimes they work against you.

The other is the attack ad leveled against your candidate. You have to determine quickly if the ads are hurting you. Some of the most virulent attack ads never gain much ground. If they're making a lot of noise but not doing much if any damage, you let it slide. But if they're damaging you, then you hit him five times harder than he's hitting you. Your oppo research people have a few juicy bits they've been pleading with you to use. You use them the last few weeks of the campaign — the Wild West of politics. There was a Midwest campaign in the forties in which one candidate (unfortunately on our side) continued to support his opponent by saying that he was sure the other man's campaign "was not being funded in part by the Greenleaf kidnapping case," a notorious recent abduction. That was the kind of support nobody wanted, especially since no reporter had ever suggested that kidnapping money was being used to support the opponent.

Lake's new hurried-up spot. (You can get

them on the air in hours these days.) Medium close of Lake running around a track, good old all-American sweat streaming down his face, an American flag fluttering in the breeze behind him. Copy: "Sound of body." (And guess who wasn't sound of body?) "And sound of mind." (A magazine page that says: "Ever notice how many good-looking women work for congressmen? Suspicious?") Four quick stills of congressmen with true-blue babes who work for them. One of the stills was a pic of Warren at a bundle of microphones with Kate at his side. "And a man who honors his wedding vows." Medium close on Lake's kids and wife standing camera-frozen in front of an SUV with a dog hanging out the window that really looked like it needed to piss.

One way or the other they wanted to assault you with two facts. Maybe Warren was gravely ill and covering it up. And as for the good old family values — now that you mention it, Mr. TV commercial — maybe Warren, who'd been known to carouse in his early days, really hadn't *stopped* carousing. Look at some of his female staffers in Washington.

We'd have to decide fast how to respond to this commercial. I already had some thoughts. One of the oppo research guys had given me the thought two months ago. Then, I thought it had been out-of-bounds and might destroy us instead of Lake. Now I wondered. Now I had a notion of how we could use it without seeming to use it.

I called my secretary at the shop and asked her to get Warren's unabridged medical records and have them couriered to me right away. I didn't want them online. Docs knew better than to put anything menacing into a computer where important people were concerned.

Billy came in late. He had the haggard visage of a man who'd been worn out by alcohol, sex, or worry. We were alone in the office at the moment. "I couldn't sleep for shit."

"I kinda got that idea."

"Huh?"

"You look beat."

"Oh. Yeah. Beth's just as bad."

"Well, it's over."

"What if they come back?"

I had to play it confidently: "They won't."

"Easy for you to say, Dev."

"They know there's nothing there. Why would they come back? By the way, what did they take?"

"That's the funny thing. We went through

227

everything carefully but nothing seemed to be gone. That's why we didn't call the cops. We figured we'd look ridiculous when they asked us what was stolen and we had to say, nothing."

"You're making my point for me, Billy. No offense, but you don't exactly live in luxury digs."

"Thanks."

"I didn't mean it that way and you know it. All I'm saying is that if they didn't turn up anything the first time, why would they go back for seconds?"

"God, I hope you're right." Then: "Man, did you hear the new Lake spot?"

"Got the copy on the TV spot. I'm sure they're just using the same track for radio. There's just one problem. They've got a family values radio spot implying that Warren's fly is still unzipped. If Warren's as bad off physically as they claim, how can he be schtupping all these women on the side? I mean, as much fun as sex is, it does require a little energy."

He had a nice rich laugh. "Thanks for trying to cheer me up. That's a good one."

"We've got a little ammo tucked away."

"The oppo people?"

"Yeah."

"What is it?"

I knew he'd take it personally. "I can't tell you right now."

"I guess I'm not important enough, right?"

"Shit, Billy, give me a fucking break, will you? Warren and I are the only two in the whole campaign who know what it is. If I'm snubbing you, then I'm also snubbing Kate and Laura and Gabe, too."

He shrugged. "Yeah. That's right. Sorry. I better get to work on his speech for tomorrow night."

No interruptions for the next half hour. I wondered if there'd been a nuclear attack that had knocked out phone lines. I wrote and three times revised the spot I had in mind for the big bomb. It was a risky idea. These kinds of spots are similar to the traps of declaring war. You never know where it will all end up. It could well do you in. Warren and I would both need some Xanax before the afternoon was over.

Laura came in late but appeared to be in control of whatever was troubling her so deeply. "Gym."

"It shows. You're more beautiful than ever."

"Sure."

"You're telling me you're not beautiful?"

"A bit above average is all."

But I could tell she was enjoying herself.

It was nice to be with the real Laura again. The playful one. "Well, maybe a little better than above average."

"There we go, that old Laura arrogance I love."

"Not as beautiful as Kate."

"Matter of taste."

A giggle. "I can hear you saying the same thing to her only reversed."

"You think I'm insincere?"

"You're in politics aren't you?"

"Guess you've got a point there."

Then she, too, got down to work.

Last in was Gabe. In my idle times I thought about Gabe a lot. He still had the best reason that I knew of to do Warren in. Greaves had videotaped Warren only to get money. Gabe had a personal reason and personal reasons are usually the ones that burn hottest in the mind. Aging hippies don't like being in hock to peacock politicians.

"You hear that new Lake radio spot?"

"Yeah, Gabe, we talked about it a little earlier."

"To me he sounds like asshole number one."

"That's because he's on the other side. He's not saying anything that's not in the wind. Warren taking that tumble the other night left a lot of questions in people's minds."

If I wanted some kind of guilty expression, I didn't get it. He just said, "Maybe. But it still could come back to haunt him."

"It's got less than three weeks to do that."

He smiled. "You don't believe in happy endings?"

"There're a lot more happy beginnings than happy endings. The internals are in from yesterday and they ain't good."

"Lake picked up?"

"Picked up and at least tied us."

"Shit."

Then we were in the bunker. Phones, faxes, e-mails. And we all got them. Work became something you grabbed between responding to queries of all kinds from outlanders and barbarians who dared interrupt the holy process of getting our man elected. Insensitive bastards.

Somewhere during all this Kate came to the office. She'd spent the morning with Warren at a breakfast fund-raiser, then accompanied him on an inner-city school visit. Warren was very good with kids. And most of them took to him. If it were earlier in the election I'd have seen this visit as a photo op. But we were past that now. Now was the time when both sides took off the scabbards and went in heavy for disemboweling each other.

When it was just about time for a lunch break, Kate shared with us, as she did so often, new photos of her daughter, who, at three years of age, was a gleaming being of otherworldly splendor. Just like her mom. For all Kate's fashion and record of breaking hearts, only her daughter truly seemed to matter to her. But as wonderful as these moments were for Kate, they were miserable for me. I always thought of how much time I'd spent away from my own daughter and wife. The man who'd fathered Kate's child, whom she'd met on a fling in London, hadn't been the type she'd wanted as a husband or as a father. She had no resentment of him. She preferred being a single mother anyway.

After the photo display with all the oohs and ahhs, Kate came over to me at my desk. I'd turned back to work. She put her hand on my shoulder. "How're you doing?"

I put my hand over hers. "Better than I should be, given the internals."

She leaned down and kissed me on the cheek. "You're a good man, Dev. I wish you'd let yourself believe that once in a while. You judge a lot of people, but you judge yourself harshest of all." Then to cover that sticky compliment, she turned to the eavesdropping group and said, "Dev gave me one of his speeches yesterday about what a royal shit he is. But he's a good man, isn't he?"

Billy led the applause. My cheeks got warm. Laura knew how to whistle real loud and man she did so real loud right then.

"Thank you, everybody. And thank you especially to Kate, who bullied you into it."

Everybody laughed and then started hurrying out the door to lunch.

I called our oppo group and spoke with a man named Neal Walsh. He was the one who'd found our secret weapon. I'd asked him to get me printed evidence of what he was claiming.

"It wasn't easy, Dev. But I got the page we need."

"And there's no doubt about it."

"None. In fact I got two different pages. You'll see what they are. I'd rather not discuss them over the phone."

"Can you overnight them to me?"

"They're already on their way. You think you'll use them?"

"I'm drinking Maalox trying to decide."

"You run the idea past Nichols?"

"I'm meeting him for lunch in half an hour."

"It'd take some balls. But the beauty is, it's mixed in with so many other things, we can always claim that we didn't realize the significance of it. You know, we thought what was interesting was another bit of information on the page."

"Yeah. But my gut's still in knots."

"Well, you can always not use it. I mean, I know the risk here. Pols overshoot all the time and the public feels sorry for the other guy."

"Exactly. Anyway, Neal, thanks. Talk to you later."

I was getting ready to go when Teresa came in. She was wearing a brown suede coat, a white blouse, a rust-colored skirt, and brown leather boots that came to her knees. With her blond hair combed out, she resembled one of those older models who always attract me far more than the anorexic nineteen-year-olds.

"I stopped by for some flyers. I'm visiting hospitals this afternoon. There are voters there, too." She smiled. "I'll hit every floor except the morgue."

"Maybe a couple of them aren't really dead."

"I guess I don't have to ask about your taste in movies, Dev."

She walked around, touching desks and

chairs as she did so. "God, Dev, how many campaigns have you and I been through? And you're not even forty-five yet. If you asked me for a count, I couldn't tell you. They all blur together."

"I'm starting to get that way myself. A blur. This is all I've done since I was in high school."

She smiled. "I remember you told me one night that you got into politics to get laid. Did that ever come true for you?"

"Only twice. And I had to use a gun and a bag of cash both times."

She smiled again. "That sounds like something Phil would have said. He knew how charming it was for a man of his looks and wealth to be self-effacing. When we first met him we both thought it was just an affectation. That he was really this arrogant rich guy who was sleeping his way through the Gold Coast. But when we got to know him, we knew he was being sincere." She tried to put a twinkle in her next words and she came close. But not close enough. "He was like you, Dev. He hated himself."

"I don't hate myself."

"Sure you do. You won't admit it to yourself, but you do. You think you're a very bad guy. And Phil was that way." She laughed. "My husband could use a little bit of that."

"And speaking of your husband, I need to go meet him for lunch." I got my coat. As I was shrugging into it I said, "You knew Wylie pretty well. Did he really have a reason to kill himself?"

"If he was drinking — which he did more and more I'm told, we'd lost touch with him after he left — he'd get despondent sometimes. Again it was mysterious to everybody around him. What could a man like him have to be despondent about? But it was always with him if you knew how to recognize it. People said he loved to laugh and he did, but when you watched his eyes they never seemed to be happy." She took a deep breath, exhaled. "That was a long answer and not helpful in any way. To answer your question, Dev, knowing what I know of him, he probably was suicidal deep down. But you make it sound as if it might not have been suicide. Or you're hinting at that, anyway."

"Not really. It's just that everything I've heard about him — all the glamour, I guess — it just seems odd that he'd kill himself. That's all. If the police and the ME say suicide, so be it. What the hell do I know?"

She walked up to me and gave me my second kiss for the morning. Right about the same spot on the cheek Kate had planted hers.

I held the door for her and we walked out to our respective cars together.

Clean, soft breeze that touched the face lovingly, filled the nostrils with air that wouldn't dare be full of pollutants but likely was anyway.

"You have any idea who Wylie was seeing lately?"

She cast her eyes to the right of me, into the middle distance, as if balancing the effects of telling me or not telling me. "Maybe I'd better not say."

"Now there's an answer."

"What does it matter, Dev? He's dead. Why drag somebody else into it?"

"You're protecting somebody."

"Yes. Somebody I value very much." She moved toward her Volvo. "I need to go."

"Teresa, I'm not happy about this." Then I said, "Why did Phil and Warren have their falling-out?"

"To be honest, I'm not sure myself. All I know is that they went drinking one night and Warren came home with a bloody mouth. And the next time I saw Phil in the office he was packing up his things. And he had a black eye. I asked both of them what happened and they both said that they'd

237

just had a disagreement over policy matters."

"And you believed them?"

"Of course I didn't believe them. But it didn't seem that important. People come and go all the time in political campaigns."

"But they were friends. Good friends, from what I hear. That's different than ending a business relationship."

She opened the door of her car. "Well, maybe you can get Warren to tell you the truth. I couldn't. And poor Phil's beyond helping anybody. He obviously couldn't even help himself. I'll talk to you later, Dev. I need to get going."

"Why did you and Phil Wylie part company?"

I thought he might gag on the Perrier he'd just started to swallow. He gulped it down and said, "We're falling behind in the election and you want to talk about Phil Wylie? What the hell's wrong with you?"

"Fair question, isn't it?"

"Sure it's fair. But since we met here at my club, I thought we were going to talk serious business. Not the past."

The club was one of those old-fashioned men's deals where all the leather chairs squeaked and the fireplaces blazed even in summer, the way Nixon's did in the White House of his years. Why Robert R. McCormick himself, old robber baron and long-time right-wing power behind the *Tribune,* had probably farted in the very chair I was sitting in now. I was having the salmon and Warren was having the chicken salad.

"So what happened?"

"What happened was very simple. We had a disagreement over policy."

"What policy was that?"

"What the hell is this, Dev?" A passing waiter gave us a look. Warren leaned forward, spoke in a lower voice. "It was over affirmative action. He thought I should push it harder, I didn't. It was a stupid argument, really. But it got heated and he said a lot of things he'd been wanting to say and then I said a lot of things I'd been wanting to say and all of a sudden it was all gone. Our friendship, our working relationship, and any trust we had in each other. It was painful as hell, believe me. I loved the guy and I think he loved me. He was my best friend. And it was over and it was irreparable and we both knew it. Now, is that good enough?" He sat back in his chair, angry. "It started out very much like this conversation, Dev. He pushed me too hard and I exploded and then I pushed him too hard and he exploded. Now, is that good enough for you?"

"Yes."

He laughed. "Good. Because I was about to put those vaunted boxing skills of yours to the test."

"Yeah, that's all we need this week, a candidate with a busted nose and bruises all over his face."

"You've got a lot of confidence for somebody approaching middle age."

"I still work out on the bag two or three times a week. I can handle myself. Nothing more. Now, let's get down to business."

The waiter came. We turned him down on dessert but both requested small glasses of wine. While we waited I reminded him of what Walsh had come up with a while back.

"I thought that was pretty much off the table. Too risky."

"All I'm saying is there's a way to bring it up."

"And how would that be?"

"His new commercial implies that you're not physically fit enough to stand for office. So we challenge him to release his total medical history. And we'll reveal yours."

He grinned. "That is some pretty devious shit."

I grinned back. "It sure is."

"You really think we should risk it?"

"If we make the challenge, then we have ourselves a new issue. We know he can't afford to release it because if he does, then his records will show that Mr. Family Values was treated for gonorrhea three years ago. So he can't release it, but we release yours and then start hammering on him twenty-four/seven to release his. And of course somehow somebody in our office will let it slip that Lake had a problem a few years back. And the press'll be all over him."

"I really appreciate how you fight for me."

I said it in such a way that he might finally understand it and quit flattering himself that I was his champion. "It's your voting record, Warren. Personally I think you're a piece of shit."

He gave a little start and said, "Well, fuck you."

"You lie to everybody around you. Nobody is ever sure what's going on with you. And I'm tired of it. Damned tired of it."

His face was flushed with real rage. "You think I have to sit here and listen to this shit?"

The passing waiter did a double take this time. So did the gentlemen sitting at the small tables in the center of the restaurant area.

Our voices dropped again.

"Yeah," I said, "I know you have to sit here and listen to this shit because I'm the only hope you have. And if you don't know that, you're dumber than I think you are. And that story you told me about Phil Wylie? No way, pal. I buy the fact that you had an argument that ended your relationship. But it sure as hell didn't start out over some small policy point. It was about something that meant something to both of you on a personal level. And I'm going to find out what it was."

"What if I insist that you stop wasting time on Phil?"

"Then fire me, Warren. I've already told you I'm quitting the day after the election. If you want to fire me now, fine."

"What the hell brought this on?"

"Are you crazy? What the hell do you think brought it on? I'm waiting for some piece of information you haven't given me to blow us out of the water. To hear it mentioned at a Jim Lake press conference. You just don't grasp the concept of trust, Warren. Not on a personal level or a professional one."

I stood up and threw my cloth napkin on the table.

"I've got things to do. I'll talk to you later.

Right now I'm too sick of your face to sit here anymore."

CHAPTER 23

My cell bleated just as I swung into the headquarters' parking lot. Billy said: "Beth got sentimental this morning. Wanted to stop by her father's office. The woman down the hall, this exporter, said that she's been holding some of Greaves's mail. I put it on your desk."

"I appreciate that, Billy."

"I'm sorry I didn't tell you about Beth. It made me look bad when you just showed up at her apartment. I'm just glad I still have a job."

The mail turned out to be junk with one exception, a bill from something called Shadows, International, which was pretty damned melodramatic for a Chicago firm that had bought the cheapest envelopes and letterhead I'd ever seen. Not only was the paper already yellowed, it was also streaked down the center with a printing malfunction of some kind.

Shadows, International sent Greaves a bill for $425.17 for "client observation." That meant following somebody — hence, being someone's "shadow." Clever. The dates of this observation put the work done at two weeks previous. The "client" who was followed was not listed. The bill was signed in sprawling fashion by "Kenny Tully." I had no idea who he was, but now I had his address and phone number. The rest of Greaves's stuff I pitched in the wastebasket.

Gabe was first back from lunch. "Just caught the new Lake TV spot. You were right. Same audio track. Visually they're not that impressive."

"No, but they do the job."

"Lake's a scary guy."

This was something Gabe would say. But was he saying it now to cover the fact that he'd stiffed Warren's Diet Pepsi in order to stop Warren from winning?

He sat down at his computer.

I tried the number of Shadows, International. I got a scratchy answering machine. I didn't leave a name or number.

Laura came in wearing a new tailored gray coat. She even modeled it, giving us a twirl. "I decided to treat myself."

"You done good," Gabe said.

"You sure did."

"Thanks, guys. I appreciate being appreciated."

This should have been said happily. But the tone was somber. I remembered her tears of the other night. Her great grief. Because it had come so soon after Warren's performance at the debate, I wondered if she'd been part of it in some way. Stupid, yes, but I had to suspect everybody because only somebody close to Warren could have done it.

Midafternoon I got the call I'd been waiting for. Money was being sent from Washington to our campaign. We'd have what we would need for the final two weeks. I should have run down to the liquor store and come back with three bottles of champagne. But my lunchtime anger at Warren was still with me. I was sick of him. I just wanted the campaign to be over. I wanted him to win because people like Lake needed to be stopped.

By four o'clock I'd tried Shadows, International three times in all and got the answering machine each time. I was thinking of driving over there when our door opened up and Detective Sayers, the dapper black gentleman, walked in. He didn't need to say anything. He just nodded at me. I got up and walked over to the coat tree. "I'm finishing up for the day," I told everybody.

They were all watching Detective Sayers. They didn't know his name, but they certainly knew his profession. He had that unmistakable cop air of superiority and impatience. I followed him out the door. "Anyplace we can sit down and have some coffee?"

"Right down the street."

The coffee shop closed at six. They didn't get a rush-hour business. The counter man was already cleaning the grill. The place had that lonely closing-up feeling.

Sayers had coffee and a bagel. "This'll be dinner until about nine o'clock. You having anything?"

"Just the coffee. I'll be having a five-star meal in about forty-five minutes or so. Unless you're planning to put me in jail."

I assumed that would draw some kind of humorous response from him. It didn't. And that bothered me.

We started in on our respective coffees and he said, "How long have you known Nichols?"

"Any particular reason you're asking?"

"You know how uniformed people have ticket quotas? They have to hand out so many for a time period?"

"Uh-huh."

247

"Well, detectives have question quotas. We have to ask so many a day or we get our asses kicked when we get back to the cop shop."

"Makes sense to me. And you guys should get your asses kicked a lot more than once a day."

"So how long have you known him?"

"He's been a client of the place where I work for a long time. Ten years at least. I've worked with him off and on for five, six years. Why?"

"You trust him?"

"He's a politician."

"That's cute but it's not an answer."

"I trust him, yes. I wish I knew why you were asking me these questions."

"You were with him in the dressing room when his drink was queered, right?"

"I was with him in the dressing room. We're assuming that that was when the stuff was put in his drink. Around that time. Maybe a little bit before."

"You got any idea who might have put the stuff in there?"

"Afraid not."

"You could've put the sedative in his glass."

"Yes, I could've."

"But you didn't, right?"

"Right."

He finished his coffee. He was a bit loud about it. He went "Ah!" and smiled. "This is some of the worst coffee I've ever had."

"We don't come here for the coffee."

"Oh? Why do you come here then?"

"The atmosphere. Don't let all the wobbly furniture and the greasy walls fool you. This is a high-class joint."

"It is, huh?"

"Just don't use the toilet."

"Bad?"

"So bad that people go in there and are never heard from again."

"I'll remember that."

He spoke without taking his eyes off me. "Way I've got it figured, it was somebody on the staff put that sedative in his glass. You considered his staff?"

"Of course."

"You got any leads?"

"Not so far."

"Who looks good for it?"

"Nobody."

"Maybe you don't know the staffers well enough."

"Pretty well."

"Background checks?"

"Yep. Or they wouldn't have been hired."

"Grudges against Nichols?"

"Distinct possibility. Lots of hurt feelings in campaigns. But nothing stands out at the moment."

"You ever consider the possibility that Nichols himself put the stuff in his Diet Pepsi?"

Fastball right across the plate. Breathtaking in its simplicity and fury. It stopped me clean and cold. I'd never even considered that possibility. "I don't believe that for a second."

"We got a tip."

"My advice is burn it. It's bullshit. Why the hell would he do it?"

"The race was tightening."

"Not that much."

"The race was tightening and he figures he can nail Lake with queering his drink. But it doesn't work out that way. Lake becomes the hero. But now there's not jack Nichols can do about it."

"Agatha Christie."

"What?"

"That's an Agatha Christie plot. I don't remember which one. But I've read all of her books and I'm sure she used that same trick in one of them."

"Maybe I should read her."

"Mostly I read noir. But Agatha's fun every once in a while."

"This sounds like the literary society. How about you tell me what you think about my idea. And don't just say it's bullshit."

I finished my own coffee, carefully setting the cup down. I cleared my throat. I stared across the table at him. "He didn't do it. Too risky and he's very conservative when it comes to risk. And he'd screw it up."

"What's that mean?"

"He's not a competent man. He was raised with money. He never had to learn how to survive on his own skills. If he was to do something like this, he'd have to have somebody help him with it. He's not stupid but he is lazy. He'd have to have somebody figure out which kind of drug to use. Then he'd have to have somebody figure out what the best way was to make everybody else think somebody had put it in his drink."

"Maybe he had help."

"If you mean me, I like my job too much. Too many things wrong with a plan like that. Bound to come undone somewhere along the line."

"There are plenty of dudes floating around who'd help him for some serious money."

"Right. But we're back to risk. He gets help like that, he instantly sets himself up for blackmail. You don't meet a high class of people in that particular trade. I don't suppose you'd tell me where you got this tip?"

"As a matter of fact, I will. Came to me in a letter. Unsigned, of course. It was just off-the-wall enough that I thought I should look into it."

"And now you have."

"And now I have."

"So you're not going to worry about it anymore?"

He smiled with those big white teeth of his. "Of course I am. I think it's a very interesting idea."

CHAPTER 24

I drove from there to the co-op building where Phil Wylie had lived. A black doorman was on duty tonight. He was middle-aged, but from the appearance of his graying hair and the broken ridge of bone above his eyes and the condition of his nose, his boxing days had likely left him capable of taking care of himself even today. He wore dark blue woolen gloves that matched his uniform coat. I couldn't get a glimpse of his knuckles. I asked him where the other man was.

"Night off."

"Be back tomorrow?"

He nodded. He watched me carefully. "Cop?"

"Pardon?"

"You a cop?"

"Long time ago. Military intelligence."

"Thought so."

"Don't hold it against me."

He had a chesty, full laugh. "I'll try not to."

"You interested in a little money on the side?"

"I don't have a police record if that's what you're asking. And I plan to keep it that way."

"Did you know Phil Wylie?"

"Mr. Wylie? Sure. He was a very nice man. He gave a damn about people. My little granddaughter, she got sick and her mama didn't have no insurance, he picked up the hospital bill. About four thousand dollars. Not many folks'd do something like that."

Wylie's death was beginning to have its effects on me. I was getting to know him through the people who'd loved him. "He must've been a damned good man."

"He was. Half the people who work here went to his funeral." He allowed himself a quick smile. "Some of the people in this building, they die and we want to celebrate instead."

I realized that I should start carrying my wallet in a holster. Easier to get to. I slipped a hundred-dollar bill from it and offered it to the man.

"What's this for?"

"I want to know about his visitors."

"What visitors?"

"Anybody you saw come here more than two or three times."

"I only work here two nights a week. Rest is days."

"Then tell me about the two nights."

"This what you gave Ralph?"

"Ralph?"

"The other doorman."

"I gave him a little more."

"How much is 'a little'?"

I took out another hundred. "How's that?"

"Passable."

"Tell me about his guests."

Before he could respond, a limo pulled up out front and dispatched a young couple who were trying awfully hard to be Scott and Zelda. They were both drunk and giggling and each waved a bottle of champagne. They stumbled and staggered through the front doors. By this point the young man, who had his hair greased back and his white tuxedo shirt covered with red lipstick wounds, kept trying to kiss her exquisite neck, but her fur wrap kept getting in the way. I wanted to call PETA and have them beat the shit out of these two on general principle. They stumbled on across the echoing marble floor to the elevators. If they'd seen us they'd decided we weren't worth acknowledging. More likely they were too drunk to see anybody who didn't appear regularly in their mirrors.

"I'll bet they're your favorites."

"Believe it or not, they're pretty decent compared to some of them."

"There're worse?"

"You kidding? Wait till you meet the Sullivans."

"Bad?"

"She always tells me it's nice to meet 'a colored man who knows how lucky he is' to have a job."

"I see what you mean."

Now he gave the subject of Wylie and his visitors some thought. "Last month or so, this one guy kept showing up a lot. He didn't belong here."

"What'd he look like?"

He gave me two sentences. He gave me R. D. Greaves.

"He stay long when he came here?"

"Once he stayed over an hour. Most of the time it wasn't that long."

"Anybody else?"

And then he said it. I knew right away the who of it. What I didn't know was the why. And then I remembered the night in the office when she'd been sobbing but wouldn't tell me what was troubling her.

"She was a real babe. Real North Shore.

A very classy number."

"She here a lot?"

"Just about every night I was."

"She stay long?"

"Most of the time overnight. I'd leave at six when the day man came on and she'd be coming down in the elevator about then."

Laura and Phil; Phil and Laura. Nothing wrong with that. Perfectly fine. Office romances happen all the time. And nothing sinister about it, either.

Then why did it seem sinister to me?

As soon as I got back to my car, I called her on my cell. I got her voice mail.

Kate was on the phone when I got back to the office. I'd just sat down when she said good-bye and hung up. "I hear we got the money."

"Yeah. I don't know what moved them all of a sudden."

"Would you like to see Jim Lake in office?"

"You've got a point there."

She went over and got her coat. "I left a number there. A man called twice for you. He sounded sort of — agitated."

"He leave a name?"

"You won't believe it. Shadows, International. He sounds short."

" 'Sounds short.' "

"Yes. It's this ability I have. Even over the phone I can tell if a man is short. There's just this aggression in their voices. Sometimes it's very subtle and almost nobody else can hear it."

"Like a dog whistle."

"If you insist," she laughed. "It's just like a dog whistle."

I dialed the number as soon as she was gone.

"Shadows, International. Tully speaking."

And damned if he didn't sound short.

"Mr. Tully, my name —"

"I know who you are. I've got caller ID."

"Good for you."

"Kind of a wise one, are you?"

"That's what they tell me."

"You called three times. I wondered why."

"You sent R. D. Greaves a bill for services rendered. I wondered if you'd tell me why."

"Hell, no, I wouldn't tell you why."

"That's what I figured. Is there a bar near where you are?"

"Lots of them. Why?"

"I've got three hundred and fifty dollars in my wallet that I've really got to get rid of because it's too heavy to carry around. I've also got a Glock nine-millimeter in case anybody might get the idea of taking the money from me before I'm willing to give it. But you sound like a deserving type of guy. So why don't we have a couple of shooters and see if we can do a little business."

"Five hundred would interest me a lot more."

"For five hundred I'd want a pretty full story. Not just a brief explanation. I'd want to know who you were following for him and why."

"What if the person I was following doesn't have anything to do with what you're looking for?"

"Then I'm out the three hundred and fifty dollars I'm going to give you."

"Five."

"Four."

"Four fifty."

"Four ten and fifty cents."

"What are you, some kind of asshole?"

"Yeah, but I've never figured out exactly what kind."

He named a bar. Forty minutes later I pulled into the parking lot.

Middle-management white-collar employees. More upscale than I would have figured for Mr. Tully. He wasn't hard to find. The shortest man in the place. Plus an idiotic trench coat with enough epaulets, flaps, and buttons on it to embarrass even real secret agents.

He was chatting up a very nice-looking blond woman who towered over him at five-eight or so. A real Amazon compared to his five-five. Her dark eyes kept furtively searching the long, narrow room. She wanted to be rescued.

"Excuse me, ma'am," I said, stepping up to them. "This man recently escaped from our psychiatric hospital and, as charming as he is, I'm afraid we'll have to take him back there for another round of two hundred electroshock treatments."

"My faith in God has been restored." She smiled. And fled.

"You've got a way with the women, I see."

"You prick."

He was a munchkin. The real kind. Sort of a Kewpie doll–face male version and short arms that made long-sleeved shirts and jackets hard to buy. "She was going home with me."

"Yeah, I noticed that."

"What? You think I don't get my fair share of pussy?"

"Why're we having this conversation?"

"Because you chased off my babe."

"Tell you what. Let's find a booth and I'll buy you a couple of drinks."

"Oh, no, man. You chased off my woman for tonight. But you're not gonna chase off my regular fee."

"Your fee? For what?"

"For talking to me. That comes extra."

Anita Baker came on the sound system. I'd had a music crush on her back in the eighties and early nineties. I wanted to sit in a booth by myself and think about the impossible woman I was going to meet real soon now. Instead I had to deal with this sharpie. "So I pay you a fee up front even though I'm not sure you have any information that would be of any interest to me."

"Hey, you called me. So if you want a sit-down here it's the same as a sit-down in my office. Seventy-five an hour. And that's seventy-five even if you get up and leave in five minutes."

"You're sort of like a shrink."

Somebody was having a birthday. A group of drunk men and women laughed their way through "Happy Birthday," drowning out Anita Baker. Nothing good lasts very long.

"You mean I don't even get one freebie?"

"Man, this is what I do for a living. No freebies."

We took a booth. A good-looking middle-aged waitress came over and took our orders. Tully said, "I don't see no ring on your lovely hand."

"My wedding ring's so big, it's hard to carry around."

"You're kidding. You're not married."

"You a psychic?"

"I just have married radar. You know, like gaydar. Only it's about which babe is married and which isn't."

"You should be more like your friend there."

"Yeah?"

"Yeah. And not pester the waitresses."

As soon as she left, I said, "Another triumph."

"Some of 'em you have to work awhile. But eventually most of them come around."

"Yeah, hit 'em with a crowbar, they'll give in every time."

"You're so smart, let's see your money."

I hadn't kept track of all the bribes I'd delivered in the past few days. The amount had to be twelve hundred or around there. Our accountant would frown and sigh. She was not only very good at accounting, she was even better at frowning and sighing, especially when it came to the sloppy way I kept track of things.

I laid out a one-hundred-dollar bill. I didn't have anything smaller. "Bonus."

He shrugged. "I'll call the networks and

let them know what a high roller you are."

"Did Phil Wylie hire you?"

"You're with Nichols, right?"

"Right."

"I Googled you."

"Good for you. Now answer my question."

"Greaves hired me to help him with the Wylie case."

"To do what?"

"To shadow a couple of people."

"A couple meaning two?"

"A couple meaning two."

"Do I get the names?"

"That's where the negotiations start."

"I could always come across this table and pound your face in. Would that start the negotiations?"

"I pack heat."

"Mickey Spillane, 1948. That's an old song, pal. I pack heat, too. But I'd hate to mess up this pretty booth with your blood."

"Two thousand dollars for the reports I gave to Wylie."

"Believe it or not, I don't have two grand on me."

"I want it in cash so there's no way to trace it to me."

"You don't like to pay income tax."

"Not only that, but selling this kind of

thing, this gets around I have to think of my reputation. People might get the idea that I'm double-dealing them. You know, I get information on one guy and he pays me. And then I turn around and sell the same information to his enemy. That could put the hurt on my business."

"And trench coats don't come cheap."

"You don't like my trench coat?"

The waitress came with our drinks. "I told my friend here that if I worked on you long enough you'd go home with me."

She smiled at me. "He really say that?"

"Well, he didn't say it specifically about you. He said it in a more general way. But you were included."

"He couldn't get me to go home with him if he had an Uzi and a bag of gold coins."

Shadows, International smiled. "You'd be a challenge but I think I could swing it."

She shook her lovely head in disbelief and walked away.

He said, "Bitch. She just wanted to embarrass me in front of you. Wanted to make my work harder for me. Wants me to work real hard for my nookie tonight."

Say what you want about delusional people, they're an awful lot of fun to listen to sometimes.

"Okay, rock star, let's get serious here. I

can have the money for you tomorrow morning. How do I get it to you?"

"You leave it at the front desk of your hotel?"

"That sounds easy enough. And you leave the reports for me when you pick up the money. And you'll be damned sorry if the reports aren't there."

"Man, you think I'd try and screw you or something?"

"Gosh, no. A man of your integrity?"

"So get outta here and let me work. That waitress don't want to go home with me, I'm sure I'll find some broad who will."

"Probably a line around the block there'll be so many."

He didn't like me much, but then the feeling was completely mutual. He worked both sides of the street and didn't make any secret about it. There are some things you just don't want to know.

I bought a Repairman Jack paperback in the hotel lobby. I'd been reading F. Paul Wilson since I was in college. The Jackster was his greatest creation. I liked the idea of somebody who helped people just for the sake of helping rather than somebody who did good for self-aggrandizement. Superman kind of digs his power a little bit too much, don't you think?

I read fifty good pages. I turned out the light, expecting to get to sleep. But that didn't happen until I spent a useless half hour on a lot of what-ifs, a lot of dead ends, a lot of pointless speculation. Who'd killed Greaves? And where was the tape?

I finally got to sleep a little before midnight, but it didn't last long. The phone woke me at 12:49, according to the night-stand digital clock. My first thought was, as always, about my daughter. The parental terror that something had happened to the most precious person in your life. I rolled over, reached long, and grabbed the receiver.

"Hello."

The voice was being filtered through some kind of electronic device. No gender. The words so muffled a few of them were lost to me. Like a bad recorded message.

"I'm picking up where Greaves left off. I have your tape and I want what Greaves wanted for it. One million dollars. I want it at nine p.m. the day after tomorrow. You'll leave it in your car in your hotel parking lot. I'll" — muffled — "in the front seat." Muffled. "There will be no other contact. If you cheat in any way the tape will go to a TV station immediately."

I hadn't even had time to wake up properly. I was in a dream state for a few minutes after the call. I knew the call was real, but it remained unreal somehow. I went to the john and took care of myself and then washed my face in icy water.

My guess was that I'd just been contacted by the person who'd hired Greaves. Maybe Greaves had passed the tape off before he'd been killed, making the search by at least two parties useless. Or maybe the person who'd just called, Greaves's boss as it were, had been unhappy with Greaves and had killed him and taken the tape.

Whatever the case, we were back where we started. The tape in exchange for one million dollars. The way it was set up, they saw the money before I saw the tape. If the money wasn't there, the tape wouldn't be there. That simple.

I slept. Maybe it was pure escape. A retreat from reality. But I slept straight through until eight-thirty and even then I didn't want to get up, could have slept a few hours longer.

By the time I got to headquarters, the staff had been at it almost two hours. I slipped into desk position and went to work immediately. The third new e-mail I opened was from a friend of mine at a large TV station. He said that there would be a new Lake spot premiering at eleven a.m. our time, that the substitution was made early this morning. Which had an ominous sound to me.

The spot would air half an hour from now. Gabe and Kate were the only two people in the office at the moment. I told them what was coming up.

"Maybe their oppo research people found something," Gabe said. He sounded properly nervous. But there was amusement in his eyes. Though he might pretend otherwise, he'd be happy to see Warren brought down, even if it meant that Lake would win.

Kate said, "Don't we have anything, Dev? We really need to fight back with something powerful. Everybody knows that Lake gets a lot of money under the table from lobbyists."

"If that was a crime," I said, "you couldn't get a quorum for a vote in Washington. We need something a lot stronger, something that's unique to Lake."

"Any idea what he came up with?" she asked.

"Wish I did."

"This could blow us right out of the

water." The glee in Gabe's voice was unmistakable.

"I know, Gabe. You're going to start crying any minute now."

"Hey, what's that supposed to mean?"

"Forget it."

I turned around in my chair, faced my screen, and went back to work. Difficult to concentrate. Most politicians come to think they're irreplaceable. That's why term limits have never gone anywhere. The divine right of kings has nothing on most pols in our country. They have manipulated the laws so that getting rid of them is virtually impossible. It can be done, but it usually takes a major seismic shift in public attitude to do it. And it usually comes as a surprise late in an election cycle. The last debate started us on our downward slide. And we hadn't recovered yet. Maybe this new commercial would contain a charge that would knock us even lower.

"It's almost eleven," Kate said. "I'll turn on the TV."

The three of us grabbed quick coffees and stood in front of the TV, pagans before a false god.

The spot was scheduled for 11:08, premiering on a statewide talk show that had a large audience.

The first seven minutes were spent with the host asking two female reporters which candidate — Nichols or Lake — held the most appeal for women. One of them laughed and said, "Neither." Then they got down to some serious assessing of the implications in the question. Both were manly men, though Lake was the manliest. Both were intelligent men, though Nichols was the most intelligent. And then came the health question. One of the reporters said that that was "the wild card." And the other agreed. "I really felt sorry for Senator Nichols and what happened to him at the debate. But it made me wonder about his fitness to serve." That was reporter one. Reporter two said: "He just looked so old and frail suddenly. That's probably being unfair. You can look old and frail when you're eighteen — if you're sick enough. But this was the image that a lot of people took away from that debate. That here was this old man being helped by this younger, more vital man. This is one of those times when health really becomes an issue."

The spot opened on a long shot of a man swimming laps in an Olympic-size indoor pool. We go into a medium close shot of the man swimming toward us now. The man is Jim Lake. We cut to Lake rising out of the water like a sea creature, water pouring off his tight, muscled body. And the voice-over accompanying all this: "A swimmer in college. A winner in Congress." And then suddenly a long shot of Lake, surrounded by a six- and seven-year-old mixed-race group in swim trunks on the edge of the same pool, Lake demonstrating swimming strokes. Now they are all in the pool, Lake swimming slightly ahead of the pack, still showing them how to swim. "A family man, a fit man, a man who never tires of fighting for the right things, the good things in American life." And we end on a freeze-frame of sea creature Lake in all his trim, muscled glory coming up out of the pool again.

"Motherfucker," said Laura, who'd come in just as the spot had started to play.

For half a minute or so, hers was the only comment.

Gabe said, "I thought he played football in college."

"He was out one year because of an injury, so he swam," Kate said.

"What'd you think, Dev?"

"Corny and obvious, but it keeps on message that Warren is a broken-down old man too tired to do anybody much good."

"That's such bullshit," Teresa said, coming through the door. "I watched it out front with the volunteers. I should do a spot about how virile he is."

"Yeah," I said. "If you could work the phrase 'sex machine' in there a couple of times, that'd be helpful."

Teresa blushed, as if just now realizing what she'd said. "Well, you know what I mean. This is ridiculous. Somebody put something in his drink. He's fine now."

"Do you think they'll stay with this health thing for the rest of the campaign?" Laura asked me.

"Unless we can force them off it. Put them on the defensive."

"Is that possible?" Kate said. "Do we have anything that could do that?"

"Maybe," I said. "I need to talk to Warren. Anybody happen to know where he is?"

Teresa said, "He's between TV interviews. He should be back here in another half hour or so."

"Great. Thanks. Guess I'll get back to work."

Teresa came over and said, quietly, "We could lose this, couldn't we, Dev?"

No point lying. I nodded.

"They blame him for that stupid drug he took. It's not fair."

"No, it isn't. But it's politics."

Then she said what was *really* on her

mind. "Maybe we should've accused Lake right away. You know, of hiring somebody to put the drug in the drink."

Her voice still wasn't loud, but it was enough that everybody heard her. Everybody started paying attention to the conversation now. Everybody knew what she was saying. That this was my fault because I'd told Warren we shouldn't make any kind of accusation until we could prove it absolutely.

"If you're asking me if I handled it correctly, Teresa, maybe I didn't. Maybe I should've suggested that we go on the attack. Make Lake the bad guy right away. But we had no evidence — and we still don't."

"People make unsubstantiated claims all the time, Dev."

"Al Sharpton comes to mind. I don't think I want to throw in with him, do you? Bush, Cheney, people like that? They made a lot of unsubstantiated claims, too."

"You're being silly. If you think you made a mistake, you could at least admit it."

Now she was the typical political spouse. Protecting her husband from the stupid consultant whose stupid mistakes were about to deprive the nation of one of its finest leaders. I'd made mistakes in my time and had apologized for all of them. But I didn't see this as a mistake. Lake had cleverly shifted the subject from the drink Warren had taken to the general subject of Warren's health. The only tactic we could have used was a dubious accusation.

"Well, I'm not happy about this, Dev. I want you to know that."

"I'm not happy about it either, Teresa. And believe it or not, I think there's a way to respond to it. All I need is Warren's approval."

Tears now. "I just hope you know what you're doing. We're a part of Washington now. We have a beautiful home and a lot of important friends."

And a lot of important friends. When senators are forced from office, many of them stay in D.C. and make enormous amounts of money as lobbyists. But there is no amount of money that can compensate them for the power and prestige they've lost. There are only a handful of United States senators. Except for the president and the vice president, there is no more significant role you can play in our government. Each man or woman is sought out by powerful people from around the world. People who want favors. People who give favors. No lobbyist ever gets that kind of treatment.

"I guess I'd better go," Teresa said. The tears were flowing openly now. I wasn't angry, I was just disappointed. I'd always felt that she hadn't been seduced by all those dos in Georgetown. All those dinners for visiting potentates. All those evenings at the White House. But I'd been wrong.

"Sorry you had to go through that, Dev," Laura said.

"Wasn't so bad."

"That's a side of Teresa I've never seen before," Kate said.

"She's a limo junkie. She digs the red carpet," Gabe said.

"She wants her husband to win, Gabe. Nothing wrong with that."

"C'mon, Dev, they're both addicts and you know it. They dig the red carpet and all that shit."

"You think Lake would be any different?"

"We're talking about Nichols. Not Lake."

Nichols, I thought. The guy who kept loaning you money when you needed it for your stupid gambling problem. The guy who could've ended your political career with one phone call. The guy who at least votes the right way ninety percent of the time. I was sick of Warren, but Gabe's attack was hypocritical and annoying.

"You ever think there'll be a day when you

help put somebody in office you actually have respect for, Dev?"

"I guess you don't want to let this go, do you, Gabe?"

"It's a fair question."

"Give it a rest, Gabe," Laura said.

"It's a stupid question anyway," Kate said.

"What's so stupid about it? Just because you people don't mind working for whores —"

I forced a smile. "And here I thought that *I* was the sanctimonious one, Gabe. We're human. That's what you're not factoring in here. If I ever got to be a senator, I might be the biggest whore who ever hit Washington."

"That's not true, Dev," Kate said, "and you know it."

"No, I don't. We've all seen it happen to people we thought we respected. They start living with all those privileges and perks and having their staffs do everything for them — I don't think you can predict how most people would react."

"There're a few you can predict," Laura said.

"Yeah, a few. Just a few. Men and women who don't get their heads turned by all the fuss made over them. But everybody else —" I shrugged. "I need to get back to work."

Over the next half hour I wrote copy for the spot that would respond to the health issue. Then I wrote a statement that Warren would give at his appearance at a luncheon for retired party officials. The press would be expecting a droner. Few pols used an appearance like this to make news. We didn't have much choice. I did all this presuming that Warren would agree with it. One look at Lake's new commercial would convince him that we needed to move quickly. Especially given what oppo research had been able to find out about Lake. All this was predicated on the hope that they weren't holding back any oppo material of their own. The conventional belief being that any major attack coming in the last two weeks of the campaign was virtually impossible to counter. You just didn't have the time to make your case effectively.

Warren came in just after noon. He said, in a tone as harsh as I'd ever heard him use, "Everybody out except Dev. And I mean now."

When we were alone, Warren said, "Let's nail his balls to the wall."

"Great," I said. "But now we have another problem."

"The bearer of good tidings, eh?" He was ready to be angry.

"We've got another blackmailer in the picture."

CHAPTER 25

By midafternoon every news source available to us, including all the cable news outlets, was carrying the story of how Senator Warren Nichols, slipping in the polls, had made available online his complete medical records dating back to age sixteen. We'd stored them this way in case we ever needed them. And now we needed them.

That was point one of his attack. Point two was that he was challenging Congressman Jim Lake to do the same in the next twenty-four hours. Everything in his medical history.

Point three was an ominous but vague suggestion that Nichols's drink had been tainted by "forces against my voting record," which he then listed highlights of. He emphasized how hard he'd fought for both the middle class and the working class. And how he'd managed to improve the lot of the working poor, "folks who Jim Lake once called in one of his more reckless and inhumane moments 'disposable.' "

He concluded with, "I get a physical twice a year at Walter Reed. I'm healthy in every respect. And I've never suffered from any disease that would embarrass me."

I'd rewritten that last line five or six times. I'd wanted to soften it. But then I decided the hell with it. Lake had dominated the news since the debate. Now we were going to dominate it; "that would embarrass me" would put the press on him day and night. "What did he mean by that, Congressman Lake?" "Are you going to release your records in the next twenty-four hours?" "You've been in Congress three terms, but you've never released any medical records as yet. Why is that?"

I'd told everybody on the staff to play it coy when reporters called them. Never say it was Lake behind the drink plan, just say, "Anything's possible." Never say that Jim Lake had been treated for gonorrhea in the tenth year of his family-values marriage, only that we'd heard there was a shocking fact to be found in his medical records.

Even without Teresa pushing me, I'd known when I'd seen Lake's new commercial that I was going to tell Warren that we should go after him. No other choice.

I'd overseen this kind of bombast twice. Once it had worked, once it hadn't. In the case of the former, a congressional opponent had managed to cover up a hit-and-run in a small town his father basically owned. In the case of the latter, the oppo people had come up with three counts of spousal abuse on a man who'd also managed to keep these off the official records. I knew this would be risky because he'd gone through AA five years ago and was now, by all accounts, including those of his wife, a very good husband. The electorate chose him over our man, who had a few problems of his own that the oppo folks on the other side had somehow missed.

We had pizza and beer as we watched the Chicago evening news. Three sets going so we didn't miss anything. We were slotted either story number one or story number two on each of them. And the leads all played heavily on the "suggestion" that Lake might have something to hide in his medical records. His press spokesman, a kid usually given to smirks, was somber and somewhat dazed when he faced the press, assuring them that Lake had nothing to hide and would address this question as soon as he returned to Chicago from Springfield later tonight. The kid, happily, looked miserable.

Only one station picked up on the inference that "anything's possible" might mean that Lake had had something to do with tampering with Warren's drink. "Asked for a clarification, the Nichols camp would say only that no accusations were being made, but that many possibilities were being considered both by them and by local police."

Beers were hoisted. Big, wet, beery kisses were exchanged. Teresa and Warren got so intense people started flickering the lights on and off to the great amusement of the lovers. For once the psychic rush was positive. We had reclaimed the argument. Somewhere lurked the information that Lake had been treated for gonorrhea while in the tenth year of his marriage. And the press was going to find it. And the press was going to ask him about it in the context of his constant criticism of our "libertine" society — single mothers, gay people, lurid TV shows, and, of course, the centerpiece of his attack, "those who would destroy the basis of our civilization, the sacred institution of marriage." You shouldn't be saying those things after requiring heavy doses of penicillin.

Somewhere along the line I got drunk and ended up making out with a thirty-seven-year-old nurse who worked as a volunteer. It was pure high school. By the time I thought I was going to get to third base in her nice warm Chevrolet, she had to go to the hospital, where she was on the night shift this week. She'd been drinking ginger ale.

One of the other volunteers gave me a ride to my hotel. I stopped at the desk and asked if anything had been left for me. The clerk, assessing my blood alcohol level, handed me a large manila envelope. In the elevator, I studied the reports that Tully had left for me. I'd spent two grand on nothing. He'd left a note inside saying that he'd actually worked two jobs for Wylie, the second relating to a painting of Wylie's stolen from a gallery he'd loaned it to. Wylie had hired Tully to follow two prominent fences. Not a damned thing to do with Warren being blackmailed.

I sprawled on the bed, not even bothering to take off my suit. It had been a long time since I'd had a beer drunk and it would have its revenge on me in the morning with a swollen head and dehydration.

Sometime in the process of falling into REM sleep, I realized that tomorrow night I

was expected to drop off one million dollars . . .

CHAPTER 26

I took a cab to headquarters, then decided I'd best hit the café down the street first. I poured three cups of boiling coffee directly into my eyes. Faster that way. Soon now I'd be able to check off "human" in one of those little boxes where they ask the name of your species. It would be a proud moment for me and the entire clan.

I went to relieve myself and when I returned, Warren and one of his bodyguards were there. The guard was an ex-Marine. In his blue pinstriped suit and white shirt and tie he looked almost civilized. Now that Warren was big in the news again, he needed protection. The crazies would be coming out for sure now. Hopefully just the harmless crazies.

"Karl," Warren said politely, "would you mind sitting over there at the counter? I need to talk to Dev here privately."

"No problem, sir."

"He's the best of the best," Warren said as Karl left. "He has laser vision. You wouldn't believe what he sees that I miss every time."

Warren had a pol's love for celebrating people. It becomes an instinct after a certain number of years and a certain number of rubber-chicken dinners where you have to extol the virtues of a tubby little man who'd contributed X amount of dollars to the party for the past X number of years. Thank God there are such people, but by the time the speechwriter has had at them they sound as if they were a combination of astronaut, scholar, and clairvoyant.

"Guys like him are the reason we win wars, Dev."

"Yeah, except for the last two."

The smile was sour. "Never can let it lie, can you, Dev? Always have to spoil the moment."

"Guess I can only gag down so much bullshit, Warren. Sorry. Now let's talk about tonight."

This time the smile was coy. "Oh, I don't think we'll need much discussion."

"You have the money?"

"I have the money. Every penny of it."

"That's amazing." And it was. When R. D. Greaves was shaking us down, Warren had had to struggle to raise three hundred thousand. And now he had a million?

"I cashed some pretty heavy-duty bonds."

"I thought you couldn't do that."

"My CPA showed me a way to do it without attracting much attention."

"But I mean you said they were tied up and you couldn't get to them."

"A little white lie, Dev."

"Gee, you telling a lie. Who'da thunk it?"

"There you go again. Spoiling the moment."

I sipped some coffee. "I've never seen anybody this happy to be losing a million bucks."

"That's the thing. I'm not going to lose a million bucks."

"You're not?"

"No. And it'll be thanks to you. Because you're going to follow the money. You're going to wait in the shadows and see who makes the drop and then you're going to follow them."

"Ah."

"Just make sure you have your Glock. And make sure your car is all ready to go."

"This is just like TV."

"You see something wrong with it?"

"I see a lot wrong with it. Mainly that we have no way of verifying what's on the tape we get."

"We have to trust them."

"Nobody I trust more than a blackmailer."

"Then what the fuck is your idea, Dev, you sitting there so smug and everything?"

"I don't have a better idea, Warren."

Warren looked idiotically triumphant. The Hollywood smile was back in place. He'd kidded himself into believing — at least for a few giddy moments here — that everything was just hunky-dunky. "Things are going so well, Dev. Three different newspapers ran editorials this morning saying that Lake should release all his medical records."

"He respond yet?"

"Not yet. But we've got him boxed in. If he releases all his records, he's dead on the spot. And if he doesn't, we've got a club to beat him over the head with from now till Election Day. I just can't believe how this has turned around."

He was a kid again and that ten-speed he'd been wanting had just been wheeled up to his front porch and he was experiencing an orgasmic moment here.

It was all coming back to him — the power, the glamour, the glory of being a United States senator.

"You hit everything just right, Dev. And I really appreciate it."

"I'm going to spoil the moment again, Warren. We've still got two weeks to go. We don't know what their oppo people have on us. Fine to be happy but, man, don't take anything for granted."

His face crimped in distaste. He'd been junkie high and I was forcing him back to drab winter gray. "I'll do my best not to be happy, Dev. You know, I sure wouldn't want to piss you off by feeling better about the campaign."

"You're being stupid, Warren. All I said was —"

"All you said the other day was" — he leaned in — "that I was a piece of shit and you'd be glad to be rid of me. You think I've forgotten that, you're fucking crazy."

He stood up, signaling Karl. To me he said: "You'll have the briefcase about five this afternoon. I'd appreciate a call as to how it goes."

"Are we breaking up, Warren? You want your ring back?"

"The ladies think you're real cute. I don't. For what it's worth, I'd planned on firing your ass anyway, Dev."

A pretty good line to leave on.

Around two that afternoon Jim Lake's press person announced that all of the congressman's medical records would be released in twenty-four hours. That brought a lot of smiles from the staff. Kate seemed particularly amused: "Maybe he'll use the Latin word for gonorrhea. It sounds classier."

"There's no way he's releasing that," I said. "He's going to trick it up some way. The press already has a pretty good idea of what he's hiding and if it's not there, they're going to jump all over him."

"I could almost feel sorry for him," Laura said, "if he wasn't such a hater. That's what he's built his career on." She smiled and snapped her fingers. "There. I'm cured. I don't feel sorry for him at all." She addressed the rest of us. "Let's get together and tear his throat out."

We all went out for pizza and beer together. Even dour Gabe was enjoying himself. "I'm going to miss you people."

"God, if I didn't know better," Billy said, "I'd say Gabe is getting sentimental."

"I can't help it. I really like working with you people."

Kate said, "Well, we're going to miss *you* too, Gabe. We go back a long ways."

"Yes, and I've been a hail-fellow-well-met through every one of our times together. Always smiling. Always with something positive to say. Always there to make people glad that they're alive."

At first we all thought Gabe was being serious and had to wonder if he'd had some kind of mental breakdown in front of our eyes. Then he gave us his hippie grin and we all started laughing.

Back in the office, everybody drinking coffee to compensate for the two or three beers they'd had, I polled several of our key sites to see how the volunteers were doing getting out the message. You always expect some marginal exaggeration — "They are as the legions of Rome, Master!" — but even chopping the enthusiasm down twenty percent, it sounded as if the volunteers were working hard and taking on extra duties the closer the election drew.

Next I called three Chicago reporters I knew to see if they'd heard anything yet from Lake and his people. I didn't tell them the exact nature of what he was trying to hide, but I did say that it would be interesting if he claimed to be presenting his entire medical history. One of the reporters asked if she could "see all his records in case he doesn't come through. I'm assuming here, Dev, that *you* have them." "What a sordid accusation." "Yeah, right, babe."

Near the end of the afternoon Karl the

bodyguard showed up with a stout black leather briefcase. It was padlocked. He handed me the key. "The senator said you'd know what this was."

"Thanks, Karl. Where's the senator now?"

"He's at the house in Evanston. He has the night off and he wants to relax."

"I appreciate you bringing this by."

He nodded as he surveyed the staff. "Nice to see people working this hard for the senator. We've got to make sure he wins."

Like most pols, Warren was most comfortable when he surrounded himself with true believers. They had their own doubts, of course, but they expressed them rarely if at all. Each entourage usually had one skeptic — in this case, me. But when the news got really bad, the rest of them stared at you as if your skepticism had caused nasty things to happen. And right after the campaign manager — almost always the first to get canned — you the consultant were next up. At the very latest you'd be fired the day after the election, win or lose. You had, merely by being honest with everyone, brought the campaign bad luck. You know, voodoo.

One by one people left for the day. All but Kate were headed back to the pizza place for more of the same. Kate said, "I'm going to bake a very special cake for my daughter tonight."

"Her birthday?"

"No, but I just feel like celebrating. That whole thing with the debate — seeing Warren that way . . ." She shrugged. "Past history." Then: "Oh, that report from the detective's been over here on the fax all day. I'm surprised nobody gave it to you."

The phone rang seconds after she left. It was Detective Sayers himself. "You get the report?"

"Haven't had time to look at it."

"Nothing special from what I can see. Thought you might look at how the crime scene broke down. Stuff we found."

"I'll bet you want to hear me say that I figured out who stiffed Warren's drink and who murdered Greaves."

"I thought you might have something. I sure don't."

A decent enough ploy — the sad, lonely cop who had nary a clue — but a bit broad to play believably to an old cynic like myself.

"Wish I could help you."

"I'll bet you do. Well, talk to you later."

"Thanks for the report."

"My pleasure."

Two minutes later the door opened. One of the older volunteers from up front escorted four high school journalists in. They wanted to interview me for their respective newspapers. I'd forgotten about it.

We spent nearly ninety minutes together and a lot of it was fun. They were bright kids for one thing and for another they had a serious interest in politics. I was surprised at the breadth of their knowledge. They knew just about every pol I mentioned in the course of citing various campaigns for this or that reason. And just at the end they focused on Congressman Lake and why he seemed reluctant — even a bit afraid — of releasing his health records.

"I'm afraid I can't give you the answer. He's the only one who'd know that. What I can tell you is that after the debate where Senator Nichols got so sick, Lake made a big deal of the senator's health. He forced us to respond the way we did. By making our entire medical history available online."

"Is Congressman Lake in trouble if he *doesn't* release his records?"

"Hard to say. The press and the public will decide that." I said this having no doubt that the press now stood ready to bring him down.

The volunteer came back and told the students that their time was up. It had been an enjoyable break.

I grabbed the briefcase Karl had delivered

from under my desk and then filled my own briefcase with two different field reports I planned to study later tonight. Then I grabbed the police report about the crime scene and gave it a quick look. The door to the dressing room hadn't been jimmied; there was no evidence that anything had been damaged inside. That pretty much confirmed that one of the staffers had put the drug in Warren's drink.

I'd shut the phone off while the students were here. Now I checked for messages. Only one. My friend in the police department said that the medical examiner was still trying to determine if Greaves's death had been a crime or an accident.

I shut off the lights, taking note of how badly my right hand was trembling.

CHAPTER 27

There was a conventioneers' dance in the main ballroom of the hotel. I'd parked my car per instructions from the blackmailer, then come inside and suddenly it was 1943. I was about to say "Nineteen forty-three again." But there was no *again* for me, of course. I hadn't come along till much later. But I'd developed a real passion for music of that era, especially the female singers, Billie Holiday and Jo Stafford and Lena Horne in particular.

So I stood near the back entrance of the place, ten minutes early, watching for signs of anybody sneaking up on my car, which was parked in the front row. My plan was to make a run for him, grabbing tape and blackmailer alike. I had my Glock, brass knuckles, and a small billy. I was ready for a war. I hated to admit that I was looking forward to it. But I realized that it would free me of my lingering depression. There's something to be said for simply taking action, a kind of purgative that doesn't do our species proud.

I had to step aside several times to let people in and out of the back door. I was in the middle of letting someone out when I saw a dark shape emerge from a six-deep row of cars and begin working its way slowly toward mine. The way it kept looking right to left, the way it hunched down slightly, the way it kept patting its gloved hand against its chest — was that where the tape was being kept? — made its purpose clear.

I got ready to move. I pushed the door open and stepped out into the dark night. The mercury vapor lights cast a strange color over all the new sports cars and Benzes and the handful of Rolls-Royces. The figure was very close to my car now.

I kept to the shadows. A narrow sidewalk stretched to the parking lot. Walls were close in on both sides. But there was enough space that I could stand on a strip of grass and watch it.

And then it stood straight up, a grandmotherly sort who clutched her purse to her chest as if she feared an imminent mugging. You get a lot of false leads in this business.

I wasn't paying any attention to the small

groups of people who came out to get their cars. They were all dressed very well, all seeming liquor happy and Black Card confident, headed to their cars and the prospect of hitting some of the tonier night-spots in the city.

So I didn't even consider that I was in danger until he brought something heavy down against the back of my skull. Not once but twice. He wanted me out. I was conscious long enough to get a mental still photo of what happened next. I fell sideways, onto the sidewalk. I hit it in such a way that my nose cut against the edge of the walk and sent a splash of blood into the air and right onto a gray trouser leg. My last thought being that there was something familiar about the material and pattern of that trouser leg —

I was aware of pain just before I opened my eyes. The picture presented was of an acoustically tiled ceiling with a square of electric light filtered through a horizontally patterned piece of plastic.

A woman said: "He's coming around. I'd appreciate some fresh water here."

She pushed her pleasing face into my view. "I'm Dr. Ryan. I'm a guest here and they asked me to help. Can you remember what happened to you?"

No memory problems. "Somebody knocked me out." I'd been shaken enough by the attack to want to say more. But I had to be careful and give no hint of what was behind the attack.

"You were found on the north sidewalk that leads to the parking lot."

"Yes, I was going out to my car."

"And somebody just hit you?" A male voice. Man in suit. Detective. Unmistakable.

"Probably a mugger."

"Didn't look that way to me. Your clothes weren't torn. You still had your wallet with several hundred-dollar bills. You've got your watch, which is expensive, and your cell phone. I don't think a mugger would leave you with all those things."

"Would you help me sit up, Doctor?"

It was a long trip to rest on my bottom. But once there I found that the pain subsided considerably. "How long have I been out?"

Dr. Ryan was a middle-aged woman with very soft blue eyes and a remarkably erotic mouth. She wore a blue cocktail dress cut just low enough to show the top of her freckled cleavage. The detective, who'd yet to give his name, was burly, surly, and suspicious.

"Do I need any stitches?"

The doctor was about to speak. The detective spoke first, over her. "No stitches, no concussion from what the doctor can see. The only blood was from your nose. We estimate that you weren't on that sidewalk unconscious very long, because of the heavy foot traffic. Somebody saw you and cell-phoned the front desk. You've been here about ten minutes. The doctor doesn't think you need an ambulance. I asked her to let me ask you a few questions. Does that catch us up to date to your satisfaction?"

The last question was sarcastic enough to bring a frown to the doctor's wonderful mouth. "I'm not quite sure why you're treating him this way, Detective Slattery, and I have to say I don't like it. Somebody knocked him out. He doesn't know who and he doesn't know why. That seems reasonable."

"Well, it sure wasn't any mugger who knocked him out. Otherwise they'd have taken everything he had on him."

My head was able to glance around the white room without undue pain. This was a real infirmary. I was on a comfortable examination table. The walls were lined with sparkling white glass-fronted cases filled with medicines and medical equipment of all kinds. No wonder I liked this hotel so much.

Dr. Ryan ignored him. "The only problem we had — and it wasn't that much of a problem — was getting your nosebleed to stop. You got very little on you but the sidewalk is a mess. There's no sign that you broke it or damaged it in any way. But the best course would be to send you to the ER, where they can X-ray your head and nose as well. That's what I'd do if I were you. You could rest here for a while and then drive yourself to the hospital — it's right nearby — or I could call for an ambulance."

Slattery moved in. "We'll need you to sign a statement."

"It won't be much of a statement. It's what I told you. I was walking to my car when somebody hit me from behind."

"And you can't think of any enemy you might have who'd do something like that?"

"I'm a political consultant. We don't usually resort to violence."

"Political consultant? Who's your man?"

"Nichols."

"Figures. I'm a Lake man myself."

I smiled at Dr. Ryan. "Why doesn't that surprise me?"

"What's that supposed to mean?"

I was irritable from everything that had happened in the last twenty minutes. I said, "You've been riding my ass since I came to. You think there was some personal reason I was attacked. I don't. I can't rule it out, but I also can't think of anybody who'd do it. I've basically given you my statement twice. I was walking out to my car and somebody hit me from behind and knocked me to the sidewalk. That's all I know and that's the sum and substance of my statement. And I don't have anything to add. And I don't plan on changing it one bit. So if you want me to stop down tomorrow morning and sign it, I'll be happy to. How's that?"

Amusement played in the gentle blue eyes of the good doctor. "For now, I want to turn the light off and let our patient here rest up a little. If that's all right with you, Detective Slattery?"

He growled something I didn't understand, nodded to Dr. Ryan, and left.

"Everywhere I go I make new friends."

A pleasing smile. "You're sensitive to what others think of you, I see. I guess I got a slightly different sense of the detective than you did."

"He was just embarrassed by how much he admires me."

302

"So that's it." She pointed to the door. "I'll be out there for another half hour. I need to check messages and call a few hospitals. As I said, you can rest here or go to an ER."

"Or do whatever I like?"

"Or do whatever you like with the understanding that I'd prefer you go to the ER and have a couple of X rays."

"So it's my responsibility."

"Yes, it is. It's your responsibility."

"Then I guess I'll go wash up and probably go upstairs to my room. By the way, shouldn't you be at the dance?"

"I would've escaped even if you hadn't had your problem. This is the awards part and it really gets dull."

"I won't tell them you said that."

"Just be careful. Remember that."

Ten minutes later I was in my room, washing up and changing clothes. The suit I'd been wearing was muddy in a few places and torn in one, under the arm. There were blood spatters on my right pants leg.

And then I remembered the gray pants leg that had been the last image I'd had before slipping into unconsciousness. Now that I was fully awake I recognized why the particular gray color and weave of the trouser leg had looked so familiar. It be-

303

longed to the uniform that the bellhops wore here. Red blazers, gray trousers. A bellhop had attacked me.

I wore a white crewneck sweater and jeans with a leather jacket and hiking boots. I figured I might be having some trouble tonight. I might as well dress for it. The Glock completed my attire for the evening.

The lobby was still crowded. The restaurant had a line of people waiting to get in and both lounges sounded full to overflowing. Either that or they had a handful of the noisiest drunks this side of the Mississippi River.

I started checking for the bellhop. There were four on duty at this hour. I was assuming that the blood would be easy to spot on his trouser leg. But the longer I looked, the more clearly I realized that as I was slipping away I was apt to see things that might not be there — yes, there'd been a lot of blood given the condition of my nose — but no, this didn't necessarily mean that he'd gotten any on him. The other possibility was that yes, he'd gotten blood on his trouser leg but he had a spare pair of trousers in his locker and had already changed.

I sat with a paperback in a chair next to

the glass elevator that worked nonstop. The most exclusive section of the hotel was the restaurant on the top floor. I'd looked at the prices. Only a lobbyist could afford them.

Who knew that I'd turn out to be the guy in all those TV private-eye shows who sat in the lobby pretending to read while actually scanning the people to find the guilty person? Well, we all had our spot in life.

He showed up about fifteen minutes into my stakeout. He got off one of the regular elevators and walked to the front desk. Even from here I could see spatters of something on his trouser leg. He was young, no more than twenty-five, with a headful of curly blond hair and an insolent smile. He was the guy who could fix you up with ladies, get you smack, even find you a cockfight to attend. You could see him on the cover of *Pimp Monthly* as "Our Man of the Year."

I didn't know where he was going and I didn't care. I followed him. He didn't become aware of me until he was in a narrow corridor. He suddenly started looking over his shoulder. But he was too late. In three steps I was right behind him, in four I had a handful of his hair, smashed his face into the wall, and gave him a kidney punch that stood him up straight and then folded him in half. His face was bloody from the wall slam. I grabbed his hair again and dragged him outside, where I stood him up straight again so I could give my knee a good target for his crotch. He instinctively tried to double up and grab his wounded area, but I wasn't going to give him any indulgences. I threw him up against the wall and said, "Who hired you?"

His wild, frightened eyes grew even more frightened. He gaped around, trying to find some way of escape. But there wasn't any escape possible.

"I want to know who hired you. If you don't tell me in thirty seconds I start working on your ribs. You understand?"

The night. Planes circling O'Hare. Giant trucks racing through the darkness. The dance music from inside the ballroom. The smells of fresh chilled air out here, and the stench of the bellhop having wet himself.

I hit him hard and square in the stomach. Blood began oozing from the corner of his mouth. His eyes told of defeat and shame. He said, the blood making it difficult to speak, "Just had a phone number. Never met her."

"Her? You must've gotten her name?"

He shook his head. "No. Honest. I never got her name."

He painfully explained the situation, grimacing every time one of his body parts sent a pain message to his brain. He'd been contacted by phone by a woman who told him that she wanted him to pick up a briefcase for her. She told him what the car looked like and what I looked like. She also told him that I would undoubtedly be watching from the sidewalk and that he was to come up behind me and knock me out. Nothing that would inflict serious damage. Just take me out for five to ten minutes. And so he had.

"But if I hit you too hard, I'm sorry."

"You got the briefcase?"

He nodded. "It's in my locker."

"You open it?"

"She told me not to."

"How are you supposed to get it to her?"

"I'm meeting her out in the parking lot in fifteen minutes. I give her the briefcase and she gives me a thousand dollars in hundreds." He was getting much better at speaking with a mouthful of blood.

"Let's go get the briefcase."

"What?"

"You said you've got the briefcase in your locker. We're going to go get it. You and I. Then we're going to wait in the parking lot for her to show up."

"I really need that thousand dollars, dude."

He must have been feeling much stronger now. Calling somebody "dude" requires a certain amount of energy.

"We'll make a trade. You lose your thousand dollars and I don't turn you over to the cops. How's that?"

He seemed to think about it, which suggested that he was a harder case than I'd guessed. I'd trade a thousand dollars to stay out of Cook County Jail for six months — his likely sentence — but he wanted that grand badly enough to actually consider risking life in a cell for a thousand dollars.

"Shit," he said.

"What's your name, by the way?"

"Tim Gaines."

I took my hands from the bunched shirt I had pressed against his collarbone.

"I can't afford no police record. They'd fire my ass here for sure. Insurance won't cover hops if they've got a police record."

"Sounds reasonable. Now let's go get that briefcase."

"I told my girlfriend we were going to Vegas on that money. I already had another fifteen hundred saved to put with it."

"C'mon. Let's go get the briefcase."

Even in the newest hotel there are sections below that remind you of the cata-combs. We went down two levels to a sub-subbasement, the effect unpleasant for a claustrophobe like me. I could smell the heat from the laundry and hear the boom and grind of different motors at work. The men's locker room had a shower area and different kinds of aftershave. Picking up the briefcase was anticlimactic.

Back upstairs, we went outside. He took up a position at the curb as I'd instructed. I wanted the arriving car to be as close to me as possible. I'd wait until the vehicle pulled up and he'd started to approach it. Then I'd appear, run around the car to the driver's side, and show the Glock. If the driver tried to pull away I'd shoot out the two tires on my side.

Gaines kept looking back at me. His nervousness started to make me anxious, too. All this had to be done quickly. Twice he walked off the curb, giving me the impression that he saw the car pulling up. But both times were false alarms. My armpits were soaked with sweat. Despite the cold I was in need of changing shirts.

Finally he made his move and it was the right one. A two-year-old Pontiac sedan pulled up and he immediately started walking toward it.

I let him reach the car and start talking to the driver before I sprinted out from the shadows and ducked down as I worked my way around the rear of the car and up to the driver's window.

I already knew who I'd see. I'd ridden in this car many times during the campaign.

While she talked to him, I tapped on her window with my Glock. She turned to face me, looking alternately shocked, angry, and then hurt, as if I'd betrayed her in some way.

I opened the door and said, "Slide over, Laura. I'm driving."

Chapter 28

"Where are you taking me?"

"We're going to drive around and you're going to tell me what the fuck is going on here."

"I don't want to tell you anything, Dev. And I don't have to."

"We could always go right to the police."

"That's bullshit and you know it. They'd want to see the tape. And it would all be over for Nichols."

"What the hell is this all about? Why did you pay Greaves to make that tape?"

"I already told you I don't want to say anything. I'll only talk to my lawyer, nobody else."

"What the hell has Warren ever done to you?"

"He fired Wylie. And Phil never recovered. He'd been sober for six years but he started drinking again." Pause. "I want to call my lawyer."

"Be my guest. Use your cell. Call him. I'll drive you over there and wait till you're finished."

"And then what?"

"Then I want you to tell me what this is all about. I think you owe the campaign that much."

"I don't owe the campaign anything."

"What were you planning to do with the tape?"

"Send it to Jim Lake."

"Great. That's loyalty."

"Yeah, Dev. The same kind of loyalty he showed to Phil."

"Phil, Phil, Phil. I don't get the connection here."

"The connection was that I was in love with him."

"Oh."

"Even though he wasn't in love with me. He saw me the way he would a sister. We even slept together but it didn't help him."

"Help him in what way?"

"Help him get over this other woman."

"Anybody I know?"

"I'm calling David. You need to be quiet."

The call didn't last much more than a minute. He was awake, and no, it wasn't too late. He'd put on some coffee for her. She knew the address. It was not far from

Loyola University, a genteel two-story brick home with white shutters and a screened-in porch running the length of the front. I parked in the driveway and cut the lights.

"You're just going to sit here?"

"I'm just going to sit here."

"There's no guarantee I'm going to tell you anything."

"I realize that."

"You could always take a cab back to your hotel."

"And miss all the fun of sitting out here?"

"You don't have any right to do this."

"You know the worst thing about this is that you're a stranger. I'm serious. I don't know who you are. You're this beautiful young woman and that part hasn't changed. But everything else has. Especially your voice. I've never heard this kind of anger and hatred in your voice before. And the way you look at me. I don't know what I've ever done to you that would make you hate me, too."

"You took Phil's place."

"But I didn't fire him, Laura. I only came on because there was a vacancy."

"Maybe I'm being irrational about you. But I'm not being irrational about Warren."

"I'm quitting the day after the election. Win or lose."

"What? Are you serious?"

"Very serious. I don't hold Warren in any higher regard than you do. I'm sick of him and all his lies."

"Well, then I owe you an apology."

"You can make it up to me by telling me what's going on."

"I'll see what my lawyer says."

She started to turn toward her door, but I grabbed her wrist. "One more question."

"Let go of me, Dev."

"Did you kill Greaves?"

"Are you fucking insane, Dev? Do you think I go around killing people?"

I let go of her wrist.

And with that she was gone. The dome light flashed bright for a moment as she got out of the car. A glimpse of that lovely face, so troubled now.

She stayed for slightly more than ninety minutes. I listened to talk shows dealing with the coming election. The vampires were out, sucking the blood from any serious discussion with wild claims and accusations. Most of the cranks hated Warren. He was described variously as a socialist, a communist, a supporter of terrorism, a sissy, and a despiser of all that was good and true in this great land of ours. Lake, on the other hand, was described as a man we could count on when the Martians attacked. Or the Venusians. I couldn't quite figure out which alien nation they had in mind.

Harsh wind sure made the lemony glow of the downstairs windows look awful cozy. Watching a late movie with a woman I was in love with, a drink or two, and then some comfortable sex before we fell asleep. All things possible. That would be my first priority after I walked away from Warren's camp. Finding a woman. I was ready to resort to sandwich boards if need be. And on Michigan Avenue. In broad daylight.

She was a bit drunk when she came back to the car. And she had the hiccups to prove it.

"Everything's going to hell," she said. "I'll probably be in prison a month from now. The thing I worry about most" — pause for a hiccup — "is my parents. I was the first person to graduate from college in my family. The Chinese" — pause for hiccup — "are proud people. Though sometimes you wouldn't know it. All that bowing and" — pause for hiccup — "crap."

"You fixed up Warren's drink, too?"

"Yeah. It was actually" — pause — "easy."

I drove slowly back to the hotel, listening to her tell me, between hiccups, what had transpired inside with her lawyer. He had told her that it was unlikely that Warren would bring the matter of taping him or extortion to the police given the nature of the tape. The police would assure him that the contents of the tape would forever be held in secret, but in this age of the media, "secret" was anything that lasted for more than forty-eight hours. But she was convinced that she was headed for prison despite all his reassurances, even when the lawyer said Warren couldn't even go after her for the stiffed drink. He'd be worried that that too would lead somehow to the tape.

"So where is the tape now?" I said.

"Right" — pause for hiccup — "here."

And with that she reached in her purse and brought forth this year's version of the Maltese Falcon. The McGuffin. The one thing everybody wanted. She held it up, streetlights and traffic lights and bistro lights flashing behind it as we moved down the city streets.

That tape should have glowed or been encrusted with barnacles or been heavy with the scrawl of some ancient and mysterious language. But it was just a standard miniature videocassette of the kind you can get at the supermarket for a buck or two.

"Are you sure there aren't any other copies floating around?"

"I made sure of that." And without a single hiccup. "The only time the tape was out of my hands was when I let Greaves use it for a few minutes to show you. I was in the other room listening. Then what I wanted was his laptop. I trashed his daughter's place looking for it but I didn't have any luck."

I decided against telling her that I had it. That might come later.

She explained to me that she'd been with Greaves the morning they'd taped Warren, never let Greaves out of her sight in case he had the idea of making a copy for himself. She had the one and only copy.

"So when he said he had the original tape, he was lying to me?"

"Ab" — pause for hiccup — "solutely."

She laid the tape on the seat between us. "All yours."

"Thank you."

A chortle. "Now *you* should blackmail the bastard."

"I just want to get away from him. Fast as I can."

"I'm with you on that."

"I'm curious. What were you going to do with a million dollars?"

She held up the briefcase and patted it.

"Give it to Kate."

"Kate? She makes good money and she comes from money."

"Her dad died a while back and her brother took over the estate. I don't know if you ever met him." Pause for hiccup. "He's a know-it-all. He lost nearly everything for them. They're not poor, but they aren't rich anymore" — pause for hiccup — "either."

"Why would Kate need a million dollars?"

"Because Warren won't give her very much for their daughter."

"Their daughter? Warren's the father of Kate's daughter?"

She nodded. And then, in between hiccups, she told me the rest. Phil Wylie had long been in love with Kate. But Kate had long been in love with Warren. The falling-out between Phil and Warren had been over Kate. Phil felt that Warren should pay an informal kind of child support. Warren felt that Kate was a "big girl" and had known the consequences of having an affair with a married man. He gave her a small "stipend" every month. But he wouldn't acknowledge paternity. Kate could have gone public but didn't because she held out hope that someday Warren would leave Teresa and marry her. This was what Phil and Warren had clashed about. Phil thought Warren was acting despicably. Warren said that Phil was being irrational. Phil resigned in a great rage. Laura watched as he declined into paranoia and helplessness, ending in suicide.

"Then nobody murdered him?"

"No," she said. "I was making us dinner in the kitchen when he jumped. I panicked and got out of there as fast as I could."

I saw a Denny's and swerved in there.

"You're going into a Denny's? Do you have any idea what kind of civil rights record they have?"

"You need coffee and so do I. I've got to think all this through."

"Denny's," she said. Hiccup. "They'll probably throw me out because I'm Chinese."

CHAPTER 29

I exercised in the hotel gym the next morning and then had room service bring me up a poached egg and a slice of toast and a pot of coffee. After the food and a shower, I called Warren.

"Where are you now?"

"I just visited three plant gates. Why?"

"I want you to come up to my hotel room."

"We finally going to have sex, are we?"

"Nobody else. Alone."

"I was hoping for a three-way."

"When can I expect you?"

"You sound pissed."

"When can I expect you?"

"You're taking over, huh? How about half an hour?"

"I'll see you then."

While I waited for him, I called my daughter and asked her how she'd like to see me for a few days. She was just as excited as I'd hoped she'd be. I sure was excited. Then I got on my computer and arranged for a round-trip plane ticket four days hence.

Warren arrived five minutes early.

He wore his tan camel's-hair overcoat, one of his best blue suits, a white shirt with the golden collar bar, and his favorite blue rep tie. He put on some swagger to back up his first words to me: "I don't like being pushed around by somebody on my payroll."

"Tough shit, Warren. And you won't have to worry about taking any more shit from me. I'm resigning here and now."

"What?"

"There's coffee on that table over there. There's also a videotape. *The* videotape. I've been assured that that's the only copy."

"Are you kidding me?"

"Sure, Warren. This is all a gag. All the shit I've been through, I did it just for fun."

"My God," he said, slipping out of his overcoat and draping it on a leather chair.

He sat down and picked up the tape. He held it up as if he could see it simply by staring at the black plastic encasement. "I don't believe this. So they fell for it, huh?"

"You mean the way you shortchanged them by eight hundred thousand? No, they knew about it right away." Laura and I checked the briefcase just before I let her out of the car. Good old Warren had cheated again.

I sat across from him at the table.

"God, Dev. I really appreciate this. All that bullshit is behind us now. That is if they were telling you the truth about this being the only copy."

"I'm positive it is."

"How the hell did you pull it off?"

"It doesn't matter. You have the tape. They have your two hundred thousand."

He leaned back. The pleasure in his gaze was replaced by suspicion. "You keep saying 'they.' Who are we talking about here exactly, anyway?"

"I have no idea."

"What?"

"Something went wrong on their end. A falling-out. Or somebody just got scared. We did everything by telephone. The guy I talked to said he just wanted it to be over. He was obviously an amateur. He was also very nervous. He brought up the subject of copies of the tape. He explained that there was only one copy, because if there were others floating around the police could trace them back to him. That's why I think they or whoever just got terrified of getting caught. A pro would never have accepted the two hundred thousand. If his motive

322

was political, he would have turned it over to a TV station. If it was just money, he would've added on another quarter million just because you screwed him. But like I said, this guy was no pro."

Still suspicious: "He have anything to do with queering my drink?"

"He said he did it and that it wasn't difficult."

After a long pause, he said, "You're not telling me the truth here, Dev. Something's wrong with your story."

There was a lot wrong with my story, but I didn't want to involve Laura. If she was to be found out, he'd have to do the finding himself.

"Accept your good fortune, Warren."

"So you're going to leave it like that?"

"Just like that."

"I want the truth."

"You've got the truth as far as you need to know it. Now take the tape and get the hell out of here."

"The cops could make you talk."

I enjoyed laughing at him. "Think about it, Warren. You sic the cops on me and the tape story'll be front and center. You really want that?"

"You don't have the right to do this."

"Sure I do. Now get up and get out."

323

I walked around to the side of his chair and said, "Let's go, Warren. I've got things to do today." I was burning to tell him that I knew about Kate's child, but I was afraid that if I did he'd know I'd learned about it from Laura.

He stood up and did a very stupid thing. He swung on me. He was a better puncher than I'd thought. He didn't hit me square in the face, but his punch landed hard enough on my ear to induce great momentary pain. He was getting ready to throw another one but I was quicker. I hit him right below the sternum, hit him hard enough to drive him back a few feet. I not only took his breath, I brought him to nausea. He covered his mouth and stumbled toward the bathroom. Even senators sound disgusting when they're puking. He stayed in there for a while washing up.

When he came out, I was holding his overcoat in one hand and his tape in the other. He angrily swiped the tape from me and shoved it in the pocket of the overcoat, which he took with his other hand. Then he walked straight to the door and out without once looking back. He closed the door gently behind him.

I wished I'd been able to beat him up, but

he had a campaign to run. Black eyes and a broken nose are a bitch to explain.

CHAPTER 30

A campaign luncheon was scheduled for Warren, sponsored by a civic group famous for the food it served. Gabe, Kate, Laura, and Billy would be there. So it would be a good time to sneak into the office, get my stuff, and sneak back out.

I sat drinking coffee in the hotel restaurant, waiting for noon and allowing myself a few moments of orgasmic self-pity.

Gosh, and here we had Mrs. Conrad's little boy Dev, always trying to make this a better world, getting stomped on for all his troubles. What a decent, righteous hero-type he was. And such a giving man, too. The perfect husband, the perfect father. If only those around him could see past his cynicism and pain and recognize him for the gallant man he really was.

But I couldn't kid myself very long. I was just as dirty as the rest of them. I pretended otherwise. I needed to or I couldn't do my job. I had to try and function as a conscience of sorts. But what kind of conscience was I? I was doing everything I could to destroy Jim Lake. I believed he would continue to perpetuate the lies and constitutional perversions of the current administration. I believed that he would continue to use the real threat of terrorism for nothing more than political gain. This crew couldn't stick up a gas station let alone win a war.

But vile as Lake was, I was just as vile. I was going to use his one-time venereal disease to bring him down. I fought his fight on his terms and had no regrets. And if Warren was a deceitful, arrogant peacock, so be it. All these stories we're taught about George Washington and Abraham Lincoln. They make me cringe with their sentimental bullshit. Most great leaders are deeply flawed men. George Washington mightily abused his open-ended expense account during his first term. But it's what they do for the common good that matters. So we put up with them because in general they're no better or no worse than the rest of us.

My trouble with Warren now was that he wouldn't do right by Kate and that he'd helped destroy a decent but troubled friend named Phil Wylie. Warren's flaws weren't all that exotic, but I cared deeply about Kate and had come to admire Phil Wylie in the days since his death.

I spent twenty minutes in my office filling up a small cardboard box with goodies I probably wouldn't be needing to look at ever again. The last things I took down were the eight hardcover books I kept on a shelf above my computer. Novels by Fitzgerald, Nathanael West, Raymond Chandler, Doctorow, Theodore Dreiser, David Madden, Joyce Carol Oates, and Richard Matheson. I read them when I needed to zone out of here, desperate to remind myself that there were other and equally important worlds.

Only after I dealt with the books did I take a closer look at the notes on my desk. There were three of them, from Gabe, Laura, and Kate respectively. Kate had also left me the two-week expense breakdown, which, for some reason, I started looking through. No reason to, now that I was no longer associated with Warren. I suppose it was just habit. Seeing if we were anywhere near our goal of containing costs.

The report ran to three pages with airline charges listed last. One line stood out. A round-trip ticket had been purchased, but the ticket holder had canceled before the flight.

The round-trip had been to Galesburg, Illinois. The trip I'd sent Billy on. The trip he'd written a very persuasive field report about.

Apparently without ever having gone there.

I wanted to check that date against another piece of information. I hadn't closed my computer up yet. I logged on and went through several days of *Tribune* headlines until I came to the story I wanted.

On the same morning Billy had canceled his flight, R. D. Greaves had been found dead in his hotel apartment.

I was shrugging into my coat when the phone rang.

"I'm calling on my cell, Bunny. I'm in the ladies' room. This luncheon is really dull." Kate. Trying hard to sound happy. But not succeeding. "What are you up to?"

"Just packing things up."

"You make that sound so final."

"Just for the weekend." I wasn't ready to tell her the truth, that I was leaving the campaign. I had other things I needed to do first. "You okay?"

"Pretty much."

"That's not real convincing."

Long silence. "I guess I might as well tell you."

I was half-afraid to hear. "You're unhappy. I'd appreciate knowing why. Maybe I can help."

"Not with this, Bunny. Teresa found out that Warren and I once had a little thing."

No mention of the baby.

"Enterprising lady. Hired a hacker. Went through our e-mails."

"E-mails are dangerous."

"But it was very civilized, actually. She came over to my place and told me she'd found out. What she wanted was for me to tell her that it was over. That now we just worked together, Warren and I."

"That must have been some conversation."

"I left a message on your room machine. I just needed to hear your voice."

"You think things are cool now?"

"She doesn't want any publicity. She wants to go back to Washington and pick right up where she left off. And I sure don't want any publicity. Wouldn't want anything of this to touch on my sweet little daughter."

"Your daughter's all that matters."

"What's so funny is that I don't give a damn about Warren anymore and neither does she. We were both laughing about that. All she's worried about is that the scandal might hurt him politically and that would hurt her in getting back to Washington."

"Good old Warren."

"Well, I need to get back to that boring luncheon. Bye, Bunny."

CHAPTER 31

I was on autopilot for the next forty-five minutes. I'd parked my car next to the side door, so loading my stuff into it was no problem. And then I started driving. But even if I wasn't aware of it, I had a destination. I kept on driving.

I sat in the car for a long time and just stared at the second-floor apartment. Maybe I should forget it. Just go back to my hotel. You could make a case that he'd done the world a favor. There were too many R. D. Greaveses in the world anyway.

He wouldn't have done it without a good reason. Killing wouldn't have come naturally to him. He would have been pushed into it. That I was certain of.

But then my fear for him became fear for the campaign. I was still a political operative. The implications of all this started scaring me.

Which would be worse? The public knowing that family-values Jim Lake had been unfaithful to his wife and picked up VD because of it?

Or that Senator Nichols had employed a staffer who was implicated in a murder?

But the operative in me was working fast.

How about the family-values man with VD who'd employed R. D. Greaves? Maybe dragging Greaves's history into it would be enough.

I knocked. Inside I could hear the TV. Billy answered the door.

"I thought I'd stop by and see if we owe you any expense money for that Galesburg trip. You didn't hand any chits in. And why aren't you at that luncheon?"

"I'm feeling under the weather, Dev. I didn't go in to work today."

"I need to talk to you, Billy. I need for you to tell me where you were when you were supposed to be in Galesburg." The screen door was locked inside. I rattled the knob. "Open up, Billy."

"Come back tomorrow."

"Open the door, Billy."

"You don't have any right —"

I looked straight at him through the rusted screening. "Sure I do, Billy. Sure I do."

He shook his head. Sighed. But he opened the door.

The first thing he did was shut off the TV. The second thing he did was pour more whiskey from the bottle on the coffee table into his glass. The third thing he did was say, "I filed a report, didn't I? So I had to have been there, right?"

"You forgot one thing. Your canceled plane ticket. It showed up on the printout from the airline."

"Story of my life."

"Oh, bullshit, Billy. It's not the story of your life. You're a very hot speechwriter. You just made a mistake. You made the mistake most of us would."

"You wouldn't have made that mistake."

"Are you crazy? Of course I would've. And so would Warren and Gabe. Laura and Kate, they probably wouldn't have, because they're smarter than we are."

A brief smile. "That's for sure." Then, "You want a drink?"

"No, thanks, Billy."

I sat down. The apartment was comfortably warm and smelled of freshly made popcorn. And real butter. Put that quality of popcorn together with a good movie and you had a decent time for human beings, lonely or otherwise.

He'd already finished the drink he'd just poured for himself. He was now pouring another one.

"So what did you do to Greaves?"

"I don't know what you're talking about, Dev." But his voice was shaky and he'd taken to blinking for no apparent reason. "We went to a movie."

"Who went to a movie?"

"Beth and I."

"Oh?"

"Yes, we went to a movie and then we went and got a pizza and that was when the news came on the TV about R.D."

"I see. So it was a complete surprise then?"

"I'm not a killer."

"I know you're not, Billy. And I'm not accusing you of being one. What I'm describing here was accidental. Unintentional. Remember, the police said that was a possibility, too."

"That's just about the way it happened, too."

Beth came into the living room from the kitchen. You expect people involved in a death to pull a Joan Crawford. You know, a big melodramatic snit ending in cries of "Yes, I did it and I'm glad I did!"

What you don't expect is a pretty young woman nibbling popcorn out of an enormous blue plastic bowl to come ambling in

335

and say what Beth had just said.

That's just about the way it happened, too.

She went over and sat on the arm of the sofa and said, "You want some popcorn, Dev? I can get you a bowl if you like."

"No, thanks. Why don't you finish what you were saying? You said that I was pretty much right, the way I scoped it out."

A shrug of her thin shoulders. "He found out I went to a lawyer."

"I'm not following."

Billy said, "The way her mother died. The cops always felt that R.D. killed her by pushing her down those stairs, but they could never prove it."

"But I wouldn't let it go. And two days ago I got the woman who lives in the apartment above where R.D. and my mom lived — Mrs. Neely — to admit she heard my mom screaming for help. Right after that she heard somebody falling down the stairs."

"Why didn't she tell this to the police?"

"Scared. Turns out R.D. threatened her. Told her he'd kill her if she said anything to me or the police."

"So she agreed to talk to you after R.D. was dead."

She nodded. Extracted a dainty amount of popcorn from the big blue bowl.

"You said you went to a lawyer."

"Umm-hmmm." Chewing popcorn and then swallowing it. "And my lawyer drinks where R.D.'s lawyer does and made the mistake of telling R.D.'s lawyer that I'd been to see him."

"So that when you went to see R.D. he blew up."

"And came at me with the fireplace poker. I was able to duck, but then he grabbed me by the throat. And that's when I kicked him on the shin. I got free. He lunged at me, but he couldn't get his balance and tripped right into the stone edge of the thing. I called 911 right away and got out of there. Then I called Billy. He canceled his trip to Galesburg. He knew how crazy I was over what'd happened."

The dispassion told me how little she'd ultimately thought of him. I suppose when Mrs. Neely confirmed for her the fact that R.D. had actually killed her mother, not even Beth could feel a sentimental attachment to him any longer. Suspecting is one thing. Knowing for sure is another.

"I wanted to take the blame," Billy said. He must have been feeling better. He reached over and she pushed the big blue bowl in his direction. Billy's hand was so full of popcorn, some of it was tumbling from his closed fist.

"First thing, Beth," I said. "Get a different lawyer. In fact, let *me* get you a lawyer."

"It did piss me off that he told R.D.'s lawyer."

"Second, I want to ask you a favor."

She seemed perplexed. "Sure. I mean, I guess. What is it?"

"The other night I asked you about a videotape. Did you ever find out anything about it?"

"No, why?"

"I want you to forget I ever asked you that question."

"Hell, Dev, what are you talking about?" Billy said.

I smiled. "I'm not talking about anything. I didn't ask you that question the other night and I'm not asking you that question today."

The confusion remained on Beth's face for a few more seconds and then she seemed to understand what was really going on here. "I see." She was angry.

"You see?"

"I always told Billy you were a real asshole and maybe now he'll agree with me. You're going to get me a lawyer — your lawyer — so he or she can make sure I don't mention the videotape to the police."

"We really need to win this campaign," I said.

"I hate Lake as much as you do." She glanced at me and then at Billy and then back to me. "I could go to prison here, but you don't give a damn. All you care about is your campaign."

"That's bullshit, Beth, Dev's not like that," Billy said.

She mocked him. " 'Dev's not like that.' When are you going to grow up, Billy?"

"I don't know why everybody's always picking on Dev," Billy said. "He means well. I know that."

"Poor old Dev. Everybody's friend." Now she was ready for Joan Crawford. She flung an arm in the direction of the door and said, "Get the fuck out of my apartment, Dev. I never want to see you or speak to you as long as I live. And I'll get my own lawyer, thank you very much. Now get out of here."

There wasn't much else to say. In fact, there wasn't anything else to say. I left.

CHAPTER 32

Warren won. The venereal disease played no role. Jim Lake self-destructed one night with a breathtaking racist rant that marked him as at best a rube and at worst a skinhead. I saw a couple of his people the following day. One of them joked that he was on his way to buy a burial plot and casket.

The person I was most wrong about in all this was Warren's wife, Teresa. She'd always seemed to be so unaffected by all the Washington bullshit. But faced with losing her status, she showed us who she really was. The *Post* ran a Style piece a few weeks ago about the returning senators and their spouses. Teresa was shown in a dress by an Italian designer whose name I can neither pronounce nor spell. She was hosting a party for the wives of two new senators, one from each party. She looked very happy. In the background Warren was chatting up a young woman who was undoubtedly on his hunting list.

In the eleven months since I left the campaign, I've never seen any of the principals again. The Cook County state attorney decided against indicting Beth; Laura, whose involvement was apparently unknown to the police, moved to warmer climes; and Kate still works for Warren and dotes on her daughter. Beth and Billy got married a few months back.

I'm back in my apartment. I've spent time in Virginia, Utah, and Florida talking to men and women who are eager to get to Washington and change how this government is run. I've visited my daughter twice and both times took out the lady professor she was telling me about. We had some good times and she'll be here over the holidays. If I promise to put up a tree.

This morning a woman called and said she'd like to talk to me about running for a congressional seat. Very intelligent, very nice voice. The surprise was that Warren had recommended me. I suppose that was my belated reward for not leaking anything I knew about him.

She laughed when she brought up the subject of oppo research. "I don't have anything to hide, Mr. Conrad. I really don't."

"Everybody's got something to hide."

"That's an awfully cynical attitude."

"Yes," I said, "isn't it, though?"

ABOUT THE AUTHOR

Ed Gorman has worked in politics as both a speechwriter and a TV producer. He has won the Shamus, Anthony, Ellery Queen, Spur, and International Fiction Awards. He has been nominated twice for an Edgar and once for the Silver Dagger. His other work includes the Sam McCain series and the Jack Sawyer series. A feature film based on his novel *The Poker Club* is forthcoming. Visit Ed's Web site at www.newimproved gorman.com.